JACKY

Book 3 of the Jimmy Boy Series

Terry Pankhurst

BOOK 1

Do not cast me away when I am old;

do not forsake me when my strength is gone.

- Psalms 71:9

Contents

Prologue

The midwife, Agnes, arrived just at noon. She was a kindly woman and was well respected in Milburra and its surroundings. She was known for her gentle hands and kind heart, and Clara Reagan felt a wave of comfort wash over her as she entered the bedroom.

After hours of labor, the moment came. With a final push, Clara brought forth a baby boy.

Agnes cradled the newborn in her arms, her eyes sparkling with joy, but as she stepped outside, away from the baby's mother, her expression changed.

"Congratulations Mister Reagan. You have a son."

But her voice was trembling.

Harry Reagan noticed the look at her face.

"What is it? Is the child all right?"

Agnes hesitated and glanced back at the room where Clara lay exhausted.

"The baby is, --------- is larger than most. He has a big head and a strong body, Mister Reagan. But I fear he may face challenges as he grows. He may not even reach the age of twenty. Is there anyone in your family with mental or physical problems?"

Reagan's mind raced. He thought of an uncle who had been born *different* and spent almost his entire life in an asylum.

Reagan forced a smile and lied.

"No. All my family is as normal as you or I."

Agnes nodded, but her expression had a flicker of doubt.

"Well, Mister Reagan, I am done here. I will call by tomorrow."

"I cannot thank you enough, Agnes."

Inside the bedroom, Clara was still recovering, but she had overheard the words spoken by the midwife. As Agnes left through the front door, her emotions exploded.

"I am cursed by the Reagan genes!" she shouted.

"I hate this child! I wish he had never been born!"

Charlene Reagan, the four-year-old daughter of the couple, had been playing quietly in the corner. She looked up with wide eyes at her mother. She did not understand the words, but she knew that in her tiny mind, they conveyed anger and fear.

Chapter 1

The morning sun filtered in through the bedroom window. Despite the early hour, Jacky's dark skin glistened with sweat as he draped his arm over his wife, Martha. She stirred and managed a small smile.

Despite the satisfaction Martha undeniably felt, she still managed to wake each morning with the same hollow feeling in the pit of her stomach. She snuggled into Jacky's body and whispered,

"What are you thinking about?"

"The bush," he said in a contemplative tone.

"The trees, the animals, the stories of my people."

Martha appreciated Jacky's tales, but being an avid reader, she craved more from life. The fashions, the people, and the excitement. These were the things that resonated with her. The bustle and vibrancy of the cities she had read so much about.

Jacky could always sense his wife's subtle mood changes, and this morning was no different.

"And what are you thinking about?" he asked.

She stroked his chin and smiled.

"You, Jacky."

 And she kissed him.

But Martha was thinking of her Emporium, of the latest fabrics from abroad, the dresses and the colours that seemed to draw a person's soul. She knew exactly how much Jacky loved the bush, but it was a place she could never really understand, a landscape she found fascinating and frightening.

Martha gave a sigh, an almost imperceptible sound that seemed to resonate with her husband. He knew that sigh. A sigh of a woman trapped, not physically, but a woman yearning for something more, something beyond the quiet and shared beauty of the outback.

*****

"Jimmy Boy, when's it going to rain?"

Eleanor's face was masked with a shroud of despair.

Jimmy Boy sighed heavily as he looked over the dry landscape.

"I just do not know Ellie. Only God knows those things."

Jacky

But Jacky, standing beside the pair, had the natural, even uncanny, knack of knowing. His eyes, filled with the knowledge of his ancestors, saw beyond the dry cracks in the earth and onward to the approaching clouds. Jacky had spent his entire life studying the land, reading the signs that others overlooked. The shifting patterns of ants, the restlessness of kangaroos, and the sudden bloom of certain plants all spoke to him of coming rain.

The drought had hit both *Wicklow* and *Shanghai* hard. After three consecutive seasons of above-average rainfall and good growing conditions, the seasons had come back to bite the Wang families with a vengeance. Cattle and sheep were dropping in the paddocks from hunger and thirst, and the men had the heart-breaking task of shooting dozens to put them out of their misery. Dams were dry, and the Bella River was at its lowest level that anyone could recall.

"And to think we once complained about flooding," said Jimmy Boy stoically.

"And look at these," he said, pointing to the deep fissures snaking through the ground like the veins of some horrible beast. His voice was a mixture of wonder and worry.

The ground was so hard it cracked beneath their boots, an imploring sound asking for moisture. The entire landscape was a poor work of art, all painted with one colour……brown. The air had the smell of death and carried with it the despairing cries of the parched farm animals.

"Come on, Jacky. We'll get Wells and Jennings and ride to the far paddocks and see how many more of the poor creatures we must shoot."

Jacky grinned at the little Chinaman and said quite confidently,

"We won't be killing too many more, Jimmy Boy. I can assure you it will rain before the sun rises."

Martha had been silent, listening to the men talk their tales of woe, but she spoke up and said,

"Jacky, are you sure? Or is this just one of your whimsical notions?"

Jacky displayed his white teeth with a huge grin.

"We'll see by tomorrow how whimsical I am, Martie."

Jennings, along with Wells, approached the group. They were ready for work, and both were bearing a rifle.

Jacky

"Don't go much on this shootin' cows and sheep, Jimmy Boy. Seems to be all we've done lately. Poor buggars. Not their fault there ain't no grass to eat."

Jimmy Boy acknowledged the two loyal farmhands.

"If Jacky is correct, it will rain tonight, Mister Wells."

Jennings let out a heehaw.

"Ha! Told yer Wells. Me arthritis been playin' up lately. Didn't I tell yer that meant rain?"

"Not yer arthritis, Jennin's. Yer bloody brain is always playin' up."

*****

The rain began in the early hours of the morning, not with a roar but with a gentle tapping on the corrugated iron roof. Martha rolled over in bed and strained her ears. A gentle smile broke over her face. She nudged her sleeping husband.

"Jacky," she whispered, "You were right. It's beginning to rain."

But Jacky was lost in sleep and gave no response. She slipped out of bed and tiptoed to the window, where she wiped the moisture away and peered out into the night. A streak of lightning startled her somewhat, and she scurried back to the warmth of the bed. She pulled the covers up to her neck and remained awake until morning. By the time the sun had fully risen, the rain had turned into a steady, rhythmical stream that drenched the countryside in a cold and wet embrace of greyness. Jacky sat up, and with a cheeky grin, he said, "I think I was right then, Martie."

She gave him a gentle nudge.

"Jacky, how could you have been so sure?"

"It's just built into my nature, Martha. It is not a science, as the white man would call it. It is just a way an aboriginal sees signs or patterns, that have occurred in the past. It is quite simple when you think of it like that."

"You are too modest, Jacky. I know you are a very clever man."

She stretched her arms and yawned.

"Let's have some breakfast. I am starving."

"Later, Martha," he said as he pulled her on top of him.

*****

Jacky's mother, Mia, had the fire in progress and was

valiantly trying to get a decent blaze.

"Damned wood too wet, Jacky. 'ad no idea about rain before I went to bed."

Martha winked at Jacky.

"So, I assume it is only aboriginal men who can tell when it's going to rain, Jacky."

"I think my mother has lived with white people for far too long. Forgotten all she ever knew."

He drew his mother into a warm embrace, but she pulled away and scolded him.

"I taught you all you ever knew, Jacky, and don't you be fergettin' it. And what I didn't teach yer, that no good father of yers did."

The fire had taken by now, and soon Mia had eggs frying, and the bacon smells were drifting through the kitchen. A hesitant knock at the door aroused their attention. It was Stubbs.

"Good morning, Jacky. Martha."

"Morning, mister Stubbs," they said in unison.

"I am assuming you smelled the bacon. Would you

care to join us for some breakfast?"

"I was hoping you'd ask that, Martha," he replied with a grin.

"Bit tired of my own cooking."

They sat in silence, eating and listening to the rain falling. The gentle falls of before had given way to an angry torrent of lashing rain, which was now accompanied by fierce winds.

"Taking the day off today, Jacky?" asked Stubbs, between chewing on a strip of bacon rind.

"Rain doesn't stop me, Mister Stubbs. There is always something to do. It's all right for you. A warm office and some bookwork. How would you like to ride with me this morning over to Wicklow and see Jimmy Boy?"

"Bookwork is just fine with me; thanks Jacky."

He began to sniffle and followed up with a cough.

"I think I am coming down with something."

"It's amazing how you always '*come down*' with something when Jacky mentions a bit of hard work," jibed Martha.

"Now Martha," said Jacky, "Mister Stubbs does what he does best. Bookwork."

"Men just can't seem to take a joke," she huffed.

*****

The rain hammered into Jacky's body like a barrage of bullets. He had his hat pulled low over his face, but still, the rain cut into the dark skin of his face as it struck both him and his horse. He rode at a steady pace, knowing it would be foolhardy to ride any quicker in the countryside that was barely visible. The day, although in its infancy, was as dark as a winter's night, and it took all the rider's concentration to follow the trail. A jagged cut of lightning toppled a tree off to his left, and he watched as the flames tried to take hold against the power of the water belting down. Nature was unleashing all its beasts.

In the hollow of a log, a vixen and her pup heard the horse pass by. They had no fear. They were well hidden and safe and warm. The mother fox was tired of her playful pups, but she was not inclined to leave her sanctuary and venture into the maelstrom playing outside. She nosed the pup away in the direction of the remnants of yesterday's meal. The drought had been good to the scavengers.

*****

"You think this will let up any time soon, Jacky?"

Jennings squinted out the barn doors.

What had been a rhythmic tapping on the barn roof had intensified to the solid thuds of raindrops. The men watched the droplets of water, seeking out any unpatched holes in the roof, and finding one, began to drip into Jennings' cupped hands. He gulped the sweet water down and sighed.

"Aaaah, tastes better than my poor, long gone mother's milk."

"We need the rain, Jennings. I don't really care how long it lasts. So long as we don't get a flood like we did a few years ago. The stock is far too weak to drive away from the river or creek."

'Well, there's not much we can do today," said Jimmy Boy resignedly.

"What about a game of cards?"

Wells' eyes lit up.

"I'll be in that."

"And none of yer bloody cheatin' Wells," Jennings couldn't resist a barb at his friend.

*****

The sound of horse's hooves slopping and squishing through the mud aroused the men, who were just about ready to finish their card game and go for lunch.

"Who'd be out in weather like this?" asked Jennings as he stood and walked to the barn door. He turned back and said,

"It's Mrs Header's old man. And 'e looks awful worried."

The man dismounted and was ushered into the relative warmth of the barn. His words came in a rush.

"It's me boy! Me, little boy."

He half sobbed, half shouted.

"Calm down, man," said Jimmy Boy, placing a hand on the man's shoulder.

"What's happened to your boy?"

"'e cleared out without the missus knowin'. Went to look at the risin' river. Jack and the Doc sent me out to get you and some more men to help search."

Jimmy Boy took charge immediately.

"Wells, Jennin's, fetch the horses."

Jacky had other ideas.

"My horse is ready to go, Jimmy Boy. I'll head off now."

Jacky gave no thought to his own safety as he galloped across the treacherous ground. The afternoon was closing in, and soon, there would barely be light enough to see. The dark clouds had swallowed the sky, turning day into an eerie twilight. The water was cold and unforgiving, reaching out to claim all it touched.

He was at the outskirts of Ramsay in less than half an hour and spied the townsfolk riding or walking along the river's edge, calling the boy's name. His horse was hissing steam from its nostrils as the aboriginal man reined it to a stop.

He called to Jack.

"Where was he last seen Jack?"

Jack cupped his hand to his ear to hear above the rain and the surging water.

"Just around here somewhere, Jacky."

Jacky wheeled his horse and galloped downstream, leaving his onlookers bewildered.

"Bloody fools," thought Jacky.

"Why search in an area where the boy couldn't possibly be?"

Jacky knew that the strength of the current would have the boy much further away from where he disappeared into the brown water. He slowed his horse to a trot and peered through rain-filled eyes. Even a man with a pair of field glasses may not have spotted the sodden figure hugging a gum tree in the middle of the roaring stream. But Jacky had acute eyesight and attention to detail. He flung himself from his horse and walked upstream to a carefully selected inlet, cast aside his boots, and slipped himself into the freezing water. He let the current carry him to the boy, who extended an arm to pull Jacky towards a branch.

"You all right, boy?"

The eyes that looked at Jacky gave him the answer. Now, it remained to get him back onto dry land.

"Boy, hop on my back, just like when your daddy gives you a piggy ride. Hold tight round my neck and don't let go.

We'll go with the current and let it work for us. Should be home with your Mama real soon. Ready?"

Jacky released his hold on the branch and kicked out into the stream, and as he predicted, with little effort, the current washed them ashore about fifty yards further down. It was a short walk to collect his horse, and Jacky lifted the wet and cold boy into the saddle.

"I cannot thank you enough, mister," said the young boy's weeping mother. She held him so tightly he had difficulty breathing.

But all Jacky wanted was some warm clothing.

"Back to your establishment, Jack?" he shivered.

"I sure could do with some warm gear."

"Might have a drink or two that will warm you up, Jacky."

*****

"Who's all the strangers, Jack? It's not often Ramsay has so many different faces. Although I must say it was good of them to join the search for Mrs Header's son."

"They're the crew from the telegraph company. Very

friendly chaps. I had a bit of a yarn to the foreman last night, and he said Ramsay will be connected within the week to Newcastle, and this line is meeting the Queensland line at a little place called Milburra."

"So, what does that mean for us, Jack?" Jimmy Boy enquired, eager to learn about the new changes.

"It will be good for country folk, Jimmy Boy. We will be able to communicate with the big cities and conduct our business."

"Load of horse shit if you ask me," said Jennings.

"'ow can a person talk over a wire?"

The group of friends laughed.

"I don't rightly know how it works, Mister Jennings, but you don't talk. There is some method where your message is sent along the wire on the poles the men have been rigging."

"Same difference!" snorted Wells this time.

"'ow can a message crawl along a wire? Fer once in my life, I agree with Jennin's. All horse shit!"

"I think we must accept changes in our lives, Mister Wells. And if I am correct, there will be many more before you or I die."

Jimmy Boy intimated that the discussion was closed.

*****

Chapter 2

The preacher had arrived the evening before he was to officiate at the christening and stayed the night at the Inn, whence he was brought by buggy to Wicklow along with Jack and his wife, Grace.

The Reverend cast his eyes around the outer edges of the homestead. It was far different from what he had seen the last time he had been here. The burnt-out shells of the barn and the crumbled structure of Wells' and Jennings' hut were embedded in his mind. But now he looked upon a new and much larger barn, and an extra two huts had been built. One of the huts originally housed Mia and Jacky but was now empty, and the other was Jennings' home.

"I must say, Jack, it certainly looks a lot better than when I was last here. Jimmy Boy must be a damned fine worker."

"He has fine workers, Reverend. Jimmy Boy is a smart man, but he hasn't gotten where he is without good men around him. Jennings and Wells have been invaluable to the man. Along with Jacky, of course."

"Jacky? The aboriginal? Isn't he married to Jimmy

Boy's daughter?"

"Yes. Do you recall Miss Martha? No offence, Reverend, to you, but it was a quiet wedding in Newcastle, away from the gossip of a small town like Ramsay. I think Jimmy Boy would have liked you to wed the couple, but you know how it is."

"Why should there be gossip?"

"Reverend, here's me taking you for a smart man!" Jack scoffed.

"Do you really believe folks round these parts are happy with a white girl marrying a black man?"

"We are all God's children, Jack."

"Tell that to those who would believe you, Reverend. Come on. Let's go in and see Jimmy Boy, and you can meet Meg, the mother of the boy you have been sent for to christen."

Bindi was the first to greet the two men, and her excitement level, as per usual, was at fever pitch.

"Pleased I am to see you again, mister preacher. Come on inside and 'ave some 'ot tea. Mia 'as been cookin' cakes for the party, but I dunno what they will taste like. Everybody round 'ere knows she ain't 'alf as good a cook as me."

The room stood as Bindi led Jack and the Reverend into the parlour.

"Welcome, Reverend. I guess you have seen some changes around the place."

Jimmy Boy extended his hand, and they shook warmly.

"Yes. Dreadful business, that fire. But at least our good lord saved anyone from severe harm. How did your man get on?"

"Jennings? He's fine and still full of cheek. But, reverend, I'd like you to meet my daughter-in-law, Meg."

Meg had been sitting quietly in the corner, nursing her son. She stood shyly and extended her hand.

"It is indeed my pleasure to meet you, Miss Meg. And what may I ask, will you be naming your son?"

"She ain't namin' im nothin' mister preacher," interrupted Bindi as she poured the Reverend a mug of tea.

"It is you, namin' the boy."

"Bindi! To the kitchen now!"

Angela, which was rare for her, had objected to the little black woman's rudeness.

"Yes, Missus Boss. Sorry Missus Boss."

"I will be naming him Robbie, Reverend."

"A splendid name. Do you have an Irish background?"

Meg bit her lip and looked as if she would cry. Martha spoke up to save the young mother from embarrassment.

"She likes the name because her late husband, my brother, had a teddy bear which he called Robbie."

"I see. Still, a splendid name."

Jimmy boy motioned to the preacher and said in a whisper so that Bindi could not hear,

"Would you rather something stronger than tea, Reverend?"

"You have twisted my arm, Jimmy Boy."

"And not very hard, Reverend," he laughed.

The two men walked into Jimmy Boy's office, where he had a bottle of fine whisky on his desk.

He poured them both a drink and then mentioned to the

Reverend,

"I didn't know at the time Reverend, but you have another tiny one to baptise. When the Doctor's wife heard you were coming, she jumped at the chance to get her son baptised as well."

"I see no problem, Jimmy Boy. It'll just be double the offering you put in the collection plate," he laughed, and his huge stomach rolled in tune with his uproar.

Their conversation was interrupted by the appearance of Jacky. He was sweating profusely and obviously in some kind of alarm.

"Sorry to interrupt folks, but Jimmy Boy, I need you to come with me."

Jimmy Boy, sensing something serious, placed his drink on the dresser.

"Excuse me for a while, Reverend."

*****

"Come on boy," cooed the soothing words of Jennings as his eyes locked on the stallion's panicked gaze. Jenning's voice was a gentle melody amidst the chaos, but it seemed to be lost on the creature. The horse's eyes rolled back, showing its whites as its hooves raked the air.

"Careful Jennings. Let him calm down a bit," cautioned Jacky.

"Bin doin' this longer than you, Jacky. I'll quieten the bastard."

The dust flung up by the horse's rage hung in the air, and both men could taste the dry powder. The smell of fear was potent and was mixed with the smells of dry horse shit and the cloying smell of freshly cut hay in the barn.

The stallion's powerful neck muscles bulged as it threw its head back, a piercing whinny echoing across the yard. The rope was burning Jenning's palms as the beast's madness grew stronger. Jennings knew the secret to calm the stallion was patience, but he had never encountered such a stubborn horse before. He held the rope tightly, and through cracked lips, he said,

"I'll tame 'im Jacky. Jis need some time."

Then, with a sudden jolt, the stallion struck out with its hooves, aiming for the source of its fear. Jennings felt a searing pain as one of the hooves struck his forehead. The impact sent him reeling, his vision temporarily lost as he saw stars and then blackness. He staggered back and reached for the throbbing wound. He could tell by the taste in his mouth that he was bleeding.

"Jennings!"

Jacky's voice was sharp with concern.

"I'll get help," he cried, and he was already sprinting to the homestead.

The world swirled around Jennings as he fell, the ground rising to meet him with a thud. He felt more trickles of blood, and he could taste it as it mingled with the dust that coated his face. The pain was a drumming pulse in his skull, but he knew he could not give in to the pain coursing through his body. He blinked and then blacked out.

Jimmy Boy took one look at the unconscious Jennings and barked an order.

"Jacky, ride for the doctor. I'll manage here. I'll get the Reverend to help me get him to a bed."

*****

"Guess that horse got the better of me, Doc," croaked

Jennings through lips as dry as a barnyard floor.

"Mister Jennings, I need you to follow my fingers."

Jennings squinted, trying to make sense of the double image. The doctor's hand hovered in front of his face, two fingers standing tall. Jennings' eyes flickered as he tried to determine if he could see three or four.

"Concentrate Mister Jennings."

Jennings took a deep, painful breath, willing his vision to clear.

At last, he said,

"I see two Doc."

In fact, Jennings saw four, but he was smart enough to halve the number. He didn't want a fuss made over himself.

"That's good, Jennings."

The doctor turned to a concerned group who had gathered in the room.

"He'll be fine, folks. Just a mild concussion. A few days' rest in a dark room, and he will be as good as new."

The Reverend knelt and said a quiet prayer for

Jennings, and when he stood, he smiled at the wounded man and said,

"I think I will have to stop coming to Wicklow Mister Jennings. It seems every time I am here, you meet with an accident."

*****

"What do you think about the stallion Jacky? It seems to be a bit of a rogue. Do you think gelding it might calm it down?"

"Jimmy Boy, never! You can't cut a magnificent beast like that. It would be a crying shame. I can see in that horse the makings of a fine sire."

"Then how about I give it to you, Jacky, and see what you can do with it?"

"I accept your offer wholeheartedly, Jimmy Boy. That stallion will be the best horse in the district."

"Then consider it yours, Jacky."

*****

Jimmy Boy placed his glass in the sink amidst the other dishes that Bindi was washing. He had been unusually quiet during the evening meal, and it had not gone unnoticed by both Angela and Eleanor. He went to the dresser, retrieved a clean glass, and poured himself a small nip of brandy.

"Is there something troubling you, Jimmy Boy?" asked Angela.

"Take a seat, and we'll have a family talk. Are you worried about the christening tomorrow?"

Jimmy Boy sighed.

"That is nothing to worry myself about, Angela. It's just poor Jennings."

"But the doctor said he will be fine in a few days, Jimmy Boy," remarked Eleanor, trying to reassure her husband.

Jimmy Boy pulled up a seat and sat at the table. He rested his hands under his chin and breathed deeply.

"I trust the Doc, Ellie. But it's just that I feel Jennings is getting too old to be doing the work he does. I think he needs to slow down."

"Do we even know how old the man is?"

Angela was curious now.

"Let's see, and he travelled with James on his expedition to find this place. And if I remember, he would have been in his late forties back then. So, add about twenty years to be conservative and I'd guess his age to be around the late sixties."

"What about Mister Wells?" asked Martha.

"Once again, I can only guess. But I would put him in the same age range as Mister Jennings."

"So, what are you suggesting, Jimmy Boy?" asked Eleanor.

"I really don't know," he mused.

"I'll sleep on it."

*****

Jennings was up and about in just three days' time, and already he had suffered enough of what he called "smart arse comments" from his old mate Wells.

"Hey Jennin's, that danged 'orse couldn't kick yer brains in, cos you ain't got none to kick in."

They were cleaning out the pig sties in preparation for the birth of piglets. At Wells' comment, Jennings hurled a shovel full of pig shit at the unfortunate man.

"'ere's some shit fer shit Wells!"

Jimmy Boy appeared and witnessed the incident. He grinned as he watched Wells wipe the muck from his face and said,

"Playing games, little boys?"

The men hung their heads with shame.

"Wells, Jennings, I need to speak with you both."

The look on Jimmy Boy's face did not augur well for the two farmhands.

"Sorry 'bout the tomfoolery, Jimmy Boy," said Jennings.

"Jis, that Wells gits me goat at times. Jis cos he's a married man 'e thinks 'e is better than me."

"As I said, I need to have a serious conversation with you both."

Jimmy Boy shifted his weight from one foot to the other, his eyes taking in the worn boots of the men before him. The lines on their faces spoke volumes of the years they had spent toiling under the harsh Australian sun, each furrow a line of dedication to their hard work. Their hands, calloused and strong, had been the backbone of the farm, but now they trembled slightly at the weight of the tools they were holding, a weight which was becoming too heavy for them.

Jimmy Boy knew it was time to have a difficult conversation, one that weighed on his heart like the thick, humid air that was pressing on their shoulders.

Jennings looked up from the slop of the pigsty, his eyes meeting Jimmy Boy's with a resigned acceptance. He knew Jimmy Boy had noticed the changes in him, the subtle signs that his once steadfast health was beginning to waver. Wicklow, the farm, had been his life for as long as Jimmy Boy had known him, and the thought of letting go was as painful as the ache in his back after a long day's work. Yet he could not escape the reality of what was staring him in the face.

Jimmy Boy cleared his throat and spoke nervously.

"Mister Jennings, I've noticed…" he paused and caught his breath,

"I've noticed you're not quite as spry as you once were, and…"

The words hung in the air, heavy with the weight of

their implications.

Jennings spoke softly.

"You're cuttin' me loose, Jimmy Boy?" Is that what yer tryin' to say?"

The old man shook his head sadly, tears beginning to mist over his eyes.

"If it's about money, Jimmy Boy, I promise to work for you for nuthin'."

Jennings sensed what he thought was forthcoming. Without the farm, what was he? Just an old man with too many yesteryears and far too little tomorrows.

The silence clung to the two men as thick as the dust that covered their bodies. Jennings shuffled from one foot to the other.

"You will be taken good care of, Mister Jennings," Jimmy Boy said kindly but firmly.

"You can have your hut for as long as you like, and I'll make sure you have everything you need."

Jimmy Boy paused, searching for words.

"I'll give you a sum of money each month to cover

your expenses."

"So that's it then? I'm to be let go like an old, broken-down horse. May just as well take me out the back paddock and shoot me, Jimmy Boy," said Jennings.

Jimmy Boy tried to console the man.

"Don't you see Mister Jennings? You will not have to rise at sunup each day and put in a day's work. You can rest."

"But I can't rest Jimmy Boy. I'll die with nuthin' to do."

Jimmy Boy saw a way out of the situation.

"Mister Jennings, just because you will not be working from dawn till dusk, it doesn't mean you will be idle. I will need to consult you from time to time on matters concerning the running of this place. You have a good head on your shoulders and can still teach me a lot. And, of course, there will be odd jobs from time to time. So, you see, your situation hasn't really changed that much. You will just be doing fewer hours and lighter tasks."

Jennings heaved a sigh of relief.

"Yer 'ad me scared then fer a while, Jimmy Boy. I

thought you was lettin' me go."

Jennings had a look of relief and surprise flickering in his eyes.

"Never, you silly man."

Then he added,

"This place just wouldn't operate without your expertise."

"What about me?" asked Wells, who had been silent and listening to the conversation.

"The same applies to you, Mister Wells. You have settled into married life and are entering the golden years of your life. You need to slow down as well. You have a good woman to take care of you, and I will still call upon you if or when I need help."

Wells smiled.

"Sounds good to me, Jimmy Boy. Always fancied meself as a gardener. Might jis take up growin' some veggies."

"So, it's settled then. You both will finish up this weekend. And as a treat, it'll be me buying the drinks at the Inn."

"Damned good idea, I say," grinned Jennings placing his greasy hat on his head.

*****

"Jimmy Boy is mighty good to us," said Jennings as he sipped on his rum and watched the Chinaman head out the door of the Inn. His voice carried a tone of gratitude and concern.

"He coulda cut us both loose."

Wells sighed deeply and nodded his head in agreement.

"He certainly is," he replied, "but he is right. We are both gittin' too old for farmin' work. I 'ave trouble puttin' me boots on each mornin'.

The two men shared a knowing glance, the kind that told of their years of toil together in the Australian bush. It was true they both knew the physical demands on them had become harder to tolerate as the years passed.

"Talk about putting boots on, and I can barely outpace the bloody chickens, Wells."

Wells laughed and said,

"Still, life goes on, and life changes Jennin's. Blokes

like me, and you are only part of the story fer a short while, then the book ends. We are just like an old red gum tree. Deep roots but thinning branches."

"What are you fuckin' talkin' about, Wells? Usin' fancy words you know nuthin' about. Always talk shit you do."

Wells said indignantly,

"You need a wife, Jennin's. At least Mrs Wells has put some culture into this old body."

"Not a bloody 'gan. Bloody rot, you talk Wells, is all. C'mon, time to go."

*****

Chapter 3

The household was bustling with activity, all excited for the christening of the two little boys.

Meg entered the room proudly, her heart racing with anticipation. The reverend stood at the corner of the Wang living room with a bible in his hand. His kind smile towards Meg gave her the reassurance that the day would be one to remember.

The menfolk had brought in extra chairs for the small gathering, consisting of the Wang family, Lily Beth, Alec, and Jack and Grace from the Inn. The Doctor and Violet, along with their son, were seated at the front, while Bindi and Mia, along with Wells and Jennings, stood at the back of the room.

"Welcome folks to this blessed gathering," commenced the Reverend.

"To save valuable time, I will splash the holy water on both foreheads and pray over both heads simultaneously."

Wells turned his head slyly and asked Jennings, "What's he on about?"

"Miserable bastard is gunna do them together, Wells.

Huh! Save time? For what? Cuttin' into 'is drinkin' time."

The two women walked forward and held their sons up to the Reverend.

It was then that Bindi whispered to Mia.

"Mia, that youngun' of Mrs. Violet's, he don't look nuthin' like the doctor. I 'eard tell that Violet dun slept with that mongrel Williams when 'e was about the district."

"What rubbish you on about now Bindi?"

"All I is sayin' is that that young boy ain't got a chance in 'ell of turnin' out any good if 'is old man is Williams."

*****

Among the crowd stood Connolly, dressed in his neatly pressed new Sergeant's uniform. He watched with little interest as the reverend poured holy water and embraced the two toddlers into the arms of the Lord. As the ceremony ended, Connolly found himself staring at Meg and realised that she had been the focus of his attention during the baptism. He felt an unusual longing and tried to summon up the courage to speak with the widowed woman. Her beauty on this day was radiant; her eyes were a captivating shade of emerald green that held a tinge of sorrow. Connolly felt a strange determination as he approached her.

"Meg, Mrs Wang, may I have a word or two?"

Meg turned to face him, a look of surprise on her face.

"Of course. How can I help you, Sergeant Connolly?"

Taking a deep breath, Connolly let out his emotions.

I have admired you for some time now. Your grace and strength in the aftermath of the tragic loss of Shimmy have captured my heart. I know it has not been that long since your husband passed, but may I be so forward to ask if you would allow me to court you?"

Martha's eyes ed in astonishment, her lips parting in disbelief. She had never expected such a proposal from any man, least of all the newly promoted Sergeant. Yet, as she studied his earnest face, she sensed a chance at a new beginning.

"Sergeant Connolly, your offer is completely unexpected but most certainly appreciated," she replied, her voice barely above a whisper.

"I, too, have come to admire your dedication to

Ramsay and its people. Sergeant Connolly, it would be an honour to have you court me."

A tender smile lined Connolly's face, and his heart swelled with joy. The pair exchanged a meaningful glance. A look that promised a wonderful future for the couple.

*****

"Letter for you, Missus Boss," said Bindi as she handed over an envelope.

"Goodness," said Angela,

"I wonder who it could be from?"

"Only one way to find out, Missus Boss. You got to open it."

Bindi reached to take the envelope back.

"Best let me open it, Missus Boss."

"Thanks, but no thanks, Bindi. I am quite capable of such a small task."

Angela tucked the letter into her apron.

"Go on Missus Boss. Open the thing. It won't bite yer."

She pulled the mail from her apron, tentatively tore at

the envelope, and extracted the letter.

"I only hope it's not bad news, Bindi."

"No bad news due your way, Missus. This old black git feels it in 'er bones. They sure are feelin' good lately."

Angela read the letter as Bindi watched on. She broke into a smile, and Bindi said,

"Told ya so! You're smilin', so it must be good news. Go on. Tell me Missus Boss."

"Bindi, where is Eleanor?"

"Tell me Missus Boss. Please," Bindi implored.

"Bindi, I have been invited to open the new telegraph station. All because of James. It seems people never forget those whom we have lost. They have asked me to do the honour in memory of James and his contribution in opening this area."

'Don't know too much about that, Missus Boss. What's a telegraph station?"

"Jimmy Boy will explain it all over dinner, Bindi. He is far more knowledgeable in those matters than me."

*****

Angela O'Brien looked spectacular, as she always did. She wore a simple but elegant dress, and she was wearing the special scent her daughter had given her the Christmas before. There was a quiet buzzing in the air, a gentle humming of the townsfolk as they waited in anticipation.

"This way, please, Mrs O'Brien," said Ridgeway, the Postmaster.

He ushered Angela towards a ribbon and handed her a pair of shears. People had come to see history being made, and when the ribbon was sliced in two, they were aware that a new era was upon them.

At the front of the crowd, standing with Jimmy Boy and Eleanor, were Wells and Jennings.

Curiosity grew as the machine began making strange noises. The needle danced across the paper, and Wells pulled back in alarm. He grabbed Jennings by the arm and pulled him away.

"Better be careful, Jennin's. Never know what 'arm that strange contraption can do."

The machine continued to tap out a message, and people were beginning to become impatient. A cry rang out from the back of the crowd.

"Coulda told yous it was just some trick. Messages on wires! Next thing you know, we'll be told there's a man on the moon."

The crowd burst into laughter.

"Have patience, my good man," called Ridgeway over the laughter.

Mrs Wells delivered a slap to her husband's arm.

"Hush Thomas. There is no need to make a fool of yourself."

The machine went silent, and Ridgeway pulled away the slip of paper and held it above his head with pride. He then sat down at his desk and, using a pencil, converted the message from Morse Code into words. He read the message to himself before he stood and announced,

"I am about to read the message."

The crowd became silent, all wondering what the message would say.

Ridgeway cleared his throat, and in a clear voice and over-inflated sense of self-importance, he read the words,

"Welcome to the modern age Ramsay. Congratulations. The line is open."

The crowd was hushed now; the doubters, who had claimed some sort of trick, shifted uneasily and looked at each other with disbelief. They had seen the influx of workers and their strange tools and the equipment that arrived by a wagon pulled by four magnificent draft horses. Yet as Ridgeway read the message, their scepticism wavered, and doubt gave way to acceptance.

*****

"This new telegraph system will be good for business, Jimmy Boy," said Jack as he carried a tray of beer glasses to the table.

"I'll be able to send a telegram when I run short of liquor, and it can come up by wagon the very same day. It'll be much quicker than sending an order with the coach and then having to wait for delivery."

'Yes, Jack, times have changed, that's for sure. But I just wonder if the changes are for the better," replied Jimmy Boy.

"I have never known you to be a pessimist, Jimmy

Boy."

"Not a pessimist, Jack. Just a very cautious man. And a realist."

Martha took a sip of her water and looked at her mother.

"It will be good for the Emporium, too, Mama. I will be able to order new stock and receive it much quicker."

'Don't see 'ow this new-fangled telegraph thing will 'elp me," drawled Jennings.

"Me either," agreed Wells.

*****

Chapter 4

On the outskirts of Ramsay, a figure emerged from the shadows of the trees lining the road. His name to the white folks from where he'd come from was Mad Bobby, a man who had seen more hardship than any man should ever have to bear. Years of toil under the harshness of the outback sun had etched deep lines into his leathery skin, a stark contrast to the spirit he still possessed.

Each step was a silent declaration of strength, a dance of sinew and bone; however, his body displayed the results of years spent in bondage. Around his skinny ankle hung a link of chain, which not only weighed him down physically but was draining his soul with each passing day. It was Mrs Wells who espied him. She was on the verandah of the Emporium armed with her constant companion, her broom. She raised her hand to shade her eyes and let out a loud gasp.

"Miss Martie, you'd better come as quickly as you can. There is some poor soul struggling into town. And by the Good Lord, it looks as if he is chained."

Martha put her pen down and walked out to see what the fuss was about.

"Who has a chain, Ethel?"

There was no reply, just a push to the side of Mrs Wells's head so she could see up the road.

"Heavens! It's some poor black man. Ethel, I can't leave here. Please dash across and inform Jack. The man looks as if he needs help. On second thoughts, get the doctor. Or no, better see if Connolly is at the police station. Or…"

"Too many orders, Miss Martie. I'll fetch the Doc."

*****

The man's leg was a twisted mass of red and purple, and the hair had worn away from the abrasion of the metal and left exposed a mass of putrefying flesh. Despite the antiseptic smell of the small clinic, the room reeked of death and decay. Kevin Heath did his best to clean the wound, with his wife Violet as his nursing assistant. As he worked on the man, he couldn't help but think how pleasing it was to be back working with his wife. She seemed to be a completely different woman since the birth of their child.

A slight, almost hesitant knock on the door disturbed the medical team. Doctor Kevin Heath turned to see Jack enter the room.

"I've got him on the bed, Jack, and he is sleeping. I gave him a dose of laudanum to ease whatever pain he is in."

"Has he said anything?"

"He's said quite a bit, but it's all double Dutch to me. Blackfeller talk. I don't think he understands English."

"Or maybe he doesn't want us to know he speaks English, Doc."

Jack scratched his head and poured a generous drop of brandy into his glass.

"What's the go with the chain, Doc?" he coughed as the brandy hit a raw spot in his throat.

"That's got me beat Jack. Why would anyone put a chain on a fellow human being?"

"You think maybe he's a runaway prisoner, Doc?"

"I doubt it, Jack. Not even our prison system would shackle such a frail man. You only need to look at him to see he wouldn't harm a fly."

Jack eyed off the man on the bed. He noted the emaciated state of his body and the festering wounds. But what struck him the most was the sadness in the old man's eyes.

"I think it would be a good idea if I went for a ride and see if I can get Jacky to come into town. He might be able to talk to the man and find out the circumstances."

"Makes sense Jack. He's a good man, our very own blackfeller."

Then Jimmy Boy added,

"But I think Jacky is more of a white feller than you, Jack."

As Jack walked out, he called back,

"I'll bring Wells back with me as well. We need to get the chain off the man's ankle, and Wells is the best blacksmith about."

*****

"You know, I've never been much of a handyman," chuckled Wells as he filed away at the iron chain.

"Leastways doin' a job like this. Jis 'ope I'm not freein' a runaway."

The chain gave a *clunk* as it fell to the floor, and Wells had a gloating smile on his face at his accomplishment.

"You've done a fine job, Wells," commented the Doc

in all seriousness.

Jennings piped up,

"And who would 'ave thought you 'ad the brains to wedge a cloth between the chain and 'is ankle?"

"Yes, very clever indeed, Mister Wells. That certainly saved the man any more aggravation to his wounds. Any further infection could be fatal."

The doctor addressed Jacky.

"He's still sleeping, as you can see. We'll go to the Inn and have a drink and give him a couple of more hours' sleep. Violet will tend to him and let us know when he wakes. Then I hope you can get some sort of explanation from him, Jacky."

"Could be a verrrry interesting tale, Doc. I am looking forward to it."

*****

The man looked up when he heard the door open. Jacky stepped inside and held his arms in front of him, offering no threat, and he backed this up with a generous smile. The old man was curious and a little confused. He had little recollection of being carried to this room, but he could still recall the countless days he had walked and stumbled before he arrived on the edges of Ramsay.

"Wallahh!" said Jacky gently.

With a nod of the head from the man, Jacky knew that things would be fine.

"Wallahh!" came the rasping reply.

But then the man broke into a dialect completely unfamiliar to Jacky.

"You speak *Kamilaroi*?" asked Jacky very slowly.

"Some little *Kamilaroi,* I speak yes. I *Wiradjuri*."

"Good. That's a start. Now," still speaking very slowly,

"How did you come to be here? And what was the chain around your ankle?"

The old man swung his head to the side and looked at his foot. He smiled a gap-toothed smile when he saw the iron was gone. For the next half an hour, Jacky patiently delved into the man's past. When he had gleaned as much information as he needed, he patted the old man on the head and thanked him, then indicated with a yawn that the man should rest.

Jacky

*****

"He told me he has walked for over thirty sleeps. And he was prepared to keep walking until he got back to his homeland, way south of here."

"Where's he been Jacky?" interrupted Wells.

"And wot's the go with the chain?"

Jacky became impatient. He wanted to impart the knowledge he'd gained from the old aboriginal but also wanted to reveal only enough information that people needed to know.

"Hush up for a while, Wells, and listen!"

Wells hung his head.

"Sorry Jacky. Go on."

"His name is Burra, which means *big*. But he says that the white people call him Mad Bobby. He belongs to the *Guringai* tribe, which is a tribe way south of here near Sydney."

"Bloomin' long way from 'ome," interjected Wells, who was immediately hushed up.

"Jis shut yer trap fer a while, Wells, and listen," said

Jennings importantly.

"Yes, Mister Wells. Please, let's just hear Jacky out."

Jimmy Boy wanted to learn as much as possible about the stranger.

"Burra left his country with his tribe to find new hunting grounds. Unfortunately for them, they were captured by a mob of drovers taking sheep to the markets."

"Where's the markets?"

"Shut up, Wells!"

"They were kept bound for the first few days, and then they were taken far north of here. They were kept chained and forced to work as general hands around the farm. The women are used as cooks and cleaners and…."

Jacky drew a deep breath, "They are used as pleasure for all the men."

There was a collective gasp.

"Go on, Jacky," prodded Jimmy Boy.

"Burra managed to steal a file, and over a period of time, he managed to cut through a link in the chain, and he fled overnight."

"And his family? His tribe?" asked Jimmy Boy, a sympathetic tone in his voice.

"Either still there or dead. But he thinks they are still alive, as they were too valuable to kill. The men were forced to work as tree fellers, clearing the scrub around the western edge of New South Wales. Somewhere close to the Queensland border. They'd grub the stumps out with picks and shovels and then stack the timber up and burn it. Burra said there were many others employed by the station owner, but his family and a few others were the only ones held as captives."

"Is there anything we can do?" asked Alec, who had come in on the last part of the conversation.

"There is nothing we can do. The old man is not even sure where the place is. He said it is a hard country, stony and not suited for white man's farming. Leastways until the scrub is cleared. But he did say it is a good area for sheep. He mentioned a place the white men referred to a lot. A place where they would go and buy their supplies and alcohol."

"And?"

"A place called Milburra."

"Milburra? Can't say as I've heard of it," said Alec as

he scratched the stubble on his chin.

"Milburra? That's the place where our telegraph line links up with the line to Brisbane," said Jimmy Boy.

*****

"Jimmy Boy, would you have any objections to me taking Burra home to Shanghai? He needs to be with his own kind, and me and Mama are there. I am sure Martie will not mind. And there is a slight chance that my mother will be able to communicate with him. She knows far more dialects than me. I think she has a smattering of the *Wiradjuri* language."

"Jacky, you do not have to ask me to make decisions you can make yourself. Shanghai is your property now and your responsibility. You are a man, Jacky. And a man makes his own decisions. You will find through life that some decisions you make are the right ones, but invariably, there will be wrong ones. Nobody on this earth is perfect. And I think the decision you have made to take Burra home is a very wise decision indeed. The poor man needs all the help he can get."

"Thank you for understanding, Jimmy Boy. Most white folk would not."

"But I am not white," laughed Jimmy Boy.

"I'll return to Shanghai and fetch the wagon and take Martie home this afternoon as well. She's tiring herself out a lot lately at the Emporium. It's lucky she has Mrs Wells to help her."

"Try and find out as much as you can from the old man Jacky."

*****

Burra appeared pleased to be out of the doctor's sick bed. He sat in an upright posture in the wagon, and on the journey to Shanghai, he said nothing. Jacky attempted to draw him into a conversation, but the man was either stubborn or afraid of something. His eyes were never still; they darted from side to side as his head whipped like a snake. The man was not mad; Jacky knew that. But he sensed he had lost a lot of general day-to-day knowledge of things. Maybe it was due to the lack of an adequate diet or simply due to the incarceration he had suffered and the sights he had witnessed. Jacky was determined to nurse the old man back to health and then try and help him reclaim his family. But the problem was, he pondered….

"How am I to do that?"

*****

Mia served up the two men their evening supper. Jacky had taken the old man to a spare hut and indicated that this was his to stay in. Burra had accepted the fact now that Jacky was solely in charge of him. He seemed to trust him and tried to comply with whatever the young aboriginal wanted. Burra looked at the steel cot with a mattress, a blanket, and two pillows. His old grey eyes misted over as he looked at Jacky and pointed to himself.

"Me?"

Jacky indicated sleeping by closing his eyes and saying,

"Yes, for you. Sleep. But eat first."

Martha stood nervously at the door and watched as the two men ate the lamb stew.

"At least he has a good appetite, Jacky," said Martha, who could think of nothing better to say.

"By the looks of him, I don't think he's had a meal as large as this in a good while."

Jacky turned to his wife.

"Martha, you go off back to the house. I'll stay here with Mama for a while and see what else we can find out about him."

"But Jacky, I'm as curious as you are. Can't I stay?"

"It's best you don't, Martie. The old man is still a bit nervy being around strangers, and you are far too white for him to trust. You run along, and I will tell you all later tonight."

*****

Jacky squatted in front of the old man. He tried to glean more from Burra, speaking to him in the *Kamilaroi* language, and to his surprise, the old man opened up,

"My language is *Wiradjuri,* but I learn little *Kamilaroi* from the other blacks on the farm where the white man kept me."

"So, how long did the white man keep you and your family captive?"

"Almost three winters."

"Burra, I am going to help you get your family back. I don't know how yet, but I promise you, I will do my best or go to the Dreamtime trying."

"You be a good man, Jacky."

The old man hung his head, not in deference, but in gratitude.

"But you will have to help me, Burra. You need to lead the way."

The old man's eyes glowed with a fierce determination.

"I lead the way, Jacky."

*****

"Martha, it is something I must do."

Jacky knew that despite the vastness of the outback, he also knew he must be steadfast in his conviction to help Burra. He also knew the dangers of entering the outback with a man he barely knew and was not of his clan. But he saw the desperation in the old man and that had resonated in Jacky's soul.

"Jacky, the outback is still a harsh place, even for an aboriginal. And you must remember that away from Ramsay you are not known. You are a wealthy aborigine and landowner, Jacky, and that does not sit well with people around here, let alone in places unknown. People are jealous of you, Jacky, and to many, seeing you in town with me is like a bur sitting in their backside. It's just not normal, Jacky. A black man having more land and money than a white man."

"I trust myself and my judgment, Martie. This is something I must do."

"*Must do*? Or do you just want to be rid of me for a while, Jacky?" she teased and kissed him on his cheek.

"Martie, if I knew it would be a safe trip, then I would surely take you with me. You know I will miss you ever so much."

"What about my father? What should I tell him?"

"There's no need. I will ride over tomorrow and see him myself. He will understand. Jimmy Boy won't stand in my way."

"He may not stand in your way, Jacky, but I dare say he won't approve."

*****

"Jimmy Boy, we will leave at first light tomorrow. If

everything goes according to plan, we should be back within a month. Burra arrived here on foot, but we will have the advantage of horses to find his family."

Jennings and Wells listened in, and Wells nudged Jennings and whispered,

"Told ya Jennin's. Even Jacky needs to go *walkabout*. Same as all blacks. In their blood."

But Jennings did not pay heed. He would be up and ready in the morning to meet Jacky and Burra in Shanghai. Jennings felt adventurous. And he wanted to prove a point. He was not too old to work for Jimmy Boy and certainly not too old for adventure. He slept a restless sleep but was out of bed and ready to go even before the sun had any inclination to rise. He was outside the stables at Shanghai rolling himself a cigarette when Jacky came out of the house to rouse Burra from his cabin. He smelt the cigarette smoke before he saw the intruder.

"Where would you be going at this hour, Mister Jennings?"

"Could ask you the same question, Jacky, but I know where you are goin'. And this old man is goin' with ya."

Jacky simply smiled at the man and said,

"C'mon then. Help me saddle some horses."

*****

Chapter 5

In the heat of the Australian sun, Jennings felt the rays wrapping around him like a cocoon. The golden orb that beat down upon the men stretched high in the cloudless sky, turning the rugged landscape into a shimmering mirage. The two aboriginal men rode tall and steady, seemingly unaffected by the cloying heat which caused Jenning's shirt to cling to his body.

"Can we take a spell?" Jennings called through chapped and dry lips.

"Not until we reach water Jennings. Burra seems to smell water in the distance. We'll stop then and have something to eat."

"Smell water? What rot!" muttered Jennings.

"Only water I know that smells is piss," he mumbled.

Burra turned on his horse to study Jennings, an aura of concern etched on his face. He spoke softly to Jacky.

"Maybe not a good idea bringin' the white man Jacky."

Jacky turned and looked at Jennings. The intensity of the heat and the long ride was getting to the man.

"He'll be fine, Burra. I've known him for a long time, and he has persistence running through his body. Persistence, but maybe not patience. We'll keep an eye on him. And Burra, you will have to learn to tolerate him and his strange ways. And he sure does have plenty," he added.

It was another hour before Burra raised his head and sniffed the air.

"Water soon, Jacky."

He pointed to the heavens at a flock of galahs circling a stand of trees about a mile in the distance.

"Birds know where there is water," he said knowingly. No birds are a bad sign. No birds, no water."

"Seems you must be like a bird too, Burra," laughed Jacky.

The horses whinnied softly upon spotting the glimmer of water ahead.

They eased their mounts to a stop at the small creek's edge and let them drink. Ducks burst from the reeds along the water's edge, their quacking a babbled chorus of surprise. A lone water rat wrinkled its nose in disgust at the unwelcome intrusion, and a water dragon quickly flopped off a log and disappeared underwater.

Jennings dismounted quickly, his leg and rump aching below him. It had been a while since he'd been on horseback for such a long period of time. He bent low and scooped water into his parched mouth, the cool liquid washing the grit from his lips. Each gulp was a revival, and his two companions were quick to follow suit.

"Tell Jennings not too much. Plenty here. No need to be greedy. Make him sick if he drinks too fast," said Burra as he watched Mister Jennings scoop more of the precious liquid into his dry mouth.

"Do you know if there's more water ahead before the next town?" Jacky asked Burra.

"Plenty water Jacky. Just got to know where to find it. 'sides, I thought you was a blackfeller like me. You should know."

Jacky laughed at the mild rebuke.

"Maybe I have lived with the white folk too long, Burra."

"Still got black skin, though," came the reply.

"That is one part of me that will never go away, Burra."

Jennings had his fill and had mounted his horse.

"Come on, you pair," he said with an air of assumed authority.

"I need a town where there is a good tumbler of rum."

*****

The terrain they travelled through was beginning to change. Gone were the vast expanses of trees and scrub cover, to be replaced by tracts of dry and sparsely vegetated ground.

Jacky began to sense Burra's growing uneasiness.

"Something troubling you, Burra?"

"Nothing. It's just that this country reminds me of where we are going. But if I remember rightly, we pass through some good country first. Many rivers and creeks to cross yet."

*****

Dusk had begun to settle over the landscape, casting shadows and creating an approaching blackness across the paddocks. The quietness of the afternoon seemed to cast a foreboding over a township in the distance. Jacky flicked the reins of his horse, his eyes straining to read the sign in the distance.

Gundurra

Pop'n 2,500

"We'll camp here tonight," he announced, keeping his voice soft alongside the evening hush.

"No sense riding into a strange town this late in the afternoon."

Jennings gave a groan and shifted in the saddle.

"Yeah, my arse is sore as hell from this horse. Couldn't we ride in and find a waterhole where we could have a rum?"

"No, Mister Jennings. A drink in a strange town is an open invitation for trouble. It's best we enter the town in the daylight. I don't feel like a bed in a gaol cell tonight."

With a reluctant sigh, Jennings dismounted.

'I'll git a fire goin' Jacky. Burra, wotcha cookin' tonight?"

But the aborigine, although he understood, opted to

avoid answering. Sometimes, he found the white man rather strange. And, at best, annoying.

As the night settled over the men lying huddled under coarse blankets, Burra sat up abruptly. He'd caught a flicker of movement in the bushes just out of the circle of light thrown by the dying fire.

"What is it, Burra?" said Jacky, with an edge to his voice.

The old man responded by throwing aside his blanket and hefting his spear in his hand. He stood and slunk off into the darkness while Jennings and Jacky sat upright with a pistol in their hands. They strained to hear, and when they did, it was merely laughter from the old man. He returned, a stray, mangy, and under-nourished dog following him.

"Got me an extra blanket, Jacky," laughed Burra as the dog wagged its tail.

The men rolled over to get some sleep while listening to the old man chatter to the stray in between feeding it dried kangaroo meat and holding it close to his body under the blanket.

*****

Jacky

The township they rode into was alive with revellers, all with an air of excitement and money in their pockets. It was a wealthy town, the economy bolstered by the fine fleece of the merino sheep, which numbered in their thousands. It seemed to the locals that there was so much future, with acres to be cleared and pastures to be sown. Itinerant workers made up a huge majority of the town's population, along with a camp full of aboriginals on the outskirts.

"Make sure they are watered and given a good feed of oats," commanded Jacky to the stable hand.

"Got money, mister?" came a grunt.

Jacky fished in his pocket and gave the man some coins. The three men decided to check the town out and strolled along the wide main street, with Burra's new friend, the dog, sticking very close to his mate's side.

"What's the occasion?" Jacky finally asked the wiry, balding man who had been eyeing him from a distance. The man walked over to the pair and leaned into Jacky's face, his breath reeking of stale tobacco.

"Ah, the picnic races is what. The Gilmore Cup. Named after a horse breeder who started the race about twenty years ago.".

His voice was a gravelly drawl.

"Course 'e's dead now, but the races are still 'eld every year. A rich farmer from up north puts up the prize money these days. Whole town turns out. Dressed to the nines and money to burn. Biggest social event of the year."

He looked Burra up and down and sneered.

"It's not about the fifty guineas prize money, though. It's all 'bout community spirit yer know?"

Jacky was intrigued.

"So, this race, is it open to anyone?"

The man's smile grew, showing a row of uneven teeth.

"Sure is."

He slapped Jacky on the back.

"But don't you be thinkin' you can jis show up with any old nag and win? This is serious business here. The 'orses are all thoroughbreds, and the jockeys are well trained."

His eyes narrowed, and he studied Jacky.

"You look like you got a bit of a wild streak in ya. Want

me to set you up with a horse?”

“No need,” replied Jacky casually.

“I have my own at the livery stable.”

The man threw back his head and laughed. The exertion caused him to let out a thunderous fart, which only made him laugh more.

“Bet yer ‘orse can’t catch that bit of wind darky.”

He bent over double with delight at what he perceived to be his own sharp wit.

“Anyways, where would a black feller like you get an’ ‘orse good enough to run in the race?”

He stumbled off laughing.

Jacky turned to his friends.

“We might get some more information about this race. I think it would take a good horse to beat my stallion.”

Jennings tugged at the shirt of a man walking past him. The man pulled away with fear and stammered,

“What do you want?”

“No need to be fearful of me, mister. Jis some

information."

The man displayed obvious relief. He had experienced trouble with drunken blacks before, and he did not take kindly to the look of a grubby white man accompanied by two Aboriginals.

"Information? No money?"

Jacky, in his polished voice, interrupted.

"We don't need money, mister. I want to know how to enter my horse in the big race today?"

*****

"So, this race, the Gilmore Cup, how much is the entry fee?" asked Jacky.

An overweight man adorned with a battered hat, drummed his fingers on the cigarette-scarred table outside a barber's shop.

"Too much fer you, darky," sneered the man.

His slur hung in the air like cigarette smoke.

Jacky squared his shoulders, aware of the looks fastened on him by the bystanders.

"I asked you…how much?"

"Ten shillings. And you stand to win fifty guineas."

The man turned aside, expecting the black man to walk away. But to his surprise, Jacky fumbled in the bag tied to his belt and counted out a guinea.

"It's all there mister. What time does the race start?"

The man raked the money in and said,

"Have yer nag ready at the common at two o'clock terday."

He let out a derisive laugh and added,

"And good luck, darky."

"Let's go, men," said Jacky to his companions.

"I need to find a post office."

*****

"Steady boy," whispered Jacky as he gently caressed the stallion's neck. The crowd's murmur had grown to a crescendo, charged with the atmosphere. The sudden *pop* of the starter's gun echoed around the town, sending a flock of cockatoos skyward in a chaotic flurry of wings and feathers.

The horses, all varying in colours and sizes, bolted forward, leaving the starting tape in the distance.

Hooves pounded the solid ground on the circular track and were matched by the thumping hearts of the jockeys. Jacky could feel the power surging beneath him as the stallion responded to his light grasp on the reins. He had not given the horse a free head yet and bided his time behind the leaders. The starting tape was a distant memory now, forgotten in the frenzy of the race. The horses made the first turn, and the sound of the crowd was lost in the distance.

Jacky figured there was about a half mile to run, and he made the decision to give the horse a free rein.

"Now, boy, give it all you've got!"

He slackened the reins, and the response was instantaneous. The stallion's stride lengthened, and he was covering the ground with no sign of exertion. They went by one horse and then another. Ahead of them by a few feet was the race favourite, a proud bay mare bred for exactly this. Jacky had heard talk of the mare; she had won every race she had entered, leaving a trail of defeated competitors eating her dust.

They were neck and neck now, and Jacky could see the beads of sweat on the jockey's forehead. He stared in surprise. The rider was a mere girl. He gave her a grin as he surged past her. The crowd could be heard now as they neared the finishing tape. But the girl was not done with yet and drew alongside Jacky. He could see the mare's eyes, white-rimmed with determination, and could smell the sweat given off by both horses.

Jacky gave one last light slap with the stick he had been using as a riding crop, and the stallion understood. He extended himself and, with muscles bulging, found an extra speed and crossed the tape a half body length ahead of the mare. Jacky eased his stallion up well past the finishing tape, and as he reined to a stop, the girl pulled up alongside him.

He was pleasantly surprised by her reaction.

"Nice ride mister. You have one mighty fine horse there."

She smiled and reached her hand between the two horses. Jacky accepted her hand, and they shook warmly.

"You rode a fine race yourself, Missy. I am sorry if a loss has disappointed you."

Again, he was surprised by her words.

"A loss does not bother me, mister. It had to happen sooner rather than later. We have had a good run, haven't we, Clara?"

She patted her horse's neck, and the horse whickered softly.

"I'm Charley," she said as she removed the cap she had been wearing and let her long, golden hair loose.

"Well, Charlene, actually. But ever since I can remember, folks have called me Charley."

"Both nice names, missy," said Jacky politely.

"You can call me Jacky."

"Well, I think we should ride back. You have your prize money to collect, Jacky."

The other horses and riders were making their way back now, and as one rider went by Jacky, he spat out of the corner of his mouth and cursed.

"Fuckin' blacks. Never shoulda been allowed to run in the race."

Jacky shrugged the comment off. He was more

interested in the cheering crowd as they hung over the fence, some congratulating him but most bemoaning the fact that they did not have their wager on the black man's stallion.

They turned their sweating horses around and slowly trotted back to the presentation area. Charley leaned across as she maintained her rhythm and suggested mischievously to Jacky,

"Care to have dinner with me tonight? I have a proposition that involves your stallion and my mare."

Jacky raised a brow, curiosity aroused, but he was guarded.

"A proposition? Sounds intriguing. But nothing improper I hope."

"Oh, come on now. We're both adults," she said rather teasingly.

"Horses need companionship too. Same as people."

Jacky had no time to respond as the reins of their horses were clutched by one of the race organisers. He led them towards a makeshift stage where an official-looking gentleman was waiting.

"Ladies and Gentlemen, we have a new champion. I am pleased to give you…"

He stopped and looked at the small-statured man standing beside him and whispered,

"For God's sake, man, what is the name of the winning horse?"

The man glanced around nervously, watching the expectant faces of the crowd.

"I don't know Mister Burgess. Just call the horse *Bandit*. That's as good a name as any, and nobody will know the difference. And it's only a darky riding it," he added.

The official boomed out in a voice that could be heard on the outskirts of the town.

"The winning horse is *Bandit*. Ridden by the very capable …" he paused again, but this time he was not flustered and said, "Mister *Black*."

He congratulated himself for his wit with a smug smile.

Jacky gave a wry grin. He was not perturbed in the least. He dismounted and walked to the small stage to accept his winnings.

"Speech!!!!" came the roars from the crowd.

Jacky turned and looked at the faces, a blur in front of him. When he spoke, the crowd went silent. Never had the people gathered there heard an aboriginal speak with such grace.

Jacky rubbed the sash which was draped over his stallion's mane and then began his speech.

"I certainly did not ride into your town with the intention of entering a race which has so much significance to you, the townsfolk, let alone dream of winning that race. But win it we did, didn't we *Bandit*?"

Jacky had not named his horse, but now he settled for the name it had been given. He tended to quite like it.

He looked at the young girl standing beside the mare.

"I wish to congratulate the rider and the horse that took second honours. I believe that horse is a crowd favourite, but unfortunately, my horse was too good on the day."

The crowd erupted into a wild, rousing applause. Jacky stepped away from the official and pulled at his horse's reins to lead it away. Charlene reached out and grabbed him by the arm.

"You didn't give me an answer, Jacky."

"To what?" he replied absently.

"Dinner. Tonight. Care to join me?"

"For dinner then, and if that is all you have in mind, the answer is yes."

"You can never tell what this young girl has in mind, Jacky," she said seductively.

Jacky, still disturbed by her audacity and forward manner, asked,

"And what do you stand to gain from this dinner meeting?"

Her eyes softened, and her eyes met his.

"Perhaps I am seeking more than a good offspring from my mare. Maybe I desire a connection that goes beyond the grazing paddocks."

Her honest admission shocked him.

"But I am a married man," he said with butterflies in his stomach. He thought of Martha, and her laughter rang in his ears. He thought of how she warmed any room she entered and made people smile.

"Married to a black woman? Those sorts of marriages are not recognised here."

"I am married to a white woman," he said, his voice firm but still with the faintest of trembling.

"So, your marriage is valid."

 Her response carried a certain amount of bitterness.

"It certainly is Miss Charley. I was even married in a church."

Her mood brightened, and her demeanour altered.

"Even married men have been known to stray Jacky."

He turned to walk away, his mind in turmoil at the young girl's suggestive approach.

"And where is this dinner engagement?"

"There are three pubs in town, but one of them has a bad reputation. I only ever frequent the *Faith & Hope Pub*. It is easy to find. Just walk to the end of the main street, and you will come across it."

Charley was about to lead her horse away when she remembered something that was important.

'When you come tonight to the pub, ask for Charlene Reagan. The publican runs a respectable business and doesn't allow blacks in."

"Then you can forget about dinner," said Jacky resignedly.

"I did not take you for a man who gives in easily, Jacky. I told you mention my name, and you will be welcomed. Besides, it is a bit of a boost for trade having the winner of the big race in the pub."

She brushed her hair from her eyes and called over her shoulder as she walked away,

"See you tonight, Jacky."

The black man, intrigued by this wisp of a girl, nodded and replied,

"Tonight then."

*****

There had been a curious bystander at the prize-giving ceremony. The man edged towards Jacky's stallion and eyed it with a mix of admiration and greed. The horse's muscles rippled beneath its hair, and it snorted and tossed its mane.

"This is one piece of nice horse flesh," the man murmured to himself.

"And to think a bloody blackfeller owns it," he spat.

"But not for long. That horse will be mine tomorrow, and the darky will be dead."

The two men standing with him exchanged knowing glances. They knew what their boss had in mind.

"Boys, you need to find out where the black bastard is camped. Here is the plan," he said in a conspiratorial whisper.

"Once we know where he is camped, we'll sneak in just on dawn while the bastard's asleep and cut his throat. Then take his horse and be out of this shit town for good."

"Mister Mullins, yer fergettin' he has got two others with 'im. What about them?"

"Are you tellin' me yer scared of an old white man and an even older black? You're getting soft, Newton. We can 'andle the three of the bastards."

Newton and Scanlon knew it was a risky plan, but

neither of them had the guts to argue with their boss. The three were desperate men, down on their luck, and the promise of a horse like the one they looked at could change their fortunes. Apart from Mullins, the thought of killing men in cold blood disturbed the other two.

Scanlon spoke up.

"Dawn boss? Why not night? Less chance of gittin' caught and more chance of gittin' away."

"Yer right. Now you pair skedaddle and find their camp."

*****

Chapter 6

Jacky handed Jennings a pound note.

"This is for you, Mister Jennings. I have some things to attend to. I need to send a letter home and will meet you both at the camp tonight. Use the money to get Burra a haircut and a shave and then you can go find a drinking hole. But I warn you Jennings, do not be drunk when I return tonight. If I find you drunk, I will turn you around and send you home."

Jennings noted the gravity in the man's voice.

"I swear, Jacky. I will just have a couple of drinks."

He tipped his head to one side and asked,

"What about Burra? And why a haircut and a shave?"

Jacky came straight to the point.

"I do not know this town, Jennings, but maybe the pubs here do not allow blacks like us inside. Besides, I do not even know if Burra drinks alcohol. And as for the haircut and shave, we do not want to risk anyone recognising him. I will go to a store and buy him a new pair of trousers and a shirt."

He thought for a moment, and his face brightened.

"I have an idea. Buy yourself a bottle of whatever you want and take it back to the campsite. That way, you can cause no trouble."

"So, what you got planned, Jacky?" asked Jennings curiously.

"Not that it is any of your concern, Mister Jennings, but I am off to find a Post Office, and then I have a business venture to investigate."

Jennings knew that was all the information he would get.

*****

The Post Office was a large brick building set back off the main road. It looked a sad affair, as if carrying the weight of thousands of messages had seen it grow tired. Jacky pushed open the heavy wooden doors, and the creaking sound echoed through the expansive interior, a cavernous room filled with the smell of aged paper and faint traces of ink. The walls were lined with shelves holding boxes and parcels. Several people were milling about…an elderly man shuffling through a stack of envelopes and a young mother trying to control her small child and stop him from fiddling with the set of scales on the counter. Yet amidst this flurry of subtle activity, the clerk remained engrossed in his work. He was a young man with prematurely thinning hair and a pair of spectacles resting on his hawk-like nose. Jacky watched him, captivated by his rhythmic movements as he sorted the letters. He wondered if he ever took the time to wonder what each letter contained…a message from home, a birthday greeting, or just a bill from a local business.

Jacky cleared his throat.

"When you are not busy, I'd like to buy some paper and a pen to draft a letter."

The clerk looked up and acknowledged Jacky. Then, he went back to his task as if the black man were a piece of furniture.

Jacky spoke again.

"Maybe you didn't hear me."

"I heard you. Just wait. Can't you see I am busy?"

He pushed the last of the letters into a cubicle and turned his attention to the small child.

"Leave things be, boy!" he admonished.

The boy responded with a loud round of exaggerated crying.

Then he turned back to Jacky.

"You want me to write you a letter?"

"Why do you ask?"

"Cos blackfellers round here cannot write."

"I am not from around here and I *can* write."

"An uppity, educated blackfeller, huh?"

"Mister, I don't have all day. Paper and pen please."

The clerk pulled open a drawer and extracted a pile of stationery.

"Pens are free," he said, indicating the ink well and pen beside it.

"Paper and stamps are not. Good luck with your letter," he said with a detached tone.

"Thank you. I will take my time."

*****

In the dim light of the dingy shop, a man hunched over a makeshift barber's chair, the frayed edges of a dirty towel wrapped around an elderly man's neck. He stopped mid-motion as Jacky and Burra entered the shop but dismissed them with a cursory wave and gave his razor a swipe on the strop he held in one hand. He went back to gently manoeuvring the lethal blade down his customer's scrawny neck. Jennings indicated to Burra to take a seat, and as he did so, the barber stopped his work and said in a snarly voice,

"Chairs fer customers only darky. Now you jis better git yer black arse outta 'ere before I take me razor to ya. And take the fuckin' dog with ya."

Burra understood the man's intentions but not his words and remained seated.

"The man wants a 'aircut and a shave, mister," said Jennings, putting on a brave face.

"Dun told yer, I don't shave blacks. Don't cut their 'air neither. Less they got a pocket full of money. Heads full of crawly things. Now git outta 'ere before I call the law!"

"If it's money yer worried about, I got money, mister," said Jennings as he fingered the pound note. He pulled the crumpled note from his pocket and waved it under the barber's nose.

The barber changed his stance immediately, and his face lit up greedily.

"Take jis about all that bill fer a shave and a 'aircut, mister," he uttered as he reached his wrinkled handout. But Jennings was too quick for him and pulled the money away.

"I guess we will jis 'ave to go elsewhere, mister barber man. Yer price is a bit too steep fer me. Come on, Burra. Let's git outta this shit 'ole."

"'ang about. Can't ya take a little bit of local 'umour? I'll do the darky fer a bob, and that is a damned bargain, mister. Never know what disease I'll catch off 'im."

He motioned Burra into the now vacant chair, and the old man sat down with a certain degree of grace. He'd seen white men cut beards and hair before and had no outward concerns. He reached for his dog and pushed it between his legs.

Burra looked into the cracked mirror and watched as years of hair dropped to the floor to lie with hair of every different colour and cleanliness. Once his matted locks were shorn, the barber took to his beard and, with precision, shaved the hair away from the old man, revealing a face that had not seen daylight since he was a youth. Burra traced the contours of his face and marvelled at the smoothness of his skin.

At that moment, Jacky walked in, looking for the two men. When he spied Burra, he let out a low whistle. The old man turned and grinned at him.

Jacky had a brown paper package with him and said to the barber,

"If you would not mind, I have some new clothes for my friend. Do you have a room where he can change?"

"Crikey you darkies are somethin'. Cut a bloody head of 'air, and yous want everythin'."

He indicated a room at the back.

"In there. But changin' rooms don't come cheap. Cost you a shillin' mister. And mind the bastard doesn't pinch anythin'. I'll be checkin' the room out before you leave."

The garments consisted of a plain shirt and a pair of trousers, both slightly large but serviceable, and a pair of heavy boots. The clothing hung on Burra's gaunt frame, a stark contrast to the hessian bag he had been wearing around his body, tied with a simple knot. As he pulled the shirt over his body, he felt its softness and the unfamiliar aroma of newness and freshness.

Burra had only agreed to the transformation because Jacky had told him that recognition could mean danger for them all. But as Burra looked at his bare feet, he felt a pang of defiance. He had never worn shoes and had walked the earth as his ancestors had done for generations, feeling every stone and blade of grass. The boots, well-crafted and a good fit, were a prison to him, like the chain he had worn around his ankle.

Jacky saw his reluctance and placed his arm gently on Burra's shoulder.

"It's all right Burra, no need, if you don't want. And Burra, nobody will recognise you now."

Burra grinned some more and dropped the boots to the floor.

Jennings was quick to speak.

"Reckon I can 'ave them if they fit me, Jacky?"

He scooped them up and inspected the heavy soles.

"They are yours if they fit Jennings. Now, come on, we'll head back to camp. I've told you I have an appointment tonight."

Jacky

Jennings hung the boots around his neck and whistled a tune while Burra walked behind them, continually sniffing his collar and smiling.

*****

Jacky soaped his body in the small creek near their camp. It felt good to wash the dust and grime from his body, and he lay back in the shallow water, thinking of the girl he was to meet that night. He knew she wanted to mate his stallion with her mare, but he also knew, via her incessant innuendos, that she had a further agenda on her mind.

He stood naked on the bank of the creek and towelled himself off with one of his two clean shirts.

"Lookin' good, Jacky. Must be meetin' someone important, huh?"

Jacky grunted, signalling he was in no mood to talk.

*****

Chapter 7

It was a short walk into the township, and Jacky relished the chance to exercise his legs after many days in the saddle. The *Faith & Hope Pub* was not hard to find. It was a brick structure, which made it stand out from the wooden buildings that bordered either side of it. Jacky walked up the small flight of steps towards the swinging doors, which looked as if they had seen their fair share of drama and good times. As he did so, a man came stumbling out the doors. He collided with Jacky and fell down the steps to end up in a crumpled heap. Jacky turned to go down and help him up until a voice stopped him. An old woman had come out behind the man, and she was wielding a green stick, just pulled from a willow tree.

"Leave him be darky, or I'll give you a lashin' too. Damned old fool drunk again. Jis wait till 'e gits his sorry arse 'ome. I'll whack his arse till 'e can't siddown to shit."

She proceeded to lay a good beating on the man's rump, and he pleaded with her to leave him be. She struggled to lift him and then half carried, half dragged him, down the street.

Jacky

Jacky grinned and pushed the doors open, then stepped into the bar area. The low murmur of conversation and the clinking of glasses ceased as the patrons eyed off the black man. The smoky atmosphere seemed thick with tension, and Jacky felt a rare uneasiness. A few of the drinkers, who had recognised the winner of the Gilmore Cup, offered a nod or a half-smile, but the majority cast him cold, hard stares, their expressions a blend of hostility and suspicion. Jacky stared back at the men, a collection of hard faces that seemed to be as hard as the wooden tables their elbows rested on.

Jacky's eyes scanned the room, taking his time to adjust to the dull light given off by the lanterns on the walls. The bar was a long plank of beautifully treated timber but was scarred by the years of crushed cigarette butts and bar room brawls. Behind the bar, an overweight man with an unkempt beard was drying glasses. He looked at Jacky and growled,

"Darkies ain't allowed in 'ere, mister. So piss off."

He looked Jacky over and shook his head.

"' specially ones dressed to the nines like you. Where would you come by the fancy shirt and that bandana you got 'round yer neck?"

Without drawing breath, he continued,

"Go on now, piss off! Told ya, no darkies allowed."

Jacky sidled up to the bar and placed his battered hat down. His hand hovered over the knife he had strung from his belt. He was not after a fight, but he knew the value of showing he was ready for one.

"I'm not here to cause any trouble, mister," Jacky said, his voice firm.

"I am here to meet with Miss Charlene Reagan. She is expecting me."

When the girl's name was mentioned, the bartender's attitude immediately altered. Nobody dared trouble the daughter of Harry Reagan.

"She'd be in the dining room, mister. Go on through. That way."

He indicated a door to the side of the room.

Jacky collected his hat and smiled at the onlookers.

"You can all just get back to your drinking now folks. This black man will not be troubling anybody."

Mutterings and curses followed him as he headed to

where he was directed.

*****

Jacky walked past a tinkling piano and found himself in a hallway where he read a sign saying *Dining Room*. He pushed the door open and spied Charlene Reagan sitting alone. Jacky had to look twice. The girl he had met that afternoon was barely recognisable. Gone were the dusty riding clothes, to be replaced by a simple yellow frock that highlighted her curves as she stood to greet him. Her hair was pulled back into a tight bun, a far cry from the long tresses flying from beneath her cap as she had galloped alongside him earlier that day. But the most striking change of all was the dark crimson lipstick she wore, giving her an allure and a mystery blended into one.

She extended her hand.

"I am so glad you could make it, Jacky."

She stood close to him, and he was bewitched by the scent of her perfume and her incredible smell of freshness.

They sat and ordered their meals. There seemed to be a tension between them, as thick as the faint wisps of cooking aromas wafting from the kitchen.

"The meals here are simply wonderful," she said, trying to break the ice.

They dined on lamb chops and a variety of fresh vegetables, the flavours surprisingly rich and vibrant, considering they had come from the dusty town gardens. The lamb was tender, and the potatoes soft and creamy, but the conversation was still dry.

"Miss Charlene," Jacky began, but she interrupted him.

"Charley is fine, Jacky. It is what I have become accustomed to."

"Charley, then, I have been thinking about our horses. How are we going to manage the breeding?"

His question hung in the air, as potent as whatever drink Charlene Reagan had in front of her.

Charley took a slow sip of her drink, her eyes never straying from his.

"Ah, the horses. They are quite the prize, aren't they?"

She leaned towards him and almost whispered her words.

"How well do you trust me, Jacky?"

"In what way? Is there any reason for me to mistrust you?"

Jacky was on edge now. He wanted a solid and reliable agreement on whether he was to put his stallion with the girl's mare.

"None at all, Jacky. I am an honest woman who believes in being upfront in all my business dealings."

"But I barely know you, Charley. That is hardly grounds for me to give up my horse to a stranger. Tell me more about yourself."

She leaned back in her chair and sighed.

"I am the daughter of Harry Reagan. My mother, bless her soul, is a mystery to me. She disappeared when I was very young, leaving myself and my brother Bruce in the care of my father. In fact, I have no recollection of her whatsoever. The talk is she ran off with a shearer, but I don't believe that. I grew up around men, Jacky, so do not let looks deceive you. I am a very worldly-wise woman."

Jacky gulped, beginning to feel more ill at ease.

'So, what you are suggesting is that I loan you my

horse. You stable it here in Gundurra and hope to breed a very handy foal."

"Correct, Jacky," she replied bluntly.

"Except for one thing. I am not in Gundurra. I am merely here for the Gilmore Cup. I arrived a week ago with a couple of my father's trusted farmhands and am due to return tomorrow."

"Just where do you live then?" asked Jacky, his interest piqued.

He fiddled with his fork, rolling peas around his plate.

"I live on my father's sheep station up near the Queensland border. It is about ten or twelve-day ride from here. We take it steady on our trips, as we do not like to push Clara."

"Clara?"

"My horse. It was named after my mother."

Jacky changed his tack and adopted a serious approach.

"Charley, I do not think this arrangement will come to fruition. I have business to take care of up north of here. And I cannot see myself leaving *Bandit* with a virtual stranger. And may I ask, just what is in this for me?"

The girl took her turn now to play with her food. She picked up one of her lamb cutlets and put it delicately to her mouth, where she proceeded to run her tongue provocatively over it.

She appeared to be thinking.

"What is in it for *you*?" she repeated him.

"Whatever *you* desire, Jacky," she smiled.

Jacky was disconcerted now and becoming agitated.

"Charley, please stop talking in riddles and talk some sense."

Her mood suddenly changed from a carefree young girl to a cold and calculating woman.

"You appear to me to be a man who does not like a bit of an adventure, Jacky. And I am the adventurous type."

"I see where you are coming from, Charley, but I have already told you I am a married man."

"Married! Schmarried! Who cares?"

Jacky stood up and said politely,

"It's time for me to head back to camp. I need to be on my way to Milburra tomorrow."

The girl looked up with an astonished expression.

"Milburra? Jacky, my father's sheep station, *Dingo's Retreat*, is just out of the township of Milburra."

Jacky's first reaction was to jump up in amazement, but he managed to control himself. The last thing he wanted was for anyone to know the reason for his journey. And he knew now, no matter how devious he had to be, he had to find out more about Charley and the township of Milburra.

Charley had noticed the change come over Jacky and asked him,

"What business do you have in Milburra, Jacky?"

He saw the perfect opportunity and carefully crafted his lie.

"I have not told you, Charley, but I own a considerable sized property way down south of here. I run both cattle and sheep, and it just so happens, not long back, a traveller came through town and was talking of the fine Merino sheep stations up Milburra way. So, here I am, as they say. I want to buy some stud rams. You want a foal from my stallion. I want some quality rams. It seems we can do each other a good turn."

She screwed her face up with curiosity mixed with disbelief.

"Excuse me for being so forward, Jacky, but how is it that an aboriginal man owns a '*considerable sized property,*' as you put it?"

"The truth be known Charley, is that aborigines have more claim to this land than the white man. It has belonged to my people for untold generations. But my property, acknowledged by the white man's law, is named *Shanghai* and was a wedding gift from the father of the woman I married."

"Some gift huh? You must be special to him, Jacky. But then again……."

She licked her lips lasciviously.

"I can see you just might have some special qualities. I think I might just have to set my sights on finding them."

Charley had become quite animated and exuberant. She was going to get what she wanted, while at the same time, Jacky would get his sheep. And she, being a young girl full of spirit, wanted some fun along the way. And she wanted to see firsthand just what special qualities the black man possessed.

"Although I did not win the race, Jacky, everything has turned out better than I expected. Let us have a drink to celebrate our partnership."

"Hold on Charley. No one has said anything about a partnership. And I will not take you up on the offer of a drink. I do not see the need to celebrate anything in a white man's way. Besides, I have my man back at camp. I would best be going. And you should make that drink your last one as well."

Jacky was wise enough not to mention Burra, for if, as he suspected, Burra had been held captive somewhere near Milburra, then there was the possibility that the girl may know of him. Or, at the very worst, recognise him.

Charley stood and walked around the table and placed her hands on Jacky's shoulders. She bent low to his ear and whispered as she nibbled on his lobe. He smelled the sweet scent of the wine she had been drinking, and this aroma, coupled with her perfume and the rubbing of her breasts on his back, began to agitate him.

"I have a room here in this very hotel, Jacky,' she

whispered, although there was nobody to hear,

"And I am a girl who gets awful lonely at night. Why don't we go back to my room and discuss some sort of agreement?"

She ran his hands down his back and then placed her arms around his waist. Jacky felt his body responding to the girl's gentle touch, and he did not pull away as she sought his lips. Jacky fought the idea of Martha knowing he was with another woman, but his lust was beginning to control him.

She pulled him up from his chair and led him out of the dining room and into the hallway, where a flight of stairs led to the rooms above. He gave a furtive look around him and allowed himself to be taken by the alluring white woman.

*****

"Do you realise how silly you look standing there, Jacky? I don't bite, you know," she laughed.

Jacky stood, unsure of himself, in front of the girl, his hands covering his nudity. She wiggled her finger at him, blew a kiss, and motioned him towards her.

Jacky cast all inhibitions aside and pulled her to him.

The feeling was wonderful; the warm, growing excitement was a special thing. And as he kissed her, their mouths moistly exploring, probing, widening, he realised Charley was trembling, not with fear of him, but with pure lust. He lowered her gently to the bed and kissed her, while she unbuttoned the front of her dress and directed his hands to her breasts. She closed her eyes as he caressed her body.

"It has been a terribly long time, Jacky," she whispered.

He pulled away and exclaimed,

"You're so young, Charley! Are you telling me you have done this before?"

She laughed and said,

"I told you I am a woman of the world, Jacky."

She cupped a creamy breast and pushed the nipple into his mouth, and Jacky suckled like a newborn lamb.

When they were spent, they lay beside each other, naked, under the soft covers. Charley rose on her elbows, her hair falling over Jacky's face, and looked at him. She traced his lips with her fingers and bent down, kissing him, outlining his lips now with her tongue.

"I'm absolutely shameless," she said, laughing.

"I want to do this all night long and again all day tomorrow. I am parched, Jacky, and now I've been to the water hole. I want to stay here."

He reached up and let her hair fall through his fingers. He followed the strands downward to the swell of her body and cupped her left breast.

"Do you know how handsome you are, Jacky? All over?"

"You're right. You are shameless."

"Are you upset with me, Jacky?"

"Of course not, but I really must be going."

He stood up, his tall body glowing almost purple in the dim light of the lantern, and he looked back at Charley. She was curled up, her hair sprayed over her shoulders, and her face buried in the pillow.

"She had been magnificent," he thought.

"*They* had been magnificent."

"What was the word she had used? *Parched*. Yes, she had been parched."

And yet he sensed she was not even fully sated.

He walked towards the door, and she pulled her head from the pillow.

"I will see you in Milburra, Jacky. Everyone knows my father's station. *Dingo's Retreat*."

"Till then," he said offhandedly.

But then she added,

"Jacky, nobody must know about tonight. My father would kill you if he knew you shared a bed with his daughter. Not to mention, he hates blacks."

Jacky placed his hat on his head, pulled the door open, and stepped out, calling back,

"Sounds like the sort of gentleman I'd like to meet. And I suppose your brother is just as protective as well."

The words she replied with sent Jacky into a state of confusion.

"Oh, don't worry about my brother. He was born stupid. My father keeps him confined to the house. His room is locked for his safety and for the safety of anyone in the house who has no business being there. The only time anyone is safe is when he is with his pigs. They are more of a friend to him than any human could ever be."

*****

Chapter 8

Jennings and Burra sat around the dying embers of the campfire. It was late, and Jacky had not yet returned. Burra sat with a stillness that emphasised his age, his eyes reflecting the faint coals. The quiet of the night was a marked contrast to the boisterous singing of the drunken white man he had endured for the past few hours. Burra's eyes remained fixed on the blackness of the edge of the camp, his thoughts a mystery to the drunken Jennings.

The old man had seen a lot in his time, and he knew that patience was a thing to cherish. But as time stretched on and Jacky's absence grew more pronounced, he had a gnawing feeling that something could be amiss. He rose for the third time that night and limped over to the three horses. Satisfied that they were settled for the night, he went back to the cleared space he had made and lay down to get some sleep.

*****

The three men tethered their horses some distance from the camp. They knew the risks of their plan and knew that if the townsfolk awoke, they would not stand a chance.

"No shooting," whispered Mullins.

"We cannot chance any noise. We will sneak in and see if they are sleeping, then untie the stallion and piss off as fast as we can ride."

As they approached the camp, the air was still, the only sound the gentle breathing of Burra, almost masked by the loud rasping and occasional farting sounds emitted by Jennings.

Mullins turned to Scanlon and Newton and spoke in a hushed tone.

"They're sleeping," he whispered.

"But I can only see two. Where is the other one?" he added with a degree of fear creeping into his voice.

"It is all right, Mister Mullins. Two makes it that much easier. Other bastard's prob'ly in town pissin' up 'is winnin's. "'e won't have much change outta his fifty guineas this time tomorrow."

Mullin's eyes raked the campsite.

"The horses are over yonder. Scanlon, you go and untie the stallion while we keep watch."

Mullins' hand rested reassuringly on the butt of his

pistol. They had formulated the plan, and now it was time to execute it.

*****

Jacky walked slowly out of the town. Most of the lights had been extinguished by now, and the only sounds were the occasional yapping of dogs. He had a smile on his face as he thought of Charley.

"She certainly is one hell of a woman," he mused.

But then he felt a pang of guilt. He had betrayed the woman he loved more than life itself. And he vowed never to fall into that trap again.

The night was darker than usual with the clouds obscuring what little moonlight there was. A playful smile covered his face as he took in the inky blackness. His heart was light as he thought about the passion he had shared with Charley. He knew that Martha would never know of his infidelity, that is, of course, unless he confessed. But his thoughts of the two women were quickly erased as he heard the loud voice of Mullins ahead. He increased his speed and moved lightly over the ground.

*****

As Scanlon inched his way towards the stallion, Burra's dog, sensing something was amiss, grew restless between the old man's legs and growled a soft warning. Burra's eyes snapped open at the noise, and he reached for the spear lying beside him. A faint noise caught his attention, just enough to break the stillness of the night. His heart thumped a quiet rhythm as his ears tuned in to the sounds of the darkness.

Burra sprang from his resting spot.

"Who's there?" he called in the harsh tone of the *Wiradjuri* dialect.

The stallion's ears pricked up, sensing the tension, and the dog's growls grew louder.

Burra lashed out with his bare feet and kicked Jennings in the ribs.

"Jennin's," he said.

The man rolled and groaned but suddenly became alert as the three men appeared in the dull light of the fire.

"Stay where you are, you black bastard," Mullins shouted as his hand tightened around his pistol.

"And keep that fuckin' dog back."

"Waddya want?" asked a trembling Jennings.

"We ain't gunna cause you no 'arm. We jis want to relieve yous of the 'orses yous got tied up over yonder."

Burra raised his spear into a throwing position, but Jennings grabbed his arm and pushed the spear down.

"No good Burra. They got the drop on us. Where the fuck is Jacky when we need 'im?"

Scanlon paused in his task, his hands hovering over the rope that held the stallion. Meanwhile, Jacky, having reached the edge of the camp, edged silently towards Mullins and pushed the tip of his knife's blade just far enough in for the man to drop the arm holding the pistol. Jacky's voice was cold and caused the man to shiver in fear.

"I don't think you are taking my horse anywhere, mister," he said, the words laced with a chilling calmness.

Jacky's hand remained firm, the knife's blade pressing slightly further into the fabric of Mullin's shirt, just far enough to pierce the skin and draw a faint trace of blood. He felt Mulllins' body quiver and pushed the blade a tad more into the man's skin.

"Now, just drop your pistol, or this knife will find itself deeper in your back."

His voice was low and steady but bore an ominous tone. The campfire gave a sudden crackle, making the situation even more tense.

Mullins swallowed hard. He could feel the cold steel against his skin. He loosened his fingers and let the pistol fall to the ground. Scanlon and Newton, both never known for their bravery, watched on nervously.

"I suggest the three of you get on your horses and get away from here before I let my man use his spear. He needs the practice."

Jacky looked at Newton and grinned, then said,

"You best be changing your trousers when you get to where you are going mister. They seem a bit damp on the front, and if my eyes are seeing things straight, we haven't had a drop of rain."

The men looked at each other and the unwavering figure of the aboriginal warrior. They needed no further bidding. It was almost comical to see them trying to avoid tripping over each other in their attempt to flee. They scrambled with their horses, fumbling with the reins as if they had suddenly forgotten how to ride. Once mounted, they galloped into the blackness.

"Pack everything now, Mister Jennings. We are leaving. It will be dawn soon, and I don't think we have seen the last of those three."

*****

The family sat around the long wooden table on the verandah and listened as Martha read out the letter.

To My Dearest Martha,

This is a message to keep you informed of our progress to reunite Burra with his family and set them free. We make steady progress each day, and I marvel at some of the countries we pass through. Some areas are extremely beautiful, while in stark contrast, there are areas where even a blackfellow would not live. Please pardon my attempt at humour. Mister Jennings has been a tower of strength and very helpful, but he still manages at least a hundred complaints a day. While we are gone, you might ask Mrs Wells to make him an extremely soft cushion for his return, as he is forever bemoaning a sore bottom from his saddle. You can tell Jimmy Boy that I am thankful he gave me the stallion. I entered a race in a small town we passed through and won fifty guineas.

I do not know when you will receive this, but it was sent on the 6th day of our journey. Burra has recovered a great deal of his strength, and he has been invaluable in supplying us with native food. We have had our share of setbacks in towns we have passed through, but I will not trouble you with details to cause you any undue worry. I will write again the next chance I get.

Your Loving Husband

Jacky Wang.

Martha kissed the letter, folded it, and then tucked it into her bosom. There was silence for a time until Mia spoke.

"My boy Jacky, he plenty smart man for a blackfeller."

She looked at Bindi with a superior look on her face.

"See Bindi, my side of the family 'as got some learnin'."

"You sayin' my side of the family is uneducated, Mia? Why, you can't even count."

Angela put a stop to their bickering.

"Would you two desist your childish banter and fetch some tea."

"And some cake, Bindi," added Martha.

*****

Chapter 9

Burra squinted into the early morning light. The smell of eucalyptus hung heavy in the air as he raked the coals together and reignited the fire. Jacky lay on his back thinking and listening to the gentle snoring of Jennings. He wondered if he had done the right thing, leaving Martha and setting off with Burra to find his people. And he still could not get the thought of Charley from his mind. Was he headed into danger?

Away from the fire, the horses were restless, and Jacky's stallion was tugging on its halter.

Burra handed Jacky a stick with meat threaded on it. His teeth sank into the charred flesh of the kangaroo with a satisfying crunch.

"Mmmm, good Burra," he said as he savoured the meat.

"Best save some, or Mister Jennings will be upset. He eats as if every meal is his last."

The smoky flavour, mingled with the sweet taste of the freshly roasted yams Burra had dug before the sun had risen, created a warm taste in Jacky's mouth. The morning was still, save for the occasional crackle from the dying fire. The day was already steamy, and the few wispy clouds were giving no relief to what promised to be a stinking hot day.

Burra nodded in approval as he watched Jacky savour the meal. His weathered hand reached into the fire to pull off another piece of meat from the carcass. He shoved the whole piece into his mouth and chewed it quickly as if there was a marauding dingo ready to snatch it from his grasp.

"We must be moving, Jacky," he said, his words carrying an urgency about them.

"Do you hear something I don't, Burra?"

Jacky cocked his head and listened, but the only sounds to be heard were the occasional rustling of early morning wildlife. Somewhere in the distance, a kookaburra's laughter could be heard, and the mournful cawing of a crow set the mood for the day.

The white men behind them had been relentless in their hunt, driven by greed to capture Jacky's stallion and to take revenge on the two aborigines.

"They're like shadows," murmured Jacky.

"Always there but never close enough to grab."

Jennings stirred and peeled off a fart.

"Somethin' smells good," he said as he sniffed the aroma of the roasting meat.

"Well, it certainly isn't you," admonished Jacky, but Jennings pretended not to hear.

"What you got cooked up fer us this time, Burra?"

"Just hurry, Jennings, and eat. We need to put some distance between ourselves and our followers."

Burra went all around the site and swept it clean with a branch from a gum tree and scattered the ash from the fire. Then he picked up the bones of the kangaroo and buried them under the leaves of a fallen tree while at the same time pocketing the smaller ones to feed his dog.

"We got to make sure, Jacky; we leave no sign of where we stop. When you ride off from here, I am going to trail you by about half a day and see if the white men are still after us."

"You think that's necessary, Burra? Surely, they have given up by now."

"Should know me by now, Jacky. This old blackfeller does not trust the whites. And if you want to keep your horse, then we best be one step ahead of them."

Burra's experience with white men taught him that their thirst and greed were as unquenchable as the harsh outback they were riding through.

"Jacky," he said, his low voice almost inaudible, "these men are like dingoes. They will not stop till they have their prey in their jaws."

"Whatever you think is best, Burra."

Jacky cocked his head and looked at the rough country ahead.

"How much further do you think Burra?"

*****

Burra pushed his horse to catch up with Jacky and Jennings. He had seen the three white men trailing them, and they were only a few hours behind. He could see Jacky and Jennings ahead in the distance, just on dusk, and he kicked his mount into a gallop to reach them. The riders heard the approaching horse and were grateful to dismount, stretch their aching legs, and wait for Burra.

"Jacky," Burra said gravely,

"They are not that far behind us. We need a plan."

Jacky looked at him and nodded.

"You are right, Burra. But what can we do?"

His eyes searched Burra's face for answers.

"We need a place to hide. Somewhere they will not expect."

Jacky looked around, his expression one of confusion.

"But where? There is nowhere to hide."

Burra squinted into the distance, his aged eyes piercing the dust and the haze.

"There. Do you see that?"

It was Jacky's turn to squint now, trying to make out what Burra was staring at. Then, he slowly made out a shape looming in the distant reaches of the approaching night.

"What is that? A mountain range? A rock formation? What?"

"No, Jacky. It is neither. That is a town you can barely

see."

Jacky's eyes widened with hope.

"A town? Are you sure, Burra?"

"This old blackfeller never says anything unless he is sure. It is a town, all right. If we make it there, we will be safe. Nobody, only a fool, would try anything in a town where there is the white man's law."

"It is still a distance to ride, but another couple of hours should get us there," said Jacky, with a growing optimism.

Jennings had been silent until now.

"You blacks must 'ave bloody good eyes. All I can see is nothin'."

"Maybe it's time you got a black woman for a wife," laughed Jacky.

"She could teach you a thing or two."

"Yeah, and end up like poor old Wells," muttered Jennings to himself.

*****

They approached the town as the sun dipped over the

small range beyond, painting the sky with a canvas of red and orange. The settlement was larger than they had envisaged, sprawling out from the large town hall and extending as far as they could see in the gloom. Lanterns flickered to life in houses, casting a warm glow over the town. The streets were eerily quiet, with only a few stray dogs wandering the dusty streets and a handful of children playing a last game of tag in the twilight.

Once again, on Jacky's suggestion, they set up camp just on the outskirts of town. The laughing of the kookaburras next morning woke two of the three men. As was his custom, Burra was an early riser and had a low fire started.

"Jennings," Jacky said firmly as he chewed on a piece of bacon rind, his voice cutting through the morning chill,

"You and Burra are to stay here with the horses. I will walk into town and find the police station. I have a plan that hopefully will get those men off our tails."

Jennings nodded, understanding the gravity of the situation, while Burra said nothing. That is what Jacky liked about the old man. He did not ask questions; he was a man of action and a man to rely on.

Jacky

*****

Hardwood's police station was a modest, unassuming building, surrounded on one side by the town butcher, and on the other side stood the town's red brick Post Office.

All the time the three men had been tailing their quarry, Mullins had been cleverly devising his plan. He smiled with smugness like a cat lapping up a bowl of fresh cream. With a flourish, he swung out of the saddle and clomped up onto the verandah. He pushed open the heavy wooden door, which slammed onto the wall behind it. The room was filled with stale cigarette smoke and the stench of unwashed bodies. He wrinkled his nose with disgust and shouted,

"I wish to report a theft!"

The lone policeman, a burly man with a handle-bar moustache, looked up with a mixture of curiosity and annoyance and said,

"Nobody comes into my office shoutin' mister. Now tone yer voice down and give me yer details."

Mullins took a deep breath. He was used to lying so it came easy to him.

"It is my stallion! It has been pinched! Two aboriginal fellers and a white bloke. Me and my mates have been trailin' them for days now. They're 'ere in yer town somewhere, mister lawman."

The policeman's expression was one of interest now. He stood up, pushing his chair to the floor in the process.

"Now, hold on," he said with a grunt,

"You are reporting your horse stolen by blacks. That is serious business, mister…?"

"Mullins. Just Mullins."

"Mullins it is then. I am Sergeant Robinson. Now, I need more details."

He pulled open the drawer of a very untidy desk and retrieved a pencil.

Outside the building, Jacky had watched as Mullins entered the police station. He scratched his head with jumbled thoughts running through his mind.

"Why would his pursuers want to visit a police station?"

Jacky looked around the street and could see the two

other men standing in the shade, waiting for their boss to come out from the police station. Jacky decided to bide his time.

Meanwhile, inside, the Sergeant was leaning back in his chair, the leather groaning from his weight.

"Now tell me your story Mullins," he said with an air of authority, his pencil having been prepared with a thorough licking of the man's tongue.

"Me and two mates are seasonal workers Sergeant, and we were headed north for the shearing season. We stopped over at a town down the track and…."

The Sergeant interrupted.

"What town?"

"Gundurra. We stopped over to have a few beers and watch the running of the Gilmore Cup. We camped just outta town on the creek, and that night me 'orse was stolen. 'e is special to me, Sergeant," said Mullins morosely, trying to garner sympathy.

"How do you know it was blacks what took yer horse?"

"One of my men saw them."

Mullins' heart was racing as he found himself

fabricating more lies.

"Two darkies and a white feller. We bin trackin' them 'ere to Hardwood."

"Ya got a description of these would-be thieves?"

"The leader of their gang was dark, but not as dark as the old man with him. He looked as if 'e'd been dipped in tar; that's how black 'e was. Anyways, the young abo was a good-lookin' sort of feller. Fer a darky, that is. And they had another man with them, a white man. He looked like 'e could be the town drunk."

"Weeelll' drawled the Sergeant, "that description could fit any one of a dozen men in this shithole town. But there ain't much I can do till my other men show up fer work later. Me arthritis is playin' up somethin' bad today. You go on over to the hotel and 'ave a cold beer and wait fer me there."

Mullins—with his intense dislike of anything to do with the law, was quick to head out the door.

Jacky was a curious onlooker as he saw Mullins speak with his cronies and watched them walk across the road to the hotel.

Jacky

*****

Sergeant Robinson looked up with a stunned look on his face. He looked at the figure of a black man; a man that had some two minutes ago been described to him. His first reaction was to reach for his pistol, which was in the holster dangling from his chair. But Jacky was prepared for anything and everything. He raised his arms above his head to show he was no threat. He surprised the policeman even more when he spoke. The Sergeant listened, intrigued by Jacky's version of events.

"Now you fuckin' listen to me, darky! You are the second bastard that has showed up 'ere this very mornin' claiming their horse has been nicked."

"I have not said my horse was stolen, Sergeant. Not yet, anyway. I am telling you, Sergeant, that whatever that man has told you is a pack of lies. It was him and his cronies who tried to steal my horse. They have been tailing me and my friends since we left Gundurra."

The Sergeant was not fully awake when Mullins had presented his accusations, but with Jacky now on the scene with a different story, he had a clearer head on him. And that head leaned towards believing the white man, Mullins. He had an intrinsic dislike of black people.

"Just where would an aboriginal man get a supposed valuable stallion? Do you have any proof this horse belongs to you?" he sneered, his voice betraying his accusation.

"The whole town of Gundurra saw me ride in on my horse, Sergeant. I even earned fifty guineas. I won the Gilmore Cup on my stallion."

The Sergeant began to show some interest now.

"You don't say. That's a pretty good achievement, mister."

But then a thought came to him.

"But just because you say you won the Gilmore Cup, it don't mean you own the horse. And besides, where is yer bloody horse anyway?"

"I am camped just out of town, Sergeant. I left my stallion in the hands of my two friends."

He chewed on a dirty fingernail and spat the fragment out onto his desk, where he made a careful show of wiping it clean.

"Folks in Gundarra wouldn't have liked an outsider winnin' their cup. I am surprised they even let you enter the race."

"And why is that, Sergeant? Because people saw a good horse or because I am black?"

The question went unanswered as the door behind him was pushed open, and two junior constables walked in. Robinson ignored Jacky now and spoke to his two underlings.

"Late again? I am warning you, pair, I'll start docking yer wages."

The two men ignored the threat. They had heard it all before. The shorter of the two men spoke up.

"What's with the black?"

He looked Jacky up and down.

"You ain't from 'round here, mister. Leastways, I don't remember ever 'avin' to lock you up."

The Sergeant turned his mind back to the business at hand.

"It's a looong story," he drawled, "and one that coulda come straight outta a fairytale."

His teeth began to attack the nails on his other hand, and he spat fragments onto his desk.

"Had a man by the name of Mullins in here earlier claiming this blackfeller and his two mates pinched his horse. Then, just minutes after he left, this very same blackfeller waltzes in 'ere as pretty as you like, and he claims that Mullins has been tryin' to pinch 'is horse. Jis do not know who to believe Ibsen. But mind you, it was blackfellers who invented lies, I think."

He studied Jacky before commenting,

"How come you speak like a white man? Talk better than me by the sounds of ya."

"I see you are a bigoted white man who is under the assumption that all Aboriginals are uneducated, Sergeant. I am not one of those. I am a respected man where I come from and own a considerable amount of land."

"Land? You blackfellers think you own all this goddamned country. I think the best place fer you at the moment, till I can sort all this out, is in the lock-up. Now you jis go along easy with my two men and 'ave yerself a nice camp in my nice gaol cell."

Jacky was stunned.

"You cannot gaol a man on suspicion. And lies," he shouted.

Robinson laughed.

"I cannot, can't I? We will see about that. Take him, men. And give 'im a good thrashin' if 'e resists."

Robinson then remembered something.

"Turn your pockets out," he ordered Jacky.

"Huh? You plan on robbing me?"

Robinson's brows furrowed.

"Ain't you ever been in gaol before?"

"No. I have not. You are making a big mistake, Sergeant."

"Yeah, I know. I have heard that all before. Now turn out your bloody pockets."

Jacky saw no point in arguing. He emptied his pockets of everything and smiled rather insolently.

"There. Happy now?"

"You ain't exactly a rich man, my friend. It's lucky for

you that you won the Gilmore Cup."

The two constables had been watching on and had their guns drawn and determination etched on their faces. Jacky knew it would be of no avail to resist. They had blocked the front doorway, their boots firmly planted as if daring the black man to make a run for it.

"Take it easy there, gentlemen," said Jacky calmly.

"There is no need for weapons. I am sure this can all be cleared up soon. It's just a case of misunderstanding."

He looked at the two constables. A flicker of recognition appeared in the eyes of one of the men. Jacky racked his brain. He knew he had seen the man before and realised that the man had also recognised him. The constable turned his eyes away, causing Jacky to wonder whether he did so in fear or bewilderment.

"I said take him to the cell," snapped Robinson.

"You pair fuckin' deaf or what?"

Jacky's eyes went to the cell door, a heavy wooden slab with rusted iron bars. He feared the cramped, damp place that awaited him, a place where a man, especially an aboriginal, could lose their mind. Or die!

The two constables got a firm grip on his shoulders and guided him towards the cell. As they neared the door, they both pushed him, causing Jacky to stumble.

"Move! Black bastard!"

He was pushed roughly through the narrow door opening and heard the cold metal bars scrape against the stone wall as the cell door was slammed shut. The sound reverberated through Jacky's bones, sealing his fate for the night.

"The night? Or how long?" he pondered.

Jacky stood for a long time in the middle of the floor, staring at the bars of the cell, wondering if there was something more sinister and significant behind the whole baffling episode. Presently, he lifted his shoulders in a fatalistic fashion, for the time being accepting the turn of events. After a while he thought he heard voices in the outer office. Someone was talking to the Sergeant in low tones. He tried to catch what was being said, but it was impossible.

Then silence reigned.

The barred windows were set high in the back wall of

the cell and allowed air and light to seep in. Jacky heard a variety of noises as the day advanced; children playing, kicking a can about in some kind of game. Then came the sound of a couple of dogs fighting, with the battle ending with high-pitched barking and yelping and then a scurry of

He heard Robinson call from the front room to his two men.

"You pair git yerselves over to the pub and bring back that other bastard and his mates. Mullins is 'is name."

"Will do Sarge."

"And don't you pair even think of having an ale."

*****

Chapter 10

Jennings was trying to speak with Burra, but verbal communication was a difficult task. The black man was smart, however, and knew what the white man was trying to say. They both knew that it had been far too long for Jacky to be away. It was already midday, and both men sensed something was amiss.

Burra pointed towards the town and Jennings acknowledged with a nod of his head. They set off on horseback, with Burra leading Jacky's stallion. The streets were busy with parasol-shrouded women gazing in shop windows and men lazing about in the shade. Jennings realised the easiest place to garner information was a pub, and he and Burra hitched their horses outside the first one they came to.

Jennings motioned to Burra to remain outside, and he walked up onto the high landing. The pub's doors creaked a greeting as he pushed them open and stepped inside. Jennings felt in his pockets and was reassured to feel that he still had money left over after paying for Burra's shave and haircut. The sight of men drinking frothy cold beer cheered him up, and he sidled up to the bar.

'What'll you have mister?"

"Just a cold beer, mate, and some information."

"I don't give information out to strangers," was the response.

'Well, my good man, what I ask could not be considered anythin' harmful. Jis wonderin' if you 'ave seen a black man about? Young strappin' man 'e is."

"I can give you that kind of information, mister. Easy enough. I ain't seen no young blackfeller on accounts; no darkies are allowed in my pub. That satisfy yer curiosity?"

He shoved a glass of beer in front of Jennings and held his hand out.

"Tuppence mister," and then he added,

"Try the police station across the street. Our Sergeant 'as the 'abit of lockin' up darkies."

Jennings drank the beer in one long swallow. He knew Jacky would be angry with him if he left Burra alone for too long. He plonked his glass down, put on his dusty hat, and walked out without a word. His eyes strayed across the street to the Hardwood Police Station. With a pat on Burra's shoulder and a nod of his head, Jennings made his way across the street.

"Jeezus! Not another one. No fuckin' crime in Hardwood fer ages, and now I got more troubles than a man could ask fer. What the fuck do you want, mister?"

The Sergeant slammed down his pencil and folded his arms.

"I'm lookin' for a mate who's gone missin'. Young blackfeller."

At the mention of an aboriginal, the Sergeant sat upright and leaned forward. Jennings smelt the remains of his last meal on his breath, coupled with the unmistakable odour of sour rum.

"Blackfeller you say?"

The Sergeant's voice was gruff and rolled off his tongue like a rock over gravel.

'And don't be tellin' me you 'ave 'ad a horse pinched too." he sneered.

"Jis so 'appens I got a darky locked up at this very minute fer pinchin' a horse."

"Jacky's no horse thief, Sergeant!" Jennings shouted and thumped his fist on the desk. His outburst did little to appease the lawman.

"You jis better be watchin' where you plonk yer fist, mister. Else, you will join yer mate in me spare bedroom."

*****

"Never figured the day I'd be seein' you in a lockup, Jacky."

"Never mind Mister Jennings. It's just a mistake. I'll be out as soon as the Sergeant has proof I own Bandit."

"And jis 'ow do you plan on doin' that?"

"Jimmy Boy's word carries a lot of weight, Jennings. He can verify that I own the stallion."

"But Jimmy Boy ain't here, Jacky."

Jacky thought for a moment, and then,

"Call the Sergeant in here. I need to talk with him."

Jennings strode out to the front office and returned, not with the Sergeant, but with the constable that Jacky had thought he recognised.

"You got something to say, Jacky?" said the man as he ran his wooden baton across the bars of the cell.

Jacky turned to meet the man's eyes.

"How do you know my name? I have not told anyone here."

The constable leaned into the bars.

"A town as small as this does not keep secrets for long. Besides, word has got 'round you pinched a stallion the day of the Gilmore Cup."

"You still haven't told me how you knew my name," Jacky persisted.

The constable grinned.

"You work for a Chinaman, don't you?"

Jacky's eyes lit up.

"I did work for a Chinaman, yes. But not anymore. I married the Chinaman's daughter."

'Well, I'll be blowed down with a feather! Are you pullin' me leg, Jacky? You married Jimmy Boy's daughter?"

Jennings interrupted.

"He's dead serious, constable."

He stared at the man, and recognition was ignited in his eyes.

"I know you! You are one of the men Jimmy Boy hired to 'elp drive the stock back from Newcastle after the flood."

"You are correct. And if I am correct, you are Jennings. I am Eric Howson. If you remember, it was me who shot the aboriginal for pinchin' a sheep. I'll never forget Jimmy Boy's kindness. He coulda laid me off, but 'e jis gave me a good talkin' to. Seems I have a chance to repay him. Tell me the full story, Jacky, and 'opefully we'll 'ave you outta 'ere soon."

"So, you will vouch for me, Howson?"

"I surely will, Jacky, but I must warn you. I pull no weight here. It all rests on the Sergeant. And he is a real moody bastard. And he 'as a particular aversion to blacks. 'Cept fer the pretty young one's he 'as in his bed," he added.

*****

"Sounds like a reasonable story, Howson," said Robinson,

"But we will still have to wait and see what the judge

says. Get yer arse over to the telegraph office and send a message to the copper in Ramsay. Meanwhile, I will go and see if I can round up those other bastards jis comin' in and tellin' me a pack of lies."

*****

"Freedom is a funny thing, darky," muttered the Sergeant as he jangled the keys and unlocked the cell.

"Somethin' you blackfellers will never understand."

"Oh, we understand, Sergeant. Probably better than a white man. The land around us is our freedom, and the only gaol for us is the white man's restrictions."

"Smart arse!" came the retort.

"Anyway, you are free to go. But you ain't to leave town. Jis do not go makin' the same mistake again."

"I made no mistake, Sergeant. You are the one who made the mistake."

"Jis git and shut yer bloody trap before I 'ave second thoughts and lock you up again. Them other bastards that come in 'ere tellin' lies 'ave scarpered. Good riddance, I say."

"You have no intention to pursue them? What does the

law do all day in Hardwood? Sit on its fat arse!"

"I warn you, mister. Watch yer bloody mouth. And chase those men? They can go to 'ell as far as I am concerned. Now, there is the matter of the court case."

"What court case?" asked Jacky, confusion crossing his face.

"Yer not free to leave town, ya know. Jis cos I let you out, don't mean you're innocent. The judge has heard about this, and he wants to try the case in his courthouse. And be warned, mister, he has a certain penchant for bein' hard on blacks."

The two men stood on the verandah of the Police Station, a spectacle for the town gossips to begin their tongues wagging.

Jennings and Burra waited patiently, with Jennings keeping a firm rein on Jacky's horse. Jacky leaned across and patted its neck.

"I can see why someone would want to pinch that horse. It's a mighty fine piece of flesh," said Robinson as he admired Bandit.

"But I will jis 'ave to keep it out back in the police stables till after the court case."

Jacky gave no argument to this. He knew the safest place for his horse would be right under the noses of the police.

"Then mind you take good care of him, Sergeant."

*****

"How can a man steal what he owns, Connolly?"

Jimmy Boy, exasperation etched on his face, needed answers.

"Jimmy Boy, I am only the messenger. Jacky was nabbed by the local police in a place called Hardwood after claims he pinched the stallion you gave him."

He scuffed his boots in the dirt and held out the telegram he'd been given.

"What can you do about this, Connolly?"

"The world sometimes does not recognise rights Jimmy Boy. You and I both know that Jacky is the rightful owner of the horse, but you must remember one thing. You are not the law. And you and everybody else must remember that they cannot just buck the law because of who they are."

"I asked you Constable Connolly, what can you do about this? I don't need a lecture."

"If you care to read the telegram, Jimmy Boy, you will see that a judge wants three men of good character who can testify that Jacky is the rightful owner of the stallion."

"What! A court case! Where? When?" roared Jimmy Boy.

"Slow down, Jimmy Boy! There is no need to worry. We just need three men to travel to Hardwood for the trial."

'Where the hell is Hardwood?"

"It's a large township up north of here. About a week's ride. The court does not sit for another ten days, so there's no hurry. Just treat it like a holiday, Jimmy Boy," laughed Connolly.

"I see no need for laughter, Connolly. Nor a holiday, for that matter. And as for three men, there will be myself and you, and I will take Mister Wells along."

"I cannot be one of the witnesses, Jimmy Boy. I cannot leave Ramsay. The town would be without any law. But I can write a letter for you to take."

Jimmy Boy pondered on this before saying,

"Mister Wells and I then. For the third man, I think the Doctor would be a sound witness."

"The town needs a doctor as much as it needs a law officer, Jimmy Boy."

"You said the whole affair shouldn't take long. The town can feel safe in knowing that the doc's wife is still available. She is a very capable woman."

Connolly nodded.

"I'll check with the coaching company to see if there is any connecting service to Hardwood."

"Much appreciated, Connolly. A coach trip sounds better than a week on horseback."

*****

Chapter 11

"You two ready?" asked Harry Reagan as he adjusted the tilt on his hat.

"Ready as can be, Mister Reagan," answered Kerrigan, his hand resting on the leather of his holster. Howarth, always the quiet one, simply tightened his grip on the reins of his horse, his expression unreadable behind the scarf covering the lower part of his face.

"Then let's ride," ordered Reagan as he kicked his horse into a canter. They rode for half an hour until, finally, the Lambert farm came into view. The modest homestead looked tired and worn, with faded and cracked paint and a fence that was on the verge of collapsing. The barn stood at a precarious angle, showing signs of one too many fierce storms.

Reagan took a deep suck on his cigar, and his eyes narrowed as he exhaled a plume of smoke.

"This is it," he said in a serious and somewhat ominous tone, "if Lambert doesn't accept my offer, then we do what we have to do."

The two men nodded solemnly. They knew what was

to come.

As they neared the homestead, a man emerged from the porch, a stooped and frail body, eyes that were alert but holding traces of past weariness. The same eyes widened as he recognised the trio, but he made no effort to greet them.

Harry Reagan swung off his horse and advanced towards the man, his cigar extinguished now but still dangling from the corner of his mouth.

"Good to see you, Lambert."

"Can't say the same about you," came the hostile reply.

"You've made your intentions clear enough, Reagan and the answer is still no. So, you and your men may as well jis ride on back to where yous come from."

Reagan's smile faded, revealing the coldness behind the veneer.

"Very well," he said with ice in his tone.

"You leave us no choice."

Kerrigan and Howarth dismounted, their boots stirring up the dust as they thudded on the hard ground.

"Lambert, you know you are too old to make a go of

this place. You can't sustain nuthin' anymore. You've got debts hangin' outta yer arse, mister, and a wife to think about. Take the money and run."

The old man's jaw was set as hard as cement.

"This is all I got, Reagan. All I ever had, I ain't about to sell to the likes of you."

Reagan spat out his cigar.

"Your last chance, Lambert or…"

"Or what, Reagan? You'll kill me?"

"Sometimes when dingoes got to eat, they jis gotta eat Lambert."

Lambert's wife, a frail woman, appeared in the doorway, fear lining her once beautiful face.

Reagan's gaze flickered towards her before returning to her husband.

"Think of her, Lambert. You ain't no use to her dead."

"Then I guess I will have to die before I sell you my land," the old man said as he reached for a shotgun resting against the porch railing.

Reagan sighed.

"Lambert, I don't want to do this."

Lambert's grip tightened on the shotgun.

"You ain't gittin' my land."

Lambert's wife rushed forward and grabbed Reagan's arm.

"Please, Mister Reagan, you can't do this."

Kerrigan, Howarth, and a solitary hawk circling overhead were the only witnesses as Reagan gunned down the old man and then shot his wife in cold blood. Then he casually mounted his horse and said,

"Home time, men."

*****

The judge entered the courtroom via a side door, and his footsteps were muffled by the thick carpet. Through beady eyes, he scanned the room, taking note of the aboriginal man standing in the dock with Robinson. The judge took his seat, flouncing his black robes behind him, and his wig gave him an air of importance that was hard to ignore.

Jacky stood in the crowded courtroom, crammed with

curious townsfolk desperate for something to relieve their boredom. And what better way to do that than to sit in on the trial of a black man.

"A good case is a quick but thorough one," said the judge in a stern voice.

"Jacky Wang, you are accused of stealing a valuable stallion from a man who I am led to believe is not present to press his charges. Why, in God's name, I do not know. Some people seem to think it is all right to waste the law's time. But I diverge. How do you plead?"

"I plead Not Guilty, sir."

The judge's eyes narrowed at what he suspected was Jacky's impertinence.

"You will address me as Your Honour," he barked, his voice ringing around the high ceiling.

"I plead Not Guilty, Your Honour."

Then, in a moment of recklessness, Jacky shouted,

"How is it possible for a man to steal something that already belongs to him?"

The judge leaned forward and shouted back.

"I will not have raised voices in my very own courtroom, mister!"

"My apologies, Your Honour," said Jacky through gritted teeth.

"Accepted," answered the judge begrudgingly.

"Now I am led to believe the court has three witnesses who can attest to your ownership of the stallion in question."

He looked at his notes before saying,

"I call Mister Jimmy Wang."

Jimmy stood and walked forward with his hands folded behind his back.

"I have two questions for you, Mister Wang. My first question concerns your relationship with the accused. You both share a common surname."

"That is correct, Your Honour."

"Here is the question. How does it come to be that a China man and an Aboriginal have the same last name? It seems rather odd to me."

"That is quite easy to explain, Your Honour, but before answering, may I ask what our surnames have to do with this case?"

The judge snapped back.

"I am holding court here, Mister Wang. I find the question very much in order. Just answer it."

"The defendant is married to my daughter, Your Honour. Because aboriginals, as you should well know, do not have a surname, Jacky took my name. Hence, he is Jacky Wang."

The judge sat back, apparently satisfied with the explanation.

"Now for my second question. Mister Wang, it is claimed that you gave the stallion to the accused. Is that correct?"

"That is absolutely correct, Your Honour. I gave the stallion to Jacky," said Jimmy Boy.

"There was no Bill of Sale as no money changed hands. It was merely a gift."

The judge jotted something on paper as Jimmy Boy continued.

"He was way too wild for anyone to handle and a

stallion like that one needs a firm hand. Your honour, Jacky has hands of magic. It didn't take him long, and that stallion was as quiet as a lamb. But for his owner only. It still was a handful for anyone else who tried to ride it."

"Then I am beginning to believe that a man cannot steal something he owns," the judge allowed himself a rare smile.

"Thank you, Mister Wang. You may step down."

"But I will hear from the other witnesses as a matter of protocol."

The judge had already determined Jacky's innocence, more so since he'd read the letter from Connolly. But court cases were few and far between, and the judge enjoyed his day of grandeur and pomp. His only other cases rarely involved witnesses, and all ended with the same result. The imprisonment of hapless and drunken black men.

"I call on Mister Thomas Wells."

Wells approached the stand nervously.

"Mister Wells, correct?"

"Yyesss," stammered Wells.

"That be me."

"I will be direct with you, Wells. Does the accused aboriginal man own the stallion?"

Wells took a deep breath, the seriousness of the situation pressing down on him like a sack of oats.

"The stallion," he said in a quivering voice, "belongs to Jacky Wang. It was given to 'im by my boss, Mister Jimmy Wang. Jimmy Boy and me mate Jennin's couldn't tame the animal, but Jacky sure did. He worked on that 'orse from the time 'e woke till the time he went to bed. He was up at the crack...."

"Enough!" shouted the judge.

"I don't want his life story."

"Sorry," mumbled Wells.

The judge harboured the thought of keeping the shaking man on the stand for a bit longer and having some sport with him, but it was already time for his lunchtime tipple.

"That's all Wells."

The judge fumbled with his watch and then announced,

"One final witness. A certain Doctor Kevin Heath."

Jacky

The Doc stepped forward with a confident air and offered a courteous nod to the judge.

"Your Honour," he spoke calmly.

"To the point again, Doctor. Does Jacky Wang own the stallion?"

"Not only does he own the stallion, but Jacky Wang is a man of integrity, and I doubt he has ever stolen a thing in his life. I have known and treated Jacky for years, and he is an honest man. Everyone in Ramsay knows Jacky owns that horse. This court, I believe, is a farce. Hasn't the law got better things to do than try a black man for a crime he could not have committed?"

He repeated Jacky's words.

"How can a man steal something he already owns?"

But the Doctor's words did not sit well with the judge, who detested anyone who would detract from his own self-importance.

"I did not ask for a character reference, Doctor. A simple yes would have sufficed. And besides Doctor, your expertise does not extend to legal matters. This court operates on facts."

"But the facts are clear, judge. Three men, I am one, have sworn the man owns the horse."

The judge knew he was defeated.

"On the evidence presented, I find this man not guilty of horse theft. Case dismissed."

The courtroom emptied slowly. Some left satisfied, but most left with disappointment that they had not seen a black man convicted.

The friends stood outside the courtroom and watched as sections of the crowd filed past.

"I am truly sorry about all this, Jimmy Boy. It was a long way for you and the Doc and Wells to travel. And all because of a lying pack of would-be horse thieves who did not even have the guts to attend the trial."

"I do not know about guts, Jacky. But they are very smart men. They knew that you could not be found guilty of theft. They took the easy option and hightailed it out of here."

"How's the old man holding up Jacky?" asked the doctor.

"He's fine, Doc. For an old man, he has plenty of stamina. He just wants to stay alive long enough to rescue his family."

"With all that's happened, I think we should plan our next moves," said Jimmy Boy with a serious look on his face.

"I know my next move, Jimmy Boy. I need to get back to Ramsay. To my wife and child. But more importantly, I need to be there for the townsfolk. The town needs me, Jimmy Boy."

"I know, Doc. But thanks for coming all this way."

"What will you do, Jimmy Boy?" asked Jacky.

"Mister Wells and I will stay with you and Jennings and help you in your bid to rescue Burra's people."

"Are you sure?"

"I have never been surer in my life. Let's go and see if we can buy a couple of horses and then go out to your camp and check on Burra."

*****

The fire pit lay cold and neglected. There was no sign of Burra anywhere.

"I done told 'im to stay here while I went into town to see the court case," moaned Jennings.

"He wouldn't wander far," murmured Jacky, but a knot of fear seared his stomach.

"He knows this country far better than us."

Then, as if evoked by their thoughts, a figure emerged from a grove of trees away from the campsite. Burra walked with a steady gait, a wallaby draped over his shoulder and a small sand monitor hanging from the rope that held his new trousers up.

"Burra," called Jacky with relief evident in his voice.

"Bin out getting' some food, Jacky."

He looked curiously at Jimmy Boy and Wells.

"Where you find them white fellers, Jacky?"

"Long story, Burra. They are coming with us."

The men settled around the fire which Burra had started and watched as his skilful hands prepared the wallaby and the plump lizard. He had used a sharpened stone to slit the abdomens of both creatures, and he extracted the guts and tossed them to his dog.

As they sat around eating the delicious chunks of flesh, Burra and Jacky spoke in their own language. Burra recounted tales of the Dreamtime, of realms where the ancestors danced among the stars. For a short time, Jacky forgot about all the troubles he was tasked with solving.

"The land tells me things, Jacky. It has many stories to share. And the land spoke to me today. We are getting closer to my family."

*****

As dawn broke over the rugged landscape, the men, still tired, packed up their possessions and mounted their horses, determination etched in their faces. Jacky and Burra led the way; Jacky sat tall in the saddle as he glanced back at the men behind. Wells and Jennings were adjusting their positions in their saddles with faces that betrayed their discomfort.

"Hate ridin' in this bloody heat," groaned Wells.

"Saddle's chafin' me arse raw."

Yet despite their discomfort, the five men pressed on, fuelled by the thought of Burra's family. Hours turned into a relentless march, and soon, the shadows began to lengthen. Finally, as dusk descended upon them, Burra spied a homestead in the distance.

Jacky was quick to ask.

"Is this the place, Burra?"

"No. Dunno know this place. But maybe we can camp here for the night. Best send the white fellers in first. They might not take kindly to two blacks and a yeller man."

Jacky explained to Wells and Jennings what the plan

was, but the men were unsure of themselves.

"Let's draw straws. Who goes in first, Jennin's."

"No need," said Jennings pompously,

"I ain't afraid to piss in the dark like you Wells."

As Jennings approached the houseyard gate, he could feel his heart thumping. With Wells hovering behind him, he stepped up onto the verandah and rapped on the door.

Jennings took a step back as the door opened. Before him stood a young woman, immaculately groomed and seemingly out of place when compared to the dusty landscape surrounding the homestead. Behind her, a man emerged from the shadows, his presence imposing despite his casual appearance. He was tall and broad-shouldered, with a weathered face that mirrored many hours in the sun. He was dressed in a flannel shirt and a pair of blue, neatly pressed jeans. He carried a rifle crooked under one arm. The man studied Wells and Jennings with a wary gaze and then said,

"Can I help you men?"

His voice displayed a certain sense of culture, a trait rare in the outback.

Jennings looked warily at the weapon the man carried.

"We are peaceable folk and mean no harm. We was jis wonderin' if we could camp in yer barn fer the night. And fill our water canteens, Mister. We got our own tucker. We are jis passin' through and saw yer lights and…"

Wells interrupted.

"We got three mates with us, too."

At the mention of others, the man became wary.

"Where are they? Why aren't they with you? Why are they hiding? Did Reagan send you?"

His words exploded from his mouth.

Jennings turned to Wells and said savagely,

"Why can't you keep yer bloody trap shut, Wells?"

He turned back to the man.

"Listen, mister, to be 'onest with ya. We got two aboriginal men and a Chinaman with us. If that bothers you some, then we'll jis be on our way. We mean no trouble. And we do not know anyone with the name Reagan."

Jennings's pitiful face drew sympathy from the man.

"I am not a man who has ever been prejudiced, mister. Call your friends and let me see them."

Jimmy Boy had been watching from the shadows and could see that they were in no danger. He was close enough to hear the man speaking with Jennings and Wells, and at the mention of wanting to see them, Jimmy Boy grabbed Jacky and Burra's arms and led them up and onto the verandah. He extended his hand and said politely,

"I am Jimmy Wang, a property owner far south of here. I overheard your kind words, mister…?"

"Andrews. Richard Andrews. And this is my sister, Rachel Andrews."

Andrews had a puzzled look on his face. In front of him stood strangers, and two of them were a Chinaman and an aboriginal, both of whom spoke excellent English.

Jacky and Burra had come forward, and Andrews studied them in the dim light.

"It's a good thing there is some light here," he said.

"I wouldn't have been able to see the two of you in the dark."

He threw back his head and laughed.

"My silly sense of humour. Please, won't you all come in?"

Jimmy Boy motioned to the others to remove their boots, and they filed into the house behind their host and his sister.

"You have a beautiful house here, Mister Andrews," said Jimmy Boy as he looked around the large room they were ushered into.

"Richard is fine for me. Is it all right if I call you Jimmy? I've noticed your friends call you Jimmy Boy."

"It's a long story, Richard. Jimmy is fine with me."

Then Jimmy Boy proceeded to introduce his companions while Rachel went into the kitchen to make a pot of coffee. Jennings, Wells, and Burra were not used to such opulence and remained silent, staring in wonder around the room.

"You could say this is our oasis, Jimmy, a sanctuary from the dangers that await us outside."

Jimmy Boy wondered what the man meant by dangers

but let it slide for the present.

The men sat at a long, polished mahogany table, which reflected the light from the lanterns on the dresser. The walls of the dining room were lined with bookshelves, their contents ranging from huge volumes on ancient civilisations to leather-bound collections of novels from around the world. The scent of something savoury wafted from the kitchen, and the men felt a collective rumble in their stomachs.

"You're just in time for dinner," said Richard.

"My sister is a mighty fine cook."

"Do you think we could wash up first?" asked Jimmy Boy.

"Sure. Follow me."

The men, feeling fresh and clean, returned to the table.

Rachel emerged from the kitchen with a platter of roast lamb, its skin a golden brown and the meat sizzling in its juices. Alongside the lamb sat potatoes, carrots, and parsnips, but Rachel realised she had a problem.

"I wasn't expecting guests," she said, "so I am afraid everyone's portion will be rather small."

But the sight of the steaming hot food and the thought of a small portion did not bother the men.

"That's all right, Miss Andrews," said Jennings as he spooned up some gravy.

"Beats eatin' wallaby and goanna every day."

"Rachel is fine. We have no distinctions here in the outback."

"Pretty name, Miss Rachel."

He nudged his friend and said quietly,

"Jis remember yer manner Jennin's, and don't fart at the table either."

*****

Chapter 12

"This is where you can bunk down for the night," said Andrews as he led the men to the barn. He held the lantern above his head, the soft glow lighting up the interior of the barn. The smell of hay and animals hung heavily around the interior, but it was a comforting smell and soon the men had rolled out their swags, their eyes drooping with the prospect of a peaceful and safe night's sleep.

Jimmy Boy took a moment to appreciate the kindness shown by Andrews, and he watched as the men drifted off to sleep until he and Andrews were the only ones left standing.

"Do you think we could have a yarn now, Richard?" asked Jimmy Boy, his voice low so as not to disturb the sleeping men.

Andrews nodded and led Jimmy Boy to a corner of the barn, where there was an old table and half a dozen chairs.

"What's on your mind, Jimmy?"

Jimmy Boy took a deep breath.

"You talked about dangers before. I was just wondering what you meant by that. Hostile aboriginals?

Bushrangers? What?"

"No bushrangers, thank goodness. But there is a tribe of blacks causing trouble. But I cannot say I blame them. They are only seeking justice from the biggest bastard of a man in these parts. Pardon my language, Jimmy, but the thought of the man causes the hairs on my back to bristle."

Jimmy Boy could read a man's character, and he knew that Andrews was not the type of man to use crude language loosely.

"Harry Reagan!"

Andrews spat the words out.

Jacky had been almost asleep when he heard the name. Harry Reagan! Charley's father. He pulled himself from his swag, got up, and joined Jimmy Boy and Andrews. He said nothing, merely content to listen.

"A cruel, heartless man. And though I have no proof, he is a murdering son of a bitch! His holding is a vast tract of land that borders my property, and the only thing that separates us is the river. He's been after my farm for years and has offered to buy me out."

"Is he the reason for the blacks' violence?"

"He most certainly is Jimmy. He has Aboriginals working for him, but he is a hard man. The blacks are treated like animals, and those that did work for him walked off the place, and now they do everything they can to rile him. The only blacks he has now is a tribe his men brought back from down south a few years ago, I believe. Yet I cannot understand why they stay when the rest have left."

Jacky interrupted the conversation.

"Mister Andrews, maybe those blacks do not have a choice. Maybe they are kept against their will. I heard you say that this man Reagan is a murderer."

Andrews looked at Jacky suspiciously, but Jimmy Boy eased his mind.

"It's all right, Richard. Jacky is here to seek justice. You can speak freely in front of him."

Jacky was insistent and wanted to pursue the matter.

"You said something about murder, Mister Andrews. Can you tell us more about that?"

"I have no proof, but I know it was Reagan's men who

murdered my neighbours, the Lambert family. They were good hard-working folk, and they had a holding the top side of me. Reagan tried to buy them out as well, but like me, they stuck firm. Then, one day, when my sister and I were out riding the boundary fence, we decided to call on them. A portion of the boundary fence had been pulled down. When we rode into their yard, we found them. We found them both. Dead!"

He covered his eyes with his hands, trying to shield the image of the bodies lying in the heat. Wells, his sleep disturbed, gave a cry of alarm.

"I don't want to run into that Reagan feller then."

He looked at Jacky.

"What say we ferget this business we are on, and jis go back to 'ome."

"Hush Wells," said Jimmy Boy, his impatience with the man growing thin.

"So, you believe this Reagan chap killed your neighbours, Richard?"

"The day we found the bodies, we saw a group of Reagan's men riding hard from the river, coming from the

Lambert's. But Reagan is a sharp and cunning bastard, Jimmy. The Lamberts had aboriginal spears in their backs."

"Then it could have been the aboriginals you mentioned previously?"

"A definite no Jimmy! The Lamberts were good to the aborigines and kept them in meat and necessities. You know, flour and sugar and tobacco. The blacks would never have killed them. Besides, when we found the bodies, there was no sign of blood from the wounds. And to me, Jimmy, that means the spears were pushed into their backs long after they were dead. If the spears had killed them, there would have been signs of blood. And when I checked the bodies, you know, rolled them over, there were gunshot wounds to the heart. They were shot at close range, Jimmy. It was not murder. It was a planned execution."

"What about the law? Was there an investigation?"

"If you could call it that. The local copper in Milburra is thick as thieves with Reagan. I think he gets a few quid a month from Reagan to keep his mouth shut about certain things. And free meat from time to time. Anyway, the blacks were blamed, and the case was closed."

"What about the Lambert's land?"

"They had no family that anyone knew of, so the government took it over. Reagan runs his sheep and cattle on it now. I guess by killing the Lamberts, he saved money on the purchase price. He now has free agistment for his stock at the government's expense."

Jimmy Boy decided at that moment to reveal why the men were headed to Milburra. He knew now that their mission was not just a search and rescue one, but it was a dance with danger, even death, and a fight for justice. And he knew he could not just waltz onto Reagan's land and demand justice. He needed a plan. But Andrews needed to know why he was there along with his friends.

It took about half an hour of explaining, along with Jacky's input, to fully inform the man of their plans.

Jennings, a nervous sleeper, had woken and lay rolling a cigarette and listening while Burra was also awake and trying to understand the white man's conversation.

"The black man with us, the old man Burra, it is his tribe and his family, Richard. He managed to escape and somehow reached our town, Ramsay. And Jacky here, he has a duty to help his people, Richard, and I have a duty as his friend to help him.”

“I believe every word you say, Jacky. Reagan is a callous bastard, and it doesn't surprise me he has Aboriginals chained up on his property.”

He looked at Burra, and the old man could see the sympathy in his eyes. Andrews spoke solemnly.

“We need to be very careful. If word gets out about any threat to Reagan, then we could all end up like the Lamberts.”

Jimmy Boy put forward a suggestion.

“We need a camp where we can make our plans, Richard. Would it be all right with you if we stayed here?”

Andrews nodded thoughtfully and stroked his chin.

“We will have to tread lightly. The town itself is not too far from here, and it is mostly under Reagan's thumb as well. We cannot trust anyone but ourselves, I am afraid.”

He looked long and hard at Jacky and Jimmy Boy.

“You two look like very capable men. I will be under your instructions. I just hope I am not inviting trouble.”

“We best get some sleep now,” said Jimmy Boy.

*****

The men were awake early, after the best sleep they had spent in days. The barn had been warm, which had come as a change to the bitterly cold nights sleeping in the open.

Jennings hauled himself from his swag and let out his obligatory morning fart.

"Shoulda been born a rooster Jennin's," said Wells in disgust.

"Yer damned crowin' outta yer arse is enough to wake the whole farmyard."

Jacky had woken with a head clouded with worry. He needed to speak with Jimmy Boy. While the men rolled up their bedding and stretched their legs, Jacky leaned across and whispered to Jimmy Boy.

"Jimmy Boy," he began,

"there's something I haven't told you, what with all that's been going on."

Jimmy Boy turned to look at his friend, his curiosity aroused.

"I have met Reagan's daughter."

Jimmy Boy leaned on the rail of the horse stall, his face a mask of surprise.

"How did that happen, Jacky?"

"It was after the Gilmore Cup. You remember I wrote to Martha about it? I raced my stallion and who should I race against? None other but the daughter of Harry Reagan."

He leaned even closer, and his voice dropped several pitches lower."

"We talked after the race, and she suggested we put my stallion with her mare. That way, we could breed a real champion."

Jimmy Boy's eyes narrowed, his mind working overtime.

"So……… you're suggesting we can use this to our advantage, Jacky?"

"I don't see why not. But I will have to leave here, Jimmy Boy. We can't let Reagan know I am staying here on the Andrews' farm with you and the others, and Burra must be always kept out of sight."

"What's the girl's name?"

"It is Charlene. Charley she is known as. But Jimmy Boy, I do not think she is like her father. She does not appear the type to enslave people nor the type to condone murder."

Jimmy remained pensive. Pensive and wary.

"So you think your stallion is the key to our success?"

Jacky nodded, his eyes gleaming.

"I can go into Milburra and book into a hotel. Most townsfolk are curious when it comes to strangers. Even more so when it is a black man on a fine horse with the money to afford a hotel room, I figure it would not take long for word to get around, and I get an invite from Reagan to visit his ranch."

Jimmy Boy's smile grew as he deliberated on Jacky's plan.

"We must play it smart, Jacky. I could never forgive myself if anything happened to you."

"Nothing will ever happen to me, Jimmy Boy," laughed the black man.

*****

Jacky saddled his horse to make the journey into Milburra. He rode with a sense of anticipation. His plan was simple: get noticed, get talked about, and get an invitation to Reagan's farm. And he knew that Bandit held the key to the invitation.

The streets of Milburra were already bustling. Women were shopping, and children and dogs raced around, creating havoc on the narrow footpaths. As Jacky rode in, heads turned to stare at the magnificent stallion and its rider. Jacky knew he had garnered attention as he heard whispers of "Who's that?" and "What's he here for? and "What's a darky doin' ridin' a fine horse?"

He tied Bandit to a hitching rail outside a general store and walked inside, a tiny silver bell announcing his entrance. The shopkeeper, an elderly woman, looked up in surprise. She was not accustomed to having blacks in her store, especially well-dressed and well-groomed ones. Her face went from surprise to a friendly smile.

"Morning Ma'am," said Jacky in his usual friendly tone while at the same time tipping his hat.

"I am looking for Miss Charlene Reagan. Can you tell me where I could find the lady?"

Jacky knew Charley lived out of town, but he also

knew it would be foolish to allow anyone to know that he knew. The less people knew of his connection to the girl, the better and safer it was for him. The old woman's eyes lit up.

"You are in luck, mister. She has not long left here, and she said she was off to the bakers."

Curiosity was getting to the woman.

"You after work, mister?"

"Maybe," was the curt response.

He tipped his hat again and placed it on his head.

"I'll mosey on down the street then."

His body quivered with excitement. This was the break he had been looking for.

The bakery was a small building standing alongside one of two butcher shops in Milburra. The smell of freshly baked bread wafted out the door and assailed Jacky's nostrils. He looked through the window and saw Charley Reagan, her hair loose and streaming down over her shoulders. A tremor went through him as he recalled the time spent in bed with her. And with that tremor came the irreplaceable feeling of guilt. He chided himself by thinking,

"What needs to be done, needs to be done."

He knew he would sleep with her again if it would help his cause.

Jacky waited patiently for Charley to finish her purchase and pulled the door open for her as she struggled with a bag containing bread and cakes. Her idle chatter and laughter with the baker stopped as her eyes flickered in recognition.

"Jacky!" she gasped.

"You made it. How wonderful to see you."

Her eyes widened, and her face broke into a warm smile as she extended her hand.

"I did not think you would come. I have told my father all about you…. Well, not all," she blushed, "that is our secret. And he is quite willing to give you a good deal on some fine rams in exchange for putting your stallion with Clara."

She looked around.

"Where is your horse? And your friends?"

A look of alarm flooded her beautiful features.

"Jacky, it is not safe around here to leave anything unattended. Bloody blacks will steal… Oh, I am sorry, Jacky.

I did not mean anything by that."

"It's all right. I understand," he said, having grown accustomed to disparaging remarks about his heritage.

"My two mates? They are staying at…"

Jacky realised before it was too late that he almost gave himself away. The girl must not know too much about Burra, for even though his appearance had changed, there was still every chance she may recognise him. He forced himself into composure and said,

"My mates are camped outside the town. I do not want them here in the town itself because one likes the drink too much. And the other is just a loner. They may have even gone by now. They talked about heading back south to find work. And my horse? He is hitched outside the general store. I have no doubt I would have a reliable witness if he were stolen. The old lady in the store has not taken her eyes off me or my horse."

"This town has the habit of knowing everyone's business, Jacky.

"Then I guess all small towns are the same."

He thought of Mrs Wells.

"Let me take this to the wagon, and we can go to my favourite little tea house down the street. It is much quieter, and we can talk there without the whole town listening in."

Jacky nodded, his heart racing. Everything was going better than he expected. As they walked side by side, he could not help but notice the curious looks of the townspeople. He knew what they would be thinking.

He could feel Charley's gaze on him, and for a moment, he wondered if she had seen through his cunning plan. They settled into a cosy corner in the teashop, and Charley ordered for them both. The soft murmurs of conversation from other patrons and the clinking of teacups created a soothing backdrop.

As they sat in silence, sipping their tea, Jacky wondered if it was a mistake to give in to the passion they had shared. Would it help, or would it complicate things? But looking at her, so self-assured and tantalising, he knew he would never regret it.

Charley, on the other hand, was lost in her own musings. The memory of their night together spread a warm glow through her cheeks, and she knew she wanted to experience the black man again. She wondered if he felt the same way or was just using her as a toy to be discarded when broken.

The silence seemed to stretch forever until Jacky spoke.

"Charley, I am willing to loan you the services of my stallion, but there is one condition."

"Anything," she replied, becoming more excited by the moment.

"My father will be so pleased. But what is the condition?"

"I want to come and stay at your farm and oversee the breeding. I have a way with horses, and I know my horse better than anyone. I want to ensure the breeding goes smoothly. Besides, Bandit is far too valuable for me to leave him with strangers."

"I didn't think we were strangers, Jacky," she said with a wicked grin.

Charley set her cup down with a delicate clink.

"Is that your only condition? You stay at my father's farm? Maybe I have some conditions of my own," she said rather suggestively.

"I'm all ears," said Jacky, drawn in by her playful tone.

Charley leant forward, her smile enticing.

"I was thinking," her voice had dropped to a whisper, "perhaps after we are finished here, we could do some business elsewhere."

"You mean" asked Jacky.

"Mmm, I mean," she said dreamily.

"But you are known here, Charley. And besides, we don't want your father finding out about us."

"No one knows me by the riverbank, Jacky."

Jacky's eyes searched hers, pondering over her open invitation.

"There's a spot by the riverbank about two miles from town. My wagon will be there. No one will be concerned. I stop there a lot on my trips to town."

Two miles seemed like ten under the weight of Jacky's thoughts.

Was this a meeting for lust or a bold strategic move?

The townsfolk paid him no attention as he left town. Just another black drifter, they thought. Jacky spied Charley's wagon by the riverbank, and his heart missed a beat as he saw her sitting by the water, taking in the beauty of the scenery.

She looked up as he approached.

"You made it," she said, her voice a mix of sultry suggestion and challenge.

"I'm surprised. I thought you had more important things to do."

Jacky had that same feeling again. Guilt!

Her next action took him by surprise. Before he could react, she had arched her back and pulled him down onto the grass. Her eyes searched his for a moment, and then her tongue sought his mouth with an urgency that was almost overpowering. The kiss was hungry, desperate, and full of passion.

Jacky felt her hands moving over his body, tugging at his shirt. He helped her remove it, and then, with a movement that surprised him, she ripped the front of her blouse open and pushed her breasts into his face. He could feel the heat of her body and the rapid thumping of her chest as her hands went to his crotch, her hand firm and knowing. He sucked in a sharp breath as she began to massage him, her movements sure and deliberate.

Jacky was sure now that Charley was no novice in the art of seduction. Yet he felt something else in her touch. A hunger that was not solely driven by desire. It was then he realised that Charley wanted to claim him as her own.

Her hands continued to work their magic on him, and he felt himself straining at his pants. His hands found her breasts, and he cupped one and then used his teeth to gently nibble the soft flesh. His hand slid up her thigh, and he pulled her pants aside and felt her wetness.

His other hands fumbled with the buttons on his pants, and he freed himself and stared into her eyes, searching for any sign of hesitation. With one swift movement, he entered her, filling her completely. Her hips bucked at the intrusion, and she moaned into his neck. Then they both cried out, their sounds mingling with the murmur of the river and the wildlife around them.

*****

BOOK 2

*Before you embark on a journey of revenge,
dig two graves.*

-   Confucius C 551- C 479

Chapter 13

"Jacky, you need to be careful. You cannot just think you can walk in on the Reagan's place and be accepted. Tell me, just how friendly are you with his daughter?"

Jacky gulped and thought carefully before he answered.

"Friendly enough to wangle an invite to the farm. She is a nice enough girl, Jimmy Boy, and I doubt she knows anything about her father's dealings."

The sound of footsteps on the gravel brought a halt to their conversation. It was Andrews and his sister, bearing a tray of scones and a pot of coffee.

Andrews looked tired and his shoulders were slumped. Beside him, his sister looked no better, a worried look on her face.

"Miss Andrews," said Jimmy Boy kindly, "you do not have to go to all this trouble for us. Jacky will bring us some supplies tomorrow to do us for a few days. I cannot guarantee how long we will be here."

Andrews gave Jimmy Boy a forced smile.

"You are welcome to stay as long as you like. I just want to bring Reagan to justice. I cannot sleep at night, and my sister is a nervous wreck."

Jimmy Boy looked at Rachel Andrews. Her face was lined and etched with the constant worries that had been haunting them. She was a beautiful young woman who faced the prospect of aging before her time.

"Miss Andrews, Jacky has received an invitation from Reagan's daughter to stay at their farm. Hopefully, he can find out more, and we can manage to release Burra's family."

"But what about us?" asked the teary woman.

"Are we left to fend for ourselves?"

She reached for her brother's hand.

"I will do everything I can to help you, Miss Andrews," assured Jacky, "but I suspect Reagan is a cunning man and very clever. I just hope we are not taking anything on we cannot handle."

He looked at Jimmy Boy, and there was an unspoken understanding. This was not just about Burra's family; it was about the survival of all the small farmers in the area.

"I know you will, Jacky, but we have lived under Reagan's shadow too long now. If there is a way to put an end to this, the whole district will be in your debt."

Jimmy Boy had remained silent, a million thoughts racing through his mind.

"This is something big," he said.

"I just hope it's not too big for us to handle. The law needs to step in."

"But I've already told you, Jimmy, the law around here is Reagan," said Richard Andrews.

The implication hung heavy, and the group stood in silence, each trying to come up with some answers.

"It is settled then," said Jacky eventually.

"I will stay at the Reagan's and try and win Charley's old man's favour. But it is one step at a time. We must not get ahead of ourselves."

*****

Jacky had given his stay in Milburra long and careful consideration. He decided against taking a room at the Faith & Hope Hotel and instead found another hotel further down the street. He pushed open the door of the hotel reception to be met with an interior that was dimly lit and smelt of stale tobacco and aged timber. The man behind the counter with greying eyes and a scowl on his face looked up and barked,

"Out! No darkies allowed!"

"I want a room for the night," said Jacky coldly.

"I have money."

He placed a crumpled bill on the counter, and as he did, a woman emerged from a back room, leaned in close to the clerk's ear, and whispered. The man listened intently, and Jacky watched as his face changed its expression.

He looked up and, in a less-than-pleased voice, said,

"Mr Reagan sent word about you. Said there might be a darky wantin' a room."

His tone had shifted from hostility to reluctant acceptance.

"He said to give you a room, and he will foot the bill. Goes against my policy, mister. Don't tolerate blacks, but Mister Reagan's word is good."

He gave Jacky an intimidating look.

"And nobody 'round these parts crosses Reagan."

"Thank you," said Jacky, his voice still cool.

"I will remember that."

"Come, I will show you upstairs," said the woman.

Jacky started to follow the woman but turned and addressed the clerk.

"I'd just like to tell you, mister, that I pay my own way. I don't wish to take advantage of Mister Reagan's charity."

"Suit yerself."

Jacky followed her as she pattered up to the landing, where she stopped and pushed open the door to his room.

From below came the voice of the clerk.

"Make sure you piss in the pot too, mister. And not on the floor."

"Don't mind him," said the woman in a surprisingly kind voice.

"You'll find it comfortable here. If you want anything, feel free to ask."

Without another word, she flounced back down the

stairs.

The room was small and sparsely furnished. If Reagan was trying to impress Jacky, he was doing a poor job. There was a single bed and a chair which was ready to collapse if anybody sat on it. He decided to sit on the edge of the bed, but finding that uncomfortable, he stood and walked to the window. It offered a view of the main street, and there were still people going about their business, although most shops were closing their doors.

He threw his belongings on the bed and lay down. He knew he needed a good night's sleep if he was to be ready for the day ahead. The springs of the bed groaned with his weight, but all that mattered was he had a roof over his head and a chance to be refreshed before meeting Reagan.

Jacky was awake before the sun rose. He washed himself and felt the cold water's invigorating sting. The towel was a flimsy affair, but he made do, and the roughness brought a glow to his cheeks. He studied his face in the mirror; the only thing in the room that had no flaws, he thought.

He descended the stairs, and at the bottom, he met the woman from the evening before.

"Breakfast?" she asked with a half-decent smile.

"No time," he answered.

"Can you tell me the way to Reagan's farm?"

"No need." came the curt reply.

"Two can play at your rudeness game, you know."

"I am sorry if I appeared rude, ma'am, but I am in a hurry to be on my way."

Her face softened.

"There's someone here to meet you. He was sent by Mister Reagan."

Jacky looked around and saw a stout man wearing a wide-brimmed hat. He looked far different from anybody Jacky had envisaged working for Reagan. His sunburned face carried a broad smile, and he seemed friendly enough. He extended his hand and said,

"I am Randall Mounsie. Mister Reagan's lawyer and bookkeeper. I've come to take you to the farm. The finest land on the other side of the river."

The man persisted with his rapid-fire talk.

"Where's your horse? I hope he is safe. That is what this is all about, isn't it? Mister Reagan cannot wait to see your stallion."

Jacky shook the man's hand briefly and then wiped the sweat from his palms on his trousers. Mounsie's hand had felt like a wet fish.

"Mister, you sure do talk a lot. Do you ever give yourself time to draw breath? And the answer is yes. My horse Is safe," said Jacky as he recalled giving the livery boy a handsome tip to safeguard Bandit overnight.

"He is at the livery. Come on, we will go get him. Do you have a horse?"

"I prefer to travel by buggy. Nasty accident on a horse when I was a mere lad. I will remain here and have some coffee while you get your horse."

Jacky looked at the size of the man and knew the true reason for the man's reluctance to ride a horse. He would be all out trying to get astride his mount.

Jacky pushed open the heavy barn door, and his gaze fell upon the boy, still fast asleep but clinging to the rope that hung loosely from Bandit's neck.

He stirred as Jacky approached and sat upright, wiping his eyes and straining to see in the dim morning light.

"Morning, mister," the boy said and then yawned.

"I watched yer horse all night. Didn't even go 'ome."

"You are a good lad," said Jacky as he fished for some extra coins in his pocket. The boy took the coins and pocketed them.

"Perhaps, mister," he said, patting the flank of the magnificent stallion, "I might have enough money to buy a horse like this someday."

Jacky reached deeper into his pocket and found some more coins. He tossed them on the ground.

"A down payment boy."

Then he added,

"Keep your dreams boy. One day, they may come true."

Mounsie was sitting up on the seat of his small buggy as Jacky rode out of the stables and into the street. The lawyer had a steaming mug of coffee in one hand and a cigarette in the other.

"Ready?" he asked with an overly familiar grin, one that Jacky would soon tire of.

"Finish your coffee first so you can leave the mug."

"No need. The money they get off Reagan, they can buy a hundred mugs."

He slurped the last of the coffee and tossed his mug on the ground.

The ride was a pleasant one. Jacky had to keep a close rein on Bandit, who, after a night of confinement, relished the morning air and wanted to work off some energy. Mounsie drove his small buggy slowly, and there was little or no conversation until Jacky asked,

"You were full of talk earlier, and now silence Mounsie. Any problem?"

"I didn't like the way you spoke to me."

The man had a sullen look on his face, like a child deprived of a slice of cake.

"If you did not like it then fine by me. Just do not talk to me again."

Mounsie realised he needed Jacky's onside, so he tried

to calm the situation.

"See that fence line there?"

The jagged wire gleamed with the early dewdrops and drew Jacky's eyes towards it.

"Whose fence line?"

"That is Mister Reagan's boundary."

"Who owns the land on the other side?"

"A family by the name of Andrews. A queer lot. Mister Reagan has offered them good money for their farm, but they are stubborn people. Refuse to sell."

"And over there?" Jacky persisted.

"That is government land now. The people who lived there were murdered by the blacks."

"Are blacks a problem around here?"

"Sure are."

He looked at Jacky furtively and crinkled up his nose.

"Just hope you are not."

Jacky declined to say anything further.

Mounsie, on suspicion he had upset the black man once more, hastened to add,

"Soon be there. Just over the next rise."

They breasted the hill and looked down on the Reagan homestead. A magnificent arch of sawn red gum highlighted the entrance to the houseyard. From the top of the arch dangled a sign which informed the visitor of the property name.

Jacky mouthed the words which read,

"Dingo's Retreat." then said to Mounsie,

"I see that Mister Reagan has a fine aboriginal name for his place, too. But we aboriginals know the dingo as a companion, not as a killer the way the white man sees it."

"Are you trying to make a point, Jacky?" asked Mounsie, with a trace of suspicion.

"And what point do you think I am making, Mister Mounsie? I am just making a general comment."

"You best keep your inferences to yourself when you meet Mister Reagan. There is one thing he cannot abide, and that is a smartarse."

"He can take me however he wants to. I am not going

to pretend to be anybody that I am not."

Jacky pulled Bandit to a stop, caressed the posts holding the sign, and looked into the sun at the residence before him.

"Some home Mister Reagan has," said Jacky, his eyes wide as he took in the grandeur.

It was a two-storey place, nestled amongst trees that stretched their limbs over it as if protecting the home from harm. The lawn was lush and green, and fruit trees were planted neatly around the fence. Jacky looked past the homestead and saw a collection of buildings huddled together. It was a very impressive setup, indeed. Mounsie pulled the buggy to a stop and said,

"Wait here. I will go fetch Mister Reagan."

But Reagan had been expecting them. He walked out the front door before Mounsie had a chance to unlatch the gate. Reagan strode towards them, his boots making no sound on the soft grass.

Jacky looked over the man who could decide his fate with a single command. Reagan was tall and broad-shouldered with a huge gut that filled out his flannel shirt. As he approached, Jacky saw eyes that were piercing and no doubt capable of seeing through any deception. He knew he had to be very careful. Behind him came two other men, both with the same deliberate walk and inquisitive eyes. Each carried a rifle, the barrels gleaming in the bright sunlight.

"I am Harry Reagan. You must be Jacky."

Jacky noticed that the man's eyes were focused on his horse rather than himself.

"My daughter was right. What a magnificent creature!"

Jacky dismounted, and Reagan took the reins with a trembling hand. Bandit snorted as if in acknowledgment of Reagan's words.

"You two," he said to the men rather gruffly, "take the horse to the stable and water him and give him a feed of oats. And do not dare let anything happen to him or else…"

The men understood. Reagan did not have to say anymore. Jacky could see the fear in their eyes. He watched as the men took his horse away.

"Be seeing you, Mister Reagan," called Mounsie as he set off for town.

*****

Chapter 14

"It's so lovely to have you here, Violet," said Angela warmly.

She looked at the two toddlers rolling around on the patchwork mat draping the floor, their laughter echoing throughout the sunroom.

The room smelt of freshly brewed tea and was mixed with the scent of the gardenia bush outside the window.

"And to think, these two wonderful little boys are almost two years old."

The four women sat on cushioned cane chairs, with cups of the hot tea balanced precariously on their laps.

Violet smiled as she observed her son Glen, his curly red hair catching the rays of the sunbeams streaming through the windows. His playmate, little Robbie, had darker skin and was a much smaller child than his playmate. His big brown eyes constantly wandered from his playmate to his mother, Meg.

Just then, Bindi entered the room carrying a tray of hot scones slathered with cream. Her dark eyes flicked sideways at the toddlers before turning to Violet.

"That youngun don't look nuthin' like 'is daddy," she remarked.

"e's sure got a good crop of red hair. Yer family got red hair?"

The question hung in the air, and the room became silent. The only sounds came from the birdlife outside.

Violet's smile faltered, and a look of annoyance caused her face to crinkle into a frown.

"That will be enough, Bindi," snapped Angela.

"It's time you knew your place."

Bindi hung her head and muttered,

"Sorry, Missus Boss."

Despite her lowly position in the household, Bindi was wise enough to recognise the unacknowledged truth. She had overstepped her mark.

"Leave us, please, Bindi."

Angela's tone was firm without being too harsh on her loyal servant. The toddlers continued to laugh and play but the room was now filled with an undercurrent of tension. The woman looked at Violet as she attempted to regain her composure.

Eleanor broke the silence.

"Let us not dwell on such trivialities. Children are children; they take after their parents in spirit rather than in looks."

But Violet could detect the cynicism in her words.

*****

That night, Violet found herself restless, her thoughts tangled around the words Bindi had uttered that day. Violet recalled previous conversations with her husband and remembered him asking,

"Violet, does red hair run through the blood of your family?"

She remembered telling him that her grandfather had red hair, which seemed to satisfy her husband as he dropped the matter.

Yet with each passing day, Violet could see the resemblance of her son to Bullock Williams. She had known from the time she became pregnant that the child was not her husband's. She knew, her conscience knew that she had to tell him.

"Kevin, I have something to tell you."

"Yes, my dear, what is it?" he asked as he spooned more gravy over his meat.

"You might wish to place your cutlery down," she said nervously.

"Is the news that bad you think I may throw my knife at you?" he laughed.

"Glen is not your son."

The words escaped her lips like a prayer. Violet waited for his reaction.

"So, all this time, I have been raising another man's child? I shouldn't say, man. He was a mongrel dog!"

He simply stared at his wife, stunned by the news. But Violet was even more stunned that he was not showing signs of anger towards her.

"I never wanted this to happen. I wanted to shield you from the truth."

The anger on his face evaporated.

"You should have trusted me, Violet. We are in this life together. I have raised him as my son and will continue to do so. I will not let the shadow of Williams taint our lives forever."

He reached for her and held her tightly, and from that moment, Violet knew she was on the path to redemption.

"We cannot let this lie persist," said Violet.

"We must tell Mrs O'Brien and the Wang family."

"Violet, I have a feeling they have known all along. As have I."

She gasped.

"You knew Kevin? Why have you kept it quiet for so long?"

"Why spoil our happiness, Violet? I am a man who can forgive, as you well know. We do not need to go through life in misery. And we have been so happy since the boy was born."

"You are a wonderful man, Kevin Heath. Why did I ever betray you?" she sobbed as he pulled her in closer.

*****

"Are you sure you are up to this?" asked the Doctor.

"There's absolutely no law that states we have to tell anybody the parentage of our son."

"I think it is for the best, Kevin. And as you said, it will be out in the open then. There will be no need for people to gossip behind our backs."

Their son lay sleeping in his mother's lap as the buggy creaked its way towards Wicklow. Kevin squeezed her hand tightly, offering silent encouragement.

*****

Bindi stood quietly in the corner of the room. She had been the one behind this disclosure, and she nodded sombrely as Violet spoke. Bindi had known for months, having noticed the similarities between the boy and the late Bullock Williams.

"My son does not look like the Doctor because Kevin is not his father."

There was a deathly silence as the women took in Violet's words. Angela was the first to speak.

"It is certainly not the end of the world, Violet. We

have accepted him as your son, so I think that puts an end to this discussion. Now, let's have some tea, shall we? Bindi, please."

"Yes, Missus Boss."

Bindi walked to the kitchen, muttering to herself.

"Told that uneducated Mia that boy wasn't the doctor."

*****

"Miss Martie, there is a letter done come for you. 'ope it's not bad news. Most of them damned things are," said Bindi.

'You will never change Bindi, will you? Always a pessimist."

Bindi harumphed.

"And do not you be using those swear words to me, Miss Martie. Must say, though, that swear word is a new one. Ain't 'eard it before."

She walked away, the word pessimist rolling off her tongue as she tried to determine how crude it was.

Martha had been enjoying her stay at Wicklow while Jacky was away and was looking forward to another letter from him. It came as a surprise to her when she turned the envelope over and looked at the handwriting. It was not from Jacky. She recognised it at once. The penmanship was Will's.

She tore the envelope open, her heart in a flutter, and took out the cream-colored paper.

"My dearest Martha," the letter began, "I have been remiss in not writing more often, but as you are well aware, I do not wish to be an intrusion in the life of a married woman. However, I have a proposal to offer for you and your family's consideration."

Her eyes widened as she read on.

"I have a week's holiday approaching, and may I be so bold as to ask whether I may visit you and all the good folk at Wicklow?"

She put the letter down on the bench, and her mind wandered to the last time she had seen Will. It was at her brother Shimmy's funeral and had ended in a terrible row between her now husband Jacky and Will, the man who had wanted to take her for his bride. Martha's thoughts raced as she read on.

"I have so much to tell you," he wrote,

"And I suspect you to me as well. Our conversations always made me happy, and I know you felt the same way.

I have not seen my sister for quite some time, and it would be a good opportunity to renew our acquaintance. I will arrive in Ramsay on the 18th, and I will book my accommodation at Jack's Inn. Then if your family agrees, I wish to come and stay at Wicklow as a guest of the Wang family.

She felt a pang of guilt for not having kept in touch with him.

"Martha," she chided herself, "you are a happily married woman."

Yet she could not shake off the feeling of happiness that Will's letter had given her. His words seemed to chase away the loneliness she was feeling since Jacky had been gone. She was thrilled at the opportunity to see him again, but she was also acutely aware of the potential trouble it could bring.

Jacky should be home before long and she knew she had to decide how to handle this situation. She was happily married, but that did not mean she didn't have moments of doubts and longing for the past. She realised she had buried those thoughts, convincing herself they were remnants of the past and youthful infatuations. Yet the prospect of Will's visit stirred something she had not felt for what seemed like ages.

She rose from the garden bench and strolled through her mother's garden, the letter clutched in her hand. Each step seemed to take her further from the comforts of her present life and closer to the tangled web of emotions that no doubt awaited her. The garden path was well-trodden and reminded her of the times she had walked it with Will, sharing dreams and broken promises.

Back inside, she slipped the letter into her cupboard, resting it between the pages of the small novel she was reading. She knew she could not keep the contents of the letter a secret for too long, but she needed time to process her feelings. She decided to wait until the next day to tell everybody.

*****

The morning sun streamed through the window as the family gathered for breakfast. Martha came bustling in, her eyes sparkling with excitement, the letter clutched in her hand.

"I have wonderful news," she announced.

"Meg, your brother Will is paying us a visit."

Breakfast was forgotten as they all fired questions at Martha.

"For how long? When is he coming? Is he coming alone?"

"All I know is," Martha answered, "he will be here in two days' time. He will make his accommodation at Jack's Inn."

"But that is nonsense, Martha. Will must stay here."

Angela, in all seriousness, said,

"I wonder how his law studies are going. I hope everything is all right."

Meg prodded her son Robbie and laughed.

"Little man, your uncle is coming to visit. He will see you for the very first time."

She collected herself, and her voice took on a solemn tone.

"Goodness, we have not seen him since we buried Shimmy."

*****

Chapter 15

Jacky followed Reagan as he led them over the spongy lawn to the front door. The interior of the home was as grand as the outside. They stepped into a large foyer with high ceilings and walls painted in white, giving the room a more spacious feeling. The floor beneath their boots appeared to be polished redgum, and Jacky hesitated, wondering whether to remove his boots. Reagan looked at him and knew what he was thinking.

"No need," he said.

"I have plenty of servants to clean any mess."

Jacky took a moment to appreciate the grandeur of the place, and for a short moment, he felt jealous of the man's obvious tastes and wealth. The sound of their footsteps echoed down the hallway as they entered a large living area and library of sorts. From a door off to the side, Jacky discerned the faint sound of footsteps.

"A woman." he thought.

"The steps are too light."

He twisted his body and found his eyes locked on those

of Charley, a beaming smile on her face, which still carried the seemingly painted-on expression of mischief.

"Jacky," she smiled.

"I am glad you are here. And I see you have met my father."

Jacky swallowed hard, trying to ignore the dryness in his throat. The girl unnerved him.

From another door, a young aboriginal girl appeared, her head bent down and her long dark hair hanging in tresses over her shoulder. She was dressed in a simple shift and was barefooted.

Without looking up, she asked,

"Anything to eat or drink, Mr Reagan?"

"Could she be one of Burra's daughters? Or granddaughters?" thought Jacky.

As he looked the girl over, he noticed she had the habit of shuffling her hands behind her back.

He was even more determined to seek the truth and discover the secrets of Dingo's Retreat, but for now, he must continue his charade as a horse breeder and sheep buyer.

Reagan dismissed the girl with a grunted sentence.

"Nothing, Mona. You get yourself on out of here and into the kitchen."

The girl turned and walked out, and in doing so, Jacky managed to get a look at her hands. He was not surprised to see red weals around her wrists, similar to injuries Burra had around his ankles. Reagan noted Jacky's eyes on the girl.

"A word of warning, Jacky. I have Aborigines working for me, but even though they may be your people, it is a hands-off policy while you are under my roof."

Jacky was cunning.

"I see no reason why you cannot employ my people, Mister Reagan. And as for your hands-off policy, I wish to tell you that I am a happily married man."

He caught the sly grin that appeared on Charley's face and had to look aside.

"But, Mister Reagan, I noticed the girl who just left had some bruising on her wrists. I would like to think that if you employ my people, you see that you take good care of them. She looks as if she needs to be seen by a doctor."

"My workers are my business Jacky. Anyway, she suffered those injuries unloading the supply wagon from town a few days ago."

He looked at his daughter.

"Isn't that right, Charley?"

Charlene Reagan gulped and became flushed in the face. She avoided looking at Jacky but said in a low voice,

"That's correct, Papa."

"All this talk is getting us nowhere, Mister Reagan. As you say, your employees are your concern. But my concern is our business. We both know your mare is a prime piece of horse flesh, and I want to see what my stallion can produce. I cast an astute eye over your rams as I came here and liked what I saw. What about we strike a deal? I give you my stallion to service your mare, and you give me ten of your best rams."

Reagan pursed his lips, considering the proposal.

"Dingo's Retreat rams are the best in the country, Jacky. You think a fair deal is ten of my rams for a service fee? Maybe you underestimate my stock."

"I do not underestimate," Jacky replied smoothly.

"I know your rams are worth their weight in gold, but my stallion will produce a foal that will be worth much more than ten rams."

Then Jacky added,

"You can win the Gilmore Cup every year for the next ten years."

An amused smile broke across Reagan's face.

"All right, Jacky, it's a deal. But let us put it in writing. I'll have Mounsie, my lawyer, come out tomorrow to draw up a contract. In the meantime, I will get Charlene to show you around the place. But mind you, don't stray anywhere off the path I have instructed her to take you. This is a dangerous country. The aborigines have been acting up something terrible lately."

"You do not say. I do not think I would have a problem there."

"Just do as I ask Jacky. And we will get along fine."

*****

They each rode one of Reagan's stock horses, for as Reagan had pointed out,

"That stallion is far too valuable to use for any wayward outings. A snake bite or a broken leg. Anything could happen. A careless blackfeller spear even."

"Why is your father so adamant we stick to a designated route, Charley? Does he have something to hide? Or does he think I might pinch something?"

"There are some areas where even I am forbidden to ride. The farm has its secrets, Jacky, and my father is protective of them. He's the only one who knows what they are. I just go along with him to keep the peace. Sort of, I leave him alone, and he leaves me alone."

Jacky arched his eyebrows, his curiosity becoming stronger, and probed further.

"What kind of secrets?"

"It is complicated, but trust me. We will stick to the trail he has laid out. That way, we will not cause trouble."

Jacky suddenly realised that the secrets Reagan held were completely hidden from his daughter. He breathed a sigh of relief. He had grown quite fond of the girl.

She kicked her horse in the flanks and broke into a

gallop.

"Follow me, Jacky," she called over her shoulder.

"We'll ride to the river."

As they approached the river, Charley's voice grew fainter, and all Jacky could hear was the rushing water. Charley dismounted at the water's edge and tethered her horse. Then, as if exhausted, she flopped onto the grass.

"We're all alone, Jacky," she said, her eyes sparkling with seduction.

"No harm in a bit of fun, is there?" she said almost inaudibly. She put her hand up for him to grasp and hinted he should join her.

Jacky slumped to the grass, his heart racing as she felt for his thigh.

"Charley," he protested rather weakly,

"Not here. Remember what you said about your father."

But as the words left his mouth, he knew he was fighting a losing battle.

"Jacky, what is the worst that can happen? We are

miles from home. There is no one about."

She leaned in, and her lips brushed his. He knew it was risky, but the lure of the forbidden was too hard to resist. He kissed her neck, and her moans grew softer as he explored her body. Her riding pants and shirt were damp with sweat, and her breathing was ragged as she whispered his name. Suddenly, Jacky stiffened and sat upright, his ears picking up the sound of horses' hooves and the yapping of dogs.

"Charley, someone is coming. We need to get back on our horses."

They both scrambled to their feet, their breathing heavy and their movements frantic as they tried to regain some sense of order.

Two riders crested the ridge, and Charley gave a snort of disgust.

"It's that damned Kerrigan again. I should have known he would be snooping around."

"These two men a problem, Charley?"

"No, only one of them. Kerrigan. The other man, Howarth, is a gentleman. It beats me how he remains that way working for my father."

"So, what is the story with Kerrigan?" asked Jacky as the men reined their horses in.

Before she could answer, Kerrigan called out.

"Miss Charley, and what may I ask, are you doing all the way out here?"

He gave a scorching look at Jacky.

"And in the company of the darky, huh? You better hope he does not know those other mongrel blacks that's been terrorising the place."

"You just mind your manners, Kerrigan. What I do is none of your business!"

The man chuckled.

"Touchy little girl, ain't ya? Anyway, it is time to be getting back. Your father sent us to fetch you."

Charley rode beside Jacky, her jaw set firmly and her reins held tightly.

"So, tell me, Charley," said Jacky in a low voice, "a bit about Kerrigan. It seems to me as if you two have a bit of a history."

Charley rolled her eyes.

"Kerrigan is nothing but trouble. He has got more nerve than a black snake and as much poison in his body. Do not cross him, Jacky. He thinks he is a gift for womenfolk with his silver tongue."

She spat out the stalk of grass she had been chewing on and continued.

"He tried to kiss me once like I was some common street whore or a young black gin ripe for the taking. Did not get him far. I think his cheek would still be stinging where I whacked him."

Jacky raised his eyebrows, a smile playing on his face.

"Sounds like he fancies you, Charley."

"He's like a mongrel dog sniffing around a bone, Jacky. He cannot take no for an answer."

A silence came over them now, both deep in their own thoughts. Jacky could not help but wonder if Charley had shared some of her passion with Kerrigan. After all, she had told him she was a worldly-wise woman. He knew better than to ask, though.

Jacky's thoughts were interrupted as the two men in front of them wheeled their horses around.

Kerrigan did not speak but pointed towards the vast land stretched out before them. A group of figures, dark even in the bright sunshine, were moving towards them, and every one of them was carrying a spear.

Kerrigan fingered the pistol in his belt and said,

"We've got company."

Jacky nosed his horse forward and said to Kerrigan,

"Let me speak with them. And do not even think of using your sidearm."

"Greetings, warriors," Jacky called out as he dismounted.

The Kamilaroi warriors looked hard at him, their faces masked with curiosity. The stranger was wearing the foreign fabric of the white man, but his language was undeniably their own. A tall, wiry warrior stepped forward.

"Who are you?"

His eyes searched Jacky's, seeking any sign of deceit or hostility.

Jacky

"Who are you?" the warrior finally asked again.

"My name is Jacky. I am not of your tribe, but I carry the blood of all the proud warriors who have walked this land."

He paused, gauging their reaction. A younger warrior stepped forward.

"You dress like a white man, and though you speak our language, you sound like a white man."

Jacky nodded solemnly, his hands outstretched in a gesture of peace.

"My tribe comes from further south of here, but I am a Kamilaroi man."

The young warrior caressed the shaft of his spear.

Again, the young warrior asked,

"Why should we trust you?"

Jacky decided to tell the whole story while he had the chance. He knew the others with him did not understand anything that was being said.

"Do you know Burra?"

At the mention of the old man's name, Jacky knew he

had their attention.

"Burra was another blackfeller from down south. Our warriors say he was forced to work for the white boss. But he has not been seen for some time now. I think he has escaped from here," said the tall aboriginal warrior.

"We don't know where he is. Maybe he is dead."

"He is not dead. I can assure you of that."

Then Jacky gave a brief rundown on how he came to meet up with Burra and their plans to free his family and other members of Burra's tribe.

"How do you plan to do it? The white man Reagan has men with guns guarding his house and farm. We have tried to free the people, but we are no match for his weapons. He has killed two of our warriors already. All we can do is raid his animals and kill his cattle and sheep. He has had the police on our trail many times, but we are way too smart for them."

Kerrigan was becoming impatient.

"What are you yabbering about, Jacky? Not planning trouble?"

"I am stopping trouble, mister," said Jacky with a

scowl on his face. He turned back to the group of blacks.

"Leave it with me. I will find your camp in a few days and let you know my plan."

The warriors were satisfied. They grunted in unison and set off in a slow jogging gait, the soles of their feet impervious to the burs on the ground.

*****

"Do you find it hard to have a black man staying under your roof for a while, Mister Reagan?"

Jacky stared hard at the man.

"I only ask because I have noticed you have a particular aversion to my people."

Reagan took a slow, deliberate sip of his whisky and then leaned and flicked the ash off his cigar. His eyes examined the ceiling, and there was a deathly silence in the dining room. Jacky leaned forward, his eyes staring unwaveringly at the older man. His question had been posed casually, but it did nothing but create a feeling of tension. Charley shifted uncomfortably in her seat. She had hoped that the evening meal would be a peaceful affair, not a breeding ground for conflict.

"Jacky," said Reagan, his voice gravelly from the cigar smoke,

"You are different. You have value. And you seem more like a white man than an Aborigine."

"Value?" scoffed Jacky.

"Now I understand why you tolerate me. It is because of my horse. Who is to say you won't double-cross me when your mare is in foal?"

"That's why I want my lawyer here tomorrow, you presumptuous fool."

Jacky's knuckles whitened, and he glared at Reagan.

"I am no fool, Mister Reagan."

Reagan looked back at him.

"No, I think not."

He could see the anger in Jacky's eyes.

"Reagan, what have my people done to you? Why do you think bad of them?"

"It is not what I think of them, it's what I know. They

are a wild, unpredictable lot. Not like us. They are not content unless they are killing my sheep and cattle and stealing supplies."

Jacky tried another tack.

"Have you ever thought about giving them a sheep to feed their families? Maybe if they were shown a bit of kindness, they would leave you and your stock alone."

Reagan counteracted.

"Perhaps if the blacks could learn from us the same way you have, then there'd be no trouble."

Jacky realised that the man would not listen to reason.

Reagan tipped his whisky down in one gulp and announced,

"I am going to bed. Tomorrow, we have plenty to do. Mona will take you to your room."

"Mona?"

"The aboriginal maid. And remember, Jacky, hands off."

*****

Jacky followed the young girl up the stairs to his bedroom. She was silent as she motioned towards an open door. Jacky looked her up and down. She was a fine-looking, even beautiful young woman.

Jacky said,

"Mine?" in Kamilaroi.

She nodded and said,

"You speak my language?"

She looked around, and Jacky could see the fear lining her pretty face.

"Do not be afraid of me," said Jacky in a gentle voice, "I am here to help you."

She became alarmed and pulled away as he reached out to take her arm and lead her into the room. Her eyes searched his face. She tried to leave, but Jacky held her firmly.

"What's your name?"

"The boss calls me Mona, but my name is Mara."

"I am Jacky," he said.

She pulled out of his grasp and backed against the wall.

"Please," Jacky implored her, "can you come back later when the household is asleep. I need to talk."

Her eyes grew wide at his suggestion, but she shook her head.

"I cannot," she stammered, "the boss chains us up at night."

"Us? How many more? Tell me, Mara," Jacky said urgently, but she dashed off.

He caught her by the arm as she reached the top of the stairs.

"The others are kept chained in sheds across from the stables. They are released each day when they are taken under guard to work in the paddocks."

Jacky was stunned by this news.

"Mara, I am telling you the truth. I want to get you and the others out of this place. I am here with Burra."

At the mention of that name, the girl stiffened and cast a wary glance around.

"You know my grandfather?"

"He is your grandfather? Mara, he is here with me. We

are staying close by and are going to help you. But you must help me."

"I will do anything to get away from this place. Do you really mean it? Can you help me?"

Tears were forming in her eyes as she pleaded with Jacky.

Footsteps could be heard coming up the stairs. Jacky released the girl, and she moved off as Charley's face appeared.

"I hope that young one hasn't taken your fancy, Jacky," she said in what seemed an ominous tone.

"Remember what my father told you."

"How could I forget?"

Charley smiled a wicked smile and sidled up to Jacky. She nuzzled his neck with her moist lips and breathed into his ear.

"Besides Jacky, there is nobody, black or white, that can please you the way I can."

*****

Jacky rose from his bed around midnight. He had to

see the girl. But more importantly he had to check the layout of Reagan's house. The floorboards creaked as he slid the door open and stepped into the hall. He approached the adjoining rooms cautiously, wondering what he would find. He had no idea where Reagan's bedroom was, nor Charley's, for that matter. But he reasoned that if the aboriginal girl slept in the house, she would not be upstairs but down in the lower rooms.

Thoughts of the girl raced through his head. What untold horrors had she endured? How could he gain her trust, and more importantly, how could he get her to confide in him? She was the key to gaining the information he so desperately needed.

Suddenly, a soft sound interrupted his reverie. A door opened, and before him stood Charley. Her hair was tousled and framed her sleepy face, but he could see the suspicion in her eyes.

"What are you doing, Jacky?"

She crossed her arms defiantly.

"I couldn't sleep. You know what it is like in a strange bed, Charley.

I was going downstairs to fetch some water."

"There's water in your room, Jacky."

She leant towards him.

"Are you sure you're not sneaking around to find the little black girl?"

She managed a seductive smile and whispered,

"Aren't I good enough for you, Jacky? I have told you, no black harlot can do the sorts of things I can do."

She was so close he could feel the warmth of her breath.

"There's also water in my room as well as other sweet things. And it tastes far sweeter than what is in your room. Care to sample?"

Jacky sensed her mood. He knew it was too dangerous to be caught in a compromising situation with her.

"I'm going back to bed," he said, and his meaning was clear.

"Suit yourself, Jacky," she huffed, "you are the one missing out, not me."

As he made his way back to his room, Jacky heard grunting and pig-like sounds coming from a room. When he looked, he noticed a lock on the door.

*****

Chapter 16

The mare, Clara, snorted with irritation and pawed at the straw-covered floor, sending strands into the cool morning air. Jacky and Reagan watched on with feelings of interest mixed with concern. Charley stood nearby, her arms folded across her chest. Jacky took a deep breath and slowly advanced to the mare and stroked her mane.

"Easy girl," he whispered.

"Easy now."

Then he turned to Reagan and said,

"We'll give her time, Mister Reagan. We cannot expect success this early. This is my stallion's first time, so they both must make some adjustments."

Reagan was blunt.

"We've got all the time in the world, Jacky."

Jacky walked out of Clara's stall, took Bandit's halter, and led him in. The stallion backed away, giving the mare time to relax. His eyes locked on hers with curiosity; the mare's ears flickered, but she made no attempt to move. She snorted once more, a clear sign of annoyance. His eyes flicked back and forth in a silent conversation that only people like Jacky and the horses themselves understood. The stallion seemed to sense she was not ready, and he went from eager suitor to patient admirer.

*****

"Why the sudden trip to town, Jacky?"

"I have a hunch, Reagan, there could be trouble at home. I feel like I should send a telegram to my wife and let her know I'm all right."

"Why is it that blackfellers always seem to sense when something is wrong?"

"Maybe we were just born this way, Mister Reagan," grinned Jacky.

"Then you'll have to take one of my horses, Jacky. I want your stallion here. As you well know that horse is way too valuable to take it for a joyride."

"I appreciate that. I will be back before sundown."

"I'll have my man Kerrigan take you to get a horse Jacky."

"I can handle it, Mister Reagan. I know where the

stables are."

Reagan studied him, suspicion in his gaze.

"You heard me. I will have Kerrigan take you."

"Something you don't want me to see?"

"Why do you ask? Just go with Kerrigan, and mind you don't go gallivanting around town, you hear?"

*****

The sun was high overhead when Jacky approached Milburra. He dismounted at the Post Office as he tied Reagan's horse to the hitching rail and stepped inside.

There was a different man behind the counter this time. The clerk looked up with a guilty look on his face, and Jacky smiled. He had caught the man out having a sly drink in the middle of the day. The man hastened to hide the small bottle, and in doing so, he knocked over a bottle of ink and dislodged a bundle of paper.

"Bit clumsy today, mister," Jacky laughed.

"I suffer from nerves if that is any of your business. Now, what can I help yer with?" he asked.

"I need to send a telegram to my wife," said Jacky,

placing some coins on the counter. For once, he was relieved that there were no comments about the colour of his skin. It seemed to Jacky that word had got around he was staying with Reagan, and he had learnt enough to know that the townsfolk did not want to trouble the man who appeared to rule the town.

"I can do that," said the clerk, his face flushed from whatever he'd been drinking.

"What's the message?"

Jacky took a deep breath. He wanted an innocuous message but one that told Martha he was all right. He did not want to give anyone the chance to detect what his mission was.

"Just say, All is well. Miss you. See you soon. And sign it, Jacky."

The clerk typed away at the telegraph machine while Jacky's eyes darted to the clock on the wall. Time was getting away. As soon as the message was sent, he stepped outside into the blistering heat. He led his horse down the street and stopped when he saw a man lazing back, reading a newspaper.

"Hey, mister, how far to the Queensland border, and is there a blacks' camp out that way? I do not want to run into trouble."

"You are a black yerself. What's yer problem? Frightened of yer own kind?"

Jacky hated himself for what he said next. He felt sorrow at debasing his people.

"I don't take kindly to the lifestyle they lead."

"Bit uppity for a darky, eh? And I cannot tell you where the blacks' camp is. That lot are never in one place at the one time. Like bloody ants. Always on the move. And the black bastards will bite yer arse as quick as look at ya. Especially that black bitch what lives just outta town. Best be watchin' out fer 'er."

"Be seeing you, mister," said Jacky as he tipped his hat.

"Bloody 'ope not," muttered the man under his breath.

Jacky felt a peculiar sense of peace as he rode out of Milburra. He was happy with the thought of meeting the tribe again and gleaning information from them. And he knew that the tribe would be invaluable in rendering assistance in his quest to free the incarcerated blacks.

He passed by a dilapidated shack and saw a woman hanging what were once white sheets on a strand of wire strung between two trees. She shouted something to him, but she was too far away for him to hear. He gave a neighbourly wave and rode on.

The landscape began to shift subtly, the flatness giving way to undulations that presaged hidden valleys and secret trails. Jacky's horse shied away as a young boy, no more than twelve years old, stepped out in front of them, his bare feet silent on the hard earth and his hand raised in a greeting. Behind him, hidden in the shadows, Jacky could see the outline of others, watching and waiting. Jacky had known he would not find them; they would find him.

He dismounted, and the boy took the reins. The other members of the tribe, consisting of seven warriors, emerged from the trees. Questions hung in the air over their heads.

"Why was this black man, one of them, but not one of them, determined to seek them out? What did he want?"

A man stepped forward, obviously the leader and a man who Jacky had not seen the day before. His skin was etched with the scars of many battles and a skin that had seen many seasons.

"I am Nullah," he said in a croaking voice, "and we are

keepers of this land. What brings you here, Jacky?"

"So the warriors remember my name?"

"Take me to your camp. We can speak there."

The old man studied him intently, then turned his back and walked away, the rest of the men trailing.

"Follow!" was all he said.

The crunching of the underbrush mingled with the chirping of small finches. As they emerged into a small clearing, Jacky was amazed at what he saw. Before him lay a vibrant scene. There were about twenty people in the camp, not including the many children running around, their laughter ringing amongst the trees. Further past the gunyahs, a small creek joined a larger river, which wound its way into the distance. Jacky inhaled deeply. The smell of roasting meat, mixed with the earthy scent of the camp, reminded him he had not eaten since breakfast.

"Welcome to our camp Jacky." said the old man and nodded towards the fire where warriors sat about eating. An old woman with silver hair approached and offered Jacky some roasted meat.

"Eat," she said, "to share food is to share life."

Jacky was quick to take the meat, which he found to be lamb, with no doubt it was stolen from the Reagans.

"Mmmm," he nodded his appreciation.

But then Jacky remembered he had more important things to do than enjoy the hospitality of the tribe. He wanted to discuss the tribe from down south, the Wiradjuri tribe, Burra's people, held captive by Reagan. But before he could broach the subject, the old man began to speak.

"I was told you were seen with Reagan's men. But you would be warned not to trust him. He, the Reagan feller, seemed to be a good white feller to us at first. We blackfellers don't need white man money, just some tobacco and grog. Reagan would give us that, along with flour and sugar and salt and other stuff. The only things he would not give us were guns. Then, about three seasons back, his men came back with cattle and sheep from south of here. But they brought back a whole tribe of blacks they had captured."

Nullah paused, put his right finger to his nose, and blew out a stream of snot. He watched as a small army of ants marched through the yellow spit.

"They had the blackfellers in chains. From then on, my tribe got nothing from Reagan. After all, why give my tribe things when he has blacks to work for him for next to nothing? He starved them. They get about one meal a day. Cheaper than him giving us grog and tobacco."

Jacky leaned forward. He could see the pain in Nullah's eyes.

"Go on," he encouraged the old man.

"It is about survival, Jacky. The land is changing since the white man came. The kangaroos are moving further and further away. The rivers are drying up. We need food and supplies for our people, especially our women and children. So, what we steal from Reagan is only what we need to survive. A sheep here, a cow there."

"There's talk that some of your warriors killed a white man and his woman, Nullah."

"That is not true. Reagan's men killed the white people. My warriors saw it happen. Then we saw the white men come back the next day and put spears in their backs so we would be blamed."

Jacky probed even more.

"Where did they get the spears, Nullah?"

"Those spears they stole from us. They were not merely stolen goods, Jacky, but part of their owner's soul. They took the spears from two of my warriors that they murdered some months ago. And Jacky, one of those warriors, was my son. He went to the Dreaming too, young Jacky."

Jacky could see the heartbreak in the old man, and he realised that the tribe would not rest until they had their revenge.

"Nullah, I know what you are thinking, but you cannot just storm onto Reagan's farm without a plan. His men are armed, and it would be a massacre. We need the law on our side."

"Reagan is the law, Jacky."

"Then we need police from outside the district."

"No white police will come here on the word of a blackfeller. We are not worth anything to the white man, Jacky. You should know that."

Jacky looked up at the sun and saw it was starting to drop in the west. He had to go.

"Nullah, I will talk with my friends, and we will come up with a plan. Remember, you must not try anything by yourself. I must go back to Reagan's now. I do not want him to become suspicious."

*****

Jacky arrived back at Reagan's farm to be greeted excitedly by the man.

"Jacky," the man cried out, his voice carrying across the yard.

Reagan, unable to hide his excitement, walked briskly to meet Jacky. He held the reins while the aboriginal dismounted.

"Jacky, you're not going to believe this, but I think we have struck gold with your stallion."

"What's all the commotion about?" Jacky said with a smirk on his face. He had sensed what the man was about to tell him.

"Your stallion." Reagan managed, unable to contain his excitement, "has done the deed with Clara while you were away."

Jacky's smirk broke into a full-grown grin as he followed the panting man towards the horse yard. Jacky's stallion, Bandit, was tethered in the corner, and the mare was grazing on oats, unfazed by the recent events.

"Look at him," said Reagan, his head angled towards

Bandit.

"What a stallion! I tell you, Jacky, I am going to get one hell of a foal out of this union."

Jacky pointed at the mare.

"We have to keep a close eye on her and make sure she is well cared for."

"Enough already, Jacky. Let's go into the house and have a drink to celebrate."

"Bit early for that, isn't it?" said Jacky stoically.

"Never too early for a drink, Jacky, whether to celebrate or just to enjoy. Besides, you must be dry after your ride today."

Jacky followed him into the house and took a seat in the spacious living room. Reagan went to a dresser and poured two glasses of rum.

They clinked their glasses together, and Reagan said,

"Here's to the finest foal in the land."

They sat in silence for a while before Jacky decided to play his cards. Reagan's thoughts were on the prospect of a fine foal, but Jacky had other ideas.

"Mister Reagan, I appreciate your hospitality, but I think it's best if I stay in town."

Reagan appeared surprised.

"Jacky, what's brought this on? You know you are welcome here."

But his voice carried no sincerity. Jacky knew he would be more than pleased to see the end of him.

"Again, thanks, but tomorrow, I will ride into Milburra and check into the hotel. I will ride out each day and check on my stallion. I figure another week of Bandit fixing your mare-up should be enough to ensure she is in foal, and then I will return to my own property, Shanghai."

The men had not seen Charley come into the room, but she announced her presence with a snide remark at Jacky.

"Are you missing your wife, Jacky? Surely, there's enough black gins around here to please you. But then again, that is forbidden here, isn't it, pa?"

She gave her father a very knowing look.

"Or maybe that is why you are going. To sneak into the black's camp at night."

Jacky ignored her comment and turned to Reagan.

"On second thoughts, Mister Reagan, I think I will ride back into Milburra immediately. I will return at first light."

Then he added,

"If you do not mind, I will take another of your horses. That is unless you want me to ride my own," he said caustically.

"Go with him, Charley. Make sure he only goes to the stables."

Jacky tipped the last of his drink down and walked outside, and headed towards the stables, with Charley a few paces behind. Kerrigan and Howarth were leaning on the rails, smoking cigarettes and watching the two horses.

"Where you headed, Jacky?

"My business is my business, mister. You would be advised to take care of your own."

Kerrigan bristled at this comment.

"Jis because you have a fancy stallion and money in your pocket does not mean you can come here and act all high and mighty, Jacky. You jis must remember, you are still a blackfeller, and they are not the most popular item on the menu 'round these parts."

Jacky threw in one last barb of his own, which only incensed Kerrigan even more.

"Where I come from, Kerrigan, you would not even appear on the menu. You would just be slops for the hogs out back."

As Jacky turned his back, Kerrigan attempted to land a huge blow on the back of his head. Jacky was alert, however. He knew Kerrigan's type. Wait for an opportunity and strike from behind. Jacky lunged to his left, and Kerrigan's weight propelled him forward, leaving him sprawled on the ground. Howarth laughed at his mate, which only angered him more.

"You black bastard!" he roared as he struggled to his feet, but Jacky was ready for him, and with a single punch to the side of Kerrigan's head, the man fell into the dust. He groaned and rubbed the side of his skull.

"As I said, Kerrigan, slops for the hogs."

Charley burst into laughter.

"Serves you right, Kerrigan," she chortled.

Jacky led his horse to the gate, where he mounted and rode off in the direction of Milburra. When the Reagan homestead was about two miles behind him, he veered off and headed in the direction of the Andrews' farm, taking care that nobody was following him. He stopped his horse twice and waited for a spell each time, and satisfied he was alone, he rode on.

Chapter 17

"Do you smell that, Jacky?" asked Jimmy Boy.

The wind had whipped up and was blowing everything in its path.

"Campfire, maybe. Could be the blacks," said Wells.

Jimmy Boy shaded his eyes and looked in the direction Wells was pointing. About two miles away, he could see a huge grass fire and it was headed their way.

"Mister Jennings, go and rouse Andrews. We will need all the help we can get."

"It's not my people," said Jacky.

"They are not camped there. That fire started at the boundary fence between Reagan's and Andrews' farm. Looks like Reagan has changed his tactics. He is trying to burn Andrews out."

The fire had been an almost insignificant flicker at first, but the wind was fanning it, and now it was an insatiable beast headed straight towards Andrew's wheat crop. Jennings and Wells ran as fast as their aged legs could carry them and grabbed at every available receptacle that would hold water.

Andrews appeared from the front door of the homestead and watched the approaching flames, his face a mix of disbelief and horror.

"Fuckin' hell screamed Jennings, "we'll be toast soon, Jimmy Boy."

Jimmy Boy stood with Andrews, watching the flames consuming everything in their path. Andrews could only watch on helplessly. Through bleary, smoke-filled eyes, he said,

"Looks like Reagan wins. My crops are gone. I have nothing."

"It's no good whining now, Richard. We must save your home and outbuildings. Crops can be replanted, but it takes a lot to replace farm equipment and buildings. And we cannot replace any lives if we lose them."

Jimmy Boy roared to the men,

"Leave the buckets and grab some shovels. Keep digging the earth and try and create a fire break, and you keep the water coming Miss Andrews."

The men managed to create a fire break and avoid the loss of any buildings, but the earth beyond the homestead was nothing but a scorched black nightmare.

Andrews, his eyes red and swollen, sobbed into his hands.

"I've lost everything, Jimmy. I cannot get out of this. I am ruined. Reagan has beaten me."

The man hung his head, his calloused hands clenching and unclenching into fists. The heat slapped him in the face as he walked tentatively towards the home paddock. His crop was nothing but blackened stalks. He wiped the stinging, salty tears from his face and coughed up the remainder of the smoke that had threatened to choke him.

"A man is never beaten Richard unless he beats himself," consoled Jimmy Boy, placing an arm on the distraught man's shoulder.

"While ever your heart beats and you are above ground, you can overcome anything. You must always remember, it is not whether you get knocked down; it's whether you get up."

The fire had passed, and the men sat on the ground, trying to inhale some fresh air. They looked out to where there had been a lush sea of green. Now, all they saw was a blackened wasteland.

Jacky looked around, and for the first time, he noticed Burra was missing. He coughed violently, his throat filled with acrid black smoke.

"Has anyone seen Burra?"

"Come to think of it," said Jennings, "I saw him headed towards the fire when it first started. He said something I couldn't understand, but I did understand one word he said. Reagan!"

"Damned old fool will get himself killed," cursed Jacky.

"I'll get my horse and go find him."

"I'll ride with you, Jacky. It will be good to get away from here after being cooped up in the barn for the past few days."

"I would appreciate your company, Jimmy Boy, but unfortunately, I cannot let you ride with me. I don't want Reagan's men to know anything about you. Besides, I am a blackfeller. They will not even see me," he laughed, his gap-toothed smile sparkling in the sunlight.

"You're right there, Jacky," said Wells with his dry wit.

"Jis, keep yer black arse in the burnt paddocks, and nobody will ever see you."

"I did not think of that. You are right. Reagan cannot know you are in any way connected to either the Andrews or us," Jimmy said flatly.

"Will you come back here?"

"Only if I find Burra. If not, I will stay in Milburra. That is where Reagan thinks I am going."

*****

Under the sprawling arms of an ancient river oak, Kerrigan and Howarth lay side by side, the heat of the day and the rum lulling them into a stupor. Kerrigan's eyes flickered open, and he looked in the distance.

"Fire's gone past Andrews' place now. Wonder if we managed to burn his home and outbuildings?"

"Does not matter Howarth. At least we have sent him a warning."

"Ya reckon he'll know we did it on Reagan's orders?"

"That does not matter either. Nuthin' he can do about it. He cannot prove anything. Besides, Reagan is as good an alibi as we can get."

He passed the rum bottle over to Howarth.

"Want some?"

Howarth took the bottle with a nod, twisted the cork open, and took a long gulp, the fiery liquid burning his throat.

A solitary figure with a vendetta watched the two men from the cover of the willows, their tendrils of green drifting on the water's surface. The smell of burning grass and the stinging smoke he had come through fired his anger. He was prepared for revenge.

Howarth was the first to notice the figure as it emerged from the foliage. He sat bolt upright.

"Jeezus Kerrigan. It's a fuckin black."

Burra's eyes narrowed, a fierce glimmer of anger piercing the serenity of the secluded clearing. Howarth's voice choked off as he felt the sharp pain in his stomach. He looked down in disbelief at the long wooden shaft protruding from his gut. His hand reached down in shock and attempted to grab the spear, but with his strength draining, he slumped to the ground. Burra took a step closer and, in Kamilaroi, said,

"That is for my people."

Howarth never heard the words.

Kerrigan, meanwhile, was fumbling for his revolver, but he was slow. The effects of the rum had had a profound effect on his capabilities. Burra felt for the boomerang he had been carving and shaping on the long trail from Ramsay and hurled it at the startled man. The boomerang did not return. The full force of it hit Kerrigan on the forehead and his body buckled to the ground.

Jacky had heard the commotion and galloped his horse into the clearing. Burra's arm was raised, a stone knife clasped in his hands, and he was ready to plunge it into Kerrigan's stomach. Without hesitating, Jacky leapt from his horse and collided with the old man, sending them both to the ground in a tangle of limbs.

Jacky regained his feet and looked at Howarth, who was still trying to pull the spear from his gut. Kerrigan lay unconscious, bleeding from the forehead. Jacky faced Burra.

"Stop! Burra, stop! This is not the way. Murdering him

won't help your people or right the wrongs Reagan has done to you."

He cast a glance at Howarth. The man was breathing heavily, trying to get as much air into his lungs as he could. He looked at Jacky, and through blood-splattered lips, he croaked,

"Jacky? You? And here was me thinking you were a decent black. Never can tell with your kind, though."

He coughed up a decent amount of blood, his eyes rolled to the back of his head, and he died. The two men who watched him die felt no remorse.

"Let's get out of here, Burra. You have a murder on your hands now. It is just lucky Kerrigan is unconscious. He will not know I was here. Come on."

He helped Burra onto his horse, and they rode back to the Andrews' farm, the horse kicking up the blackened ash from the ground as they went.

*****

Kerrigan sat up with a groan, his head throbbing like it was on a blacksmith's anvil. The acrid smell of burnt country assailed his nostrils, a grim reminder of the inferno he and Howarth had started.

Howarth? Where was the man?

Kerrigan looked to his side. A few feet away lay the body of his accomplice, a spear protruding grotesquely from his stomach and reaching for the heavens. The recollection of the attack slammed into his head like a sledgehammer. His hand instinctively reached for his head where the boomerang had split him open, and he winced as he felt the tender spot.

He stumbled to his feet, his legs wobbling as if they had forgotten how to stand. He had to get back to see Reagan. Panic swept through his addled brain. Were the blacks still around? Were they waiting to finish him off?

A soft whickering came from the two horses tethered to a gaunt stringybark. Clumsily, he made his way to his horse and, with difficulty, managed to mount it. Kerrigan headed for home leaving the body of Howarth to the scavengers. He called back over his shoulder,

"Be back to git you later, Howarth."

*****

Chapter 18

The ride back to Dingo's Retreat for Kerrigan was a blur of guilt mingled with pain. He gripped the reins tightly, steering the horse through the scrub with sheer determination. The sun had long passed its peak, and the shadows were lengthening. Every jolt of his horse's hooves sent waves of agony spearing through his body. In his semi-dazed state, Kerrigan's perception of the countryside looked eerie, and he felt himself tremble as the shadows began to play tricks on his mind. Was that a tree branch moving in the breeze or a black man waiting to spear him? His thoughts kept returning to the attacker. The eyes! They looked at him as if they knew him. There had been a flicker of recognition. Think man! Think! Where have you seen those eyes?

Kerrigan's heart was pounding as he reached the homestead gate. The only sounds were the barking of dogs and the squawking swarms of galahs overhead as they headed to roost. As he opened the gate, he saw Reagan walking towards him. He would no doubt have been with the two horses. As Howarth had said, God bless the dead man's soul, "The boss is like a kid with a new toy."

"Where's Howarth?"

Kerrigan appeared to be in one of his moods.

"He's dead," Kerrigan said, his voice flat and his whole body tired. He needed to rest. He was not up to facing Reagan and the relentless barrage of questions he knew would come.

"We were taking a rest after the fire went through the Andrews' farm, and a fuckin' black came out of nowhere and speared him. Knocked me out with his fuckin' boomerang. But I swear to you, Mister Reagan, I am sure I have seen that blackfeller before. There was something about his eyes."

Kerrigan swung his leg over the horse, and when his feet hit the ground, he gave a soft moan of pain.

"I need rest, Mister Reagan. My head is splitting in two."

Charley had come from inside the house and stood beside her father.

"Get him inside," he said, his voice firm but surprisingly gentle.

"You mean in our house Papa?"

"Yes. He needs to be seen, too. Get Mona to fetch some

water and clean him up. Put him in a room on the ground floor."

There was a thud, and Reagan turned round and saw that Kerrigan had collapsed onto the dusty ground.

"Go and get Bruce and get the big lazy bastard to lug him inside. No, on second thoughts, go across to the men's quarters and ask them to come over to the house. Bruce might take him to the wrong place. I need to talk with the men. Tomorrow, there must be some form of justice. The blacks will soon learn they have no right here. This is our land now."

*****

"Where did you find him, Jacky?

Jimmy Boy's voice was lined with concern.

"He was right where I figured he'd be. At the spot where the fire began."

Jimmy Boy looked hard at the old man.

"You went seeking revenge, Burra?"

The old man did not understand the words, but he understood the look and implication on Jimmy Boy's face. He nodded his head sadly and grunted.

"There's worse, Jimmy Boy. Burra killed one of Reagan's men."

"What? Are you telling me we have a murder on our hands?"

"'fraid so, Jimmy Boy.

Then Jacky said,

"Realistically speaking, we are safe, Jimmy Boy. Reagan will think it was the Kamilaroi tribe. The other man, Kerrigan, was unconscious when I arrived so he does not know I was there."

"That is one good thing anyway, but now we have the Kamilaroi tribe to think of. Reagan will want revenge, Jacky. We need to warn them."

"I can handle that, Jimmy Boy. And Reagan, as well. You and the others will just have to stay put till I see Reagan and sort some things out. And Jimmy Boy, make sure you keep Burra here."

*****

Reagan sat proudly in the saddle, flanked by eight men, all mean-looking and ready for action. The men were armed with pistols, shotguns, and rifles. Jacky knew Reagan meant business.

"Didn't expect you back so soon, Jacky. We're just off to do some hunting of the black kind. You would best stay here and watch the horses."

"Hunting? You mean you are going on a murdering raid! Reagan, what have my people done to you this time?"

"They murdered my man, Howarth, yesterday. It is time they got a wake-up call."

"These are my people." Jacky asserted.

"You cannot murder them! Killing them will not bring Howarth back."

"And who says so, Jacky? You ain't got no call 'round these parts. Those who killed Howarth might just kill me or more of my men. There's no room for them here."

He crossed his arms defiantly.

"Let me ride with you," said Jacky.

"I can talk with them and get them to move on to new hunting grounds. That way, you will be rid of them and won't have blood on your hands."

Reagan scratched his chin and thought deeply. He grinned as the formulation of a plan came into his mind.

"Why not take Jacky and get rid of him as well as the tribe? That way, I will have his horse as well."

"Sure, Jacky, you can ride with us."

Jacky nodded, unaware of the malice hidden behind Reagan's facade.

Jacky rode at the head of the men, his eyes constantly flicking back to the hardened men trailing him.

"Stay sharp, men!" Reagan barked as he cradled his shotgun.

Unbeknownst to the riders, they were not the only ones with watchful eyes. Deep within the scrub, the warriors moved silently and invisibly, spears at ready.

Reagan called a halt.

"Jacky, you are a blackfeller. Where do you reckon their camp is?"

Before Jacky could answer a spear came whirring through the air and struck one of the horses in the rump. The horse collapsed to the ground, dislodging the rider. A shot was fired, and more spears appeared, soaring through the air.

"Shoot to kill!" roared Reagan as he aimed his shotgun at a warrior who was charging at him.

Jacky wheeled his horse and slammed his arm on the barrel, knocking it from Reagan's grasp. The other men were in a state of panic and were firing blindly.

"You're a traitorous bastard, Jacky!" roared Reagan as he pulled a pistol from his belt and aimed it at Jacky's chest. Jacky reefed on the reins and urged his horse into a wild gallop and was gone before Reagan had a chance to open fire. The aboriginal warriors were gone as quickly as they had come.

The horses were snorting and pawing at the ground with excitement, but Reagan's moment was lost.

"We will never find the black bastards in this thick scrub. It is way too dangerous in here. There will be a tomorrow. Let's go home."

On the ride back to his homestead, Reagan's mind was working overtime. He smiled to himself as he finally came up with the ultimate plan.

*****

"Charley, I need you to go into Milburra and deliver a message to Mounsie."

Mounsie, Reagan's shady lawyer, was a man who could make anything appear as legal as a gathering at a church picnic. Reagan instructed his daughter to tell Mounsie to draw up a Bill of Sale for something very specific. Jacky's stallion.

"But you can't do that, Papa." remonstrated Charley

"I can do what I want. Now, don't you even think about bucking your own dear father. And I want the Sergeant to come out here as well. I am going to report Jacky for associating with the blacks who murdered Howarth."

"But you know Jacky had nothing to do with that."

"I know, and you know, but the law does not know. Besides, the law does what I say, Charley. You know that."

The journey to town was a silent one; the only sound was the clip-clop of Charley's horse's hooves. As she neared town, she saw a rider coming in the opposite direction from the Andrews' farm. She squinted her eyes and made out the figure of Jacky. Her mind was in turmoil. Should she warn him? Or keep her family's pride intact? She decided for now to say nothing and to pretend she knew nothing of her father's attempt to slaughter the blacks. And to steal his horse.

The two came together at the signpost, indicating the town and its population.

"Morning, Charley," said Jacky cheerily.

He also had decided to be cunning and find out how much the girl knew.

"And a good morning to you, Jacky," she smiled and fluttered her eyelids.

"How's your father this morning, Charley?" Jacky asked offhandedly.

He's fine, Jacky. Why do you ask?"

"Did he tell you we went looking for the Kamilaroi tribe yesterday?"

"No. His business he keeps pretty much to himself," she said, but now she knew Jacky had been with the men.

Jacky had no reason to disbelieve her. It appeared she knew nothing of the incidents of the day before and nothing of Reagan's attempt to kill him. But what she did know, and he didn't, was the plot her father had hatched to steal his horse.

Charley had guilt gnawing at her stomach. What she

had to do was against her nature. She liked the black man and thought she saw a future with him. In her naivety, she had daydreamed of leaving her father and Jacky's horse behind and riding off into the proverbial sunset with the black man. But her thoughts always returned to the same thing. Her father's farm.

Her future was here, and soon, with her father not getting any younger, she would own everything he had built with his evil ways. But there was still no harm in satisfying her wants with the black man.

"What business do you have in town, Charley?"

"My father has sent me to see his lawyer and ask him to draw up an agreement about the sheep and your stallion," she said, the lie slipping from her tongue.

Jacky knew there would never be an agreement drawn up. Not by a man who wanted him dead.

"After I am finished there, would you care to meet me at the tea house?"

"Why not?" he answered.

"I'll just go back to the room at the hotel and tell them

I will be leaving tomorrow. The papers should be signed later this afternoon, and that concludes my business here. Oh, and I want to scout around and hire a man to assist me in driving the sheep back to my farm."

*****

Mounsie's office was dimly lit, befitting the man sitting in the tattered leather chair. He looked up from his cluttered desk as Charley walked in.

"Reagan's girl," he drawled, stroking his long moustache.

"What brings you here?"

"My Papa needs your help. He wants you to draw up a Bill of Sale."

Mounsie's expression shifted from nonchalance to curiosity.

"What's for sale?"

"A stallion. The man you brought with you to my father's farm has sold it to my Papa."

"Jacky? The blackfeller? Must need the money for some grog. Personally, I would not part with such a magnificent animal."

"Mister Mounsie, it is simple. We need a Bill of Sale to prove the stallion is rightfully my father's."

He stroked his chin thoughtfully.

"Well, I suppose I could draft something for him. But it will cost you."

"Mister Mounsie, you know my Papa does not care about money. Just make sure the paper looks legal."

"I'll get on it right away, Miss Charlene."

As she walked out, Mounsie called after her.

"The paper will need the darky's signature, Miss Charlene."

"I'm sure you can manage something, Mister Mounsie."

Mounsie stared at the paper and then picked up his pen and dipped it in the well. With a grand flourish, he scrawled a large X. Then he set about making a duplicate of the document and stowed it in his drawer.

"Black bastards can't write anyway," he grinned to himself as he penned another X on the second document.

Jacky

*****

Jacky drained his cup and gently placed it on the table.

"More tea, Jacky?"

"I reckon this man needs an afternoon nap, Charley. Tell your father I will be out there in the morning to pick my horse up. And I will be expecting my sheep to be ready."

But Jacky had no thoughts of going to the Reagan farm the next morning. He knew a bullet would be waiting for him. He would get his horse that night.

"Jacky, what say we go for an afternoon ride? We have unfinished business at the river," she said as she ran her tongue over her top lip.

Jacky wanted to refuse the invitation. He knew what it would lead to.

"But then again, the girl might just come in useful," he thought.

But on the other hand, would it help his cause if Reagan found out he was with his daughter?

******

It was a slow pace, and it suited their respective moods.

Charley was daydreaming of a faraway place, and Jacky was taking the chance to try and relax. A half-hour of the slow ride saw them come across the river.

Charley dismounted gracefully and then flopped onto the grass.

"I love this spot, Jacky. It takes all my cares away. There's nobody here to disturb us."

She pulled him down, and without hesitation, she kissed him. He could feel the heat of her breath and feel the slight trembling of her body. He rolled her over and raised her skirt. The world seemed to fade away as they sought each other. Nothing else mattered. Charley's hands explored him, hesitantly at first, then with an overwhelming urgency. She fumbled at his trousers and grasped him with a fierceness that surprised him, and then she guided him in. A soft moan slipped from her mouth, and then they were both lost in the moment.

They lay on their backs, their naked bodies open for the sky to see.

"Jacky, what sort of woman do you think I am?" she asked as her breathing steadied.

He paused, taking in the beauty of her body before

answering.

"You are a woman of passion and beauty, Charley."

"Jacky, what will we do? I think I love you."

At those words, Jacky hurriedly stood and pulled his trousers on.

"Charley! Never say that again!"

She turned aside, and a small sob escaped her lips.

*****

Chapter 19

"Jimmy Boy, we need to go in tonight. I want my horse back, and I know Reagan will shoot me on sight if I go tomorrow."

"What about the captives, Jacky?"

"I may be selfish, Jimmy Boy, but my horse comes first. Once he is safe, we will devise a plan to rescue Burra's people."

"Then I will come with you tonight, Jacky," said Jimmy Boy, his voice full of concern.

"Thanks, Jimmy Boy."

Jacky looked around him at the other men. Burra was silent, concentrating on smoothing a spear shaft with a piece of flint. Jennings and Wells were doing what they did best. Eyes closed and resting. Jacky leaned across and nudged Jennings, who sat up with a grunt and let out a loud fart.

'What's up, Jacky? Can't a man get a sleep 'round here?"

"I'm sorry, Jennings."

Wells stirred.

"Jimmy Boy and I are going to the Reagan farm tonight. But you two are to stay here. It is too dangerous if there are too many of us."

*****

The night was dark and moonless, the only light a smattering of silver stars. The air had the scent of pine, the sour smell of moist undergrowth, and the only sounds were the scurrying of nocturnal animals. They crept around the side of the barn with their hearts beating, not knowing what lay ahead of them.

Between them and Jacky's stallion, there stood only a couple of workers' huts. Outside one of them, a campfire flickered and gasped for oxygen. Two men lay on their backs, empty bottles lying beside them. Jacky could make out the familiar shape of his horse, and then he saw what he had been dreading. A man was leaning against the rail, gun under his arm and a cigarette in his mouth.

"Who's there?" came the startled cry of the sentry.

Jimmy Boy had been careless and stepped on a dry twig.

"Stay still, Jimmy Boy. Not a sound." Jacky

whispered.

They exchanged panicked glances, knowing the element of surprise had been lost.

"Easy, it's just me," Jacky said.

He stepped into the open, and the man's eyes widened as he recognised him.

"Jacky!" he called, loud enough for anyone to hear him. He swung his rifle up, but it was too late. Jimmy Boy, moving like a shadow, knocked the rifle from the man's arm and punched him to the ground.

Shouts erupted from the huts, and doors flew open. Lanterns flared to life, and men came rushing out with pistols and rifles. Jacky's heart raced as he realised the odds had turned against them.

We've gotta get outta here," yelled Jacky.

"What about your horse?"

"We will have to come another time. Right now, we have got to save ourselves."

The yard was in complete pandemonium now. Men were scrambling from huts, and dogs were going berserk on their chains. Reagan had been sleeping. He had good men, and he knew he could sleep soundly, knowing he was fully protected from harm or theft. He hurriedly pulled his boots on and, wearing nothing but a nightshirt, raced down the stairs and into the houseyard. The lights of the lanterns would have painted a beautiful picture had it not been for the backdrop of alarmed and armed men.

"Set the dogs loose," barked Reagan.

In his haste to get to the gate, he tripped and fell. Charley was behind him now and she helped him to his feet.

"Must be the fuckin' blacks again, Charley. You get yourself back inside in case they start throwing their spears."

The woman ignored her father and sprinted towards the horseyard. She was relieved to see the two horses still tethered and unfazed by the commotion. Suddenly, she was knocked off her feet as two horses galloped past her. As she regained her footing and her breath, she stared horrified at the back of Jacky as he sped away.

*****

"Who was the night guard?" demanded Reagan.

"That be me, boss."

A tall, lean lad stepped forward, his head drooped and his arms dangling uselessly.

"Come here, boy," ordered Reagan.

The lad stepped forward, fear etched in his youthful face.

"Sorry, Mister Reagan," he stammered. "But I swear I was awake. It's jis the fact them blackfellers are too sneaky. I never heard them till it was too late."

The blow came unexpectedly, and it struck the young boy so hard that he collapsed to the ground, blood spraying from his mouth. He spat out an eye tooth and began sobbing.

"I'm sorry, Mister Reagan."

"Sorry ain't good enough, boy. Get all your miserable belongings and git on back to the whore who done spawned you. Git!"

*****

"Papa, Sergeant Tanner, and Mister Mounsie are here."

Reagan pulled himself up from the wicker chair in which he had made himself comfortable and had been reading one of his many books. He closed the book with a thud, blew the dust away, walked to the open door, and looked out. The Sergeant was on horseback, while Mounsie preferred to travel by buggy.

"Show them in Charley," he called to his daughter.

The two men approached the house.

"Good day to you both," said Reagan.

"I've been waiting for the two of you."

Reagan's heart was racing. These visitors could be the solution to all his problems. He would own the stallion and be rid of Jacky and the tribe of marauding blacks.

Mounsie held out a leather satchel as if it were a sacrificial offering.

"Mister Reagan, I've brought you the Bill of Sale as promised."

Reagan's eyes lit up as he took the bag and fingered the worn leather. Inside, a crisp white sheet of paper awaited him. The proof that the majestic stallion, now securely locked in the barn, belonged to him. The Sergeant was curious and stepped closer to Reagan and looked him over.

"What am I doing here, Mister Reagan?"

Mounsie cleared his throat, his eyes wandering from Reagan to the Sergeant and back again.

"Perhaps we might take care of our business first, Sergeant, and I'll be on my way."

The Sergeant's gaze was unwavering, watching the pair with curiosity and suspicion.

"I just need a signature, Mister Reagan," said Mounsie, eager to be gone. He did not like the Sergeant one bit, although both were cast from the same mould.

Mounsie offered a pen to Reagan, who scanned the paper.

"It seems to be in order, Mounsie," he said as he scrawled his signature.

"What's that paper?" asked the Sergeant.

"It's a Bill of Sale," replied Mounsie.

"The blackfeller sold his horse to Mister Reagan to try and stop him pressing charges of murder."

"Murder! What are you talking about?"

Mounsie placed the paper in his satchel and walked to the door.

"I will leave you two men. I've got more business in town."

The Sergeant watched Mounsie's back as he exited.

"Bit nervy, isn't he Reagan?"

"No, that's just him. A nervy type. Now, care for a drink, and I will explain why I asked you here."

The flies were busy around the neck of the whiskey bottle as the Sergeant craned his neck forward.

"Tell me about this murder."

"Yesterday, a man named Jacky, the man I purchased the horse from, speared one of my men. He was murdered, Tanner."

"Are you telling me Jacky murdered one of your men? That's a mighty big accusation to make, even if it is against a black."

"He isn't one of the local tribe, though, Sergeant. Have you seen the flash blackfeller that has been getting around town?"

"The one that has been hangin' with your daughter. He is the talk of the town, Reagan."

Reagan chose to ignore the insinuation.

"I have a witness to prove it."

Charlene had been standing silently in the corner, watching and listening. Reagan beckoned her over.

"Charley, go and fetch Kerrigan."

*****

"How reliable is this man, Reagan? If we are going to arrest the blackfeller, we will need a good case. Seems to me that there are too many sympathisers of the blacks these days."

"Tell him the story, Kerrigan, so he can judge for himself."

"Same as I told Mister Reagan, Sergeant Tanner. Me and Howarth was ridin' the boundary fence and caught the blacks lightin' a fire. Damned near burnt the Andrews' place out. Anyways, we fired a shot over their heads, jis to scare 'em, you know, and next thing I knew that Jacky feller come hollerin' outta the scrub and chucked a spear at Howarth. End of story. Howarth was dead before he hit the ground. The blacks jis buggared off then.”

Reagan interrupted now.

“That was the reason for Mounsie’s visit today. Jacky came here and offered to sell me his horse if I did not tell anyone he killed Howarth. Luckily, I never blew his black head off with my shotgun. But you know me, Sergeant. A law-abiding citizen. I like to do things legally. I even sent the money owed to Jacky with Charley yesterday for Mounsie to pay him after he signed the Bill of Sale. Now you can find him and arrest him for murder.”

Reagan paused and took a swig of his drink, then added,

“Oh, and by the way, Tanner, the money Jacky has on him is all yours when you catch him. Know what I mean?”

“Reagan, yer thieving ways will git you caught sooner than later. You’ve been good to me over the years, but I got to draw the line somewhere. I’ll do this for you, but this is the last time I will get caught up in yer illegal business.”

Reagan scoffed.

Last time? You will do as I say, Sergeant bloody

Tanner! You are in too deep now. I own you, and don't you forget that!".

The threat was obvious.

*****

Chapter 20

As Will stepped from the buggy, memories came flooding back. The Wang family, the social gatherings, and most importantly Martha. Their laughter and shared moments were a reminder of their youth. But he had to face the harsh reality. Martha was a married woman now; he had to remind himself. But he could never forget their stolen kisses and their tender moments together.

It was not extraordinary for Bindi to be the first to see Will pull up in the buggy he had hired from the stables in Ramsay.

"Oh, my Lord," she squealed with delight.

"It is Mister Will. Maaaartha! Mister Will is here."

Martha had been up since dawn waiting for this moment. She emerged from the house with trepidation, holding her body captive.

"Will," she said softly as she walked towards him.

"Martha."

He swallowed, feeling the weight of time and the memories that had passed between them and disappeared into another world.

"It's been a while."

"Do come inside, Will. My mother and grandmother are dying to see you. And let's not forget your sister and your nephew, little Robbie."

*****

"So, city boy, do you remember how to ride?" Martha teased Will.

"Or have you forgotten your country boy roots in the cobblestones and fancy carriages of the city?"

"I may be a city boy now, Martie, but a good horse, a good view, and a beautiful woman can awaken any forgotten instincts."

They set off at a steady pace, Martha leading the way. The pace quickened as they left the homestead behind, and it wasn't long before Martha's adventurous spirit took over. She urged her horse into a gallop and soon arrived at the river, its waters reflecting the golden hue of the sun. Both dismounted and sat on the grass, the silence filled with the trickling of water and the gentle sounds of nature, a perfect backdrop for the unspoken feelings between them since Will's arrival.

"Do you remember our very first kiss here?"

Martha's voice was barely a whisper.

Will hesitated, his mind trying to bring back the past, and he hesitated before answering.

"I do," he said with a bittersweet smile painted on his face.

Then, with a sudden rush of nostalgia, he turned away. All he could think of was the laughter, the whispered secrets, and that kiss.

"Martha, you are married," he said, shaking his head.

"Everything has changed. We have changed."

Then, in a moment of weakness, he reached for her. She melted into his body, and their lips met softly. Their kiss deepened, filled with memories of their youth and the dreadful present. When they pulled away, Will searched Martha's face for answers.

"Will, what will we do?" was all she could say.

"I've never stopped loving you, Martha. I thought time might ease my feelings, but unfortunately not. They have only grown stronger."

Her eyes were wide and filled with anguish.

"Will, I don't know if I can walk away from my marriage."

"I know."

His eyes were sad.

"But I had hoped… "

"Please, Will…no."

Tears brimmed in her eyes.

"You were my first love, Will, and that makes you special."

"You deserve happiness, Martha, even if it's not with me."

He went to stand, but she reached for his arm and pulled him down to her.

"Will. Oh, my darling Will," she moaned softly, so softly that she could not be heard over the sweeping of the willow tendrils in the water.

"Will, please don't do this to me," but her body offered

no resistance.

Martha's heart raced as Will became more insistent, his hands both tender and possessive.

"Why, Will? Why?"

Her voice trembled, but her body betrayed her desire. Every part of her responded to his touch, and ripples went through her to the core of her body. A fierce urgency took them, and she pushed aside any thoughts of Jacky as Will carefully slipped her riding jeans down. She offered no resistance and felt for, and unbuckled, his belt. A sudden thrill went through her. The thought and danger of being here with a man other than her husband fuelled her desire.

"Martha, I cannot fight this any longer," he panted.

"Do not fight it, Will. Go with the moment. Never let it stop."

She was an untamed beast now, clawing at his back, and she pulled him onto her, her legs spread instinctively, and her head flung back. In the moment that followed, they forged a bond, an intersection between danger and desire, a whisper of a union that went against the norms of a married woman.

"Will, you don't know how long I've waited for this moment," she panted.

"Our bodies have cried out for each other for too long."

Will rolled from above her and caught his breath.

"Martha, I know it is wrong. We are wrong. But I love you and always have and always will."

She covered her nakedness with her shirt and quietly sobbed.

*****

It was a lively affair at dinner that night. Little Robbie wouldn't be put down for his sleep, and his Uncle Will was keeping him amused.

"He sure is a good boy, Meg. I hope one day I can have a child as mild-tempered as him."

She laughed.

"You do not see him all the time, Will. I think he is making an exception for his uncle."

Martha laid down her fork; her appetite was gone. Her grandmother had been giving her strange looks. Bindi and Mia arrived on cue and began stacking up the plates and clearing the table.

Will suggested an early night after his travels. It was his second night staying at Wicklow, and he had not had a chance to take a proper rest.

He bade the women goodnight and headed to the guest room.

Angela was the one to broach the subject.

"Martha, I could not help noticing the looks you have been giving Will. I am a wise woman, my child, and I see danger in your eyes."

Meg could sense what was coming.

"I'll put little Robbie to bed. Good night, Mrs O'Brien. Goodnight, Ellie."

"Goodnight, Meg," they all spoke in unison.

The three women watched her as she carried her son to bed.

"I might go to bed myself, Mama," said Martha.

"No. We need to talk, Martha."

Angela's voice had a firm ring to it.

Martha looked long and hard at her grandmother, her eyes brimming with tears that threatened to spill over.

"You cannot know how I feel. This is me you are talking about," she said, her voice trembling.

"The feelings I have are my feelings, and I don't know if I can control them."

"You must, Martha!" her mother interjected, her voice as hard as the wooden dining table they sat around. She had been quiet up till now, but there was a fierce resolve in her gaze.

"You are a married woman now and have responsibilities that should overrule any fleeting emotions."

Then Angela continued. Martha was almost at breaking point.

"Do not fall into the trap that some women do, and let the past distort your judgement, Martha."

Martha's heart sank under the weight of their expectations.

The looks she had exchanged with Will were like ghosts haunting her thoughts, whispering promises of what once was. She stood and turned away, knowing her future depended on her own strength and not the interference of her mother or grandmother.

"I will go to my room."

"Goodnight," said Angela.

"We will talk again tomorrow."

*****

The long breakfast table had been laid meticulously by Bindi and Mia. Plates were neatly arranged, and there was an assortment of breakfast items…fluffy scrambled eggs, crispy bacon, and buttered toast, along with pots of steaming coffee and tea. Yet the breakfast spread was overshadowed by the sombre mood of the diners.

In the corner, the grandfather clock ticked away, its sound soothing to the ears.

It was then that Martha entered, the last to join the gathering and almost half an hour late. As she stepped through the doorway, the room turned its collective attention to her, but she appeared oblivious to the questioning looks. Her hair, usually neat and tidy, fell limply round her shoulders, and her face bore the marks of a sleepless night. Dark circles framed her eyes and bore evidence of the tears she had shed through the night.

"Good morning, Martha," her mother said, attempting to bridge the silence that had enveloped the room.

Martha looked up and stared vacantly around the room.

"Good morning, everyone. I must have been overtired. It's not like me to sleep so late."

She avoided looking at Will, who sat stony-faced at the head of the table in the chair normally reserved for Jimmy Boy.

Martha had no sooner sat when her chair scraped back, and she stood and rushed from the room, calling,

"I am not hungry."

She went to the lounge room where she flung herself down and sobbed. Back in the breakfast room, the walls seemed to close in on the others as they pondered the situation.

Angela broke the silence.

"Leave her be. She will return."

After a time, Martha's heaviness seemed to lift, and she composed herself and walked back to join the others. She took her seat and then a sip of her now cold coffee.

*****

"Will, now the others have gone, would you kindly remain. My mother and I have things to discuss."

At the mention of his name, Will's face paled, dread etched across his handsome face.

He had been sitting opposite Martha, and the fear of what lay ahead loomed large in his mind.

Yet he nodded, almost mechanically.

"Of course," he replied, but the tremor in his voice betrayed the impending doom he felt.

"Ellie, I am sorry if I have intruded on your family."

"Intruded? Is that what you call it? Will, I suspect," she paused and then said,

"Let me rephrase that. Not suspect! I know what has been going on between my daughter and yourself. Have you no shame, Will? She is a married woman."

Will decided it was time to defend himself.

"Shame? Do you think I should be ashamed of being in love with Martha? Who are you to judge us, Eleanor? Or you, Mrs O'Brien? What matters is our happiness. We are in love, and you can never stop that."

"How dare you, Will? How dare you raise your voice to me? I want you gone from here before lunchtime."

Will leaned across the table and almost spat his next words.

"I will leave for sure. But I will make you a promise. I will return and take your daughter with me."

"Get out!" shouted Eleanor.

"Get out of my sight!"

*****

Chapter 21

Jimmy Boy wouldn't take no for an answer.

"Richard," he had said, "here's some money for the food and supplies. I am a man who believes in paying his way."

"I do not want your money, Jimmy. I would rue the day that I couldn't do the Christian thing and feed good men."

Jimmy Boy ignored him and walked to the front seat of the wagon, stood on his toes, and shoved a roll of notes in Rachel's apron pocket.

"Rachel, please take this."

She smiled at the Chinaman and patted his arm.

"You are a good man, Jimmy. Thank you."

*****

Andrews and his sister returned from Milburra carrying supplies in their wagon. Rachel had found it taxing trying to feed all the men, but she knew she had to. They were hopefully her and her brother's saviours.

The men came from the coolness of the barn to help

Richard and his sister unload the supplies. Richard pulled Jimmy Boy aside and said,

"I need to talk."

Jimmy Boy noted the desperation on the man's face.

"Any problem in town, Richard?"

"There's no problem for us, Jimmy, but Jacky is in serious strife."

Jimmy's face screwed up with concern.

"Has Reagan found out about Jacky being here with us? Does he know about us?"

"No, it's worse than that. The talk of the town is Jacky is wanted for murder. One of Reagan's men, Kerrigan, has claimed to have seen Jacky throw the spear that killed Howarth."

Jimmy Boy looked around just as Jacky returned from carrying a sack of flour into the house.

"Jacky!" called Jimmy Boy.

"We've got a problem."

*****

The men sat around the dining table. Rachel Andrews was clearing the dishes, and the men had settled in to have their nightly rum and whiskey. Burra was sitting alone in the corner. He knew there was no point in his joining them. Besides, he knew Jacky would do whatever was best for him.

Andrews passed the bottle across to Jacky, but he waved it away.

"Thanks, but no thanks, Richard. This blackfeller can only tolerate one a night."

"I'll have his share," said Jennings willingly.

"No, you won't, Mister Jennings. You've had enough already."

Jimmy Boy gave Jennings a warning glare.

Jacky leaned back in his chair and in a calm voice said,

"I have reached a decision. I'll stay here with Burra until the heat dies down a little, then I'll try and sort out this mess."

Andrews interjected.

"But staying here puts my sister and I in danger, Jacky."

"When I said stay here, I meant around the district. I would never endanger you or your sister, Richard. We will go and live with the Kamilaroi tribe."

Jimmy Boy's eyes were full of concern.

"All right, Jacky. But you must be careful. They're not going to stop looking for you."

Burra was listening closely. He had picked up enough English to understand what was being said.

In his own language, he spoke to Jacky.

"You should remain here, Jacky. Just keep out of sight. They won't trouble me. And with my new look, they will not even know me. Dressed like this, I can even go into town."

He ran his fingers down his once-new shirt and fiddled with the buttons, and for the thousandth time, he sniffed the collar.

"Burra, you know I cannot do that. Your people are my people, too. We cannot let them down. My idea makes sense. We will go to the Kamilaroi tribe and stay with them. We just need to be patient. If Reagan thinks we have left the district, then he will let down his guard."

Jacky

*****

Jimmy Boy was the first to awake the next morning. Or so he thought. He looked across to where Jacky and Burra normally slept, but they weren't there. His first thought was that they had deserted him, but then he realised their bedding and bags were still in place. Jimmy Boy walked out into the already hot day to alleviate himself from the snoring of Wells and Jennings. A small wisp of smoke was coming from the homestead chimney. Jimmy Boy pondered on Richard Andrews and his sister. They were good people, and he wanted to help them. But the man he needed to talk with was nowhere in sight.

During the night, Jimmy Boy had come up with a plan. But Jacky was not there to share it with. He ambled across to the side door of the house, and as he did, he caught sight of Jacky and Burra in the distance. They were carrying something, and as they edged closer, he saw a small wallaby slung over Burra's shoulder, and Jacky had a couple of fat possums.

They waved at Jimmy Boy, and Jacky called,

"Breakfast, Jimmy Boy. I need to get accustomed to

blackfeller tucker if I am going to live with them."

*****

"Would you move away with your cigarette, please, Mister Jennings," said Jimmy Boy as he waved the smoke from his face.

The men were sitting under a large ghost gum. Wells was mending a halter, and Burra was shaping a spear.

"Jacky, last night I had an idea. It may be a little risky, but I think it might just work."

"Fill me in."

"We need to get in touch with Kerrigan. He is the key to solving all our problems."

"How can he help Jimmy Boy? He has it in for me and would like nothing better than seeing me hanging from a noose."

"Jacky, do you remember our trip to Newcastle to restock a few years back, after the flood?"

"I could never forget that. You ended up with some mighty fine stock. But what's Newcastle got to do with Kerrigan?"

Jacky did not know where Jimmy Boy was headed with his conversation.

"When we went to Newcastle, I took a chest of gold, Jacky. And that gold has been sitting in Mister Loomes' bank ever since. With the price of gold rising and the interest accrued, I should have quite a sum of money sitting in Loomes' strongroom."

"Go on," a puzzled Jacky said.

"The idea came to me, if I was to offer Kerrigan a decent sum of money, he might be persuaded to tell the truth and admit it wasn't you who killed Reagan's man."

"You are asking Kerrigan to betray Reagan? It just will not work, Jimmy Boy," said Jacky, shaking his head.

"He knows too much, and Reagan no doubt has ways to be rid of him. Permanently! Besides, Kerrigan would still face the law if it was him who murdered the Lamberts and carried out any other killings we know nothing about. He would not risk his life for your money, Jimmy Boy."

"Maybe he would, Jacky, if I added a sweetener."

"Sweetener?"

"An added incentive. We could persuade Kerrigan to disappear."

"The law in Australia is getting better, Jimmy Boy. He would be tracked down and hung. That is, if Reagan didn't get to him first."

"The law would not find him in America, Jacky. Or England. Or Canada, for that matter."

Jacky's mouth grew into a grin.

"You are a very clever man, Jimmy Boy."

He slapped Jennings awake and said,

"You know, Mister Jennings. I just have the feeling Jimmy Boy's plan might work."

"What plan? And keep yer bloody 'ands to yerself, Jacky or I'll backhand ya one."

"A sweetener, Mister Jennings. Jimmy Boy is going to give Kerrigan a sweetener to convince him to change his story."

"You talk nonsense, Jacky. 'ow the bloody hell would a cup of sugar make a man change 'is mind?"

"Go back to doing what you do best, Mister Jennings,"

Jacky

chuckled Jimmy Boy.

Jennings farted and rolled over. He needed more sleep.

*****

Jacky controlled the reins of the horse, and Burra sat behind him.

"I'll turn it loose at the boundary, Burra," Jacky said, glancing at the man behind him.

"It will find its own way home. Too risky hanging onto it. If we are caught, we will also face a charge of horse theft."

Burra nodded.

"Good. I would rather travel by foot, Jacky. I have never got used to sitting on one of these things."

They dismounted, and Jacky gave the horse a whack on its rump. It galloped off into the distance.

"If we cannot find the tribe Burra, I am sure they will find us."

They trudged through the scrub and suffered the stinging of nettles and grazes of the brambles. Hours slipped by. And shadows lengthened and began to merge into one.

Burra was leading the way, his senses attuned to the land, but then, without warning, he halted and lifted his head slightly, his nostrils flaring as he sniffed the air. The dog, silent until now, began whining.

"Smoke, Jacky. Close," he declared, his voice a mere whisper.

Jacky breathed in; the familiar scent of smoke carried with it both comfort and caution. This could mean the tribe was near…or there was an unseen danger ahead.

"Can you tell which direction, Burra?"

Jacky's gaze shifted across the landscape.

Burra squinted,

"That way," he nodded his head, and Jacky followed his line of sight. Without another word, they continued in the direction of the smoke. They found themselves pushing through the thick scrub, the air heavy with the earthy smell of wet undergrowth. As they moved further into the scrub, they both sensed they were not alone. Just then, a figure emerged from the bushes behind them.

Stepping into view was a young Kamilaroi man, his

presence commanding but with a smile that was welcoming. His long black hair hung over his shoulders, and the faint fuzz of a developing beard could be seen on his face.

"Welcome and greetings," he said, his voice calm and steady.

"I have been watching you for some time. Follow me."

Without waiting for an acknowledgment, he turned and walked off, a spear held loosely by his side. Jacky could tell that he had been with the white people before. He was dressed in an old pair of cut-off trousers and wore a cotton shirt missing all its buttons.

*****

Jacky and Burra had been with the tribe for two days now. It was a completely different world for Jacky, who had spent much of his life with white people. He was calm, calmer than he could remember. He wondered if this was the life for him.

Jacky lay in a gunyah, sweat dripping through the leaves above. Warm rays of sunshine mingled with nature, the only sound a kookaburra laughing in the distance, and the smooth flow of the river a short distance away. He closed his eyes and let the tranquillity overtake him. He slept for a while, and when he woke, he felt refreshed.

He pushed himself up and wiped sweat from his brow and headed for the river, the soft earth a soothing balm on his soles. When he came to the river, he knelt and placed both hands in the water and let it trickle through his fingers. He peeled off his trousers and, naked now, he dived in. The water, unlike the day, was cool, and it caused him to raise his head and shake it vigorously. It was then he sensed a presence. He looked to the bank and saw a young woman, also naked.

Jacky had become accustomed to nudity. Mostly all the warriors and lubras were naked, with only a handful wearing clothing. But the sight of this woman had a profound effect on him. He found himself staring at her and noticed she returned the look, with a mixture of curiosity and playfulness. Then, like a leaping kangaroo, she dived into the water and sliced through it to the other side, where she lay on her back like a lizard and dried herself. Hungry frogs croaked from reeds, and a lone eagle soared overhead.

The sight of her drew Jacky like a thirsty man to water. With short, determined strokes, he swam to her. He pulled himself up the bank and settled himself on the grass beside her.

"What is your name?" he asked as he stared at her small, firm breasts.

She stared at him, her eyes wide and brown, and her long eyelashes fluttered in a way that was charming and alluring.

"They call me Tarni. It means river or stream. And I know your name is Jacky. I am Nullah's granddaughter. My father, our tribe's best warrior, was murdered by Reagan's men."

"You have a very beautiful name. Tarni."

Jacky let the word roll off his tongue.

"I am sorry about your father, Tarni, but that is why I am here. I want to free Burra's people and at the same time bring Reagan to justice."

"My tribe knows of the southern blacks he has prisoner, but our warriors can get nowhere near Reagan's farm. He has many men, and their guns are no match for our warriors' spears."

"Tarni, it will take more than violence to free the people. While I rest up at your camp, I hope to come up with a plan."

"I want to help you, Jacky. My father's spirit needs to rest in peace."

She placed her tiny arm on his knee, and he felt a shiver course through his body. He reached for her, but she jumped up and laughed and dived back into the water. She was across the other side and gone before Jacky had managed to stand.

*****

Later that night, Jacky and Burra listened as Nullah recounted stories of the dreamtime. He had found a new respect for the Kamilaroi people. No longer did he feel an outsider, but more an integral part of their community. And he found himself growing fonder of the young aboriginal girl Tarni.

As he slept that night, he realised that for a long time he had given no thought to his wife Martha.

"Was this a warning sign?" he wondered.

*****

Chapter 22

Four days had passed, and Jacky was becoming impatient. He was edgy like a fox lurking at night outside a hen house. His mind was clouded with thoughts of Mona, the aboriginal maid. He decided he could not wait any longer. Tonight, he would act.

He thought back to the words of Nullah the previous night.

"The first thing you need to do, Jacky, is to stop your white man's hurry. You have lived like them for too long. My tribe will help you, but in Kamilaroi time, not white man's time. The sun and the wind, the earth and the sky, these things will still be here when you are gone."

But Jacky cast the words aside. He knew that in his attempt to hurry things along, it would work for him rather than against him.

Under the shroud of darkness, Jacky crept from the camp. He would not target his stallion as he knew that it would be heavily guarded, but he would attempt to get into the house and find where Mona was chained. She was his focus, the key to the whereabouts of the other imprisoned blacks.

Reagan's farmhouse loomed ahead, and Jacky crept under the wire fence and edged his way along a side wall. He peered through a window where the light from a lantern spilled out onto the lawn, and then he looked up to the second storey and noted no lights on. That would mean Reagan and Charley were in bed. He raised his eyes to the level of the windowsill and peered inside. There she was. Mona, sitting on a mattress, sewing a button on one of Reagan's shirts by the dim light. He tapped gently on the glass. Mona dropped the shirt, and with terror etched on her face, she looked up and into the eyes of Jacky. He pressed his fingers to his lips to hush her. She cowered back and watched as he raised the window sash and climbed inside.

"It's Jacky. I told you I would help you."

"They will hunt you down and kill you, Jacky."

He looked at the chain around her wrist.

"I need you to tell me where Reagan keeps the key," he whispered.

"I will have you out of here tonight."

"I am afraid, Jacky."

"Don't be," he reassured her.

"Everything will be all right. Tell me where the key is kept."

"I have only ever seen one key, and if it is the one to my chains, it is hanging by the clock in the library."

With calculated stealth, Jacky made his way through the house to the library where he and Reagan had sat drinking whiskey not more than a few days ago. He looked for the clock in the gloom, and its sound gave him the location. Beside it, on a nail, hung a key. He paused, listening intently. There was no sound. He unhooked the key and crept back the way he had come.

Mona was chained to the back wall of the small room. Her only provisions were a jug of water and a small bucket for use as a lavatory. Her hair seemed to hang sadly tonight, and her eyes were red. She smiled weakly at Jacky as he tried the key in the lock. A satisfying click signalled it was the right key. He pulled the chain away and pulled the girl up and over to the window.

"Me first. When I see all is clear, I will tap on the glass. You climb out and follow me. We need to be silent, and we need to be fast. Understood?"

She blinked and nodded blankly.

Jacky was out and in the clear, but he had to pull the frightened girl through the window. Then Jacky froze. There was the sound of footsteps coming down the stairs inside the house.

"Hush, Mona. It must be Reagan. The footsteps are too heavy to be Charley."

Reagan had been unable to sleep. He had always been like that. A man on edge all the time. A man waiting for the unexpected to happen.

"Stay still," said Jacky as he felt the girl's trembling body.

"He doesn't know we are here."

Regan pushed the front door open and walked out onto his lush lawn. He stretched his arms above his head then pulled his nightshirt up and pissed on the grass. He gave a sigh of relief, shook himself then walked back inside.

"Let's go."

Jacky pulled the girl by the arm, and they headed off

on the three-hour trek to the Kamilaroi camp.

*****

It was breaking dawn when they arrived back at the camp. Already the tribe was up, about, and busy. Numerous fires had been lit, and the sweet smell of roasting meat filled the air. Jacky and Mona arrived unseen. Burra was the only one who had missed Jacky. The other tribal members had assumed he had gone hunting on his own. But what Burra didn't expect was Jacky to arrive with his own flesh and blood. It was a joy for Jacky to watch as the old man looked at his granddaughter.

Burra stood on his frail legs and extended his arms.

"Welcome home, girl," he said in barely a whisper.

Mara beamed as she returned his smile.

"It is good to be free," she said and looked at Jacky.

She stepped towards Burra and embraced him, her heart swelling with joy at the reunion.

"Ah, my sweet Mara. You have no idea how much I have missed you."

They settled down in front of his gunyah and sat in

silence for some time. Then Burra spoke.

"Do you remember the stories of the Dreamtime Mara? The tales of how our ancestors walked this land. You are part of this land, girl, and now you are back."

They sat and watched as the sun climbed higher, and Burra looked at how its rays illuminated his granddaughter's face.

*****

"It sure is a big help, Jimmy, you are loaning Mister Wells and Jennings to me while you go home to your family."

"They are both good men, Richard, and will do whatever you ask of them. They may be a little slow, but very hard working."

Jimmy looked across at his two loyal men. They were carrying armfuls of wood that they had spent hours chopping to the back door of the homestead. Jimmy Boy cared deeply for the pair, almost as much as he did for his own family. Realising they did not carry their youthful vigour still tugged at him; they deserved rest, not endless toil.

"I promise not to overwork them," Andrews chuckled.

"And Rachel will keep them well fed. It will be a comfort just to have them around, knowing that Reagan is so unpredictable."

They kept their eyes on the two men, both maintaining a silence now.

Then Andrews said,

"Do you want me to take you into Milburra to catch the coach, Jimmy?"

"Does a coach run from Milburra? That would sure help some saddle soreness."

"Yes, all the way to Newcastle. I am not sure if it runs through to Ramsay, though."

"So long as I get to Hardwood. I know a coach runs from there to Ramsay. I'd like an early coach tomorrow if there is one."

"Then let's ride in this afternoon in my buggy and see. If it gets late, we can stay at the hotel for the night."

"This afternoon is good, Richard. I want to keep a low profile, and hopefully, the town might be quiet in the afternoon."

*****

Jimmy Boy's heart was buoyant with the thought of seeing Ellie. He had been away only for a short while, but to him it felt like a year. The buggy lurched and swayed as it made its way into Milburra. Jimmy Boy had his hat pulled over his eyes and was daydreaming when he felt a nudge in his ribs.

"Hey Jimmy, we have company."

Jimmy Boy immediately sat up and watched as three riders made their way along the road towards them. The lead rider hailed them from a distance and kicked his horse into a trot until he pulled up short of Andrew's buggy.

"Afternoon, gents," he said.

"Bit late to be journeyin' into town, is it not?"

"We have business there," said Andrews with measured caution.

"We all have business in this world at some time or another. I won't ask you your business, mister, but I do have a question."

"Go ahead," said Andrews with suspicion building in his bones.

"Is this the road to the Reagan farm? We were told he was hirin' men."

"Reagan? Yes, follow this road."

Andrews pointed behind him.

"My place is the road to the left. You turn right to Reagan's."

Andrews leaned forward with his arms crossed.

"But I'll give you a warning, strangers. Reagan is a hard man."

The trio shared a glance before the taller of the men, and obviously their spokesman, said,

"We'll take our chances. We've worked for some hard arses before now."

Andrews remained impassive, his eyes cold and unrelenting in their gaze.

"Don't say I didn't warn you."

"And just who are you to be giving advice?" the smallest of the men spoke up.

"I am Richard Andrews. A man who's seen firsthand

what happens to those who cross Reagan. Now follow this road and don't turn left to my place. Remember, Reagan's to the right."

The three men exchanged glances. Then,

"C'mon, you pair. No good listening to poor advice."

And Mullins and his partners, Scanlon and Newton, would be horse thieves, come anything thieves, kicked their horses into a trot and headed down the road, towards Reagan's.

*****

Charley heard her father from the bedroom. He was in a terrible rage, and she heard glass breaking and the sound of a table being upturned. She pulled herself from bed and wrapped a dressing gown around her naked body, and tentatively descended the stairs, the creaks echoing through the house as mournful as a funeral dirge. Her heart fluttered as she approached the dining room. The smell of alcohol was potent, but not from her father having an early morning drink, but rather from smashed bottles. The room was a mess, with shattered glass and splintered wood from the table strewn over the floor.

"The fucking bitch has escaped Charley!"

He turned to face his daughter.

"But how?"

He stared at the empty hook where the key had been.

Charley had no rage in her, and in fact, she was quite composed.

"She did not escape Papa. Someone has found the key and freed her."

"But who? And who knew the key was there? Only me and you, Charley."

He looked at his daughter with a threatening snarl on his face.

Charley backed away; her arms raised as if defending herself from an invisible attacker.

"Surely you don't…… why should I? Papa, I swear I didn't touch the key."

"Then who?"

Her father's glare didn't waver. His voice came in raw gasps.

"You had better come up with an explanation."

Charley didn't know if she was saying the right thing, but she said,

"It had to be Jacky."

"Jacky?" he roared.

"I thought we had seen the last of that black bastard!"

His eyes searched the room and settled on his cigar box, lying on the floor.

He retrieved it and extracted a cigar and fumbled in his pocket for a light. The inhalation of the acrid smoke did nothing to calm the man. He fell into a bout of coughing and, with a rasping voice, said to his daughter,

"I will have the men scour the entire bloody district and find the bastard. And then I want him dead and his black hide hanging in the scrub as a warning to the other black bastards. Nobody crosses Harry Reagan!"

*****

Reagan pulled his trousers on and then his boots, forgoing any socks. Then bare-chested, he put his ear to Charley's door. Satisfied she was asleep, he went downstairs and walked across the yard to where the blacks were chained for the night.

He stood in the doorway of the dilapidated shed, his bare chest gleaming with sweat in the light of the lantern, and his ponderous belly hanging over his trousers. The flame from the lantern cast a shadow on his face, making him appear even more horrific in the eyes of his captives. He looked around the make-shift prison, with the women and children shackled on one wall and the youths and men on the other. Reagan had made sure there was no possible physical contact between the two groups.

"Which of you lovely women is itchin' to please this handsome white gentleman tonight?" he asked with a leer in his tone.

The chains that held them rattled softly, and the children whimpered in fear. The women cowered back while the men sat tall, their chests taut with anger. They watched Reagan with a fiery hatred and defiance that could never be contained by the chains holding them.

Reagan's gaze raked over the trembling women and stopped as he met the defiant eyes of a young mother with a child clinging to her legs. The woman knew what was coming, and she was prepared to fight back, all the while knowing that her resistance was futile.

The men began to chatter in their own tongue.

"Good, you bastards! Yabber all you like!"

Reagan liked his fun with a degree of defiance. It excited him.

He took a key from his pocket and his hand hovered over the lock for a while, savouring the power he had over her. Then he unlocked the shackles that bound her and dragged her across the floor, where he tossed her in a heap. He leant down and with his hot and smelly breath spoke in her ear.

"You are going to do everything I tell you. Understand?"

The woman didn't understand the words, but she did understand his intentions.

"Watch this you black scum!" he bellowed, his words slurred slightly by his intoxication.

"This is how a white man does it!"

He unbuckled his trousers and let them drop to the floor, his erection standing proud and tall.

"Look at this," he laughed almost maniacally as he waved it at them.

"She is going to taste this and she will love it."

His laughter bounced off the walls as he threw himself on top of her and pushed in, feeling her body tense and quiver. She made a sound somewhere between a scream and a whimper, but it was a sound he was used to, and it only fuelled his depravity. Each thrust brought an extra agony, and all she could hear was his grunting and the howls of the menfolk. At the exact moment a dingo howled mournfully far off in the night, Regan exploded inside her. She felt the relief of his weight removed from her, and he fumbled with his trousers.

"Fucking stinking black whore!" he spat.

His hands were shaking as he dragged her back and shackled her ankles.

*****

Chapter 23

"I am not sure when I will return, Richard, but I need to bring the money back as soon as possible. Money and freedom should be enough to entice Kerrigan to give Reagan up."

The men had stayed at a hotel in Milburra and were in the process of settling their bill.

"But as I said, in the meantime, you have two willing workers and a good man in Jacky if you ever need help. I know if anyone can free Burra's people and bring Reagan to justice, it is Jacky."

"I hope you are right," said Andrews with a lack of optimism in his tone.

"Come on, I will walk you down to the coaching station where you can board the coach."

*****

It was just after seven in the morning when the stagecoach pulled out of Milburra. Sitting beside Jimmy Boy was an elderly woman, her hair neatly pinned up, but with enough loose ends to flutter in the breeze. The coach creaked and groaned as it rolled over the rough track, its wooden body echoing the ravages of time.

Jimmy Boy had tried to start up a conversation with his fellow traveller, raising his voice to compete with the clatter of the wheels.

"It's a lovely day, isn't it?" he had said, glancing at her expectantly.

She smiled politely, but there was an unmistakable image of confusion clouding her eyes. He repeated himself, hoping he might garner some attention this time. Yet the only response he received was a tilt and a nod of the woman's head. After several more futile attempts, Jimmy Boy cast his attention to the scenery on the outside.

Every so often, a flock of birds would take flight and soar up and over the rolling hills in the distance. Jimmy Boy could almost hear their calls, a melodic call of freedom which stirred something inside him. Freedom. Could Jacky deliver this to Burra's people?

The elderly woman shifted her gaze as well, as she turned her stare away from him and marvelled in the beauty of the countryside. Jimmy Boy wondered what thoughts occupied her mind. Were they thoughts of family? He felt a pang of homesickness at the thought of family.

The coach passed a small farmhouse with smoke spiralling from the chimney, a homely sight that evoked even more homesickness. He thought of a warm meal with his family, the banter that accompanied each meal, and the loving warmth and humour of the irreplaceable Bindi.

The sun began its descent, painting the sky in orange and pink and purple. Jimmy Boy glanced at the woman. She was sleeping now, her features softened in the gathering dusk.

Jimmy Boy had just nodded off when the sound of a gunshot stirred him from his reverie. The sharp crack reverberated around the valley walls, and he was immediately awake and alert. He felt for his pistol and placed it beneath him. The old woman continued to sleep, confirming his suspicions that she was deaf. There was silence for a while, and then Jimmy Boy heard the crunching of gravel and a voice.

"Bail up! And don't go hoisting yer shotgun driver. I jis want to relieve you of yer strongbox. Any passengers?"

He walked to the coach and reefed the door open. Jimmy Boy sat there and stared at the man. The old woman had still not woken.

"Out! Bloody Chinaman!"

The voice was harsh and aggressive. Jimmy Boy thought back to his son Shimmy. He could never imagine his boy using such a strident tone. But then again, he never imagined his own son would grow up to be a bushranger.

Jimmy Boy stepped out with his hands in the air. He decided prudence was a better option and left his pistol on the cracked leather seat. With deliberate calm, he faced the thief.

Then, in a soft tone, he said,

"Take what you want. But would you have the Christian decency to allow an old woman to sleep? I don't think she has anything valuable on her."

The bushranger just stood there, and the two men eyed each other off. Jimmy saw echoes of his son…the defiance and the spontaneity, but he saw something else. A flicker of vulnerability.

"This is your first time, isn't it?" asked Jimmy Boy.

The young man hung his head and shuffled his feet.

"How can you tell?"

"I can see through you, mister. And I can see you don't want to do this."

The bushranger lowered his weapon.

"I'm just a man trying to survive, mister."

"What's your name?" asked Jimmy Boy.

"Billy."

Billy, you really don't want to do this. What about if I give you all I have, and you leave the old woman and the coach driver alone?"

The coach driver, silent till now, said,

"Can't make deals with his type, son. Let me just give him the strongbox and we'll be on our way."

Billy looked up at the driver

"Good idea. Hoist it down, mister."

Then he added,

"Throw the shotgun down first."

The driver kicked at his weapon, and it fell to the ground at Billy's feet. He bent to pick it up, but in doing so, he took his eyes off the driver, who pulled out a pistol and fired.

The bullet struck Billy in the forehead, and his bushranging career had come to a halt. He was dead before he came to rest on the gravelled track.

The driver clambered down and placed a neat kick in the dead man's ribs.

"'ere mister, give me a hand to heave this box back up and we can scarper. Should be at the next changeover station in about an hour."

Jimmy Boy shook his head and said softly,

"Why? Why kill him? I could see he meant no harm. He was just a kid."

"Kids grow up to be men. I don't take no fuckin' risks, mister. Seen too many coach drivers shot by the likes of that bastard."

*****

"You're too soft on young Shimmy, Jimmy Boy."

He could still hear Jennings' words ringing in his ears.

"Maybe I was too soft on him," he thought.

"But how could I have done things any differently?"

The aching in his heart grew stronger at the memory of Shimmy lying at his feet, dead. He could almost smell the blood and the gunpowder, and as he looked back on his son's life, he realised the truth. He couldn't have done anything differently. Shimmy was like a young colt, one that had tasted the thrill of the open paddocks.

People would never really know the son he had raised, the laughter and tears they had shared, and the dreams that would never become a reality. And the same question that never would be answered came to him.

"How? Why did it all come to this?"

The ache in Jimmy Boy's heart had now become a physical pain that seemed to pulse with the rhythm of the turning wheels of the coach. With the faint trace of tears, Jimmy Boy recalled the sound of the shot and the look Shimmy had given him one last time.

"I am sorry, Papa. Please forgive me."

*****

The coach pulled into Ramsay just on dusk, the twilight casting long shadows over the main street. As Jimmy Boy gazed out the window of the coach, he could see the outline of the Emporium, its silhouette striking against the fading sunlight. There were no lights shining from within, a clear indication that his daughter Martha had gone home for the day. He clambered down from the coach, his muscles sore and his body weary from the many miles he had travelled. He stretched his arms, and it felt as if he was pushing them through a barrel of molasses.

"Thanks for the ride, mister," Jimmy Boy said, with not an ounce of gratitude, but the driver dismissed him with a careless wave of his hand. They hadn't spoken since the coachman had killed the bushranger.

The scents of Ramsay welcomed him, and he thought how wonderful it was to be almost home.

The townspeople had already settled into their nightly routine, and the town had a certain stillness about it. He made his way towards Jack's Inn, passing the warm, lamplit windows of the townsfolk, and he could smell the homely scents of meals being prepared. As he drew closer, the sounds from the Inn became clearer…the distant clink of glasses and rounds of laughter and the low hum of conversation. He pushed open the door, and the familiar creak greeted him like an old friend. The Inn was alive, and Jimmy Boy realised it was a Friday night.

"Jimmy Boy," Jack called above the din.

"You are back. Come on and grab a drink."

Jimmy Boy smiled as he approached the bar. It was good to see Jack's welcoming face.

"Just one Jack. Then I want to get home."

"One it is then. I'll send someone to the stables and arrange for your horse to be saddled and ready. She's been well looked after since you've been gone."

He placed a cold beer in front of Jimmy Boy, who studied it for a while, as if deciding whether to drink it.

"Many a story to tell, I suspect," Jack winked at him.

"Long story, Jack. But not tonight."

Jimmy Boy drank his beer and excused himself.

"I'm tired, Jack. I will see you tomorrow."

*****

A short time later, Jimmy Boy was astride his mare called Josie. It pawed at the ground as if signalling to him that it could sense freedom from being corralled for too long. With a quick pat on her neck, Jimmy Boy steered her out of the stables and onto the road to Wicklow. The trail stretched out in front of him, and he urged the horse into a gallop. The rush of the wind in his ears carried whispers of home and his family.

He reined in at the garden gate and was not surprised that there was no one to greet him. His trip home had been a secret. But then he espied Ellie in the garden. In the moonlight, to Jimmy Boy, she looked just like an angel. He crept up behind his wife and kissed her on the back of the neck. Startled, she spun around.

"Jimmy Boy!" she cried as she threw her arms open, her eyes shimmering with tears.

"You're home!"

He enveloped her in an embrace, feeling the familiar form of her body and enjoying the sensation of her face pressing against his. Within moments, the others had come from the household, all followed by Bindi, who was trying to keep some calm.

"Leave the man be!" she chastised.

"He must be 'ungry and thirsty. I need to 'urry up and make him some supper."

*****

It was late in the evening, and all but Ellie and Jimmy Boy had retired for the night. He gazed around the room. He could feel the love and the familiarity, and he knew. This was home.

His reverie was broken by the soft voice of Eleanor.

"Jimmy Boy, I have some matters to discuss. I know you are tired from your travels, and I wanted to leave this matter until tomorrow, but I just know I won't sleep."

He looked up, an element of worry crossing his face.

"Is there a major problem, Ellie? I am tired of everything of late. There seem to be more and more problems facing us every day. What with Burra and Jacky now, it is becoming too much."

He took a small sip of his brandy.

"So tell me, Ellie, what is the problem?"

Eleanor stared blankly across the room.

"Jimmy Boy, Will McKenzie has paid us a visit."

She waited for her husband to speak.

"Will? When? Where is he now?"

"He left two days ago. I asked him to leave Jimmy Boy."

"Why? Whatever for Ellie?"

He turned his gaze to her, searching for answers he already knew. Ellie drew in a shaky breath, her mind racing to the moments that had led to the final confrontation. Memories of joyful dinners where Will had been the life of the party, but those thoughts were mingled with recollections of fleeting glances she had observed between Will and their daughter.

"Jimmy Boy, our daughter, who is a married woman, I suspect, has rekindled her interest in Will."

Her words spilled out; each one heavy with the implications.

"I have seen the way she looks at him and how she laughs a little too easily when he is around. It is not just an innocent friendship, Jimmy Boy. I can feel it."

The amber light from the lantern cast long shadows. Jimmy boy recalled the young Will. The lad who brought a smile to everyone's face and had a boisterous laughter that filled the room.

He leaned back in his chair.

"What if you are wrong, Ellie? What if it is just your imagination?"

"I only wish it was my imagination. But I have seen firsthand the connection between them. And what do you expect me to do? Just stand aside and let this happen? She is married to Jacky for God's sake."

Jimmy Boy nodded, his arms crossed.

"Martha did seem livelier around him, Ellie. But she is more like a sister to him. Looks between them do not have to mean anything but innocence."

He took another sip of his drink

"So what do we do?"

"You need to speak to her," replied Ellie, her voice growing in strength.

"And what if she gets angry? What if I push her away from us and headlong into his arms?"

"Then at least we will have tried, Jimmy Boy."

****

Chapter 24

Mullins and his two accomplices arrived at the Reagan farm around lunchtime. The road they had been directed to follow was a good two hours from where they had encountered Andrews and Jimmy Boy.

As they approached the gate, they spotted Reagan as he came from the stables. He had a cockiness and an air of superiority in his carriage, but today he carried with it something extra. Pride. He was leading a handsome stallion, its coat glimmering in the sunlight.

Scanlon was the first to react.

He whispered across his horse's neck to Mullins,

"Fuck me Mister Mullins. That is the blackfeller's horse. The one we tried to pinch."

Mullins was quick to shut him down.

"Keep yer fuckin' mouth closed, Scanlon. We don't know what's happenin' here. Jis gotta hope the darky ain't about. You two just hush up. I will do all the talking."

With brow furrowed, Reagan's abrasive voice cut through the warm breeze.

"Who are you men? What do you want?"

His brusque demeanour hinted at no nonsense.

Mullins dismounted and said,

"You'd be Mister Reagan. Jis wonderin' if there's work fer three hardworking men. We was told in town you was hiring."

Reagan narrowed his eyes and sized up the trio. He could see they had travelled a long distance. They were dusty and worn and dirty.

"Work, huh? What can you do?"

Scanlon piped up, his excitement getting the better of him.

"We can do most anything, mister Reagan. Muck out the stables, tend to the livestock and the horses, and ride yer boundaries."

Then Newton chimed in.

"Yeah, mister, we ain't afraid of hard work. We can do most anything."

Reagan studied them, weighing up his options.

"You ever hunted down blackfellers?"

The three men were surprised at the question.

"What do you mean?" asked Mullins.

"Just what I said. I have got a tribe of blacks camped somewhere near here," he waved his arms in all directions, signalling the tribe could be anywhere.

"I want to be rid of them. Bastards are causing me no end of trouble. Think you can handle that?"

"As we said, we can do most anything," responded Mullins with a grin.

Reagan liked what he heard. Here was a way to get rid of the *Kamilaroi* tribe while keeping himself in the clear. The men would be just pawns to be played by him in the game of life. Or death.

"C'mon over to the house. We'll have a chat."

*****

"So, Mister Reagan, what sort of trouble have you had with the blacks?"

"The usual. Stock theft, fences torn down, and any petty theft you can name. The bastards steal anything that is not nailed down. I want the whole district to be rid of the bastards."

"Never could take to blacks meself," said Mullins.

"And just how are we to get rid of them? "

"Use your imagination, Mullins."

"How many are we talking about? "

"Maybe thirty or forty. They are like blowflies. It's hard to count them. But there is one major problem. They have an educated black with them. He might cause some trouble. Jacky, a black bastard who thinks he is white."

"Jacky, you say?"

Reagan gave Mullins a querying look.

"You know him?"

Mullins thought quickly.

"No. I don't know him personally, but I was there when he won the Gilmore Cup."

"Yes. The bastard beat my daughter."

Mullins' face took on a perplexed look.

"So that was your daughter we saw the darky with?"

Reagan gave him a savage look. The mention of his daughter with a black man rankled him terribly.

"Correct. Now I will give you the story, albeit just enough that you need to know. Jacky killed one of my best workmen and then sold me his horse cheaply on the condition I did not report the murder. So, what did this astute man do? I had a legal document drawn up, paid the black man, and then I did the right and honourable thing and reported the murdering bastard to the local police. The law is after him at this very moment, but I want him first. And I want him dead. No questions asked. If you men can do this for me, you will be well paid. But then you must disappear from this district forever. Understand my drift?"

The three men grinned with expectation. Then, almost in unison, they spoke,

"Understood."

*****

Jacky left the camp before the sun was up. He carried two spears and one of Burra's boomerangs. It felt good to feel the warm earth under his feet and the freedom of being almost naked, save for the trousers he wore, which he had cut off at the knees. Today was special to him. He wanted to show his gratitude to the tribe by bringing back some meat. And if he couldn't bag a kangaroo or capture some ducks, then he saw no harm in spearing one of Reagan's sheep.

As he walked, he could not shake off the feeling that someone was following him. He stopped in his tracks and listened carefully. The continuous sounds of leaves rustling and twigs snapping filled the air. He *was* being followed! His instincts kicked in, and he quickly hid behind some low bushes. As the footsteps approached, Jacky prepared to pounce, but to his surprise, it was Tarni. She had a mischievous smile on her face, and her long hair was ruffled by the slight breeze.

"Gotcha!" Jacky exclaimed as he leapt out and grabbed her around the waist.

Tarni pulled away and laughed.

"Why, Jacky," she teased, "if I was a dingo, I could have eaten you way before now. I have been tailing you since you left the camp."

It was then that Jacky realised she had wanted him to catch her.

"Can I go hunting with you, Jacky? Please?" she asked, her eyes sparkling with anticipation.

Jacky paused, taken aback by her question.

Hunting was man's business. But as he looked at her eager face, he couldn't bring himself to say no.

"Fine. But you must prove yourself first," he replied, trying to hide the doubt in his voice.

"And fine by me," she said as they headed deeper into the scrub.

As they came into a clearing, Jacky spied a stump, a gnarled, horrible thing, alone and desolate.

There, he handed her a spear.

"Hit that."

She took the spear and threw it, then listened as Jacky roared with laughter.

"I knew it! Hunting is man's business," she said with disappointment.

He patted her shoulder and reassured her.

"Never mind. You can do women's business. I am sure

there are many tasty yams to find."

She cheered up and followed him. The sun was climbing now and augured a hot day with rain to come. Already, dark clouds were building.

They approached a small billabong, and Jacky immediately pushed her shoulders down.

"Shh!" he whispered

"Maybe ducks."

They sat in silence and listened to each other breathing. The closeness of the girl stirred Jacky, and he glanced sideways at her. He was not surprised to see that she was not looking for ducks. She was staring at him. He reached a hand towards her and stroked her cheek. Meekly, she surrendered, flopping herself backwards and lying prostrate on the mossy embankment, her dark hair fanned out around her. His fingertips, although calloused from hard work, were gentle to the touch, and they brushed against her with sensual intimacy.

Tarni closed her eyes, giving herself to the moment and the timeless beauty of the scrub surrounding them. She could feel their heartbeats, keeping time, and she could smell the scent of the warrior who was now pinning her body beneath his.

"Do you want me, Tarni?" asked Jacky with a laboured breath.

Her answer was not spoken. She took him in hand and stroked him gently, as he pulled aside the possum skin she had covered her treasure with. He entered her gently, and then they moved as one, giving themselves to a primeval urge.

They rolled apart, and Tarni lay still, taking in the splendour of nature that surrounded them. She was thinking of the earth, the sky, and the stars…they were all a part of her, as the blood flowing through her veins, and just as Jacky now flowed through her.

The peacefulness of their encounter was interrupted by a loud shout from Jacky. He had made an almost fatal error by putting his hand on a small spider in the grass. He drew back at the fiery bite. Tarni glanced at the spider and then thumped her fist on it, causing its guts to spew over the ground. She lay Jacky's head back and rested it on a large stone, then proceeded to construct a temporary shelter. The scrub was an untapped source of raw materials. She snapped branches, their bark rough against her fingers, and then she worked methodically gathering reeds from beside the billabong, and then with precision she began weaving them into the branches.

With each item she gathered, she conjured images of her mother and the stories that were told at night in the shelter of the gunyahs. When she finished, she had built a shelter that would protect them both from the elements. Then she settled beside Jacky to keep vigil over him. She knew that in the end, survival was not merely a fight against the elements, but a connection to the land and the promise of healing through their resilience.

Within an hour, Jacky knew he was in danger of death. Terrible belly pains and nausea racked him. He began to shiver and sweat out precious body fluid. The bitten hand swelled and cracked open.

He lay in the brush gunyah for the rest of the day and overnight, half conscious, aching and trembling. By the following morning, he had begun to feel better. During his delirium, he had seen ghostly shapes of his wife Martha and images of Charley and Tarni. He woke with a shiver to a clear dawn, feeling weak but clear-headed. He crawled from the humpy and saw Tarni, with a small fire burning and chewing leaves. She pulled some of the plant matter from her mouth and pressed the mush onto the bite wound. Then she placed the rest of the bush medicine in his mouth.

"I thought I was going to the Dreaming Tarni," he said with relief.

"You could have left me. Why did you stay?"

"I would have left you if you had died, but I knew you were a strong warrior. Besides, a woman does not leave the man to whom she has shared her spirit with."

'We best be getting back to the tribe, Tarni. People will be worried."

"Sometimes I fear for our future, Jacky."

"What do you mean?"

"You are whiter than you are black, Jacky."

"To fear is to care," he smiled.

"Let's carve our own path together."

"I trust you, Jacky," she whispered, her heart laid bare.

"And I will always protect that trust," he vowed.

*****

"It's a fine day to be huntin' blacks, Mister Reagan.

But where exactly is their camp?"

"No one knows. They move about too much. Bastards never shit in the same spot twice. But don't worry. If you do not find them, they will find you."

"Well, we will be off now. We will be back later this afternoon. Or earlier if things go well."

Mullins was the first to see smoke rising above the gums in the distance. It twisted upward, a spiral of grey against the blue sky, and Mullins' eyes sparkled with malevolence.

"I think that's the blacks' camp," he said wickedly and pointed ahead.

He looked back at Scanlon and Newton. Both men, he noted, were on edge. As they had left the Reagan farm earlier in the day, Newton had remarked,

"I don't like this idea of killin' blacks for fun, Mister Mullins. They ain't dun us no harm."

"We do what we are getting paid for, Newton. Stop yer bloody complainin'," was the response from the leader.

Mullins halted his horse and drummed his fingers on the barrel of his rifle.

Jacky

"Now for some fun. Make sure your guns are ready to fire."

The men cracked nervous smiles at Mullins' nonchalance.

Their horses trotted along the rough trail, and they approached the plume of smoke.

"Remember, lads," said Mullins in a hushed tone, "these people are no fools. Be prepared for anything. We'll leave our horses here and go on foot."

They tethered their horses and inched their way forward, their senses overwhelmed by the scent of roasting meat. Mullins gestured for silence and crept further ahead.

*****

Jacky and a handful of warriors were returning from the morning's hunt when they heard the faint crack of a rifle shot echoing down the valley. They quickly broke into a loping gait and headed for the camp.

*****

When the three white men emerged from the scrub and entered the clearing, they were surprised at what they saw.

They were not greeted by murderous savages but a small camp with makeshift gunyahs and children playing at the feet of their mothers and the elders too old to join in the hunt. Tarni was immediately alerted to the danger, and she sped to Burra's gunyah to warn both him and Mona.

As she led them from the camp, she spied the old man Nullah sitting in the shade and fashioning a spear.

She called to him in an urgent voice,

"Grandfather, you must come with me."

She grabbed them by the arms and led them on a trail that led to the river, where she knew a spot where they would never be found. They squatted in silence and listened.

The three men moved into the centre of the camp now and were met with looks of bewilderment and fear. Scanlon fired the first shot. It hit an old woman in the chest, and she gave no sound as she dropped to the ground, one arm landing on the hot coals of the fire. Panic ensued. Mullins and Newton both began firing, and the bodies began to pile up around the camp. It was over in less than a few minutes. The only ones still alive were a couple of young girls and some babies, no more than a year or two old.

The men were panting and flushed with adrenaline. They took time to gather their breath and inspect the carnage. Babies were wailing, and the women were lying on the ground, beating their fists on their chests and shouting unintelligible threats to the white men.

"Didn't take long," puffed Mullins.

"Easy money."

But Scanlon was still very edgy.

"Where are the men, Mister Mullins? They are the ones we should be worried about. Anyone can kill women and old men, and children."

"Huh! It's simple, you fool. We come back tomorrow and find the rest and finish all the bastards off."

But Newton was not convinced.

"They are not idiots, Mister Mullins. They will not be here tomorrow."

"It doesn't matter," said Mullins.

"We go one step at a time. Now let's have some fun," he said as he leered at a young woman who was nursing a bullet wound to the shoulder.

"She's mine. You men can take your pick of what's left. And if you're a bit testy and nervy, Newton, you can have one of the old men."

Mullins grinned as he walked towards the woman, who cowered back in fear.

"I won't hurt ya," he said.

"Just play a little game with yer titties and yer breedin' hole."

He undid his belt and dropped his trousers, and threw himself on top of the helpless woman. She screamed as he forced her legs open.

The spear made no sound as it arced through the air. And Mullins made no sound as he died with the spear in his back. Newton and Scanlon turned to flee, but the spears kept coming until the three white men were dead.

The once vibrant camp lay in ruins. The air smelled of burning flesh and fear and death. Normally, at this time of day, the camp was filled with the sounds of nature. Of birds in the trees and the laughter of children. But now there was a cacophony of sounds. Crying toddlers, wailing women, and the frenzied barking of native dogs. The flimsy gunyahs had been ransacked and set alight, and the smouldering fires cast an ominous light on the lifeless bodies strewn around, with faces frozen with looks of terror and pain. Old men, who once held the stories of centuries past, lay slumped over, their bodies riddled with bullets. Women and children, who should have been safe in their camp, had been carelessly gunned down, their blood staining the earth a dull crimson.

The whole scene was simply a senseless act of violence and made no sense to the distraught warriors.

Jacky was desperate to locate Burra and Mona and Nullah, but most of all, he wanted to know if Tarni was safe.

He saw a small figure behind a gunyah, and he dashed across.

"Tarni!" he cried out, but his eagerness turned to despair. It was a young boy, trembling in the dirt, his eyes wide with terror.

"You are safe, boy," said Jacky in a calming voice.

He stood up and called "Taaaarniii! Buuuraaaa! Monaaaa! Nuullllllaaah!"

There was no answer. He squatted and felt the onset of

tears forming in the corners of his eyes.

The rest of the warriors began tending to the wounded and the children, after dragging the already bloating bodies into a central heap. They worked methodically and unemotionally. Death was something that happened. But this death, an unnatural and terrible death, was something that had to be avenged.

Jacky felt numbness spreading through his body. His world was shattered. His only thoughts were for Tarni.

*****

Tarni pulled at Burra's arm.

"No, Burra. Stay here. It is not a place for an old man like you. You don't want to get yourself killed."

"I am a warrior," he said as he pulled against her grip.

"Tarni is right, grandfather. You cannot help them. It is safer here."

Mona was more frightened now than at any time she had been chained up in Reagan's home. The three huddled in silence until the noises and howling had died down. Once again, Burra went to rise, and once again, Tarni restrained him.

"Not yet," she said.

"You two wait here while I go and see if the white men have gone."

She crept along the stony ground and in some places, she slithered on her stomach like a snake, oblivious to the cutting edges of dry twigs and burs which dug into her breasts and belly. She raised her head, aware of the absence of sound. Tarni peered over a bush and saw the regal figure of Jacky standing in the centre of the camp, surveying the carnage. Then she leapt to her feet and raced towards him. She took him by surprise as she fell into his arms.

"Tarni," he breathed a sigh of relief, "you are safe. Where are Burra and Mona, and Nullah?"

"I took them away when the white men came. To the one spot where I knew we would be safe. The spot where you and I joined our spirits."

He shielded her eyes from the hideous sights around them.

"This has to stop, Tarni."

"Who were those men?" she said as she pulled out of his grasp and spat at the bodies, which had already begun attracting flies.

"Just some losers, I had a run in with some time ago, Tarni. But I guess they must have been hired by Reagan."

*****

Chapter 25

"Papa," Charley called out, her voice carrying the urgency of a storm just about to burst.

"You'd better quit spending your time watching those two horses and spend more time looking after the men you hire."

Reagan emerged from the barn and let out a gasp. There were three lost and sorry-looking horses wandering around the yard, and each horse had a bloodied body draped over the saddle. Reagan took in the scene with a single glance, his jaw tightening as he recognised the lifeless form of Mullins. The spear in his back was unmistakable, the same craftsmanship as the one he had pulled out of Howarth.

"Fucking black bastards!" he cursed as he threw his hat to the ground.

"Get inside, Charley!" he ordered.

She hesitated; her eyes still fixed on the three bodies. But she knew better than to disobey her father, especially at a time like this. With a peculiar sadness in her heart, she turned and walked to the door of the house. Charley was beginning to sense that things were not looking so good for her father and his farm.

Reagan approached the horse cautiously, reaching out to stroke its neck and calm it down. He took a moment, sucked in a deep breath, and then he lifted the body down. It was heavier than he had anticipated, and he could not manage to take the weight. He dropped the body onto the dusty ground and pulled at the spear: it was embedded deep in Mullin's back, suggesting the strength and skill of the man who threw it.

"Kerrigan!" he shouted.

"Where the fuck are you?"

Kerrigan came from his hut, wiping sleep from his eyes, which immediately grew wide awake at what he saw.

"Fuckin' hell, Mister Reagan. When did this happen?"

"It doesn't matter when it happened. It matters as to *why* it happened, Kerrigan."

Kerrigan looked puzzled.

"But we *know* why, Mister Reagan. Surely you did not think the blacks would just lie down and surrender. We sure have mighty big trouble on our hands. And Mister Reagan, I do not really know if I want any part of what's about to go down."

"Just do not forget, Kerrigan, you work for me. And if *I* have a problem, mister, then *you* have an even bigger one."

Kerrigan understood the veiled threat.

"What about the bodies?"

"Call Bruce. He will know what to do with them."

*****

Reagan's farmhands moved quickly, following Kerrigan's orders as they prepared themselves for an expected retaliation. All the horses were taken to the barn, and the working dogs were unleashed, free to roam the perimeter of the house yard. Kerrigan sent two men to ride the distant hills and report on any movement, and then he went in search of Bruce.

"Hey, Bruce, your Papa has a job for you."

The gawky man looked up; a mud-caked piglet nestled in his arms. Kerrigan hated being around the man, with his weird ways and fondness for pigs. He recalled Charley telling him once that she had to take a piglet from his bed one night.

"Come on, boy. I haven't got all day."

But Bruce was reluctant to leave his beloved "friends." He loved the way they rooted around in the mud and rolled in their own shit. Just as the swine were oblivious to life outside their pen, so too was Bruce. He spent his whole day at the pig sties and had names for every hog. This was his world, and he hated being taken from it, except when it was time to eat. The pigs were the only ones who didn't judge him, didn't look at him with fear or pity in their eyes.

"Stop your gawking, boy, and put that creature down. Your Papa is waiting."

"Are we gunna feed the piggies, Mister Kelligan?"

Try as he might, Kerrigan could never get the fool to say his name correctly.

"Yes, Bruce. But not me. *You*! *You* are going to feed *your* pigs!"

Reagan had gone back inside the house. When it came to Bruce and his love of pigs, he was just the same as Kerrigan. And Kerrigan, having witnessed it before, vowed never to watch Bruce at work again. He also left and went to his hut.

Bruce took a step towards the horses. They were one thing the brute of a man was afraid of. He took two of the men down from the saddles and carried them like rag dolls to the pig pens. Their combined weight was nothing to the giant. He had been known to hoist a full-grown boar on each shoulder. He returned for the other, all the while singing a nonsense tune to himself. Bruce was happy. His pigs would soon be happy. Their squeals grew louder, eager with anticipation.

Then Bruce, with the same precision as he threw bags of meal to the hogs, threw one of the corpses into the pen. The hogs charged forward, a mixture of snouts and tusks, and the body was lost in a sea of ravenous swine, the mud churning as the hogs devoured what had been human, not even a day ago.

Bruce was aroused now, and taking care there was nobody to see him, he slipped off his overalls.

*****

Back at the camp, Jacky was using similar words to those uttered by Reagan.

"Burra, we have big trouble in front of us. Nobody is safe from Reagan. The tribe has almost been wiped out, and

Reagan won't stop there."

"We fight Jacky," said the old man defiantly.

"No! You and the remaining members of the tribe must go on one big walkabout. You must get out of the district altogether. You need to go South Burra. Go back to my country, to my land. You can camp by the river there. There is plenty of tucker there, Burra, and I don't mind if you kill one or two of my sheep to feed you all. You are these people's leader now, old man. You cannot let them down."

"What about you, Jacky?" asked Tarni.

"I will remain here. I have friends with guns. It is time we took the fight to Reagan. And I still need to find and free the other members of Burra's tribe."

"Jacky, why are you risking your life for our people?" asked Mara.

"Because they are *my* people, Mara."

He sucked in his stomach and then exhaled heavily.

"Time Burra. That is what you said to me. I will take my time. Reagan will be expecting an attack, but I will disappoint him. I will wait until he drops his guard. With the tribe gone from here, he will naturally assume there are no more blacks in the area."

"You are a very wise and brave man, Jacky," said Tarni.

*****

As dusk settled, Jacky saw the Andrews' farm in the distance. He was relieved; his body craved water after the long trek. He found Andrews tending to his pigs and laughed as the man gave a start when he greeted him.

"Hell, Jacky, do you think it is funny to creep up on a man?"

Jacky patted the man on the back.

"It's good to see you, too, Richard. Where's Mister Jennings and Wells?"

"They have gone to the far paddock to bring some steers into the yards. We are running short of meat, and I need to slaughter one."

He threw the last of the pig swill into the pigsty and wiped his hands on his trousers.

"Any good news, Jacky?"

Jacky hesitated, unsure where to begin. The enormity of what he had to disclose threatened to overwhelm him. He took a deep breath and steeled himself.

"There's been a massacre, Richard," he finally managed to say.

"Massacre? The blacks? Reagan?"

Andrew's words flew from his mouth.

"I am afraid so. It happened while I was out hunting with the other warriors."

Jacky went on to describe the incident as Richard Andrews gave his full attention. He spoke of the fear and the chaos and the senseless slaughter.

Andrews listened in silence, his face grim, the only sound now the *chirping* of crickets, soon to be drowned out by the *chhhirrring* of cicadas.

"I don't know what to say, Jacky. This is terrible."

He kicked at the ground in frustration.

"What happens now, Jacky?"

"I cannot stay here and be seen with you. It will only bring more danger to you. I am a blackfeller, Richard. I can live off the land. I will return and see the rest of the tribe off on their way south. Burra knows the way to my farm. The tribe will be safe there. Then I will give Reagan some time to think everything is over and spend some time going back to my roots."

He finished off with a laughing comment.

"I am rather enjoying being a blackfeller, Richard."

He pulled the last of the witchetty grubs he had stored in his pocket and dangled them over his mouth.

"Ugghhh! Jacky. How can you stomach those things?"

"I am a blackfeller, that's how," and he popped the grub into his mouth.

*****

The early morning light filtered through the curtains, casting the sun's rays on Jimmy Boy's face. He could hear the rattling of pots and pans coming from the kitchen and could smell the faint aroma of bacon cooking and coffee brewing. Ellie's voice, a comforting hum, reminded him of what went on in the household each day. God, he loved that woman!

He rolled onto his back with his eyes still closed and

thought back to the previous night. His sleep had been a troubled one, and he tried to push the unsettling thoughts from his mind, but he knew he had to speak with his daughter. With a heavy sigh, he swung his legs over the side of the bed. He realised he could not ignore the situation any longer. It was time to discover the truth about Martha's heart. Did it still hold a place for Jacky, the man she had married? Or had it been swept away to be replaced by rekindled feelings for Will?

Jimmy Boy walked to the kitchen, his bare feet feeling the chill of the polished floorboards. The smells of breakfast assailed him as he pushed open the door. Ellie looked up. She knew of the demons he had been wrestling with all night. They were the same demons that had been troubling her for days now. She nodded her head as she handed her husband a mug of coffee.

Then she looked out the window and said, "She's out there, Jimmy Boy."

He stepped outside to be greeted by a chilly breeze. Martha was wrapped in a shawl and was sitting on a garden bench, idly pulling petals from a flower. The sight of her filled him with a feeling of fatherly love, but it was almost overshadowed by a feeling of dread. She looked up with a guarded expression, then gave a cautious smile.

"Would you care for some company, Martha?" he asked, his voice trembling a little. Jimmy Boy was not a man who was good at intimate talks. He sat down beside her and sipped his coffee. And for a while, they shared the quiet of the morning.

It was Martha who spoke first.

"I know what you wish to discuss, Papa."

He looked her in the eyes and asked the question she had been waiting to hear.

"Are you becoming too close to Will?"

Jimmy Boy stared at his daughter. She was a beautiful young woman, and her beauty was even more pronounced with the sad smile she managed to offer him.

"Papa, I am so confused. Please try and understand me. Mama does not. She makes no attempt to understand my feelings. She just wants to chastise me."

"Unburden yourself, Martie. Tell me everything. I am a good listener. I think," he gave a small laugh.

"Papa, I married Jacky because I loved him, I thought.

But now……Now I think I was too young to know what a woman wants. It is not just a lack of passion. It is just a hollow feeling. It is as if I am trapped. Since Will has been here, I doubt myself even more."

She thought of her husband. Jacky was the complete opposite of Will. Whereas Will was spontaneous and given to adventure and frivolity, Jacky had a predictability that was like a cage. Martha did not know what to do. Leaving Jacky would be like betraying him, and everything she believed in, but in staying, she could see a slow and agonising future.

"I do not know if I am in love with Will, Papa. It is just that he makes me feel alive."

Jimmy Boy's heart was heavy. He hated seeing his daughter this way.

"I am afraid I cannot help you, Martie. This is one of those decisions you must make. Let us just hope it is the right one."

Martha leaned across into her father's chest.

"I love you. Papa. You are the kindest and best father anyone could ever wish for."

Jacky

*****

Jacky stood on the perimeter of the camp, watching as the last of the fires petered out and died, the embers' final glow dancing on the faces of those about to make the long journey south. He watched as they packed their meagre belongings into *dillybags*, the children chattering and playing, unaware of the long trek in front of them.

Burra approached him, his eyes a milky white.

"Jacky," he said, "Stay safe. We will meet again, where the fish swim in schools and the kangaroos roam in numbers."

"Stay safe, Burra," replied Jacky, but his eyes and thoughts were on Tarni.

The tribe moved off, their bare feet padding in the soft earth. Then Tarni left her place in the line and dashed across to Jacky. She grabbed his arm and pleaded,

"Jacky, I want to stay with you. I know this land better than you, and I am good with a spear."

"You? Good with a spear? Tarni, the other day, you could not hit a stump from ten feet away."

"Please, Jacky," she implored him.

"My mind is made up. There are too many dangers here, Tarni. We will be together again. Now go!"

With tears in her eyes, she rejoined the group. Jacky's heart ached, but he had a job to do.

*****

That night, Jacky lay on his back by the low fire he had kindled in his new campsite. It was a far better site than the spot where members of the Kamilaroi tribe had been murdered. It was more secluded and could only be reached by following a narrow cutting through a gorge. It had reminded him of the gorge country near Wicklow, a place where he had disposed of three bodies in what seemed like centuries ago.

A sudden noise alerted him to possible danger. He felt for his spear, and the smooth shaft eased his nerves. He slowly slipped his pistol from the kangaroo hide strap he had wrapped around his waist.

"Jacky, you're jumpy tonight."

He let go of the spear and sat upright.

"Tarni, what are you doing here?"

She laughed.

"So, the brave warrior thought I was of no use to him, huh? I have been tracking you all day. If I had any evil intentions, you would be dead by now."

Jacky had to acknowledge the fact that the girl was good. He had no idea he was being followed.

"I cannot shake the feeling of danger, Tarni. Every twig that snaps or creature that moves feels like a ghost, a spirit from the *Dreamtime.*"

Tarni stepped into the dull light of the fire.

"They're just bad memories, Jacky," she said as she placed an arm on his shoulder.

"The past cannot harm you."

"I know that, Tarni, but I can still see the faces and hear the screams and the sounds of gunfire."

"We just must look ahead, Jacky. We cannot change what has happened."

She sat down beside him, and he put his arm around her slender waist.

"I am glad you found me, Tarni."

He looked into her eyes and found comfort and

urgency. He knew he had to protect this girl from the horrors she had seen. She had experienced a nightmare that would haunt both their dreams for a lifetime.

The warmth of her body was a comfort from the cold, hard ground beneath them. Tarni leaned into Jacky, and he could feel the rising and falling of her chest and smell her sweet womanly scent.

"Jacky," she whispered, "What will we do? What will become of us?"

Jacky sucked in a deep breath.

"We are safe here, Tarni. For now."

The urge to hold her was overwhelming, a primal need to take her. She could feel his urgency, and she lay on her back. Despite the horrors she had witnessed, she felt safe with the black man. She placed a trembling hand on his cheek and rubbed his stubble, and the contact between them stirred them both. She closed her eyes, and Jacky positioned himself on top of her. She whimpered, and they gave themselves to the heat of the night.

*****

Reagan was a troubled man.

"I don't like it, Charley," he said to his daughter as he pulled on his cigar.

"Then why do you smoke them?" she asked with her childish humour.

"You know damned well what I am talking about girl. The blacks haven't been sighted in days."

"Perhaps they have left the district," she responded, almost hoping that wasn't the case. She felt her thoughts drifting towards the black man and the times they had spent together. She wanted to see Jacky again, but she knew it was dangerous. Her father would not hesitate to horse whip her if he knew she had given herself to a black man.

"It's as if they have vanished into thin air. I tell you, girl, something is brewing."

"You worry too much, Papa. I think they have long gone from here."

"I am starting to worry, Charley. There have been too many deaths. Both blacks and whites. And I cannot afford the police to come snooping about."

"But you have nothing to fear from Sergeant Tanner, Papa. He is not backward in taking his money each time it is offered."

"The thing is, Charley, I don't trust Tanner. He is a coward and like a mongrel dog, he's liable to turn and bite the hand that feeds him."

Charley stood and walked behind her father. She placed her hands on his neck and massaged his weary muscles.

"Papa. Do you think Jacky is behind everything that is going on?"

"I don't *think*, Charley. I *know*!"

He lapsed into a bout of coughing and stubbed his cigar out.

"I told you, Papa, those things will kill you before the blacks do."

Then, for no known reason, a black and macabre thought crossed her mind. She shivered as she thought of it.

"What if Jacky killed my father? Then there would be just me. And a very prosperous farm. And then I could have any man when and where I wanted."

She just as quickly banished the thought to the back of her mind.

*****

Chapter 26

Jimmy Boy had a hint of excitement about him as he saddled his horse. But while doing so, he thought of Mister Wells and Jennings. Both would have pushed each other over to do this job. He smiled at the thought of the two men, like competitors in a race, each one determined to come out on top.

He rode off to the old camp. The journey to where he had the last of the gold stashed was unsettling. He had too many recollections, but he smiled at the thought of the gold and the money convincing Kerrigan to turn traitor.

Jimmy Boy couldn't help the feeling he was being watched, but he knew it was just nerves—a hangover from his past. Still, every creak of a branch and the rustle of leaves sent a shiver down his spine.

The earth was soft, and he soon had the stash uncovered. He took two decent-sized nuggets and shoved them into his pocket, and then rested in the shade. He looked around him with an air of nostalgia. He could see Jarrah tending the fire and hear his melodic laughter. He cast the happy memories aside and mounted his horse.

The ride back to Wicklow was a more comfortable one.

The two gold nuggets in his pocket gave Jimmy Boy a glimpse of the future.

*****

Jimmy Boy lay awake, the weight of his decision pressing into his chest. He knew he had to return to the Andrews' farm and check on what had been happening.

Was Jacky still safe? Was Andrews' farm still under threat?

And then there were Wells and Jennings to consider.

Ellie stirred beside him. The sun was just poking its morning smile in the window.

"Jimmy Boy, what time is it?"

"It's still early, Ellie," he said as he climbed from the bed and pulled his trousers on. He looked down at his wife.

"Ellie, there is something I must tell you. I need to go back to the Andrews' farm tomorrow."

"Tomorrow?" she said drowsily, her eyes still heavy with sleep.

"I must."

She propped herself up on an elbow.

"It has been wonderful having you home, Jimmy Boy. Can't you stay a little longer?"

He took a deep breath.

"I really must go, Ellie. If I don't get this money to Kerrigan soon, it may be too late, and I will have the deaths of many on my conscience. And Ellie, I don't want anything to happen to Jacky or Mister Wells and Jennings."

Her eyes fluttered open.

"But what if something happens to you?"

He squeezed her hand.

"Nothing will happen to me. I have it all planned."

"What plan?"

"I will slip into Milburra without any fanfare. Nobody knows me there. I will wear a suit and just pass as an ordinary traveller in town for business. Then I will wait for a man by the name of Kerrigan to come to town and offer him the money I will take with me."

"What money? What are you talking about?"

"Ellie, that is part of the reason I came home. I couldn't be seen in Milburra just yet. I sent a telegram to the bank in Newcastle and drew a money order on my stocks of gold. And yesterday I went to the old camp and dug up the gold and pocketed two nuggets. I will use the money to bribe Kerrigan into testifying against Reagan, the man who is holding Burra's family captive."

Ellie nodded her acceptance.

"Just promise me, Jimmy Boy, that you will come home to me."

"I promise. And Ellie, if there are any problems, then send a telegram to the Milburra Post Office. I will check in there every few days."

*****

Jimmy Boy sat drinking his nightly tipple of brandy. The room was unusually quiet, except for the soft crooning of Meg as she put young Robbie to sleep on her lap. Both Angela and Eleanor were reading, while Martha was busying herself with her needlepoint. She kept casting surreptitious glances at her father. She needed to speak with him alone. Finally, when the others gave no signs of retiring for the night, her frustration overcame her.

"Papa, can we have a quiet talk?"

She nodded her head towards the study. The others pretended not to notice as father and daughter left the room, but as soon as they had gone, Angela and Eleanor came together for a worried conference.

*****

"You have me in a difficult spot, Martie," said Jimmy Boy as he scratched at a non-existent itch on his head.

"What do you mean, Papa?" asked his daughter, the pain of her request etched on her face.

"You know I would do anything for you, Martie, but to travel to Sydney alone is far too dangerous. You would need someone with you."

Martha nodded, understanding his words. She knew it was not merely about the journey, but the outcome of the whole proposal.

"Papa, I am not a child anymore. I can take care of myself."

"You are right. You're not. But things are different out

there. Sydney is not like Ramsay, Martie. It's a bigger and even worse version of Newcastle."

"I found Newcastle quite safe, Papa. Please?" she implored him.

"You know how to twist a man's arm, Martie. I will give you my permission on one proviso."

"Anything, Papa," she answered, her excitement building.

"You must take Bindi along with you."

Martha felt her excitement dissipate. She loved Bindi, but she seemed to be always there, a tangible presence in their lives. She was always there… watching… listening. She had never travelled any further than Ramsay and a handful of times to the outskirts of Newcastle, and the thought of her tagging along to Sydney seemed inconvenient and troublesome at best.

"But why Bindi, Papa? Why not Meg?"

"You know Meg cannot leave her child, Martha. You need to reason, my dear child. You have the Emporium to think of. And Meg will no doubt have to take charge of it while you are gone. It is either Bindi accompanies you, or you will not receive my permission to leave."

Martha screwed her face up.

"Mrs Wells is quite capable of tending my business. I do not want to put any extra burden on Meg. She has her son to think of."

"I stand firm, Martha. It is either Bindi, or there will be no trip to Sydney."

"Then I will take Bindi with me."

She flounced from the room, her spirits buoyed at the prospect of freedom and the chance to see Will again.

*****

"Ellie," he looked up as she came into the room, concern lining her face.

"What's wrong?" Jimmy Boy asked.

He did not realise she had overheard the conversation with Martha, and it had made her visibly upset.

"Jimmy Boy, I cannot believe you would agree to this. It is just not safe. And Bindi, of all people, to accompany our daughter! You are going crazy, Jimmy Boy."

"Ellie, Martha is a grown woman, and a smart one at that. A trip to Sydney is an opportunity for her to grow and explore her independence."

"But you know the reason why she is going, don't you?"

"Yes. And I think I am right in letting her go. She is in a troubled state, Ellie, and this trip will go a long way to helping her make some very difficult decisions. We can prevent her from going, but we cannot prevent her from following her heart. And Bindi is part of our family. She will ensure she is safe."

"We both know that Bindi will be no help in the bustle of the city. Why, she even gets rather nervous when she goes into Ramsay if it is a particularly busy day."

"She is far wiser than we can imagine, Ellie. At any rate, I have made my decision. I need to sleep so as I can get an early start tomorrow."

"Fine, Jimmy Boy. I will sleep in the guest room. Good night."

Her sleep would be a troubled one—troubled with both tears and fears.

Jacky

*****

"Finally," Jimmy Boy said as the coach lurched to a stop. It was late in the afternoon, and it had been an agonising three-day journey by coach.

"Much better than riding though," he had thought as the coach lumbered over the well-worn track.

Dust swirled around his well-polished boots as he stepped down from the coach, adjusting his wide-brimmed hat to block out the last of the sun. He wore a well-tailored suit which he had borrowed from Martha's Emporium… a well-crafted façade that exuded respectability and success. Beneath his garments, however, his heart was filled with apprehension. He just hoped he looked like the businessman he was trying to appear.

He had decided that it was much too late to hire a horse and ride to the Andrews farm. He would check into a hotel for the night.

He walked into the brightly lit foyer and smelled the aromas of home cooking and tobacco and stale beer. He was followed in by two others who had been on the coach with him, a friendly couple, a husband and wife.

"It has been a pleasure travelling with you folks," said Jimmy Boy in his usual polite manner.

"Thank you, Mister Wang. I hope your business enterprise takes off," replied the man.

Jimmy Boy approached the front desk where a middle-aged woman greeted him.

"Good evening, sir. May I be of assistance?"

"I would like a room for the night, please."

She reached behind her for a key and handed it over.

"Sign here, please," she said as she pushed a tattered register towards him. She watched his hand move deftly over the paper and scrutinised his signature.

"You have beautiful handwriting, Mister Wang."

"Thank you. I must thank my teacher for that."

"You are in Room 6. You cannot miss it. It's up the stairs and first on the right."

"Thank you, ma'am."

"The name is Myrtle, Mister Wang. Myrtle Peterson."

As he turned towards the stairs, the woman called after

him.

"Mister Wang, your face is familiar. Have I seen you before?"

Jimmy felt his blood turn cold. Had the woman seen him when he had boarded the coach several days before?

He composed himself and said softly,

"I think not, Mrs Peterson. Maybe it was another Chinaman you are mistaking me for. People say we all look alike anyway."

*****

Once settled, he unpacked only his necessities, one of them being a pistol carefully hidden under his clothes.

Then, with the night closing in, he ventured out. He wanted to be seen. Already, to while away the hours on the coach, he had fabricated his story. He was Jimmy Wang. He thought it was pointless to use anything other than his real name for fear of slipping up, and he had come to Milburra to evaluate the prospects of opening a Farmer's Co-operative.

He assumed an air of nonchalance as he stepped through the doors. After all, it was crucial to be seen as a man of means. He allowed himself the pleasure of walking the length of the street, and when he returned, he decided on a drink before having an early night.

The bar room was pulsing with energy—card games, laughter, shouting, and cursing. He found a quiet spot at the end of the bar and ordered a whisky. As he sipped on his drink, he listened to the gossip… anything he overheard could be very beneficial to what they were about to do. He kept his ears open for names. He wanted to hear the name of Kerrigan.

But tonight, he was out of luck. There were Sanders, Jenson, Millers, Hopes, Penders, Bells, and even a smattering of foreign names like Rosenbaum and Brandolini. As the evening wore on, he engaged with the locals and recounted fictitious tales of his business dealings in other towns. Each laugh and nod from his companions signalled that his ruse was working.

When he felt it appropriate, Jimmy Boy slipped out of the bar and went upstairs to his room. He stripped naked and climbed under a freshly laundered sheet with his pistol under the pillow.

*****

"Good morning," said Jimmy Boy to the deliveryman, a burly man with a bushy grey beard that matched his tousled hair.

The man simply nodded and continued polishing a well-worn saddle.

"I need a horse," said Jimmy Boy, his voice steady and friendly.

"Just for the day. I want to ride around the area and check on the farms."

"And why would you be doing that?" asked the man, suspicion lacing his tone.

"Can be dangerous ridin' around here checkin' on people's farms."

In the corner of his mind, he thought of Harry Reagan.

"Better be careful which farms you check out, mister."

"I mean nobody any harm. I have travelled here to assess the viability of establishing a Farmers' Co-operative if the region is suitable. It would be a boon for the town. And for me, of course," he added with a grin.

The stableman turned away.

"That there is a fine horse, mister."

He nodded to a roan mare grazing on a nosebag of chaff.

"She's a good ride, sure-footed and gentle."

"That sounds good to me. As you can see by my attire, I am not very familiar with riding."

The man looked him up and down.

"Yeah, mighty fancy outfit fer ridin'. Still, the horse won't let you down. And if you get lost, it will even bring you back to town on sundown. It knows where its tucker is."

Jimmy Boy's aim, however, was not to assess the area but to ride to the Andrews farm and check on the welfare of the men.

*****

After an hour's ride, Jimmy Boy reined in at the Andrews' home. There appeared to be nobody about. Then a voice came from the washing line at the back of the house.

"Jimmy, is that you?"

"Rachel!" he exclaimed.

"It is wonderful to see you. But where is everybody?"

"They are due back soon, Jimmy. They have gone to ride the boundary fence. Leastways, that is what Richard said. But I think the real reason is that he wants to see if any of Reagan's men are about."

"Has there been more trouble, Rachel?"

"I will let the men explain when they return, Jimmy. Come in and take a load off your feet and have a cool drink."

"Sounds good, Rachel."

He cast an eye over the house paddock and followed the woman.

*****

"That's all there is to tell, Jimmy. The tribe was murdered in cold blood."

"Where's Jacky now, Richard?"

"He's gone bush, Jimmy," said Andrews in a low voice, as if the walls had ears.

"He said he would stay in the bush and spy on Reagan and give the man time to start thinking he has left the area."

Jimmy Boy nodded, but he had his doubts.

He knew Jacky well and knew the black man's intentions were often shrouded in secrecy, and this worried the Chinaman. Reagan was too powerful and too dangerous to meddle with lightly.

"Where is the tribe camped?"

"There is no tribe, Jimmy. The remainder has gone south to Jacky's country. To his property. Shanghai, I think."

"You mean to tell me that Jacky is alone out there?"

He waved his arms and pointed to the seemingly endless scrub in the distance.

"Jacky appears a very capable man, Jimmy. He knows what he is doing."

"Capable, yes. But sometimes he can be too headstrong."

"If anyone can get us out of this mess, I am sure it is him."

"The good thing is, Richard, I have the money with me to buy off Kerrigan. It is just a waiting game now. I will continue staying in Milburra and keep up the pretence of being an investor until I can get near Kerrigan."

"You think the townsfolk will buy your story, Jimmy?"

"They already have," he grinned cheekily.

*****

"It's probably safer in the daytime," whispered Jacky.

"Reagan would not expect that. He would be more worried about a nighttime raid. We will just creep in a little further and see if we can find the shed where Burra's tribe is kept."

They moved with practised stealth, using anything they came across as cover. As they neared the barn, a banging sound caught Tarni's attention. A loose sheet of iron was being buffeted by the breeze which had sprung up, revealing a dark space within.

"There," she whispered.

"We'll take a look in that shed."

The opening was barely large enough, but they managed to climb through. As their eyes adjusted to the dim light, their lungs were filled with dust and the scent of old wood.

"Look!" exhaled Tarni, pointing to the darkest corner.

Quietly they moved across the room, the floorboards creaking beneath their feet.

"It's just old blankets," said Jacky.

But Tarni's instincts were sharp.

"No, they're not just blankets. There's something here."

She picked up a small white object and brushed the dirt away from it.

"It's a bone," she gasped.

"Jacky, what if…?"

He took the bone from her and studied it carefully.

"No, it is not a human bone, Tarni. This is a sheep's bone. But the evidence is here. Someone was kept here and slept and ate here."

"Burra's people?"

"Maybe. I cannot say for sure. But it is obvious that nobody has been in here for a while. Come on, let's get out of here and try the next shed."

The next shed they tried was larger and just as dimly lit and filled with an array of objects—barrels, ropes, and farming tools. Jacky moved towards a barrel, but upon opening the lid, he found it empty, while Tarni pulled aside cobwebs to uncover a large chest.

"There's nothing here but junk, Tarni."

"Wait while I check this box out, Jacky," she said as she raised the lid.

But again, the chest contained nothing but dust and the mummified remains of a large rat.

"Let's not give up yet. There is one last shed to check, Tarni. Are you up to it?"

She nodded.

"I am ready."

"Keep low to the ground as we cross the open area," said Jacky, and he sprinted across the yard and flung himself through the door.

Once inside, they were surprised at what they saw. Unlike the previous sheds, this one spoke of life. Discarded clothing and food platters were strewn across the floor, and in the centre of the shed there was a large bucket with fresh water. Around the walls there were makeshift beds constructed of straw and covered with grimy blankets.

"We are not alone, Jacky. Look!"

They moved deeper into the shed, and crouched in the corner, partly obscured by shadows, a group of people huddled together. They were the people Jacky had been searching for.

In the little Wiradjuri he had learned from Burra, Jacky said,

"Do not be afraid. We are here to help you."

"Who are you?" An old woman pushed herself forward.

Jacky uttered one word, which set the group to low wails.

"Burra," he said.

The old woman crawled across and grabbed Jacky's ankle.

"My Burra?" she said with tears forming.

"Your Burra," he replied, and then he turned to Tarni.

"There are no men here, Tarni. Only children and old women. The men must be out working for Reagan. We cannot take them today, but now we know where they are, we can come back at night and take them all away from this rat-hole."

He turned back to the bedraggled group and thumped his chest and said,

"I am Jacky."

Some of the women repeated the words, pointing at him.

"I am Jacky. I am Jacky."

The black man spent the next five minutes explaining things to the old woman and then informed Tarni.

"We must be out of here. Every minute we are here, the more risk we are taking with our own lives."

"But we must take these people," protested Tarni.

"Tarni, we cannot. Think about it. If we take them now, we will never be able to free the men. Reagan will have the rest of the people guarded so well that we won't get near them. Besides, if we take this lot, Reagan will know I am still around the district. And as sure as hell, he will have a whole bunch of his men scouring the countryside for me.”

She looked at him, obvious admiration creasing her face into a smile.

“You are one smart blackfeller, Jacky.”

“I know,” he said with a cheeky grin.

“C’mon, let’s go.”

*****

Chapter 27

Jimmy Boy decided to try his luck. It was a Friday night, and he knew that farmhands invariably let their hair down at the end of a back-breaking week. He swirled his drink around, the amber liquid catching the light from the lanterns, and he took the occasional sip. The air reeked of tobacco smoke, something Jimmy Boy had never quite become accustomed to. He pretended to take a further sip of his drink. The last thing he wanted was to find himself drunk in a room full of strangers.

Conversation around him was a muted buzz, a mixture of laughter and complaints about the week's work. He nodded along, trying to appear interested, while his ears were tuned for the name Kerrigan to be uttered.

He checked the clock above the unlit fireplace. It was getting late, and there was no mention of the name Kerrigan by any of the drinkers. Just as Jimmy Boy was about to leave and go to his room, the doors opened, and in walked a man who could be just the person Jimmy Boy was waiting for. The conversation suddenly went quiet, and he sensed then that it was Kerrigan.

No one else could command such fear. The man's eyes centered on Jimmy Boy for a fraction of a second, but then they went back to the barman.

"What'll it be, Mister Kerrigan?"

"The usual, Jake," he rasped.

Jimmy Boy took a deep breath, trying to look at ease, but his heart was racing. From what he had learned from other drinkers in the bar, Kerrigan was a shrewd man and not to be trifled with. He had to play it cool.

The barman slammed a shot of whisky in front of the man and said,

"Just like you have it, Mister Kerrigan. A warm glass as usual."

Kerrigan quaffed the drink and pushed his glass across.

"Another."

Jimmy Boy swirled his drink around, the ice clinking against the glass. He decided it was now.

"I like mine with ice," he said, trying to initiate discussion.

"You talking to me, mister?"

"I am looking at you, aren't I?" replied Jimmy Boy, trying to keep his voice steady.

He had been waiting for this moment with Kerrigan, and now was not the time to blow it.

Kerrigan sucked on his cigarette.

"They don't work unless they're alight," said Jimmy Boy.

"Mister, what do you want? You're not just another smartarse Chinaman, are you?"

Jimmy Boy leaned into the man's ear.

"You are Mister Kerrigan, right? I need to talk with you. I have something important to discuss."

The drinkers had been listening but now relaxed. They assumed the Chinaman was simply checking out Mister Reagan's man to see if he would come on board with the Farm Co-operative proposal he had been spruiking.

Kerrigan tightened his grip on his glass.

"I don't talk with strangers."

Jimmy Boy extended his hand and politely said,

"Jimmy Wang. Now I'm not a stranger, Mister Kerrigan."

Kerrigan ignored the hand he was offered.

"Over there."

He nodded towards a table in the corner.

The two men sat down. Jimmy Boy continued to swirl the ice in his drink.

"That habit is getting a bit annoying, mister. You said you wanted to talk. I have better things to do than sit around and watch a man play with his drink."

Jimmy Boy smiled and swirled the ice again. The frustration was beginning to show on Kerrigan's face.

"I'm fucking warning you, mister. Speak your piece or leave."

It was now or never, Jimmy Boy decided.

"Are you a rich man, Mister Kerrigan?" Jimmy Boy asked, his voice as smooth as silk.

Kerrigan was momentarily stunned.

"What the fuck you on about? What's my financial

situation got to do with you?"

He kept his voice low, but it was edged with irritation and carried the trace of suspicion.

"It has everything to do with me. I have a proposal for you."

Jimmy Boy leaned forward, the confident grin on his face hiding the game he was playing.

"What do you have in mind?" Kerrigan asked cautiously, still wary but wondering at the Chinaman's audacity.

"Well, let's just say that if you're already a rich man, then you can leave now and forget you ever talked with me. But if you're a man who could do with some easy money, then feel free to stay and hear me out."

"You've got me taking your bait, mister. And just how can a man come by some easy money?"

Jimmy Boy leaned across the table and whispered,

"How much money would you need to renounce your claim that my friend Jacky killed Reagan's man?"

"The black bastard is your mate? That's one hell of a

strange combination. A Chinaman and a blackfeller."

"Our relationship has no bearing on my offer. I want you to say that Jacky was not the man who murdered your mate."

"Howarth?"

Kerrigan pushed back his chair and, in a loud voice, said,

"And why would I do that?"

Jimmy Boy felt a tremor run through his body. This was going to be harder than he thought. He looked at the drinkers in the bar and gave them a friendly smile. Anything that would not arouse their suspicions.

"Keep your voice down, Mister Kerrigan. Please. What I'm saying is for our ears only."

Kerrigan was a stubborn man. Years of servitude under the iron rule of Reagan had made him careful and watchful. He rubbed the back of his neck, feeling the pulsing dread of betrayal and the consequences simmering below the surface. If he angered Reagan, it would be dire for him, yet the prospect of easy money made him consider the proposal in depth.

"Listen," said Jimmy Boy quietly, "I can make this easy for you. All you have to say to the local police is that Jacky was not the murderer."

"And what's in it for me?"

"Fifty thousand pounds, Mister Kerrigan. Enough to get you out of the country and start a new life."

"Fifty thousand pounds! Mister, you ain't got that kind of money."

Jimmy Boy reached deep into his pocket and pulled out a letter from Loomes. He waved it under Kerrigan's nose.

"A piece of paper ain't worth horseshit, mister."

"Oh, I beg to differ. This is a letter entitling the bearer to withdraw fifty thousand pounds from my bank account."

Kerrigan let out a low whistle and leaned forward, his face almost coming to rest on the man opposite him.

"Show me that bit of paper."

Jimmy Boy passed the letter across the table, and Kerrigan made a point of studying it. He had only the basic reading skills, but the letterhead and the figures of fifty thousand were enough to convince him that the Chinaman was on the level.

"But questions will be asked, mister. People will want to know why I had a sudden change of mind."

"We can think of something, Mister Kerrigan."

Jimmy Boy decided on another tactic.

"Do you care for Reagan's daughter at all?"

"Of course. Who would not? She is one beautiful young girl."

"I hear tell that her and Jacky are very close. You can say you were jealous of Jacky and made up the whole story of him killing Howarth."

"Do you think that will work?"

"Of course, if you stick to your story. Then you say you had a racking pain of conscience and decided to come clean. You could not bear to see an innocent man hung."

Kerrigan went silent. Jimmy Boy could see the man was troubled.

"What you're asking… it's not that simple," Kerrigan replied, his eyes darting around the barroom, ensuring there were no interested listeners.

"Maybe this will help you make up your mind."

With a calculated slowness, Jimmy Boy reached into his pocket and pulled out a handkerchief and placed it on the table.

"Go ahead. Unwrap it, but let nobody see."

Jimmy Boy felt in his other pocket. He hoped he would not have to rely on the remaining nugget.

Kerrigan looked around suspiciously and placed his huge hand over the handkerchief.

"Doesn't feel like money to me."

"It's something better than money, Mister Kerrigan. I told you. Take a look."

Kerrigan opened the handkerchief, and his face broke into a masked smile.

"Is that what I think it is?"

"It's real, Mister Kerrigan. That bit of gold and the money I will pay you could change your life. No more dirt scraping, labor, and dirty work, and facing Reagan's wrath every day."

Kerrigan's eyes widened momentarily, but then his

apprehension returned.

"And if Reagan learns of this? You think he will let me live?"

Jimmy Boy shrugged, his indifference masking his desperation.

"Reagan does not need to know. Not at first. You go to the Sergeant and tell him the truth, then you leave town. You have enough to set yourself up for life."

"Kerrigan is a powerful man, Mister. If I betrayed him, he would not rest until he scoured the whole country to find me and kill me."

"Haven't you ever wanted to see America, Mister Kerrigan? Or England or Canada?"

The weight of the gold nugget weighed heavily between them: a temptation and a betrayal.

Kerrigan's mind raced, and he conjured up an image of the confrontation between him and Reagan.

"If I do this, I seal my fate. There is no turning back."

"If you help Jacky, Kerrigan, you will help yourself. You can't let fear rule your life. I will give you the night to

Jacky

think it over, and we will meet here again tomorrow night."

*****

Chapter 28

The cool morning air bit at Eleanor's cheeks as she watched Martha and Bindi prepare to board the stage. Martha appeared quite calm, but Bindi bustled with nervous energy, her simple attire of a cotton shift contrasting starkly with Martha's fine long dress and woolen shawl.

Both Ellie's and Angela's hearts ached… Angela's with pride and Ellie's with apprehension. The two older women had spent the night, along with Bindi and Mia, preparing their bags with supplies… dried fruit, water, biscuits, and a small Bible— all the things meant to ease their journey.

But it was not the physical journey that worried Ellie. It was the unknown dangers that lurked in the bustling streets of Sydney. A place of both opportunity and peril, especially for a young girl and her Aboriginal companion.

Ellie tightened her shawl and hugged her daughter.

"Be careful," she said, her words choking in her throat.

"Look out for each other."

The coach awaited, and the driver was getting restless.

"Shoulda said yer goodbyes hours ago, ladies. I have a schedule to meet."

He hefted the women's bags onto the coach and then helped them up.

"My first time," said Bindi excitedly.

Martha leaned out the window and blew a kiss to her mother and grandmother as the coachman whipped his horses into motion. Ellie watched the coach until it disappeared on the long road to the Newcastle dockyards, a lone tear rolling down her cheek.

It was then that the reality of her daughter's departure settled upon her. She knew little of Sydney beyond the vague descriptions of travelers. Some spoke of a vibrant place, full of opportunity and promise, while others were contradictory and painted a grim picture of disease, poverty, and prejudice. She worried about Bindi, and she knew the little Aboriginal woman's vulnerability would be tested.

*****

The coach lumbered into Newcastle just as evening was closing in. Bindi had been awake for the entire two-day trip, but Martha had managed to doze on and off, lulled by the rocking of the stagecoach and the almost melancholy rumbling of the wheels.

The coachman poked his head through the window and announced to the passengers,

"Newcastle folks. A mighty big thanks for traveling with Wilkinson Coach Lines. I do believe that it is the end of the line for you, sir," he said, acknowledging the elderly gentleman who was just rousing from an afternoon nap.

"And you pair of fine young ladies, I have it in my logbook, are catching the steamer to Sydney tomorrow."

Martha yawned and stretched her arms.

"Are we anywhere near our hotel?" she asked, her eyes now wide open and taking in her surroundings.

"Most folk stay at the hotel just down the road. It's the closest one to our depot and only a ten-minute buggy ride to the wharves. I am not allowed to take the stage any further than this, but I can help you with your luggage if you want," he offered generously.

$$*****$$

After a solid night's rest, Martha and Bindi made their

way downstairs, struggling with their luggage. The hotel clerk was dozing behind his counter and jumped in alarm as the heavy suitcases bumped their way down the stairs. He jumped to his feet and stroked his rather large handlebar moustache.

"I am dreadfully sorry, ladies. You should have asked for someone to come up to your room and fetch your luggage."

"We have managed, thank you," said Martha.

The clerk made a grand gesture of flourishing his pocket watch and said,

"I have done as you asked last night and have arranged for your buggy to be here shortly. It will take you to the docks."

Newcastle harbour was a hive of activity, a chaotic space filled with cranes, shouting dockworkers, and the constant thumping and banging of cargo being loaded and unloaded. The air hung thick with the smell of salt, smoke, and the scent of spices… a potent cocktail from around the world crammed into a single space.

People of all nationalities and occupations thronged the docks: sailors with sun-weathered faces and tattooed arms, merchants haggling over prices, and families huddled together, their belongings piled beside them.

Bindi had never witnessed such a spectacle. She had seen the ocean, of course, but never such activity as she was witnessing now. The immense ships and fishing trawlers held her in awe. She had never seen a sailboat so big. She was used to the small wooden dugouts her people had used for centuries.

Martha, sensing Bindi's mood, grabbed her hand and squeezed it reassuringly, while Bindi maintained a firm and nervous grip on the side of the buggy.

"It's quite something, Bindi, isn't it?" asked Martha, her own breath caught by the sheer energy of the place.

The buggy finally lurched to a stop at the edge of the docks, the jarring halt throwing them forward.

Bindi yelled at the driver,

"Hell, mister! Where did you learn to drive one of these?"

The Bingera, the ship that was to carry them to Sydney, lay at anchor in front of them. It was far larger than both had ever imagined, and it promised a journey into an unknown world.

They walked nervously towards the gangplank, the buggy driver lugging the two crammed suitcases. Then they heard a voice shouting above the noises around them.

"Ahoy there! You must be Miss Martha Wang. I was told to be on the lookout for a young woman with a darky servant in tow."

"An Aboriginal friend is a more acceptable term," chastised Martha.

He stepped nimbly down the wooden gangplank and extended a hand.

"Aboriginal friend it is then. I'm Frost, the first mate."

"Ain't no mate of mine, mister," Bindi mumbled.

"Welcome aboard," he said cheerily, and with a practised ease, he helped them aboard.

Martha, noticing the wonder and trepidation lining Bindi's face, said,

"Ready for an adventure?"

*****

Martha and Bindi spent the day on the ship, having

been told by Frost that there were various items of freight to be carried and most of it would not be loaded until mid-afternoon.

"We will haul anchor at eight p.m.," he had said to them, "and if the seas are favorable, we will dock in Sydney roughly twelve hours later. Just in time for your first breakfast in Sydney."

As the Bingera pulled away from the bustling port, leaving the chaos of Newcastle behind, Martha felt a sense of exhilaration wash over her. This was a journey into the unknown, a chance to explore a whole new city, and at the same time, a chance to explore her own heart.

The rhythmic churning of the propeller, the gentle rocking of the vessel, and the warmth of Bindi's hand in hers created a sense of profound peace. As Newcastle receded, becoming a distant smudge on the horizon, an unknown fate stretched out before them like the endless ocean itself.

*****

The Bingera, a sturdy if somewhat aged ship, sliced through the waters of the Pacific Ocean. The voyage, as promised, proved to be uneventful. They shared a small cabin and tried to get some sleep, comforted by the creaking of the timbers and the endless cries of the crew. The cabin smelled of salt and old rope, but the bunk that Martha lay on was comfortable and clean. She soon drifted off into a deep sleep. Bindi, however, found no such peace. She lay on the narrow bunk, her small body tossed and turned by the gentle rocking of the boat, a restless spirit confined to a small cabin.

The next morning, as the sun rose, painting the sky in hues of orange and faint pinks, they were wakened by a cry.

"Land ho!"

Bindi, startled by the interruption to her short sleep, sat upright, her eyes wide with a mixture of fear and wonder.

"I think we are there," she said to a drowsy Martha.

The rolling of the ship seemed to cease and drew out a feeling of excitement from the two travelers. The uneventful voyage, so testing and even frightening for Bindi, had come to an end. The two women made their way on unsteady legs up to the deck. The restless expanse of water from the day before was now replaced by the distinct line of the coast.

"I think I see it, Miss Martie," yelled Bindi excitedly.

Martha squinted through the salty air, her heart racing. The distant silhouette of Sydney appeared as a mirage. As the Bingera edged closer, the outlines of the city became clearer.

"Look, there's the harbour," Bindi shouted again, bouncing on her feet.

Martha followed her gaze, eyes alight with awe. The harbour bustled with activity; ships docked alongside one another, men shouting orders and children scurrying between ships hawking fresh produce.

It was then that Bindi spied the solitary figure of a man standing, shading his eyes from the easterly glare of the sun.

"Miss Martie, I believe I can see Mister Will."

They grabbed at their suitcases and stepped down onto the solid wood of the dock. Will strode forward and greeted them warmly, his laughter ringing like music.

"Well, and what do we have here? Two of the prettiest women to ever set foot on the precious soil of Sydney."

Martha felt ill at ease, unlike Bindi, who was like a child on a Sunday outing.

"It is so nice of you to meet us, Will," said Martha

rather shyly as she extended her hand. He took it and held it for longer than was necessary.

"I wouldn't have missed your arrival for anything," said Will, pushing the hair from his eyes.

"Welcome to the big smoke."

"Sure is plenty of that," said Bindi as she sniffed the air.

Martha offered her right cheek, and Will gave her a light kiss.

"I have my own place now," he said excitedly.

"It's not as fancy as your home, Martie, but it suits me until I start earning some bigger money with my law career. But it has a reasonably sized kitchen for you to work your wonders in, Bindi, and there is a large bedroom where you both shall sleep."

"I don't judge a person on their home or what they have in terms of material possessions, Will. You should know me better than that."

Will hailed a coach, and the three of them piled into the cramped but cozy space with worn leather seats and windows adorned with faded blue curtains, which fluttered with every bump in the road. The city sprawled before them, revealing a variety of street life—children playing in the streets, dogs chasing each other, and street vendors selling their wares.

"You jis gotta tell me everything, Mister Will. What is Sydney like? Is there a magic garden? Are there black people here? Are there ghosts? Are there orphans?"

"Hush, Bindi," said Martha.

"Just enjoy the place. You will get to know Sydney soon enough. We are here for three weeks."

"It's all right, Martie. She is just curious."

He gave his attention to the little black woman.

"Bindi, it's much like Newcastle, only busier and bigger. There are gardens here, of course, but the only magic in them is their beauty. I will take you both to the Botanical Gardens one day. The flowers there smell just like the sweet smell of your baking, Bindi. And there are docks and sailors and... Oh Bindi, you will see it all for yourself."

Martha felt herself leaning too close to Will. She adjusted her seating position and ensured there was a respectable distance between them.

Bindi and Martha gazed in wonder as the little buggy clicked its way through the cobbled streets of The Rocks, a beautiful but, at the same time, forbidding and often dangerous area. The smell of salt from the harbour was dissipating now, to be replaced by the smells of smoke and the delicious smells of freshly baked bread. Laughter and chatter filled the air, interspersed with the clip-clop of other buggies.

"Where in Sydney do you live, Will? Is it far from here?" enquired Martha.

Will turned to face her, his cheeks flushed with excitement.

"Not too far. Up this street and we are nearly there. It's quite a humble abode, and you will have to mind the books."

"Books? Law books, Will?"

He laughed.

"No. Although I do have some law books, Martie, I have acquired a taste for reading. I find it helps beat the loneliness. The stories are mostly adventure tales. Stories of a handsome knight rescuing a fair maiden."

When he said that, he looked hard at her, and she felt the redness infuse her cheeks.

As the buggy rolled along, the three of them shared laughter and stories and marvelled at the grand sandstone buildings they passed.

"Well, here we are. My humble home," said Will as he fidgeted in his pocket for some coins to pay the driver.

They were outside a recently whitewashed bungalow with a beautiful bougainvillea growing up the side.

"What makes it humble? It is beautiful," said Martha.

"Much better than my hut back at Wicklow," Bindi threw in.

"Come on. I will show you in and come back for your luggage."

Will picked up a sandstone block and located a key, which he used to unlock the door, which he pushed open with a flourish.

"Welcome to my library," he said.

"My house may be modest, but it holds treasures like these."

He pointed at the shelves lining three walls of the room. Martha made her way across the room and traced her fingers along the spines of some books.

"You have really read all these, Will?"

"I have devoured every word of every book, Martha," Will said, becoming thoughtful.

"These books have been my companions on many a lonely night."

He moved toward Martha and whispered,

"I have missed you, Martha."

Martha's heart skipped a beat. The last thing she wished for was any undue pressure put on her by Will.

"I have missed you too," Martha responded, her voice slightly cracking.

Will took a step toward her, his arms open wide, but Martha reacted by stepping back, her gaze flicking to Bindi. With Will so close, Bindi's presence was an unwelcome one.

"Where shall we sleep?" asked Martha in order to calm her trepidations.

Will turned his head and nodded to a room off to his

left.

"There is a large bed in that room, and I have a small cot to sleep on in this room. You will find the room quite comfortable."

He turned to the door and said in a rather jubilant voice,

"I will go and fetch your things."

*****

The evening sun cast a warm glow over the street as the three walked down the road to Will's favourite pub, The King's Arms.

"I eat here most nights," he said. "But sometimes I go to my parent's house for a home-cooked meal."

"Why doncha you live with your mum and dad, Will?" asked Bindi.

"Bindi, why are you so full of questions?"

Will stopped and said,

"I like my independence, Bindi. Besides, my home is close to the office of the law firm I work for, and when I was studying, it was nice to have a place of my own where I had peace and quiet."

The King's Arms was alive with the chatter of drinkers and diners and smelled of the usual cigarette smoke and spilled ale. They took a table in the corner, as far from the bar as they could manage, and Will ordered roast beef and vegetables for them all. Conversation was light, and at times they had to raise their voices to be heard over the ever-increasing noise of the other patrons.

Bindi pushed back her chair and stood up.

"Too much tucker, Miss Martie. I think I will go for a walk."

"Be careful, Bindi," said Märtha, a teasing edge to her voice.

"This isn't Ramsay, you know."

Bindi laughed loudly, a sound that matched the noise in the room.

"This old black git can take care of 'erself, Miss Martie," and with a wink to both, she headed for the door.

Will called after her.

"Don't go beyond the end of the street, Bindi."

As the door swung shut behind her, the atmosphere shifted, with an undeniable tension hanging heavily between Will and Martha.

"Martha," Will began, his voice low and hesitant, "Why did you bring Bindi with you? We cannot be alone together."

Martha's heart sank at the implication.

"Will, I had no choice. My father insisted I bring her, or else I would not have been allowed to come."

But Martha knew that Bindi's presence was a risk to both. After all, Bindi was her husband's aunt.

"We need to sort this out, Martha. Love isn't just thinking about what has happened in the past; it is about facing today and whatever tomorrow will bring."

At his words, silence resumed its tight grip.

"Maybe Will is right," thought Martha.

"Perhaps it is time to face past shadows and either embrace them or banish them forever."

Just then, the pub door opened, and Bindi came in carrying a small bunch of flowers.

"Look at what I found, Miss Martie. Pretty, ain't they?"

"Yes, very beautiful, Bindi. But where did you get them?" asked Martha, taking special notice of the soil-encrusted roots.

"They was just sittin' in a fancy pot outside the pub door, Miss Martie."

Martha pulled a face.

"Whatever am I going to do with you, Bindi?"

*****

As they made their way back to Will's home, Martha's heart raced. Was it anticipation, or was it fear? Her mind drifted between thoughts of her attraction to Will and thoughts of guilt.

The trio settled in what Will termed his library, and the warmth of the fire embraced them as they sat in silence, staring at the flames.

Martha's restless gaze flitted between Will and Bindi, feeling the pain in her heart pressing heavily upon her.

"Good night, Martha," Will's voice interrupted her

reverie, his tone tinged with a hint of longing.

Martha's body tensed at the finality of his words, knowing this night held the key to her heart's desire.

As the hours passed, Martha found herself tossing and turning alongside Bindi. The whispers of the past swept through her mind, and with a resolute determination, she quietly and carefully, in order not to wake Bindi, slipped from the bed and made her way to the library where Will was asleep on a cot.

She stood and studied his shape, a silhouette enhanced by the moonlight filtering through the window.

Will stirred and rolled over and, in a whisper, said,

"Martha."

In that moment, all pretence slipped away, leaving the raw reality of the truth that bound them together.

Their reunion was a storm of passion and desperation, and in the quiet hours of the night, they found comfort in each other's bodies.

As the first light of dawn painted the sky, Martha retrieved her nightgown, kissed Will lightly, and made her way back to her bed and Bindi, leaving the man she now knew she loved, fast asleep.

*****

"You will soon get the hang of it, Miss Meg," Mrs. Wells reassured her as Meg walked into the Emporium.

"Anything you cannot find, just ask me. I know every nook and cranny of Miss Martie's Emporium."

Meg nodded, her body energised with excitement. She looked forward to the challenge of running the Emporium while Martha was holidaying in Sydney, and it would be a welcome break from her son, Robbie.

She strolled around the interior, seeing it in a different light as a manager rather than a customer. The shelves towered over her, filled with bolts of fabric, menswear, bottles of sweets, and tinned vegetables.

"Now you just remember, dear," said Mrs. Wells with assumed authority, "everything has its rightful place here. We wouldn't want something in the wrong place, would we?"

After her first week at the Emporium, Meg was pulled aside by Mrs. Wells.

"I cannot work it out, Miss Meg. Why is Sergeant Connolly here every day, standing on the verandah? We certainly don't need police protection. Ramsay is a safe place now. Ever since you have been here, his presence has been like a bad penny."

Meg ignored her, but Mrs. Wells continued.

"You cannot fool me, Miss Meg. It's because of you. You are a fine figure of a woman, and a good catch for any man in the district. It's not just the tea and biscuits that draw him in."

She clucked her tongue.

"Ah, the joys of being young and pretty."

*****

Chapter 29

Jimmy Boy took up the same position at the same table he had shared with Kerrigan the night before. He felt nervous—an unusual sensation for him, a man who prided himself on keeping a steady head.

In the dimly lit room, the clock above the bar showed the time as almost nine.

"Have patience, Jimmy Boy," he said to himself, with his eyes glued on the door. The minutes dragged by like the tail on an overweight goanna after a solid meal of a decaying beast.

The ice in his whisky had long melted, diluting his drink into a lighter amber, and the glass deposited its oozing moisture on the tabletop. His eyes went back to the clock for what seemed like the hundredth time.

But then the door swung open with a gentle squeak, and Kerrigan walked in. His boots thumped on the wooden floor, and his eyes rested on Jimmy Boy. He gave a nod to the barman and took a seat opposite the Chinaman. Jimmy Boy's hand tightened around his glass, and he felt his heartbeat accelerate considerably.

"You're late," said Jimmy Boy, his voice a little shakier than he would have liked.

Kerrigan grunted in response.

"Nobody said anything about a time, Jimmy. 'Sides, I had some serious thinkin' to do."

"Look Kerrigan, Jacky is in big trouble. And you are the only one who can get him out of it. I have the gold nugget and the bank letter with me. All it takes is for you to say you will accept my offer."

He paused, watching Kerrigan's face, trying to read the man, but Kerrigan's face remained as unreadable as a statue's.

Jimmy Boy slid a small bag containing the nugget and a bank letter across the table. Kerrigan's hand shot out, snatching both before the Chinaman had a chance to change his mind.

In the far corner, Mounsie sat at a table he knew well, and if tables could talk, then it knew him too. His arms rested in the same spot each time he sat, and his glass was very familiar with a dent in one corner. He had few, if any, friends in Milburra, and it was his norm to imbibe alone and listen to the town gossip—anything that may in some way be of an advantage to him. And tonight, the sight of the strange little Chinaman talking with Mister Reagan's right-hand man piqued his interest.

The candles began flickering, and the barman was beginning to extinguish the lanterns. Still, Mounsie did not take his eyes off the two men and saw the nugget and bank letter being pushed across the table. He wiped his mouth, the taste of his own treachery beginning to sour his tongue. He knew Mister Reagan would want to hear about this little deal, whatever it was.

But it was late. Mounsie decided to take a buggy ride in the morning to Dingo's Retreat. He smiled as he thought to himself,

"No matter how small something may appear on the surface, there is always money to be made if one is clever."

Back at the table, Kerrigan had a wide smile on his face. He reached his dirty hand across and offered it to Jimmy Boy.

"The deal is settled, my foreign friend. I will visit the Sergeant tomorrow and tell him the truth. The truth? As far as he knows it will be. I figure if I just stick to my story and say that I was jealous of the black man being around Miss Charley and decided to get rid of him by framing him for the murder of Howarth—that should suffice. Tanner is as dumb as dogshit, so he will believe my story. Then this man Kerrigan is out of here and bound for lands unknown."

Kerrigan downed the last of his drink with one gulp and said,

"Nice doin' business with you, Jimmy."

Kerrigan stood and cast his eyes around the room, which was almost empty now, save for the pitiful figure of Mounsie sitting alone in the corner. He tipped his hat at the man in recognition and headed out the door.

*****

Mounsie's eyes glanced nervously around as he steered his buggy through the entrance gates of Dingo's Retreat. Despite the hour, the farm was already bustling with activity. The clucking of chickens and the low murmuring of cows added to the noise of the dogs' raucous barking.

Reagan's towering figure was framed in the doorway of the homestead, and the look on his face was one of curiosity and annoyance.

"What brings you here so early, Mounsie?" he called out.

"I have no need of your services today."

Mounsie alighted from the buggy, his legs slightly wobbly, and wiped his sweaty brow with a grimy handkerchief. He approached Reagan with a servile step and said,

"Pardon the hour, Mister Reagan, but I have some information that you may find interesting."

Reagan's curiosity was aroused now. The man looked agitated. He stepped aside, and Mounsie scurried through the door into the huge reception area. The room reeked of tobacco and the sour smell of spilled whisky.

"Speak," Reagan ordered, his voice echoing off the high ceiling.

"I was in the pub last night, Mister Reagan, as is my habit most nights, and there was a Chinaman sitting alone, drinking."

"I fail to see the relevance of a yellow man having a drink, Mounsie."

"But the important part comes next. Your man, Mister Kerrigan, came in and sat with the Chinaman."

"Interesting, Mounsie. Tell me more."

Reagan scratched his chin.

"Who's this bloody Chinaman?"

"He is a businessman, supposedly evaluating Milburra to test its viability for the establishment of a Farmers' Co-operative."

"Go on."

"Well, next thing I knew, the Chinaman gave a small bag to Kerrigan and a letter. I didn't get a close look, but it appeared to be something of an official nature."

"So you have no idea what the letter was or what the bag contained?"

"None at all, Mister Reagan."

"Then there is only one way to find out. I will send for Kerrigan at once."

Mounsie's face yellowed.

"Mister Reagan, can I leave now? I don't want Mister Kerrigan knowing I have anything to do with this."

Reagan threw back his head and laughed.

"Go on. Get out of here and back to town before you shit yourself, you weak little bastard!"

Mounsie was quick to stand and, with his hat in his hand, looked pitifully at Reagan.

"Mister Reagan, if the information I gave you is of any interest, do you think you could see fit to pay me some……"

"Get out!" roared Reagan.

*****

"Charley, get your lazy arse down here. I need you to round up some men whilst I have a little chat with Kerrigan."

The young girl bounced down the stairs, a smile covering her beautiful face.

"What's up, Papa?"

"Nothing just yet, Charley. But things may get a bit savage during my conversation with Kerrigan. So fetch him here as well."

The girl knew enough to ask no further questions.

*****

Kerrigan walked into the room, his face bearing the same cocky smile it always did. He had no reason to suspect what was about to happen. And nor did the three men who had tailed him in, with faces lined with curiosity and tension.

"You armed, Mister Kerrigan?"

The question came as a surprise.

"Why? Should I be? Is there going to be trouble?"

Kerrigan was confused.

Reagan, satisfied that the man was not bearing a weapon, indicated towards his gun rack.

"You three men, select a piece and cock it, and hold your aim on Mister Kerrigan while I ask him some questions."

Kerrigan's words spat out.

"What the fuck is happening, Mister Reagan?"

"That's exactly what I intend finding out, Kerrigan."

Kerrigan held his hands up in a non-threatening

gesture, his eyes wide open.

"I want answers, Kerrigan. What were you and the Chinaman discussing last night? And what did he give you?"

Kerrigan's face paled. Someone had seen them. He thought back to last night and conjured up the weasly face of Mounsie.

"I don't know what you are talking about. Sure, I had a drink with a Chinaman, but we only discussed his plans for a Farmer's Co-Operative."

"A discussion only? He gave you nothing?"

"I swear, Mister Reagan. He gave me nothing."

Reagan's face screwed up. He knew the man was lying.

He drew back his arm and then smashed his fist into the side of Kerrigan's head.

Kerrigan fell to the ground and, in fear, he uttered,

"All right. All right. He gave me something. I just forgot it, that's all."

"Now we are getting somewhere. And what was it he gave you?"

"It was only a leaflet about the business he was tryin' to set up in Milburra. I forgot all about it, as I didn't think it was important."

"You seem to forget, Mister Kerrigan, it is I who decides what is important."

"Yes, Mister Reagan. I am sorry, Mister Reagan."

"Take him to the shed where we first kept the blacks and tie him up. We'll give him a day in the heat to think things over. A man could cook in that tin shed."

*****

The two silhouettes moved silently through the underbrush. Both Jacky and Tarni were well versed in the art of moving unseen and unhurt. It had been Tarni's idea to do another scout of the Reagan farm to determine what guards Reagan now had, and to ascertain the best time and way to free the Wiradjuri tribe.

"We should have come at night, Tarni," whispered Jacky.

"Too stinking hot in the daytime," he mouthed silently as he brushed the flies from his lips.

"Jacky, it was you who said the daytime would be best. Nobody will suspect us of snooping around in daylight."

Before she had a chance to say anything further, Jacky pressed his hand over her lips.

"Over there!" said Jacky urgently.

"They have Kerrigan."

Tarni peered over the log they were crouched behind.

"Why do you reckon they have guns on him, Jacky?"

"It's plain that someone has got word to Reagan about Jimmy Boy's offer to him. And that means Kerrigan's life is worthless."

He punched the ground in frustration.

"Damn it, Tarni. Now we have two rescue missions to carry out. We will return tonight and free him."

*****

As they approached the farm, the air was heavy with the scent of eucalyptus, and in the distance, the howling of dingoes echoed through the night. Their cries were both eerie and mournful, and set the backdrop for the task ahead. Jacky's sinewy frame moved silently through the shadows, and Tarni matched his step with unwavering resolve.

"I don't know why you want to help Kerrigan, Jacky. He's nothing but a murdering white bastard!" spat Tarni.

"Tarni, there are some things you do not understand," Jacky whispered as he edged forward.

"You must remember he promised Jimmy Boy that he would testify I did not murder Howarth. He took the money, and I believe the man just wanted a clear conscience and a new start in life."

Tarni tugged on Jacky's trousers and pulled him back. She placed her hands on his cheeks and, looking in his eyes, said,

"Jacky, he's only doing it for the money. He doesn't care about you or the rest of the natives tied and chained up in Reagan's sheds."

"Tarni, you might not understand certain things about people, but I am a man who cares about others. And I know what will happen to Kerrigan now Reagan has him. He will be a dead man."

*****

Jacky

Kerrigan had no clear idea of the time until the door was prised open, letting in a trace of moonlight.

He was able to make out a dark shape, nothing more than a blob through his swollen eyes.

"Who's there?" called Kerrigan weakly.

"It is me. Jacky. I have come to get you, Kerrigan."

"Jacky! Come to get me? It was because of you, mongrel black bastard, that put me in this position in the first place."

Kerrigan tried to push his aching body into a crouching position, but he did not have the strength.

"You know what I am gonna do with you, Jacky? I am gonna kill you!"

Jacky just smiled and said,

"Kerrigan, I mean it. I am here to save you."

Both men froze as they heard footsteps coming across the yard.

Jacky said,

"Just hold on as best you can, Kerrigan. I will return

tomorrow night. No good us all being caught."

And then he was gone, and so were the footsteps. Kerrigan knew that there was nobody coming to him. The hours passed, and he must have dozed a little. Each time he jerked awake, it was with a sense of terror and foreboding. He was caught in a web from which there was no escape.

"What did Reagan plan to do with him? Did he intend torturing him until he admitted betraying his boss?"

A thousand thoughts scurried through his brain. And they all came back to the same thing: the hiding place which contained the gold and the bank letter.

*****

Kerrigan's mind was beginning to desert him. Imprisoned in a tin shed for a day and night in over forty-degree heat had sapped his whole resolve. He edged backwards as he heard the door open.

"Hold it right there, Mister Kerrigan."

But Kerrigan was too slow to react, and the man behind the voice managed to score a direct blow to the side of Kerrigan's head. He whirled around, only to capture another stunning blow from a flying rifle butt. He stumbled and tried to concentrate on clinging to his senses. But then a second man was on top of him, and a booted foot was being driven against his ribs. He was endeavouring to twist aside when a huge form fell on him and his right arm was twisted and levered back against his shoulder. He managed to look up; the pain was agonising and added to the blow he had taken on the forehead.

Kerrigan stared into the face above him, a malicious face filled with hatred. It belonged to his boss, Harry Reagan. What followed was like a nightmare. Kerrigan rose and staggered a few yards, then lost balance and once more hit the earth. All the while Reagan kept goading him, reminding him of what happened to traitors. Somehow, he stumbled forward, but once again the strength rushed out of his legs and the earth came up to meet him, all the while the men were chuckling with amusement.

Kerrigan's next sensation was of a veritable torrent of icy water sweeping over his head and body. The cold water clawed at his bones, and while partly reviving him, sent shivers through his aching body. He heard voices, but they seemed far away, and when somebody laughed, he clenched his teeth in fury and frustration. Then he felt himself lifted by the shoulders and dragged across the dusty yard. A quick heave launched him into a well of darkness, where a fetid smell forced his stomach to heave and retch.

Then there came such a silence; it was enough to send a man mad. He could hear nothing but the insistent ringing in his ears. The inside of his skull felt as if there was honey being slowly stirred inside him.

*****

He knew when the night had elapsed by the first glimmering of grey light filtering through the door of the shed. Then he heard a key rasping in the lock, and the door was hauled open. Reagan stood there, an image of cruelty, and in his right hand, he caressed a bullwhip.

"Come, Mister Kerrigan. It's time for breakfast."

Kerrigan stooped quickly and clutched a log in the

corner. He had it raised above his head by the time two other men rushed him and tried to trap his arms, when a third man appeared and hit him over the head with the stock of his rifle. The three men seized the opportunity to overpower him, dragging him outside and throwing him on his stomach on the dry and dusty ground.

Reagan barked an order,

"Rip his shirt off, boys. Let me give him a taste of this."

The initial lash of the heavy whip on Kerrigan's shoulders and the sheer agony brought a groan from his lips. Reagan grinned and brought down another cruel strike. Kerrigan could only grit his teeth against such treatment. Sweat was pouring from his forehead and running down his cheeks and jaws. He never knew when the punishment ceased, for mercifully he relinquished consciousness about halfway through the whipping.

He had a vague sense of being totally engulfed in a devouring fire, then fancied he was swimming in a river, with the water getting into his mouth and throat and clogging his nostrils as he choked. Then there was movement and the harsh sound of horse's hooves galloping madly over a paddock, taking him into a black and deadly oblivion.

"Mister Reagan! That's enough!" shouted one of the men.

Reagan pulled his cigar from his mouth and turned to the dissenter.

"I say when enough is enough! That is, unless you want the same treatment."

Reagan raised the whip and cut across Kerrigan's back one last time.

"He sure is one tough bastard, I will give him that. A whipping like that should be enough to make any man talk."

"I think he is dead, Mister Reagan."

"He's not fucking dead! Death is too good for a traitor. Tie him to a horse and take him to the river."

"Leave him there?"

"No, you fucking idiot. Weigh him down and sink him."

He turned and stalked off to the house, calling over his shoulder,

"When you are done with him, I want his hut searched. Whatever the Chinaman gave him must be there somewhere."

*****

Jacky and Tarni watched on with horror as Kerrigan was subjected to the flogging. It eventually became too much for the young girl, and she covered her eyes.

"C'mon, Tarni. They are taking Kerrigan somewhere. We have to follow."

*****

The men they followed made no attempt to be cautious. Besides, the blacks had not been sighted for many days now. The burden they carried was unmistakable—even from afar they could see the limp form of Kerrigan, a grim reminder of the fate that awaited him. Jacky and Tarni exchanged glances, an acknowledgment of the horror they had witnessed at Dingo's Retreat.

As the men approached the riverbank, one of them said,

"We can't jis fuckin' drown 'im. Poor bastard's still alive."

"Then he better thank his God that Regan never gave him to his fuckin' mad son. Poor bastard would have been eaten alive by his fuckin' hogs. And if you wanna go against Mister Reagan, then go ahead. Not me. I am jis gunna do what 'e said. Drown the bastard. I never much liked 'im anyways."

With a grunted effort, he pulled Kerrigan from the horse.

"Look about and find a big rock."

Kerrigan tried to struggle, but all his strength had left him.

"I'll come back and haunt you miserable bastards," he managed to say through parched lips as his legs and arms twitched weakly.

It was then that Jacky stepped out of the shadows.

"Hold it right there, men," he said, his voice firm and unyielding.

The three men straightened in alarm.

"It's the fuckin' black. The one who sold 'is 'orse to Mister Reagan."

"Yes. The black. But the black who had his horse

stolen by Reagan. Now release that man."

The three men stepped back, wary but conscious of the fact they were armed and Jacky had nothing.

"You talk big, darky, when you ain't even got a bloody spear in yer 'and."

The man cocked his pistol, aimed, and was in the process of squeezing the trigger when the spear pierced his ribs. He dropped his pistol and slumped to the ground. Tarni emerged from the bushes with Jacky's other spears cradled under one arm.

"See, Jacky. And you seemed to think I couldn't hit anything. Proved you wrong, huh?"

The two other men had lost all their bravado.

"Don't hurt us, please. We was only followin' orders."

"You need more practice, Tarni," said Jacky as he squatted on the ground.

"You surely can't miss those two."

In quick succession, the young girl hurled two more spears, and three dead men lay on the ground.

"You should have been a man, Tarni. You would have

been a better warrior than me."

Jacky, with the help of Tarni, hefted the men onto their tethered horses, balancing their weight with loose limbs dangling each side.

"Now let's get Kerrigan on his horse and get him to Andrews. Maybe his wife can patch him up."

*****

Kerrigan remembered nothing of the trip to the Andrews' farm. For two days he was delirious, in the grip of a raging fever. Rachel Andrews nursed him, applying salve to the awful wounds inflicted by Reagan's whip, wiping his brow, and trying not to listen to the awful babblings that came from his mouth. But despite her efforts to turn a deaf ear to Kerrigan's wild talk, she could not help but learn a great deal about the man's past life. She had taken him to be just a murdering thug, working for the evil Harry Reagan.

On the third day, Jacky came by to inquire about his health.

"He's lucky to be alive at all," said Jacky.

"What makes you say that?" asked Richard Andrews.

Jacky was blunt with his response.

"The whipping that man got would have killed most men. Has he said much since you have been tending to him, Rachel?"

"A lot," she confessed, "and most of it to do with his past."

"He said nothing about what happened to him? How he came by the whipping?"

"Nothing at all."

She screwed up her face and thought.

"He did mention a man's name a few times. Mounsie. Yes, Mounsie. He mentioned that name."

Jimmy Boy stood quietly in the corner.

"This is all my fault, Jacky. I was sure my plan would work."

"Don't be too hard on yourself, Jimmy Boy. You weren't to know that Mounsie would rat Kerrigan out."

"It seems as if Reagan has the whole district in his pockets. We need to be extra vigilant and trust nobody."

Jimmy Boy, for the first time, was beginning to be afraid.

Jacky scooped up his hat from the table and said,

"Then I will be off. I will return in a few days and maybe then he will be well enough to talk. I need him to talk with the Sergeant, so my name is cleared. And right now, after what Reagan has done to him, I doubt he even needs any amount of gold that Jimmy Boy can give him to take revenge on that son of a bitch."

"I will send for the Sergeant as soon as he is well enough, Jacky. The sooner all this business is finished, the better."

*****

"Boss! Mister Reagan! You better come quick!" called Franklin, the young stable boy.

Reagan looked up from his faded newspaper, a week-old copy of the Milburra Advocate. He was relaxed, not having expected trouble of any kind. Besides, he had not heard nor seen any sign of the blacks in the area for days now. Both he and his daughter had assumed they had moved on after the massacre of so many of their tribesmen.

He pulled his heavy frame from his chair and went to the partially opened front door. The sight that greeted him was grisly. Three of his men were dead, slumped over their horses and with faces contorted in silent pain. Each man had an aboriginal spear, the tips revealing caked blood, tied to the saddles. The horses, exhausted and spooked, pawed at the ground restlessly, their nostrils flaring with every breath.

Franklin's hand was shaking as he pointed at the dead bodies.

"They jis arrived like that, Mister Reagan. Not a sound, 'cept fer the horses."

"Fuck, fuck, fuck!" roared Reagan, unable to control the rage bubbling inside him like a volcano about to erupt. He had been sure the tribe had long gone, scared off by the tragic deaths of so many of their own. But here was a twisted and haunting message. It was now that Reagan realised that someone was still out there, watching and waiting.

He knew that Jacky was behind all this, a sly and at the same time clever aboriginal. The others were just mindless brutes, easily cowered and controlled. But Jacky, he was different. Reagan knew he had underestimated him.

"What will I do?" asked the frightened youth.

"Leave them there and call Bruce from the hogs' pen. He'll take care of them."

Charley came out into the yard, her eyes wide with horror. She stared at the bodies with her mouth open and said nothing.

"What's a man to do, Charley?" he asked, the question left hanging in the air like a puff of dust blown by the wind.

"What makes me sick in the guts with worry, is…"

"What, Papa?"

"If Jacky did this, then there is every chance Kerrigan is still alive. And if he is, that spells bad news for me. The man knows too much."

"We gotta fight back, Papa," but her words were soft and soon lost in the breeze.

"I don't know, Tanner. He had nothing on him."

"I will have a look through his hut, Mister Reagan. Never know what I will find."

As Tanner approached Kerrigan's hut, he noticed that the door was not just slightly ajar, but wide open, as if in welcome. The interior was cleaner than he had expected and was sparsely furnished with a single bunk, a table and chair, and a chest of drawers. The bed was neatly made with the pillow propped up against the headrest and, above it, a rifle hung on the wall. He pulled open the drawer of the cabinet and found it contained only the essentials: a few changes of clothes, a shaving kit, and a journal. He flipped through the pages of the journal and found it contained nothing of importance — a list of tasks and some weather information. Nothing that suggested anything untoward.

As he pulled away the chair to sit and read through the journal, the padded top came away, revealing a crumpled brown paper bag. He picked it up and found it quite heavy, much more so than it should have been for something so innocuous. His curiosity grew as he felt inside and pulled out a gold nugget of a size that could make a man a fortune in an instant. He looked around and listened closely for any sound and then, satisfied he was indeed alone, he stuffed the bag inside his shirt and went back to report to Reagan.

"Didn't find a thing, Mister Reagan. Maybe Mounsie is just full of horseshit."

*****

"Papa, why not release the aborigines?"

Reagan looked up from his dinner plate.

"What did you say?"

"You heard me, Papa. Why not release the aboriginals? They are people, just like us, and they have suffered enough. Since your men brought them here, we have had nothing but trouble. Your workers are always whispering about them, and it won't be long before word gets out to people in town. People who matter."

"None of my workers will ever say a word, Charley. They know what will happen to them if they open their mouths."

"The way things are going, Papa, it won't be too long before you have no workers left. The men are muttering their discontent now. They are all saying the same thing, Papa. They don't want a spear in their back."

Reagan's knuckles turned white as he grasped the knife and fork.

"That black bastard Jacky! He is the one that has caused all the trouble. It's a good thing he has decided to move on. The only good thing he did was bring me his horse. I own it, Charley, and I have the papers to prove it. He won't show his black face 'round here while ever Tanner has a warrant for his arrest."

"Forget Jacky, Papa. You must free the others. They are entitled to freedom as much as we are. Possibly more so. They just want their land back."

"Their land? This is my land, Charley! My fucking land! You hear me, girl?"

Reagan's face had turned a deep scarlet, but he wasn't done.

"If we bow down to the blacks, they will just want more and more, and soon we will be overrun by the bastards, just like rabbits."

He slammed his hands on the table so hard that the cups overturned, spilling the warm tea.

"You don't get it, do you, Charley? I need those blacks. Without their labour we won't get through the season. I have had good men murdered, Charley, and I don't have Kerrigan anymore. He was a good worker, but he turned on me. Just like you seem to be. Now shut the fuck up and enjoy your dinner."

*****

Chapter 30

The sprawling expanse of the Common, renamed Hyde Park by Governor Lachlan Macquarie, had captivated the two women.

"I never dreamed of such a beautiful place," said Martha to Will as they sat under a giant Moreton Bay Fig. The sun was high and shone on the lush greenery, and couples walked hand in hand while children raced around chasing each other and being chased by yapping dogs.

"Look at Bindi," Martha added, "she is certainly enjoying the place."

But Bindi, drawn by the sounds of an enticing melody from a park musician, wandered further than she realised. Meanwhile, Will and Martha were comfortable in their own existence and completely unaware of Bindi's absence, until Will leaned over and kissed Martha on the cheek. She reacted immediately, looking up to see if Bindi had noticed. But to her surprise, the woman was nowhere to be seen.

"Will, we must be careful. Bindi must not see our show of affection."

"Martha, you are more naïve than I thought. Do you honestly believe that Bindi doesn't know about us? For goodness' sake, Martha, she is far from stupid, and we are not children."

"It's just that I am not comfortable, Will, with this situation. I am a married woman."

His response was to kiss her on the lips, and she could feel the passion burning in his very soul. She responded by pressing her lips so hard to his mouth that they both felt pain. Martha pulled away, breathless and panting.

"Not here, Will. There is a time and place for everything."

It was then that she noticed Bindi was nowhere in sight.

"Goodness, Will. Bindi has wandered off. We must find her."

Will immediately stood and scoured the park with his keen eyes.

"I don't see her, Martha."

Martha's voice came with a tremble.

"What if something has happened to her, Will? I could

never forgive myself."

They shared a determined glance that signalled they would search together.

Unbeknownst to them, Bindi had fallen victim to two shady characters who had been lurking in the shadows, looking for this exact opportunity. Petty crime had become common in Sydney, and for the two brothers, John and Ray Thomas, their moral compass had ceased to function. John, the elder of the two, had recently returned to society after spending a month as a guest of the local police on a charge of disturbing the peace—a badge of dishonour he seemed to wear proudly. Ray, the younger brother, barely twenty years of age, was keen to follow his brother's reckless path in life. Both were drawn to a life of petty crime and easy money, rather than commit to an honest day's work. They had been watching Bindi for some time, smoking discarded cigarette butts they had scrounged in the gutter.

"That one there," said John, pointing at Bindi.

"She'd fetch a few bob. The rich bastards around here would pay a pretty penny for a wench like that as housemaid."

Ray looked at his brother with some doubt in his mind.

"You reckon we could sell 'er?"

"Of course!" John exclaimed, his voice tinged with the thrill of the whole thing.

"We'll grab the black bitch and tonight we can drink like kings. Rich people don't care where their 'elp comes from, Ray me boy."

As Bindi admired a bed of flowers, the two men seized the moment and pulled her roughly into a stand of trees, then dragged her towards the exit gates of the gardens.

John Thomas ogled Bindi and said,

"My, my, oh my. You'll fetch a good price. Got a bit of age on yer but still a few good years' work left in your old feeble black body."

He gave her a solid whack on her tiny bottom.

"Might be worth a bit of sport with before we sell you," leered the older of the brothers as he cupped his hand between her legs.

Bindi struggled and tried to pull away, but she was simply not strong enough.

"Let me go, you white bastards! Yous ain't about to be

puttin' yer white stick in me," she screamed, but a hand was quickly clamped over her mouth.

"Ain't no use in screamin', you little black bitch. Bloody seagulls drown out any noise 'ere. Now git a move on. You ain't worth putting me cock in yer scrawny body. We got some business to take care of."

Fear was crawling up Bindi's spine, but she remembered the words of Jarrah.

"Strength lies in the earth and the spirits will protect us."

Using every ounce of willpower, she pushed against her captors and with her perfect teeth bit into the shoulder of John. He let out an anguished wail and released his hold on her, and she grabbed the opportunity to break free. The two thugs were taken aback, and she used her deceptive speed to run as fast as a startled rabbit down the narrow street.

Will and Martha scoured the park, their desperation growing with each unanswered call. Meanwhile, Bindi, with adrenaline pushing her, ran through the deserted streets with the two men in close pursuit. Just as she thought she had outpaced them, she saw them closing in. Instinctively, she ducked inside an open doorway, an unassuming bookshop which smelled of mouldy paper.

The man behind the counter looked up and showed no alarm, but rather amusement at the woman who had burst through his door.

"Whatever is the matter? Are you in trouble?" he asked as he replaced a book he had been dusting back on the shelf.

"I am lost, and they are after me," she panted with an edge of fear.

Cornelius Deakin's smile faded, replaced by a look of concern.

"Who?"

He stepped closer, resting heavily on his cane, and then he walked to the door but could see nobody.

"You are safe here now," he said.

"Whoever was after you is gone. Now, take a seat and I'll fetch a cup of tea," he said with a soothing tone.

"But first, tell me what happened."

Bindi took a moment to gather her breath, her chest still heaving, then began to recount her tale.

"I was in the gardens up the road with Miss Martie, and……….."

The man interrupted.

"Miss Martie?"

"Yes, she is my charge, you know. She was not allowed to journey to Sydney without me," Bindi said pompously, enjoying the attention now lavished on her.

"I see. So, this Miss Martie, she works for you?"

The man had a twinkle in his eye.

"No. I work fer her, but I am her boss here in the big smoke. Someone needs to take care of an innocent young thing."

"You are indeed a noble woman, Miss…………?"

Bindi looked at him suspiciously. He appeared kind enough, but after her ordeal she was not about to trust anyone just yet.

"Me name is Bindi. And there ain't no bloomin' Miss about it neither!"

"I am delighted to meet you, Bindi. And I am Cornelius Deakin. Now do go on."

"Well," she began, "two rough lookin' men grabbed me while Miss Martie wasn't lookin' and they took me. I think they was gunna do the business with me."

"Business?"

"You know. What men do to women. The thingy thingy you know. Poke their white stick in me."

"You thought they had rape in mind?"

"Didn't think. I knew. Yes. That's what you white fellers call it."

Then her eyes flashed with anger as she spoke of her struggles, her biting and scratching to free herself.

"And I got loose and ran and ended up here, mister."

"As I said, you are safe here. Sit down and rest and calm your nerves, and I will fetch the tea I promised."

Bindi looked around the room.

"Lot of books, mister."

"Yes," came the response, accompanied by a sigh.

"Too many I am afraid. A lifetime's work is what you see around you. I have had this shop for nigh on thirty years, and I have seen the city evolve around it. But the books, well, they never change. Just sit and gather dust, most of them. They are just waiting for the right person to come along and give them a good home."

"My lady's friend Will has a lot of books. She's his secret lover, but she doesn't know that I know that. Cannot put anything over this old black git. Will's his name."

Bindi cast an eye around the room, fearful that someone may hear her.

"Will? You do not mean Will McKenzie?"

"Yes, that's him. He reckons he learns things from books. All rubbish to me. My people keep our stories up here."

She patted her head.

"Our people talk of the Dreamtime when our ancestor spirits made the world. They walked this land, leaving tracks that became rivers, and they carved valleys and mountains with their very steps. The stars in the sky at night are the campfires they lit and the animals we see are their children."

Cornelius, who was still standing, leaned forward on his cane and said in hushed tones,

"Your stories, Bindi, I imagine are nothing like the stories I could read in any of these books."

"These 'ere books of yours," Bindi waved her arms around the room, "are jis fer white folks. Our stories are meant to be told, not read like your books."

The old man nodded solemnly, realising the great divide between the two of them.

"I have lived here all my life, but I have never really known the land beneath my feet. Not in the way you do."

He then returned the conversation to the earlier mention of Will McKenzie.

"You mentioned Will McKenzie. What an amazing co-incidence. Will is a close friend of mine. We have done business for some time now. He buys his books from here."

"So this is where 'e gits 'is books? He's a strange one though. He tried to tell me the other night that books were a bridge between worlds. I tried not to laugh. If he thinks he can build a bridge with books, then he better spend some money on a whole lot more."

The man laughed at the woman's naivety.

"I have only known you for the space of a few minutes, but I can see you are a woman of the land, and not the city. Your eyes tell me that you are used to vast spaces and endless skies. Not these tall walls and crowded streets. But I also see a hunger for knowledge. And that, Bindi," he ruminated for a short time, "is something I can offer."

"And jis how did you know I was hungry, Mister Cornelius?"

He threw back his head and laughed at the woman's question.

"Never mind, Bindi. Never mind. I will fetch us something to eat and then I will return you safely to Will's home."

"You always this kind to strangers, Mister Cornelius?"

*****

"They have to find her," Martha murmured to herself as she peered out the window into the darkening streets.

Will placed a comforting arm on her shoulder.

"The police will find her, Martha. But knowing Bindi, she's liable to find her own way home. You know how the

Aboriginals are with their survival skills."

Martha gave him an exasperated glare.

"You seem to forget, Will McKenzie, that this is Sydney, not a small country town in the bush."

Suddenly Martha froze. Were the shadows playing tricks on her? She was sure she could make out the figure of Bindi, but the figure she saw appeared to be accompanied by another.

"It's her, Will!" exclaimed Martha excitedly.

"It's Bindi. She has come home."

There was a gentle knock, and then the door creaked open, bringing a gust of cool evening air into the room. Martha peered into the gloom and saw a tall figure silhouetted in the doorway.

"Bindi?" she asked with a trembling voice.

Cornelius Deakin stepped into the room, with Bindi clinging to his arm.

"I have brought her back," he said matter-of-factly.

"We have had a very pleasant afternoon."

Will recognised the voice of his old friend.

"Cornelius! Well, blow me down with a feather. What a remarkable co-incidence. Come in, come in."

But Martha's expression shifted from relief to anger in a split second.

"What happened, Bindi?" she asked, rushing towards her and embracing her.

She looked at the torn blouse and the dirt smudges on Bindi's face.

"Who did this to you?"

Bindi looked at Cornelius with a silent plea.

"Kidnappers," he said.

"There's quite a market in Sydney for Aboriginal housemaids. It's extremely lucky that she happened to stumble into my bookshop."

Martha's hands trembled as she examined Bindi's bruises.

"My poor Bindi," she almost wept.

"But at least you are safe now."

"I will never feel safe in this place, Miss Martie. I wanna go 'ome."

*****

"I will show you out, Mister Cornelius," said Bindi as she retrieved his hat and coat from the hall rack. The hat looked oddly out of place in her small hands, a part of his world that she handled with surprising care.

They walked out into the street and stood for a moment, breathing in the nocturnal smells of a sleeping city. Then Bindi handed him the hat and coat.

"Thank you," he said, his eyes meeting hers. He noticed they were filled with a quiet strength—something that had been lacking when she had first burst into his shop.

Then Cornelius surprised himself, and Bindi, with his words.

"I have really enjoyed my time with you today, Bindi."

His words were sincere and settled around them like a warm blanket on a cool evening.

"Me too, Mister Cornelius. You're a right gentleman, you know."

Cornelius took a deep breath and placed his hat on, the brim tilted slightly to one side. He felt a sudden awkwardness as she reached up and rearranged it.

"There you go," she laughed.

"You bein' a poshie and all, gotta wear yer 'at right."

There was silence again, then,

"Bindi, do you mind if I ask you out on a picnic tomorrow?"

"You can ask, but I can't say yea or nay till I speak with Miss Martie. Besides, Mister Cornelius, I just want to go 'ome to Wicklow. Don't fancy the city too much."

"I see. Goodnight then, Bindi."

Bindi noticed his words were tinged with disappointment.

"Maybe you be better to call around tomorrer, Mister Cornelius."

"I most certainly will."

"And Mister Cornelius…"

"Yes?"

"If it ain't too much trouble, you might jis see about takin' the scissors to the 'air growin' outta yer nose."

*****

"Miss Martie, that man Cornelius upset me some yesterday."

The two women were strolling down to the markets, a short distance from Will's home. He had left early for work but had pointed out the directions, warning them not to stray from the route he had shown them.

Martha was intrigued, as usual, by anything Bindi had to say. Despite years of endless idiosyncrasies, fantasies, and sometimes plain nonsense, she never really knew what to expect from Bindi's imaginative mind.

"In what way, Bindi?"

"Well, I like him, is all."

Martha was befuddled.

"But if you like him, then he can't have upset you."

"Maybe I used the wrong word. You know, Miss Martie, when you like someone, you get an upset feelin' in yer belly. Like grubs in yer belly."

"I think you mean butterflies in your stomach, Bindi."

"Whatever," came the nonchalant reply.

"Aaaaaah," said Martha, drawing out the syllable,

"Now I understand. Bindi, you old devil," she nudged her in the ribs, "you've developed feelings for Mister Deakin."

"Yeah. Feelin's is all though. Can't never feel with another man the way I did with my Jarrah."

"Bindi, do you fancy him, really? Now tell me the truth, you hear."

Bindi's black skin turned a shade lighter.

"Nah! It's not right. He's an old man, Miss Martie."

"Oh Bindi, age is never a barrier. Think of the immense wisdom the man must possess."

"Wisdom don't put tucker on the table, Missy."

The sounds of vendors at the markets grew louder as they wandered along, selecting fresh fruit and vegetables.

"I think I'll ask Will to invite him for supper, Bindi. You need company in your life. It's not right that you don't have a companion."

Jacky

"I is tellin' you now, Miss Martie, I don't need a man in my life. Let alone a white man at that. So jis forget all about it, right."

*****

Chapter 31

"I am so happy, Will. These past few days here with you have been the happiest days of my life. But, Will, our time is running out. Bindi and I must return to the countryside in a few days."

"I am so grateful that Cornelius fetched Bindi to take her to see St Mary's Cathedral. It gives us more private time together," was Will's response.

"I really do not think Bindi is much interested in visiting a church, Will. But on the other hand, it will give her a chance to get better acquainted with Cornelius."

"What are you up to, you mischievous girl?"

Will grabbed her by the waist and steered her towards his cot and lay her down.

"It's not what you think, Will. Bindi has already told me she will never have another man in her life. I was merely referring to the fact that Cornelius may educate her on the finer points of life."

She was silenced by the pressure of Will's lips on hers, and the warmth of his body washed over her as he lay beside her. Her heart began to race as his hands found their way to her chest, gently cupping her breasts. They found her nipples, which began to harden as he slowly stroked his fingers over the tips. She gave a soft moan, but it was immediately muffled as his lips pressed on hers again. His passion and desire were unmistakable.

Martha's body responded with a hunger which she realised she had never really felt with Jacky. She could feel him pressing against her, reminding her of the pleasure yet to come. Her mind swirled with the thoughts of their previous encounters, the way he had made her feel like never before. The way he filled her with pleasure far beyond anything she had ever known.

He took the hint and slid his hand down her hips, then to the front to raise her dress. As his fingertips caressed her inner thigh, she felt bolts of lightning ignite her very core. She parted her legs slightly, and he slid down her panties. He groaned into her neck, his breath hot and wanting. Her grip on his neck tightened, and she felt him enter her, gently at first, building her anticipation until she was quivering with desire. She felt herself being led to the very precipice of pleasure, the veins on her neck protruding and pulsing.

The room around them seemed to fade away, leaving only the muffled sounds of their moans and the creaking of the bed.

*****

Martha's eyes fluttered open. It was only mid-afternoon, and she lay there, feeling the warmth of the quilt wrapped around her and listened to Will's breathing. He had an arm draped across her, and she dreaded to move. She wanted time to stop and this moment to go on forever, but she had no idea when Bindi would return. She carefully rolled her body away from Will and went to step out of the bed, but he stirred and pulled her back.

"Will," she protested, "we must get up. We don't want to be seen like this."

"Hush, Martha," he whispered into her ear.

"Let us just savour the moment and forget about the future."

Martha nodded. She knew he was right. The moment was about them, not the future. The warmth of his body and the scent of him was all she wanted to focus on. She could feel the call of the afternoon growing stronger, but she resisted it and delighted in Will's hand tracing patterns on her back.

Then suddenly a moment of panic hit Martha like cold water being thrown on her face. She jolted upright, the warmth of Will's embrace dissipating.

"What are we to do, Will?" she gasped in a shaky voice.

"I am an evil woman. Here I am, a married woman, but lying in bed with you."

Tears trickled down her cheeks as she added,

"I am so ashamed of myself, Will. What we have done is not right. My heart bleeds for Jacky, a good man, and a man who trusts me."

She clutched the bedsheets tightly.

"I don't know if I can live with all this."

Will tightened his grip on her shoulders.

"Martha, you cannot let fear overrule your happiness. We love each other, and that is all that matters."

His eyes drilled into hers, urging her to accept his words, then he pulled her closer to him and kissed her again.

*****

Martha's voice came in gasps as Will rolled from above her.

"I never knew that having so much fun could make a person so tired," she said with a dreamy look on her face.

"I am totally exhausted, Will."

Will's chest heaved, and he managed to say,

"You are not the only one," but his voice carried the sounds of satisfaction.

Martha's eyes searched his, the weight of her sins pressing down on her.

"We cannot just ignore the reality, Will. Jacky is my husband, and what we are doing is wrong."

Will's face hardened. He sat up and said,

"Then choose between us, Martha. I cannot live in the shadows any longer, stealing moments like this."

Martha pushed herself up, exposing her breasts.

"It's not that simple, Will. I took a vow to honour my husband. I do not think I can break that vow."

"So, it's to be like this then forever? Two people in love. Two people who can only share their love at times like this. Snatching fleeting moments to satisfy our desires."

He stood up and walked to the window.

"Well, I am sorry, Martha, but I cannot live like this."

The heated words between the two suddenly ceased as Martha urged Will,

"Quickly, Will. Put some clothes on. I am sure that is Bindi's laughter I can hear in the street."

Martha hopped nimbly from the bed and covered herself with a gown and made for the bathroom, while Will fumbled with his clothing in a hasty attempt to be dressed.

The scent of bougainvillea and dust wafted in through the opened door as Bindi, with Cornelius in tow, breezed in. Will's hand hovered over the last of the buttons on his shirt. The last thing he wanted was to be caught out by Bindi. He looked around. The room was a mess, a testament to the passion that had occurred not moments ago.

"We are home," announced Bindi with a triumphant shout, but then she paused, and her smile faded as she realised

Martha was not there to welcome her.

"Where is Miss Martie?"

"She is taking a bath, Bindi," he replied.

"We have not long returned ourselves."

His voice was calm and deliberate.

It was then Martha came from the bathroom, her face flushed and her hair dripping wet.

"Oh Bindi, I didn't expect you back so soon."

Bindi noticed her awkwardness and chuckled, prompting Martha's face to turn a brighter shade of pink.

"It's alright, Miss Martie. We bought some things at the markets. I will see about gittin' us some tucker."

*****

Martha lay awake that night, the sounds of the Sydney nightlife drifting through the open window, along with a gentle breeze that tried to calm her restless mind.

What would happen if she chose Will? What would happen if she followed her heart?

The shadows of doubt would not free her from its

clutches as she considered the ramifications of her decision: the disapproval of her family, the heartbreak of betrayal, and the risk of an uncertain future.

Yet beneath the layers of anxiety, there was an undeniable truth—the pull of her heart that pushed her to pursue happiness in its purest form.

What good was life without passion, and adventure, and excitement?

As the sun rose over Sydney, Martha had made her decision. The choice was not merely emotional; it was about choosing a new life.

She found Will sitting at the small kitchen table, sipping on his morning tea.

"Like some?" he asked with a gentle smile.

Her words surprised him.

"Will, I have made my choice. I have chosen you. I want a fresh start, with no turning back."

*****

Jacky returned from the Andrews' farm late in the afternoon. He was cautious as he entered the clearing and kept his body crouched low to the ground. A small fire was burning, but there was no sign of Tarni. Jacky felt for the pistol he had taken from one of the men and pulled it slowly from the rope holding his trousers up.

"Bloody hell," he muttered, as his eyes scanned the clearing. He had only been gone about four hours. What could have happened in that time? The camp looked the same as it did when he had left earlier in the day; the makeshift gunyah and their gear were neatly arranged. It was obvious that there had been no trouble.

"Unless," he thought, "Reagan has cleaned up his mess this time."

"Tarni, get your tiny arse back here now!" he shouted.

The girl had proven herself reliable and clever, but that counted for nothing when one was alone in the harsh outback. And it wasn't like Tarni to leave without a trace.

Then, from behind a clump of trees, Jacky caught a flash of movement. The scrub parted, and Tarni emerged, a smile splitting her face.

"Bloody hell, Tarni. What do you have to prove now?"

"Jis showin' you, Jacky," she said with a mischievous sparkle in her eyes, "that you were right lettin' me stay with you. Not only can I kill white fellers, but I can even take a big warrior like you by surprise," she teased.

Jacky couldn't help but smile, and he ruffled her hair and said,

"You're a cheeky little buggar."

She moved her tiny frame into his wiry body and said suggestively,

"Why don't you take them white feller pants off and come for a swim with me, Jacky?"

Her breath was hot against his neck, and her hands slid down and gave his crotch a playful squeeze. She giggled and walked off in the direction of the billabong. Jacky followed her, the afternoon sun bouncing off her brown body, casting shadows which only scrved to highlight her beauty.

With subtle grace, she plunged into the water, surfaced, and swam as gracefully as a duck-billed platypus. Then she dove deep, and Jacky watched the ripples grow smaller until she surfaced on the far side. The water glistened on her skin, and her teeth gleamed white in the already setting sun.

The sight of her so free and uninhibited began to arouse Jacky even more, and to save embarrassment, he slipped off his trousers and followed her into the water. The shock of the cold was brief, the heat of his desire quickly replacing it, and the water was cool and soft as he swam over to her. As he approached, Tarni's eyes never left his, and he felt himself growing harder. Her bare breasts were bobbing just above the surface, and when he was close, she reached out and took his hand. It took all their strength to keep their heads above water as they locked in a passionate embrace.

"Better off on dry ground, Jacky," she laughed. "I don't want a belly full of water."

They swam to the edge of the billabong and pulled themselves onto the lushness of the river reeds.

Tarni made her intentions clear when she said,

"Might want a bellyful of something else though."

She lay on her back and closed her eyes, her skin still glistening with water droplets. Without opening her eyes, she said,

"Well, Jacky, you jis gunna sit there and look or what? If you like what you see, why not come and take a better look."

"I think I will," he said, his voice deep and sending shivers down Tarni's spine.

She adjusted her position, her pubic mound a soft, inviting mystery of darkness against her lighter skin. The rays of the sun captured every curve and line of her body, and her open eyes now danced with mischief. As Jacky lay beside her, he brushed off the few remaining water droplets from around the fine hairs covering her sex like dew on a gum leaf.

"You are so beautiful, Tarni," he murmured, his voice betraying his desire.

The sprinkling of hair around her womanhood was in stark contrast to the rest of her body, which was smooth and unblemished. He leaned down, his nose brushing against the softness of her pubic hair, and at that moment he wanted to taste her, devour her, and explore every part of the body that was calling to him.

Jacky's hands were gentle as he parted the curtain of hair.

"You are right," he said. "I am not just going to look."

Her hips bucked, and she let out a primeval cry as his lips touched her flesh.

Their eventual connection was as ancient as the land they lay upon. Their bodies danced in unison, and the world around them faded away, leaving them like the last two souls remaining on earth.

*****

"You make a lot of noise when we do that," laughed Jacky.

"Sounds a bit like one of my bulls bellowing in the paddock. That last scream you let out would have shaken the Dreamtime and woken the ancestors."

"You would have screamed louder, Jacky, if a bloody ant had bitten your bare arse," Tarni said as she rubbed a red spot on her bum.

*****

Tarni placed some small twigs on the fading coals of the fire, and it roared back into life. Soon she had a hot enough flame to roast some yams.

"I have missed native tucker, Tarni," said Jacky as they sat cross-legged by the fire.

Tarni's eyes crinkled with a mischievous smile.

"Maybe just the way I cooked them. I can cook for you every night if you want. And do other things if you want."

She put the stick she had been using for a skewer into the fire and placed her hands between his legs. Jacky ignored her subtle movement and placed another yam on the end of his stick. He relished the simple pleasure of cooking over a fire, the way it had been done by his people since the Dreamtime.

When Jacky had finished the last of the yams, he rubbed his belly and took a deep breath and turned to his woman. Her hand remained where she had placed it, and he could feel the heat of her touch through his trousers. He knew what she was hinting at, and his heart skipped as he thought of their earlier mating.

But there was something he had to tell her, something that had been troubling him for quite some time. He took her hand and moved it aside gently.

"Tarni, there is something we must speak about."

Her happy face disappeared and was replaced by one filled with curiosity.

"What is it, Jacky?"

He drew in a deep breath.

"Tarni, before I met you, before I came to your tribal lands, I married a white girl."

The words seemed to rush from his mouth.

"A white girl? Jacky, you have a white woman?"

"Yes," he said softly, his head dropping.

"Why, Jacky," she said with building anger in her tone, "why would a blackfeller choose a white girl over one of his people? Tell me, Jacky! Tell me!"

"Tarni, you know I did not plan for this to happen. I didn't know that I would meet you. And I didn't know that I wanted you to be my woman."

He braced himself for the blows which he knew were inevitable.

"Your woman? Huh! Who says I am your woman? Go on, git! Go back to your white slut!"

"Tarni, she doesn't see colour. She just sees me. She doesn't see me as just a blackfeller from the bush."

"Get out of here, Jacky! You have seen how good I am with a spear!" she said as she reached for one.

"Tarni, please?" he implored her.

"I want you as my woman. I only want you. Tarni, as soon as this is all over, everything will be alright."

The small girl, tears forming now, cradled the spear and walked off into the gloom.

*****

Chapter 32

Jimmy Boy and Andrews squatted on the ground and watched Wells and Jennings as they pulled out the burnt stumps of the fenceposts and readied the holes for the new ones.

"I don't know if it is worth it, Jimmy. No sooner will I have the fences mended than Reagan will find another way to destroy me."

But Jimmy Boy was brimming with enthusiasm. Kerrigan had eaten a hearty breakfast that morning and enjoyed his first cigarette on the verandah. The rage he carried inside his beaten body was enough to convince Jimmy Boy that the time was ripe to send for Sergeant Tanner.

He conveyed his thoughts to Andrews.

"It's best you ride in alone and fetch the Sergeant, Richard."

"But what will I tell him?" asked Andrews, with lines of worry criss-crossing his face.

Jimmy Boy considered what would be most convincing.

"You need to tell him the truth, Richard. Tell him Kerrigan is here and unable to travel, but he has some important information. And Richard, one more thing. Make sure you mention Reagan's name. That will be enough to bring the police here in a hurry."

Reagan nodded.

"All right. I will do it."

The journey was a blur of blackened earth and persistent heat, but it took Richard Andrews less than two hours to ride into Milburra. As he left the scorched paddocks of his farm behind, he prayed that this whole business would soon be over.

He dismounted at the front of the Police Station, and with nerves playing havoc with his body, he entered the well-lit room. Tanner looked up at the sound of the door creaking open and the man's boots clomping on the floor. He placed his pen down and squinted at his visitor.

"What brings you here?" he grumbled as he leant back and crossed his arms over his chest.

Andrews cleared his throat and felt the sweat dripping down his back as he replied.

"I have come with a message from Jimmy."

Tanner picked something from his front teeth and drawled,

"Jimmy who?"

"The Chinaman. The one who has been staying in Milburra. He's here to see about establishing a Farmers' Co-Operative."

"And what bloody message would a yeller man have for me? I ain't no farmer."

"Sergeant Tanner, Kerrigan is at my farm."

At the mention of the name, Tanner pushed back his chair and stood.

"Kerrigan?"

"Yes. But he is in no fit state to travel, and he has something to tell you about the murder of Howarth."

"Why should I care? It was that black bastard that did Howarth in, and the bastard has pissed off. Left the district. Gone, Mister Andrews! Fucking gone!"

"I think you need to talk with Kerrigan, Sergeant. He is willing to tell the truth about the murder."

Jacky

*****

"Jennings! Wells! You pair knock off for the day. The policeman should be here any minute," Jimmy Boy shouted.

The two men exchanged confused looks.

"What's the police got business here for, Jimmy Boy?" called Wells.

"Just mind your business, Mister Wells, but if you must know, the Sergeant is coming to ask some questions of Kerrigan. So the pair of you make yourselves scarce. Go to the barn and stay there. I don't need extra ears around, especially when they don't know when to remain silent."

He glared at Wells, who took the hint and hastened to the barn.

*****

Kerrigan and Jimmy Boy were sitting in the cane chairs on the verandah as they watched Andrews and the Sergeant ride up. The two men dismounted and clunked their way up the rickety steps where they both pulled up a chair.

"I must say I have seen you looking better, Kerrigan," observed Tanner as he pulled his tobacco pouch from his pocket. As he began to roll a cigarette, his eyes took in the man's bruised and dishevelled form, the bruising under his eyes, and the way his hands trembled slightly as they rested on the table.

Kerrigan managed a wry smile.

"I've seen better days, Sergeant."

Then his smile disappeared, and he said with venom in his voice,

"Nobody runs over the top of me. The man who did this will rue the day he was born."

Tanner took no notice of the words. He was more interested in what Kerrigan had to say about Howarth's murder. All the while, Jimmy Boy sat and said nothing, his face unreadable in the shadows of a hanging pot plant. There was no need for the Sergeant and himself to have any dealings, and the least said the better.

"I believe you have something to tell me, Kerrigan," said Tanner, leaning forward and placing his arms on the table.

"What's the story?"

Kerrigan took a quick, shaky breath and looked at Jimmy Boy, who simply nodded for him to continue.

"It wasn't the blackfeller. Not Jacky. He didn't kill Howarth."

Tanner screwed up his face.

"Then who did? And why the fuckin' hell did you lie about it?"

"I lied because I hate blacks, Sergeant Tanner. Same as you. And Jacky seemed to be gittin' a mite too cosy with Miss Charlene."

"I don't give a horseshit about your love life, Tanner. Who killed Howarth?"

"It was another black. An older man. I thought I recognised him, but from where I just cannot recall. Maybe he spent some time working on Reagan's farm. He just came out of nowhere and chucked his spear into Howarth's gut. Then he threw his boomerang at me and knocked me cold. That's all I remember till I woke up."

Kerrigan scratched his chin.

"This story seems a little too convenient, Kerrigan.

Where is Jacky now?"

"I don't know. He could be anywhere. You know how Mister Reagan is about the blacks. He's probably scared and pissed off well away from the district. And the remaining blacks have gone too, I think. After half their tribe was wiped out, I think they were spooked and all left the district."

Tanner's jaw clenched at the mention of Reagan's name. He knew too well what the man was like, and it was beginning to unnerve him. He regretted the day he took the first of a bundle of cash from the man.

"What do you mean by half the tribe wiped out?"

"What I said. Reagan hired three drifters and sent them on a search and kill mission. Some of Reagan's men claim that they found evidence days later of a mass murder."

Tanner was sweating now. Everything was getting out of hand. He had to put a stop to it. But knowing Reagan, he knew he was facing a difficult task.

"And where are these three men?"

"Dead, Sergeant Tanner. They were fucking killed by the remaining blacks."

"Dead, yes. But where are they?"

Kerrigan gave the Sergeant a scornful look.

"You have known Reagan long enough to know he doesn't like loose ends."

Then he made the sound of a pig squealing and followed it with an oinking sound.

Tanner did some quick thinking. If he was known for anything, it was not for being slow to think on his feet.

"Weeeelll," he drawled, "the way I see it, Howarth was murdered by a blackfeller who is no longer here. Jacky is in the clear and he has pissed off too, it seems."

With each sentence, Tanner ticked off with his fingers.

"Then the three men who killed the blacks are killed themselves, and their bodies ain't nowhere to be found. Then those murderin' blacks piss off too. Seems to me to be an open and shut case. I can't arrest anybody if I don't know where they are. And the district is better off with a few less black heathens anyway."

He looked hard at Kerrigan, and his mind was

working overtime.

"You realise, Kerrigan, that all you have told me won't sit right with Harry Reagan. He will come after you, and I ain't about to put myself in his firin' line by protectin' you."

"I don't need your protection, Tanner. I am leaving this fucking district for good. And you nor anyone will ever see me again."

Jimmy Boy was about to bring up the subject of the Aboriginals kept as slaves by Reagan, but on second thoughts, decided against it.

"Better to wait," he thought.

"No need for Tanner to suspect why I am here."

Then Tanner thought of something.

"Kerrigan," he said with a trace of suspicion, "how did you come by your injuries?"

"Are you such a perfect fucking rider, Sergeant, you ain't never been unsaddled from yer fucking horse?"

"A horse did that to you, Kerrigan? Reagan doesn't hire idiots. I think there is some funny business goin' on 'round here. And I will get to the bottom of it."

*****

Jimmy Boy's expression hardened as he watched the Sergeant make his way back to Milburra.

"Mister Kerrigan, I thank you for what you have done, but now your part is over. It is no longer safe for you to stick around here. You know as well as I do that there is a man who will want you dead. I don't know how many more secrets you have, and I do not wish to know. But anything else you have on Reagan, I suggest you take it with you to America, or Canada, or England. What I have given you is enough to set yourself up for a new life."

The conversation was interrupted by the arrival of Rachel Andrews, carrying a third pot of steaming tea and a plate of sliced sponge cake. Kerrigan's voice came like a sudden storm cloud on an otherwise fine day.

"I figure I might hang 'round here for a bit, Jimmy Boy. I have had enough of this place and the people, but I figure I owe Andrews and his sister. Especially his sister."

He attempted to stand but wobbled and fell back on his chair. Rachel was quick to place a steadying arm on his shoulder.

"I reckon it's time I settled down and made a new life," he continued.

"And I want a life here in my country. Not a life in some foreign land."

What he said next surprised everyone.

"And I sure would like to know Miss Andrews a heap better, if that is all right with you, Richard?"

His eyes were begging for forgiveness and making a silent plea for redemption.

"I would work your place for a bed and food and hope to repay you, Richard."

He then turned to Jimmy Boy.

"And Jimmy Boy, when I am stronger, I will fetch the bank note and gold you gave me from where I hid it from Reagan. You can have it back. I have realised that I cannot accept money for simply telling the truth."

They all remained silent, digesting the brutal truth of Kerrigan's words.

Were they the words of a hired thug and stand-over

man? Each soul listening to his words suddenly developed a completely different opinion of the man.

"I am a man who honours his word, Mister Kerrigan. You fulfilled your promise to me and cleared Jacky's name. I cannot take back what I have given you."

"But Mister Kerrigan, you cannot stay here. It is not safe for you," said Rachel.

Kerrigan's eyes showed traces of weariness and guilt.

"Where did I go wrong in life, Miss Andrews?"

Kerrigan placed a gentle arm on Rachel's shoulder.

"I know I have made mistakes, but I can change. I know what you have done for me, and I want to repay you and your brother."

Rachel knew she was torn between the help he could give them on the farm and the connection that was growing between her and the man who had stumbled into her life.

The silence stretched between them, only broken by the laughter of a kookaburra in the distance. Rachel took a deep breath.

"Mister Kerrigan, I have had sleepless nights because

of you. I have thought about us and… I am willing to give us a chance.”

She could still see the scars of the whip marks on his body, but she could see something else… a softness, a vulnerability of a man searching for his place in the world.

He pulled her into his arms and placed his lips on her mouth.

*****

Despite the fact that Jacky had now been cleared of Howarth's murder, Jimmy Boy was still far from happy. Jacky had not been sighted for days now, and Jimmy Boy was tired and just wanted to return to his home.

“We seem to be right back to where we started, Richard. Although Sergeant Tanner will call off the hunt for Jacky, we are no closer to freeing Burra's people.”

He sighed and watched as a solitary kangaroo bounced across the charred remains of Andrews' wheat crop. The sight of the big 'roo only served to remind him of the freedom so cruelly denied to the Aborigines. He knew that they had to come up with a plan.

"Richard, I think that Kerrigan knows far more than he has told us. If we can get him to open up, we might succeed in our attempt to free the blacks. Do you think that Rachel…?"

"Jimmy, you shame me and my sister!"

He thumped his fists on the table.

"Do you expect my sister to virtually prostitute herself to gain information for you? You have disappointed me, Jimmy."

Jimmy Boy was surprised at Andrews' reaction, but on second thoughts, he realised he had gone about it all wrong.

"I am truly sorry, Richard. But there has been a misunderstanding. What I meant was, if Kerrigan is so keen on your sister, then he might open up and give us some dirt on Reagan. Anything we can use legally against the man. Kerrigan has said himself that he wants to remain here and begin a new life. Well, he cannot do that while ever Reagan is around. In other words, we need to be rid of Reagan for good."

Andrews remained unconvinced.

"I don't want to use my sister as a pawn, Jimmy. We will speak with the man ourselves."

"As you wish. We will do it your way."

*****

"Mister Kerrigan, we are back to the beginning. What we set out to achieve, we have failed to accomplish."

"But you have accomplished it, Jimmy. I have told Sergeant Tanner that Jacky did not murder Howarth."

"That was an offshoot of our purpose here, Mister Kerrigan."

"Hey, how about enough of the 'Mister' moniker, Jimmy. The name is Arthur."

Kerrigan began to roll a cigarette, conscious of Jimmy Boy's eyes on his face.

"You got somethin' to say, Jimmy, then say it. No need to be beatin' 'round the bush."

"OK, Arthur. I have a certain feeling inside me that I just cannot seem to let go. I think there are certain things that you have withheld from us. And from Sergeant Tanner."

"Like what?"

"That is what I want you to tell me. Perhaps I can get you started with some prompts, Arthur Kerrigan."

"Then jis prompt away, Jimmy."

"What can you tell me about the murder of the Lamberts?"

Jimmy Boy made a point of studying the man for any reaction, but Kerrigan maintained a straight face.

"The Lamberts? They were murdered by the blacks."

"Do you have something against Aborigines, Arthur? You seem to say the word 'black' with bitterness in your voice. You talk about them like they have wronged you in some way."

Jimmy Boy could see he had hit a raw spot. Kerrigan was barely able to contain his rage. His hands thumped the table, sending cups and plates crashing to the floor.

"You wouldn't understand, Jimmy."

"Try me, Arthur Kerrigan."

He shook his head with unspoken resentments before he managed to speak.

"They took everything from me, Jimmy."

The Chinaman could see the pain in the man's eyes, but he was persistent.

"Everything? What do you mean?"

"They came in the dead of night. They were screamin' and hollerin' like animals. The blacks, Jimmy. It was the blacks. They took my sister first. I could do nothin' but watch from my secret hideout in my room. I heard her screams, Jimmy. The fear in her voice. I was a fuckin' ten-year-old boy!"

He paused, wiping away the tears that had formed.

"Then they came for my mama and pappy. Of course, my pappy fought back, but there was just too many of them. My pappy died with a black's spear in his gut. They dragged my mama and sister away right before my eyes, and that was the last I ever saw of them. But I heard their cries in the dark, Jimmy. I didn't know then, but I know now. The bastards took them into the scrub and shoved their fucking black cocks into them."

Jimmy Boy reached across and placed a comforting arm on the man's shoulder.

"I cannot help what has happened to you in the past, but I can offer you some solace. Not all Aborigines are the same, Arthur. It is the same as every race of people. White men, black men, brown men, and even yellow man like me. There are both good and evil in every race."

Jimmy Boy let the man compose himself before he added,

"Do you know how you got to this farm?"

Kerrigan smiled with a sense of satisfaction.

"Ahh, I see. You are expecting thanks for finding me and bringing me here. Well, thanks, Jimmy. There. It's done. I have said my piece. Now you can walk away and feel like the fuckin' hero you are trying to be."

Jimmy Boy was becoming frustrated with the man.

"It was an Aboriginal who saved you from a certain and cruel death, Arthur. It was Jacky who rescued you from the clutches of Reagan's men and brought you here."

"Jacky?"

His face held a mask of disbelief.

"But he hates me. Why would he bother to save me?"

Jimmy Boy gave a sad smile.

"Maybe he was just trying to tell you that not all Aborigines are murderers and kidnappers. Without him, you would be at the bottom of the river, just another forgotten victim of Reagan's ruthlessness. That is why nobody must know you are still around the district."

Kerrigan was speechless, the truth finally hitting him hard. The very race he despised, and a man who hated him, had saved him from death. All he could say over and again was,

"Why? Why would he do that?"

*****

Chapter 33

Martha stared at the clock on the wall.

"Time is something I cannot control, Will."

She turned to face him, her hands clutching the fabric of her skirt.

"Will, I know this isn't what you want to hear, but Bindi and I must return home in two days' time."

Will's hands paused mid-air. He shoved the two books he had been dusting back into the shelf.

"I have dreaded this day, Martha. But I knew it had to come. So, it's back to the farm? And back to Jacky?" he said forlornly.

"Will, don't you see? It's best for now. I can return to Wicklow and talk with my mother and grandmother and tell them of my decision. Oh, Will, you know I want to be with you. You know I will return."

His eyes fell to the floor as he realised the enormous pressure his beloved was facing—the implications of leaving Jacky, the man she had wed, and choosing to return to Sydney and be with him.

Martha leaned across and took his hand.

"I'll come back. I promise, Will. Once I have talked with my mother and worked things out, I will return."

He squeezed her hand in return and said,

"All right. But promise me, Martie, that you won't change your mind."

*****

Jacky sat at the edge of the billabong and recalled swimming with Tarni. He was a shattered man, but he knew the girl had every reason to be angry with him. He scooped up a handful of pebbles and cast them into the water and watched the ripples come and go. The ripples were like the tale of Jacky's love story—Tarni by his side one moment and gone the next.

He had warned himself about becoming emotionally attached to the young girl. And he had promised himself he would never leave his wife. But as he continued to study the ripples, he found himself unsure. His days spent with Tarni had made him feel happy—happier than he had felt for quite some time. He had tried to keep both worlds separate, but the truth, the reality of his situation, just would not go away.

Frogs began their nightly chorus, a sound which normally brought him peace, but now they only highlighted the empty feeling in his chest.

He was tired. His head ached. His heart ached.

"She will return," he told himself, but the moon had crossed the sky almost halfway and there was no sign of her. He was sure she would be back by now, tears in her eyes, and they would talk things over. But the night remained still and silent, save for the sad howl of a dingo in the distance.

*****

Tarni's legs ached as she pushed through the thick undergrowth, her eyes scanning the area for a suitable place to rest now the shadows were growing longer. She had been walking for hours, the anger at Jacky's betrayal simmering in her breasts.

She stumbled into a clearing revealing a small, even patch of ground, littered with dead leaves and twigs, where she could build a temporary shelter. She set about gathering branches and foliage and built her gunyah. It wasn't the best, but she knew it would give her some comfort through what she knew would be a long night.

Jacky

*****

"Charley, do you see that?"

Harry Reagan and Charley had been riding since early morning, checking the boundary fences. As they rode past the sweat-lined backs of the Aborigines toiling in the heat, grubbing out stumps, Charley turned her head. She hated seeing men forced to work, and she hated having to look into the sad eyes of the captives. The sounds of her father's men barking orders to the wretched souls made her spine shiver.

Charley squinted her eyes and looked in the direction Reagan pointed.

"It's not a kangaroo," said Reagan, "but I just cannot make out what it is."

Charley looked harder.

"It's a person, Papa."

"Who the bloody hell would be out walking in this heat?"

But he knew the answer.

"It has to be one of the blacks, Charley. I thought we had seen the last of them. C'mon, let's go and take a look."

Tarni heard the horses before she saw them, and she began running in a low, angling gait towards the creek. She had been careful to avoid people since she had left Jacky, but now it seemed as if her luck had run out. If she could just make it to the creek, then she had a chance of swimming to the other side and hiding amongst the reeds.

The hooves grew closer and she didn't dare look back. Even the fastest of warriors couldn't outrun a horse, and she was no match for the warriors from her tribe. She could hear the gurgling of the creek, as if calling her to safety, but then she sprawled headlong into the dust from a boot to her back. She rolled over to face her pursuer and looked into the evil eyes of Harry Reagan.

He climbed from his horse and pulled her up.

"What the bloody hell are you running for?"

Tarni hawked her throat and spat greenish-yellow phlegm on his boots.

"What do you want with me? Let me go. Please," she begged, but Reagan couldn't understand a word she said.

He raised his arm and backhanded her across the cheek. Blood trickled from the corner of her mouth, and she began to weep quietly.

"Charley, toss me down the rope. I will take this one home with us. Never know, she may come in handy as a bargaining chip if there are any more like her around."

Charley shook her head sadly.

"Papa, when is all this going to stop?"

"When I say so, Charley. Now toss me that rope. I sure like the look of this one."

*****

The shed was dark and oppressive, and it took some time for Tarni's eyes to grow accustomed to the gloom. The air was stale and smelt of dust and the unwashed bodies of people. Or animals? As her vision swam into focus, she saw them. Dim figures huddled and shackled against the wall, their eyes wide and haunted. They were women and children, and their skin was the same colour as her own. Tarni realised she was imprisoned with the very people that Jacky and herself had promised to rescue. These were Burra's people. The people that Jacky had come from a faraway land to rescue.

At the thought of him, her eyes teared up, but she

brushed them away. She saw no point in showing any weakness in front of the miserable wretches still clinging to hope. They stared at her, not with hostility but with a quiet, solemn curiosity. This was the same girl that had come in the night with the warrior. The one who had promised them freedom. But where was their saviour?

Tarni spoke to them in her Kamilaroi language, but the only response was bewildered stares. She tried sign language, but to no avail. The people imprisoned with her just didn't seem to care. They realised that their hopes of freedom had been dashed with the imprisonment of this girl.

Tarni thought for a while, and suddenly she realised what she needed to say to give the people hope.

With rising excitement, she said a solitary word.

"Jacky."

At the mention of the warrior's name, the faces of the captives became animated, and there was a silent buzz around the shed.

"Jacky is coming to save us."

*****

Jacky

Jimmy Boy and Andrews sat on the verandah, each man cradling a small glass of sherry. They were carefully studying the forms of Kerrigan and Rachel Andrews, returning from a walk to the river.

"What do you make of Kerrigan, Jimmy?"

"Well, Richard, your sister seems to have complete trust in him, and I have noted her wisdom. She is a fine judge of character. But as for me, I see a man carrying a bitter legacy. He cannot seem to let go of the past. I know it must have been horrible for him at such a young age to watch as his family was abducted by the Aboriginals. Which brings me to the next thing I wish to raise with the man. I need to know how much he knows about the southern tribe that Reagan has imprisoned somewhere on his farm."

He swallowed the last of his glass of sherry and poured another.

"If only Jacky would pay us a visit. I don't know what he is doing or where he is. And we need him, Richard."

"We only need him if both he and Kerrigan can get along, Jimmy."

*****

"Where is Jacky now, Jimmy?"

"That is a question I cannot answer, Arthur. He is like a ghost sometimes. But a trustworthy ghost at that. He would be watching every move by everyone in the district. Including us."

Jimmy Boy's words caused Kerrigan to glance around him, half expecting the black man to jump out and ambush him. Jimmy Boy decided the time was right.

"What can you tell me about the Aboriginals Harry Reagan has chained up somewhere on his farm?"

Kerrigan took a deep breath. He knew the Chinaman was not going to let it rest until he had answers.

"You have been fishin' 'round fer the past week, Jimmy. I think it's 'bout time I came clean."

He kept his eyes on Rachel Andrews as she pegged the laundry on the line and did not look at Jimmy Boy as he began his narrative.

"They're not Aboriginals from 'round here. A while back now, I led a team of men, and we drove a mob of sheep from Reagan's farm right way down south to the Hawkesbury.

After we delivered the sheep, we all got liquored up. We were drunk for a week. Reagan had promised us a bonus for our work. Anyway, after we sobered up, we headed for home. That was when we came upon the tribe you are looking for. Well, you know how men are, Jimmy. There was a couple of nice young ones in the group, and the men had some fun with them. To cut a long tale short, we decided to bring them with us. It was a big mistake. Harry Reagan saw the chance for free labour, and he grabbed at it."

Kerrigan paused for a while and took a few deep breaths. Jimmy Boy knew it was hard on the man, but he knew he needed to tell the story.

"They are treated worse than animals, Jimmy. They are worked while ever there is sunshine and are barely kept fed. At night they are kept chained up. They have become Reagan's personal slaves. Slaves to build his empire on. I hated every moment of every day working for that man."

"Sometimes I have no faith in my fellow man," muttered Jimmy Boy.

Kerrigan continued.

"He just wanted more land, Jimmy. And the local

Kamilaroi lands are prime real estate. That is why he has been trying to get the blacks to move on. Then there are the people who won't sell, so he just takes it. With the Sergeant on his payroll, there's not much anyone can do."

Jimmy Boy did not appear shocked. What Kerrigan told him he had already guessed. Tanner was under Reagan's thumb as well. And without realising, Kerrigan had told Jimmy Boy what he wanted to know. Reagan was responsible for the murder of the Lamberts.

"But you stayed loyal to him?"

"I wasn't what you could call loyal. I was fearful for my life. Anybody who went against Reagan paid the price."

"The price?"

"They were dealt with by Bruce."

*****

"He just got up and walked away, Richard. He told me how the Aborigines ended up at Harry Reagan's, and then when he mentioned a name—Bruce—he suddenly turned pale and cleared out."

"Bruce? I have no idea who that could be. Can't say as

I have ever heard the name before around here."

*****

Jennings spotted the lone figure trudging through the blackened paddock. He tossed the soil from his shovel and then put his weight on it to relieve his aching body.

"Looks like Jacky has decided to pay us a visit, Wells."

The other man raised his head wearily.

"Bout time too, Jennin's. 'e might give us a bloody 'and with this fencin'."

Jacky, having seen the two men, pushed himself into a slow trot, his feet paining from the hard ground and the thorny country he had passed through. As he puffed himself to a stop, he accepted the water canteen handed to him by Wells and gulped the sweet liquid down until the container was as dry as the country he had walked through.

"Didn't your Mama tell ya, Jacky? Never drink too much at once. Bring a man undone mighty quick it will."

Jacky ignored Jennings' advice.

"Where's Jimmy Boy?"

"Him and Richard, and maybe Kerrigan, are in the barn

workin' on the reaper. Got me buggared why though. That man jis ain't about to git no wheat this season."

Without a word, Jacky headed for the barn where he found the three men bent over the reaper. Jimmy Boy wiped his oily hands on a rag and motioned towards the chairs in the corner. Kerrigan, meanwhile, at the sight of Jacky, put down the hammer he was holding and headed for the barn door.

Jimmy Boy opened the conversation with a rebuke.

"Jacky," he said rather sarcastically, "it is certainly good of you to pay us a visit."

Jacky had never heard his friend speak like this, and he could only put it down to the stress of being away so long from his farm and his family.

"I am sorry, Jimmy Boy. But I have had more important things on my mind."

"Important things? Jacky, what is important is us freeing Burra's people and getting the hell back home. We both have a family if you have not forgotten, Jacky."

Wells and Jennings came in and saw how agitated their boss was. Jennings placed a calming arm on his shoulder.

"Steady it up, Jimmy Boy. Don't be speakin' to Jacky like that. He must have 'is reasons."

The Chinaman sighed.

"So Jacky, what is the problem now? What is so important?"

"It's Tarni. She has gone missing."

"Seems like every man and 'is dog goes missin' 'round these parts. Jimmy Boy, why don't we jis go on 'ome?" said Wells.

"Next thing you know I'll go missin'."

"Sooner the better, Wells," threw in Jennings.

"Who or what is Tarni?" asked Jimmy Boy.

"Tarni is the granddaughter of Nullah, the head of the Kamilaroi tribe."

"What happened?"

"We argued and she left. I have not seen her for two days now."

"But I was led to believe that the entire tribe went south to stay at Shanghai."

"That is correct, Jimmy Boy. But for some reason, Tarni chose to stay with me. Her father was murdered by Reagan's men, and I can only imagine she has revenge on her mind. The same as all of us."

Jimmy Boy studied the face of the handsome warrior.

"Jacky, why should one person take priority over a whole tribe?"

Jacky sensed the insinuation but remained poker-faced.

"Wouldn't you care for the safe keeping of someone who saved your life, Jimmy Boy? Not once, but twice. I could have died from a poisonous spider bite, but she knew the bush medicine I needed. And I would have been shot in the gut if not for her spear."

Jimmy Boy hung his head.

"I am sorry if I doubted you, Jacky. We need to sit down and devise a plan. A damned good plan!"

"Another of your half-arsed plans, Jimmy Boy," Jacky said under his breath

*****

"Arthur, deep down you are a good man," Rachel spoke softly.

"You are not the bitter man that people see. While I nursed you back to health, you were delirious and rambling, and most of it was nonsense. But you did say things that made me come to know you."

"Like what?"

"You talked about your sister and your parents, but what touched me the most was that you talked about regret, about a life wasted in anger and bitterness. And you raved to God, asking forgiveness."

Kerrigan's face flushed.

"I ain't never been one for God, Rachel."

"Then maybe deep down it is time to find Him. And you can start by giving thanks to Jacky for saving your life."

Kerrigan stood and walked off the verandah. He bent and pulled a wild daisy, stuffed it under his nose, and said,

"A beautiful flower but no scent whatsoever."

"Arthur Kerrigan," remonstrated Rachel, "stop trying to avoid the issue. Now will you thank Jacky or not? Prove to me that you are a good man with a good heart, Arthur

Kerrigan, please?"

He tossed the flower into the air and turned and said,

"On one condition, Rachel Andrews."

"Speak away."

"Promise me that one day, if I can prove myself, that you may consider me as a husband."

Rachel burst out laughing.

"That is one promise I can make and easily keep."

*****

Chapter 34

"You sure do make a good cuppa tea, Mister Cornelius," said Bindi as she balanced the cup in the mannerisms of Martha and the white folk. The porcelain cup was delicate and a sharp contrast to the rough and calloused hands that held it.

Cornelius looked up from his own cup, his eyes searching Bindi's.

"Bindi, there is something I must ask you."

Bindi felt her heart flutter. She had suspected this moment was coming, and she had steeled herself for it. It was the way in which Cornelius watched her, his eyes never leaving hers when she spoke, and his touch lingering a tad too long when they said goodbye. She placed her cup back on the saucer with a delicate clink.

"What would that be, Mister Cornelius?"

"Bindi, I cannot bear the thought of you leaving," he confessed.

"The city has changed you. You have grown into city life, become so much more than you could have ever imagined. I want you to stay. I know you miss the countryside, but there is so much I want to show you and teach you."

"Mister Cornelius, I know you mean me well, but I cannot live 'ere in the city. This place is way too big for me and would never feel like 'ome. This old black heart of mine is in the land, the animals, and the stars shining over my ancestors. I jis cannot leave all that to stay 'ere."

Cornelius Deakin nodded slowly and sadly. He had gotten the response he had expected. He took a biscuit from the tray and snapped it, letting crumbs fall onto the floor.

"Then I imagine it is goodbye," said Cornelius.

Bindi's eyes sparkled.

"But there ain't no harm in you comin' to visit me, Mister Cornelius."

"Yes, I think I would enjoy a trip to the countryside and see how the rest of the world lives. But Bindi, I want you to have something."

He produced a book and handed it to her.

She scoffed.

"Didn't you know this old black git can't read?"

"Then maybe it is about time you learned, Bindi."

She examined the book's cover and traced the title.

"What's this say?"

"Pride and Prejudice."

"Jis have to learn what them words mean then, won't I?"

*****

"What do you have there?" asked Martha as she noticed the book Bindi was clasping to her bosom. Bindi had her one bag already packed while Martha was folding the last of her clothing.

"Jis some silly book Mister Cornelius gave me. Told me about time I learn to read."

Martha took the book and read the cover.

"Pride and Prejudice. A very good choice, Bindi. You know, reading is like a journey, Bindi. It leads you to places unknown. Each page is a new path."

"The only path I want, Miss Martie, is the path back 'ome. And the way this bloke is driving this buggy, we'll be lucky to git home alive."

531

Will remained silent, but Bindi was excited. She had enjoyed the boat travel to Sydney and was looking forward to the ocean trip again.

"Be good to git home. Better to smell a gumtree than the rotten air in this big town."

"Yes, the bush has its own scent that is awfully hard to forget."

The buggy pulled to a stop at the dockside. The ship that would take them to Newcastle loomed large before them, swaying on the rope that tethered it to the dock. Seagulls squawked noisily above them, and the smell of the salt water was overpowering for the two ladies from up country.

Will still had not spoken. He helped the buggy driver carry the cases to the loading ramp, where a sailor hefted them on his shoulders and took them aboard.

Finally, Will broke his silence.

"Then it is goodbye for now."

Martha raised his chin with her hand and smiled.

"But it is not goodbye forever, Will McKenzie."

He kissed Bindi on the cheek.

"Goodbye, Bindi."

"Be seein' yer, Mister Will."

Martha offered her cheek but was not surprised when he placed his lips on hers. He pulled away and in a soft voice said,

"I love you, Martha Wang."

*****

"You saved my life, Jacky," said Kerrigan, his voice gruff and tinged with emotion and a trace of embarrassment.

Jacky looked up from the bale of hay he had been sleeping on and sniffed at the stale scent of the straw and the horse shit.

"What's got you saying that, Kerrigan?"

"Back at the river, you saved me from Reagan's men. They were going to drown me. If not for you, I would be dead. But you didn't only save me from drowning, you saved me from what I was becoming. I want to say thank you, Jacky."

Jacky nodded, understanding how hard it was for Kerrigan to say the words.

"You are welcome," said Jacky in a steady voice.

"We all make mistakes, but it is important that we learn from them."

Kerrigan stepped closer.

"I have never thanked a black man before, but… thank you."

He reached out and took Jacky's hands. The black man felt the sincerity in the grasp.

"I have never been a hero or saviour, Kerrigan. I just did what any man would do."

Kerrigan grinned.

"There. It's off my chest now. Rachel will be pleased."

"You mean you did this just to please Rachel Andrews?"

"No, Jacky. She asked me to thank you, but I did it of my own accord because I am man enough to show gratitude."

"I had you figured as a better man than you made yourself out to be, Kerrigan. Seems I was right."

Kerrigan's face became hard once more as he mulled over some seemingly difficult things he needed to say.

"I think it is about time I told Jimmy and the others the full story."

*****

"I was with Harry Reagan the day the Lamberts were murdered. Me and Howarth. Harry Reagan committed cold-blooded murder."

Jimmy Boy and Andrews leaned in closer, their faces a mixture of surprise and curiosity. Jacky remained aloof, his face a blank canvas.

"Can you prove it? Tell me the whole story, Arthur. Leave nothing out."

"It was common knowledge that Harry Reagan wanted the Lambert farm. Then, when the couple was found murdered, the townsfolk whispered Reagan's name, but nobody dared accuse him outright."

"What about the police investigation?"

"Again, everyone knows of Sergeant Tanner's cowardice when it comes to crossing Reagan. He did a perfunctory investigation, and everything pointed to the aboriginals as the murderers. It wasn't too long and the whole business was forgotten."

"What was your role in this?" asked Jimmy Boy, eager to hear the truth.

Kerrigan steeled his face.

"I swear that I had no part in the murders, Jimmy. I was simply a witness to the whole ghastly affair. An alibi, if you like, for Reagan. Howarth and I were under no illusions as to what would happen to us if we ever spoke of the incident."

He hung his head for a while and collected his thoughts.

"It has troubled me every night since it happened, Jimmy."

Then he turned to Andrews.

"Richard, for me to prove myself to you, and to win your sister, I swear I am telling the truth."

"So you kept all this to yourself for fear of reprisals by Reagan?" questioned Andrews.

"Why aren't you afraid now?"

"I am afraid. Fear is something that is lurking inside me every waking hour. I don't care to face Bruce."

Jennings and Wells stomped up onto the verandah and pulled up a stool.

"Who is Bruce?" asked Wells, always eager to join a conversation.

Jimmy Boy was quick to shut the inquisitive man down.

"Mister Wells, please remain silent. This is important."

He turned back to Kerrigan.

"You mentioned Bruce before. But who is he?"

Kerrigan continued.

"The townsfolk have heard the whispers, but what I tell you is the gospel truth. The truth Harry Reagan has tried so hard to keep hidden. What I am about to tell you would turn even the strongest man into a quivering, spewing wreck."

"You better git then, Jennings. Yer even afraid to take a shit in a paddock in case a snake bites yer arse."

"That is enough!" roared Jimmy Boy.

"Go and occupy yourself elsewhere, Mister Jennings."

Jennings, like a dog with its tail between its legs,

skulked off mumbling to himself.

"Go on," urged Jacky.

Kerrigan drew a deep breath.

"Bruce is Harry Reagan's son, Charley's brother. He was born a simpleton. Bruce raises pigs, big nasty things that would eat anything you threw at them. And Harry Reagan, with his fair share of enemies, folks who knew too much, or anyone who questioned him or stood in his way, well, he would just send them to Bruce, and they would disappear."

"You mean……."

"Exactly what I mean, Richard."

Kerrigan grabbed at his head and began sobbing.

"The stench of those pig pens, the screams of those tormented souls, I can never forget!"

Jimmy Boy was aghast. His yellow skin had turned a sickly orangish hue.

"Alive? He fed live bodies to swine?"

"Some," mumbled Kerrigan, "but mostly they were dead."

Jacky recalled tying the bodies of men on horseback and sending them back to Reagan, but he felt no sympathy. He visualised Tarni hurling a spear and his heart sank.

"Where are you now, Tarni?"

*****

Reagan sat up with a start, his heart thumping in his chest, and the room spun as he staggered from his bed. He knew he should not have had the extra rum, but he had needed it to chase away the panic he had been experiencing. He squinted into the darkness. His house had always been his fortress, but right now it felt like a prison.

The clock downstairs chimed midnight, and the mournful sound echoed through the house like a funeral dirge. Usually, he found the sound comforting, but right now he felt the rhythmic tone of time passing him by. The distant sounds of nocturnal animals disturbed him and felt much closer than usual, and he couldn't shake the feeling he was being watched.

His eyes darted around the room, and he searched for any sign of movement. To reassure himself, he caressed the pistol he pulled from beneath his pillow.

The floorboards groaned in protest at his weight as he

pulled his trousers on, and then he lit the candle beside his bed. The little light it gave comforted him and made him feel more secure. Reagan stumbled to the window, the glass cold against his forehead, and he listened as the whispers of the breeze carried reminders of the vengeance that awaited him outside his domain. His workmen, once loyal and feared bodyguards, had been picked off and their lifeless bodies sent back to him as a reminder of things to come. The aboriginals were not to be trifled with, and here he was, a prisoner of his own fear.

The aboriginal girl! The thought of her brought a twisted smile to his face. She was his consolation, his prize, a way of showing the black heathens that he was not to be messed with. He had seen the way she had looked at him when he had shackled her in the shed. It had filled him with a perverse sense of power. He poured another rum and tossed it down, exhaled, burped, and farted. The shed was a short distance from the house. As he walked to the door, every creak of the floorboards set his nerves on edge. But he knew every step he took brought the realisation he was closer to his prize.

As he approached the shed, the moon illuminated the lock holding his captives. As he stepped inside, he could smell stale piss, damp earth, and an overwhelming sense of fear.

Tarni was huddled in the corner, and as he entered, she hissed at him like a wild cat.

Reagan felt himself growing hard, a mixture of anger and lust driving him. He was going to enjoy her, and at the same time, in his own warped way, he would punish the rest of her tribe. Tarni's eyes fixed on the pistol tucked in his belt, and he could recognise the calculations in her head.

"Would she fight? Would she beg?"

He was hoping for both. Her skin was the colour of the earth, smooth and unblemished. He reached out and stroked her chin, and she made no attempt to move. He could feel the heat and the fear coming off her body, and it intoxicated him more than the rum he had consumed.

Reagan leaned in and whispered into her neck,

"You are mine now, girl."

He fumbled with the key and unchained one ankle so as to spread her legs, and then he dropped his trousers and stood naked in front of her.

Harry Reagan then yanked her head back and looked into her eyes. It was like looking into the eyes of a cornered animal, despairing and fierce. It only served to make his desire stronger. He grabbed the rags she had covering her and ripped them away, revealing her legs, bruised from the chains with which she was bound. Tarni kicked at him, but the chain allowed her no room at all to deliver a decisive blow.

"Fight me," he slurred, "it will only make it better."

The girl's breath was sharp and fast, her chest rising and falling, trying to contain her fury. She spat at him, and Reagan pulled back. He placed a finger to the globule of saliva and then put the spit on his tongue and savoured it, his eyes now wide with excitement.

Then the unthinkable happened. The shed door creaked open, revealing a sight that sent chills through him. Charley stood there, wide-eyed and open-mouthed.

"Papa! What are you doing?"

"Charley, what are you doing here?"

"I could ask you the same question. I heard noises and thought the aboriginals were coming for us."

Reagan covered the dwindling erection he had been so proud of, and she said,

"Papa, you can't fight aborigines with that spear."

She pointed at his half-flaccid member, signalling to her what his intentions had been.

"You are a disgusting man! Put your trousers on and leave these people alone!"

She turned and stormed out.

Reagan felt his face burn with shame as he attempted to pull his pants up. In the corner, Tarni suppressed a giggle. The man's face grew even redder, and he shouted at the girl,

"What the hell is so funny, you little black bitch?" he roared, his face contorted with anger.

The giggle she had been trying to silence turned into loud laughter and only served to enrage the man more. Then, without another word, he dropped his trousers again.

"Guess I will have to finish what I started."

Tarni's laughter stopped. She realised now her mockery was a mistake. She had only served to rekindle Reagan's lust. Desperately, she looked around for anything she could use as a weapon, but her captor had ensured there was nothing in the cramped shed. Then, with a sickening thud,

Reagan's beefy hand smashed across her cheek. She could hear the shouts of the men and the wails of the women as she lapsed into semi-consciousness.

He fell on her naked body, his corpulent shape just managing to fit between her legs. Through her pain, she could feel the tip of his resurrected erection searching for an entry. But the girl was not going to give in without a fight. As she felt him ever so slightly push into her, with a sudden surge of strength, she used one hand to yank him by the hair and pull his head away. With her other hand, she used the long nails on her fingers to claw at his left eye. His screams filled the shed, drowning out the cries of the other prisoners, and Tarni smiled as she felt the warmth of his blood spill over her fingers.

"You have fuckin' blinded me, you black bitch!" he roared as he rolled around on the ground.

Her eyes fastened on the key which had fallen from his grasp, and she was quick to retrieve it and undo the remaining chain from her ankle. Reagan was rolling around on the floor, covered in the damp earth where the prisoners had pissed.

Tarni knew she had to seize the opportunity and release the others, but before she had a chance to insert the key into the lock, the shed door opened, and light spilled in. Charley stood there with a shotgun in her hand, and her face took on a mask of fear as she saw the demonic eyes of the black girl. She raised the shotgun and levelled it at the girl, but every instinct Tarni possessed drove her forward, and her head slammed into the crotch of Reagan's daughter. Charley collapsed on the floor with a whimper, and Tarni sprinted out the door and into the night.

*****

Chapter 35

Telegrams were something Jimmy Boy still hadn't quite gotten used to, but he knew one thing for sure: they only ever brought good news or bad.

And the words he read outside the Milburra Post Office weren't good.

Come home at once. Ellie.

He folded the paper and stowed it in his pocket. Now he had to ride hard to Andrews' farm and tell the others.

*****

There were murmurs from the men, but the only voice of dissent came from Jacky.

"I know how much you want to free the tribe, but we cannot dive headlong into danger. Reagan still has the power of the law behind him, and we can't underestimate Tanner."

"But Jimmy Boy, if we don't do something soon…"

Jimmy Boy could see the anger rising in the black man's face. He held up his hand.

"Richard's farm needs tending to. And we can't forget

that. We cannot abandon the hand that feeds us all. All of you need to settle down and run the farm till I return. I have a plan."

"You always have a plan, Jimmy Boy," said Jacky, shaking his head, "and where have your plans gotten us?"

"We are still alive, aren't we?"

Jimmy Boy noted that it was the first time Jacky had ever disagreed so strongly with him on anything.

"So, what's the plan?"

"I am going to get real help. An outside policeman. Someone who can take down Reagan and Tanner."

"You're not thinking of Connolly? He won't do it."

"I am a very persuasive man when I want to be."

But Jacky was just as stubborn as Jimmy Boy was confident.

"I am telling you, Jimmy Boy, your gold will not work its magic with Connolly."

"I have no intention of buying his support. I will appeal to his conscience. Haven't you noticed? The man is a churchgoing, well-meaning, and responsible law officer. And I think he has friends in high places in Newcastle. The sort of friends we so desperately need."

"Then I will do it my own way, Jimmy Boy. I need to find the girl."

"I cannot stop you in your endeavours, Jacky, but whatever you do, make certain you do not jeopardise the lives of the others."

*****

Mia's eyes squinted as she looked over the drying clothes into the dying sun, and she could just discern the figure of a man on horseback.

"Miss Ellie, yer 'usband's 'ome," she called.

Before the dust kicked up by the horse had settled, Ellie was by its side. Jimmy Boy searched her face, with lines of worry shrouding his own.

"What's wrong? The telegram said to come at once. Where's Angela? Has anything happened to Martha?"

The words spilled from his mouth like a rushing torrent of water.

"Nothing like that, Jimmy Boy. I think those new telegrams seem to make everything worse than they seem.

Everyone is fine. But come inside and have something cold to drink. We will talk after supper."

*****

"It's Martha," began Ellie.

"We have received a letter from her, and it seems she has made a choice. She wants to leave Jacky and go to Sydney and live with Will."

Jimmy Boy swallowed hard. This was one thing he had never anticipated. He thought hard before he said,

"She needs our support, Ellie, not our judgement."

"Well, she will be home from Sydney tomorrow. I anticipate a very big family talk, Jimmy Boy."

*****

"That's the coach now, Jimmy Boy," warned Jack as he wiped the tables down, keeping an eye on the clock above the bar.

Jimmy Boy tipped his beer down and picked up his hat.

"You're right. Best not to keep them waiting. See you, Jack. They'll be tired, I figure, so I'll take them straight home to Wicklow."

With a final nod to his friend, he pushed through the doors and stepped outside. It was late afternoon, and he could hear hooves and the jingle of harnesses. The coach rolled into view, and he saw his daughter's smiling face out the window. When it stopped, the coach driver called out a greeting, and Jimmy Boy stepped forward with an outstretched arm to help the women down. The driver unloaded their bags and tossed them in the wagon with a grunt.

"Thank you, kind sir," said Bindi.

"No need fer any sir fer me," he barked.

"Only tryin' to be bloody well nice, mister."

She turned to Martie and said,

"Some people jis ain't soph——"

"Sophisticated, Bindi."

"Yeah, that too."

The trio climbed aboard the wagon, and Jimmy Boy rattled the reins. They were off to Wicklow. Jimmy Boy waited for Martha to speak, his hands holding the leather reins gently.

The silence seemed to stretch on for an eternity. Bindi

was taking a nap, the effects of the sea voyage and then the coach travel tiring her aging body out. Jimmy Boy broke the silence.

"Well, my daughter, have you anything to tell me?"

"Papa, you know I have. Please, Papa, don't be mad."

"You can speak easily with me, Martha," he gave her a gentle nudge.

"What has Mama told you?" she asked.

"Only the basics. I want to hear everything from you."

"I know you and Mama want me to stay in Ramsay and run the Emporium, but… but I can't. I want to go back to Sydney. Back to Will."

Jimmy Boy patted her on the knee.

"I thought you were happy here, happy with Jacky and the Emporium. But I guess the pull of the big city is just too much."

"Papa, I am scared. I don't want to hurt Jacky. What will I say? I am confused. All I know is what I feel for Will. Sydney is pulling me away, Papa."

"Martha, my child, I think you have made your

decision. I can only listen to your words, but you must listen to your heart."

She sighed and leaned against his shoulder.

"Why must life be so difficult, Papa?"

He laughed.

"A wise man by the name of Confucius could answer that. Life is really simple, but we insist on making it complicated."

"You mention that man quite a lot, Papa. Is he, or was he, a friend of yours?"

Jimmy Boy burst out laughing.

"Oh Martha, Confucius has been dead for over two thousand years. I think it is safe to say we are not friends."

"Then who was he?"

"He was a Chinese philosopher whose ideas and quotations are still relevant today. You really need to learn more about your heritage, Martha, being half-Chinese."

"I think I need to learn more about myself first," she said rather sadly.

Jacky

*****

The living room was shrouded in silence before Angela decided to broach the subject which had been consuming all their thoughts.

"Martha," she said in a firm voice, "as soon as Jacky returns you must tell him of your wish to leave him. It is better to be upfront and honest."

Martha closed her eyes. Visions of Jacky flooded her mind.

"When will he return?" she asked, looking at Jimmy Boy.

"I need to return to Milburra soon, Martie, and finish the business we started. Hopefully, we will all be home in a few weeks."

"But what if he doesn't understand?" she whispered finally.

"And what will the townsfolk think? I do not wish to be labelled a woman of little virtue."

Her grandmother shook her head and sighed, the whole business consuming her thoughts.

"Your happiness matters more than societal whispers and judgmental people, Martha."

"I hope he understands. I truly do," came her response.

*****

Sergeant Connolly sat forward in his chair, a look of disbelief on his youthful face.

"That is sure one hell of a story, Jimmy Boy. Aboriginals kept as slaves. A Sergeant on a murderer's payroll? Are you sure you haven't been using any of your Chinese medicine, Jimmy Boy?"

"What I have just told you, I know is the truth, and not some whimsical nonsense that appeared magically in my head!"

Jimmy Boy's face had coloured, and Connolly knew he had overstepped the mark with reference to opium.

"Calm down, Jimmy Boy, and give me time to digest what you have told me."

But the Chinaman pushed the matter.

"I recall you telling me that you had an uncle in the police force in Newcastle, Sergeant Connolly."

Connolly tapped his pencil on the desk.

"Yes, I do," he replied.

"But what makes you think my uncle can help you?"

"Your uncle is some sort of high-ranking policeman, isn't he? He has connections. He can give us the resources we need. Please, Sergeant Connolly. We need to do this."

Connolly's eyes narrowed. He knew what sort of man his uncle was—a hard-nosed cop who played it just within the bounds of legality.

Jimmy Boy pressed on.

"Sergeant Connolly, if we are successful, imagine the headlines. Your name will be in bold type in every newspaper across the country."

Connolly's face became cold and calculating. He could see the possibility of leaving the tiny town of Ramsay and joining the elite forces in Newcastle or Sydney. He thought of Meg. She would be so proud of him.

"I'll do it, Jimmy Boy. I will send off a telegram right away. Then I will set off to Newcastle today. It may take some time, but Jimmy Boy, if this man Reagan has done all you claim he has, then I know my uncle will do everything to bring him to justice."

*****

Chapter 36

"Mama, I have received a telegram today. Mrs Wells brought it to me at work."

"Telegram? From Jacky?"

"No, Mama. It was from Will."

She offered the piece of paper to her mother to read.

Am coming to visit. Room at Inn. Will.

Eleanor handed the telegram back to her daughter.

"How thoughtful. He is staying at the Inn."

The sarcasm was not lost on Martha.

"Why would he stay here?" Martha shouted.

"You told him to leave the last time he visited! I think he only wants to talk. To make things right."

"What is there to make right? You left your husband for him, Martha. Do you want a pat on the back?"

"Sometimes I hate you, Mama."

Martha fled from the room before her mother saw the tears, while Angela placed her needlework on the table.

"Eleanor, you are fighting a losing war, my dear. Young love is a powerful force, as you should well remember."

"Jimmy Boy is no help, Mama, when it comes to that child. He bows down to her every wish."

*****

Andrews wished him luck with a firm handshake and a warning to stay safe. Then Jacky set off to the place where he had last seen Tarni—their camp near the billabong. The trek across the hard country was filled with both hope and dread. The trail became increasingly familiar as he neared the waterhole, and Jacky could almost hear their laughter and feel the warmth of the fire that protected them at night.

When he reached the clearing, he saw the skeleton of their gunyah still standing, but there was no sign of life. He had hoped there would be some sign of Tarni, and he feared what could have befallen her. He crouched down and felt the firepit. The little remaining ash was cold, the rest blown by the wind. Jacky's spirits sank as he took in the desolate scene.

Where was she? Is she safe? Will I find her again?

He couldn't shake the feeling of unease that settled in

his gut. Suddenly, a noise in the bushes alarmed him. He hefted his spear into an attacking position just as Tarni leapt from the bushes, her eyes wide with relief. Jacky tossed his spear aside and pulled her into his arms. Their reunion was sweet, a moment of pure emotion that seemed to make the world stop.

Tarni was the first to break the silence.

"I knew you would return here," she said, tears rolling down her cheeks.

"I am sorry, Jacky."

"Hush, Tarni. No need to be sorry. You are safe, and that's all that matters."

It was then that Jacky noticed the discolouration on her face and ankles.

"Reagan!" he cursed.

She nodded. Jacky could feel her pain and her fear. But he felt something stronger… the hunger for revenge.

"Tarni, I swear on the graves of our ancestors, I will hunt that man down and kill him."

*****

Jacky tugged at the collar of his shirt, feeling the now unfamiliar fabric chafing his neck. He had shed the cut-off trousers he had worn for the past week or so and now, fully clad, he felt he was betraying who he was.

His footsteps echoed off the wooden planks as he headed to the Post Office, hoping for word from Jimmy Boy. He pushed open the door, and a gust of cooler air greeted him. The clerk didn't look up.

"Morning," said Jacky. The man gave a nod but still said nothing.

"Any mail for me?"

At the sound of a strange voice, the clerk raised his head.

"Jacky? Yeah. A telegram. Been here a day or so now."

He felt under the counter and found a slip of paper which he pushed across.

"Thank you," said Jacky politely and left. Once outside, he hurriedly unfolded the paper and read the simple message.

Connolly assembling team. Stay put. There soon

Jimmy Boy.

The town was coming to life, and Jacky smelled the aroma of fresh bread. He realised he hadn't eaten since sunrise. He walked past the tea-room where he had shared a conversation with Charley and later shared more than that with her. He smiled at the thought.

As he neared the door of the bakery, it was pushed open and Tanner walked out, a loaf of bread tucked under his arm. When he saw Jacky, he lifted the bread and poked the black man in the chest.

"Jacky?" he arched his eyebrows.

"Thought you and the rest of the blacks had pissed off out of the district."

"What do you want, Tanner?"

"You might be a free man, but you are still not welcome here. Look at you! Dressed up like a civilised man. But we all know what you are. A thief and a troublemaker."

"I am just here for my mail," said Jacky as he held up the telegram.

"Now you got it, you best be on your way. I don't want

the likes of you in my town."

"I'm leaving, Sergeant. And I don't know if or when I will return."

Jacky grabbed the loaf of bread and pressed his fingers into it, pulled a piece of the bread off and stuffed it in his mouth.

"Too much of that will make you fat, Tanner."

The Sergeant could be seen feeling his waistline as he watched Jacky walk out of town. He threw his bread onto the street in disgust.

*****

Mounsie was nursing a throbbing head. A stale odour of whisky lingered from the night before. He rested his arms on his desk amongst the scattered papers and half-smoked cigarettes, then he took a deep breath and tried to focus. He had important information for Reagan, and the sooner he delivered it the better.

He'd seen Jacky not ten minutes ago, talking with the Sergeant. It was something Reagan needed to know about, because the presence of Jacky meant the Aborigines had not left the area as everyone assumed.

The ride to Dingo's Retreat was excruciating. Every jolt on the buggy seemed to further loosen the screws in his head. His eyes were bloodshot and his mouth dry as a bone left in the sun for a month. He reached for his canteen, but the lurching of the buggy caused him to lose his grip, and the canvas sack fell to the ground.

"My fuckin' luck," he moaned to himself.

As he steered the buggy into the house yard, he saw Reagan coming from the stables where he had been checking on his prize possessions, the stallion and the mare.

"Got some information for you, Mister Reagan," he shouted as he fought back the urge to vomit.

Reagan looked at the shabby excuse for a man. He looked as if he had just stepped out of a barroom brawl.

"What now, Mounsie? More of your drivel?"

"It's not drivel, sir," he insisted.

Mounsie looked through his aching eyes.

"Whatever happened to your eye, Mister Reagan?"

Reagan fingered the patch covering the side of his face.

"Just a minor accident, Mounsie. Nothing for you to worry about. Now what is so important?"

"I saw Jacky in town this morning. Large and in the flesh."

"Jacky!" roared Reagan.

"Don't be telling me that the black bastard is back!"

"I swear I saw him, Mister Reagan. He was walking down the main street as if he owned the town. Had some words with the Sergeant too."

Reagan reefed the hat from his head, tossed it to the ground, and kicked it across the yard.

"Tanner was supposed to arrest the black bastard for murder! What in God's name is going on around here?"

"I don't know, sir," said the man meekly.

"But word on the street is that the charges against Jacky were dropped."

"Hmmm. Interesting. You've done well, Mounsie. But I need you to do more."

"Anything," said the grovelling man.

"I want you to keep a close eye on both him and Tanner. I got a funny feeling about our policeman. Last thing I need is for him to turn traitor as well."

'Whatever you say… but Mister Reagan, I am running a bit shy of cash. Surely my information is worth something. There hasn't been much call for my services this month. I don't suppose…?'

"You will never change, Mounsie. All you do with your money is piss it up the wall."

But Reagan was running out of allies. He needed the eyes of the pitiful lawyer.

"C'mon over to the house. I will fetch you some cash. But Mounsie, I want results! Got that? And I need you to send that fat gutted Tanner out here. He can maybe clear some things up for me."

*****

'I don't like this one little bit, Mister Reagan. I told you before, this is all gittin' outta 'and.'

"You can't back out now, Tanner. You're in the same deep shit as I am."

"I told ya, I couldn't arrest the black man. Kerrigan changed his fuckin' story. Said it was another black and he was tryin' to frame Jacky 'cos he thought he was tryin' to 'ave some fun with yer daughter."

"Leave my daughter out of this, Tanner!" snarled Reagan.

Tanner couldn't resist a barb.

"Touchy about her, eh?"

"I need to think, Tanner. We must get rid of Kerrigan. The man knows too much about me and my dealings."

Reagan pictured himself looking down on the bodies of the Lamberts. With Howarth dead, Kerrigan was the only man who could incriminate him for murder.

"Kerrigan needs to be gone. This time for good. But how do we lure him away from the Andrews' farm?"

A smile came over his face.

"My daughter."

He rubbed his hands with delight.

"Charley can be the bait."

*****

"I have come to see Mister Kerrigan," said Charley with a delightful smile on her face.

"My father would kill me if he knew I was here. He thinks I have ridden into town."

Rachel Andrews gave the girl a once-over. She could see treachery lurking behind the smiling facade.

"Then you are in luck, Miss Reagan. Arthur is in the barn, where he spends most of his time. He has almost fully recuperated from the beating your daddy gave him. But mind you, he is still somewhat weak."

"Beating? I know nothing of this. I knew my father and Arthur had a disagreement, but I assumed he left and came here to find work."

"Feel free to go on over and see him. I have work to do," said Rachel brusquely.

"Are you here alone, Miss Andrews?"

"I don't know what business that is of yours, but yes. I am here alone. The men have gone riding the boundary fences. Seems that mysterious fires are springing up and fences are being pulled down."

"Maybe the blacks?" she said and walked away.

Charley made her way to the barn, where she found Kerrigan fast asleep on a small cot. She bent over the weak-looking figure and prodded him gently.

Kerrigan roused immediately. Since his beating, he slept with a restless fear clothing him.

"Charlene!" he exclaimed with wide eyes.

She placed her hand on his forehead and stroked the hair which hung loosely almost over his eyes.

"What are you doing here?"

"I needed to see you, Arthur. I needed to know you are all right."

"After the beating your father gave me, I am lucky to be here at all."

She bent low, and Kerrigan could smell the scent she had sprayed a little too liberally on her neck.

"I have missed you, Arthur," she said seductively as she placed one hand between his legs.

He sat up and pushed her hand away.

"Missed me? Why? You showed no interest in me in the past."

"That was my father's doing, Arthur. I was warned not to flirt with his men."

"Just tell me the real reason you are here, Charlene."

She gave a false smile and said,

"I want us to go away together. Think of the life we could have. Something you have always dreamed of. Don't let life dribble through your fingers."

"Life? I lost that when I lost my trust. Your father tried to kill me."

"Then Arthur, let's go away. Just the two of us. Let us run. Time is running out for my father."

She bent her head and kissed him on the lips, all the while feeling the repulsion that shrouded her. She placed her hand on his crotch, and he felt himself ready to yield.

But immediately he pulled away and stood up.

"I am sorry, Charlene, but my interests lie elsewhere at present."

The girl knew she was fighting a war she couldn't win.

"Damn you to hell, Kerrigan! It is just a shame my father did not kill you!"

"I think it is time you left, Miss Reagan."

The voice came from behind her. She turned and looked into the eyes of Rachel Andrews, a shotgun crooked under her arms.

"And as for you, Arthur Kerrigan, I want you off this property within the hour. Never show your face around here again!"

Kerrigan rolled his eyes back in shock. Why was Rachel treating him this way? He gave her an imploring look and happened to spy the subtle wink she tipped him.

"You are one clever girl, Rachel Andrews," he said to himself.

*****

Reagan had seen his daughter's schemes unravel in disaster before, and this was no different. He had thought Charley's charm and other attributes might have swayed Kerrigan back to his side. But the failure of her seduction hadn't been a total loss.

"What the bloody hell are you telling me? The Andrews bitch run you off with a shotgun?"

"Not only me, Papa. She held the gun on Kerrigan too and warned him to leave the district and never be seen again."

The tension drained from Reagan's face.

"Well, Charley, that is one less snake we have to worry about."

*****

Chapter 37

"I need two of your best horses, Langley," said Jimmy Boy.

The livery man looked up from the saddle he was polishing. "Two horses? Haven't you got enough, Jimmy Boy?" He pointed at the three horses tethered behind his own mount.

"I have enough for three men, but there are five that need to be saddled. I've got some visitors from Newcastle arriving on the coach tomorrow. Policemen, in fact."

Langley's eyes narrowed, his curiosity aroused. "Police, you say? What's happening in Ramsay we need police from Newcastle for?"

"I can't say too much, Langley, but Connolly's uncle is one of them, and I hear tell he is a hard man." Jimmy Boy's eyes scanned the stable, taking in the horses.

"Got two real fine ones, Jimmy Boy, but don't expect them cheap."

"Nothing is ever cheap when I deal with you, Langley," Jimmy Boy gibed.

"All right. I have just the pair for you. Those two mares." He pointed to a stall at the far end of the stable. "They are fast, strong, and have good stamina."

"I trust your word, Langley."

"How long will you be wantin' them?"

"That I cannot rightly tell you. It could be a week, or even longer."

Langley's face grew serious. "You know, if there is something the people of Ramsay should know…"

"There is nothing to worry about."

"The townsfolk here in Ramsay stick together, Jimmy Boy, so…" His words were cut short.

"I know and appreciate it. But this business has nothing to do with Ramsay. We are heading way up north."

"Up north, huh? Bad country, I hear."

"The country is not bad, Langley, but I cannot say the same about the people who inhabit it. Now if you don't mind, I will leave these three horses here. That way when the visitors arrive, Sergeant Connolly can bring them to Wicklow."

*****

When Jimmy Boy had left the stables and headed to the Inn, big Georgie Khan, forever on the prowl for the articles he sent to the city papers, was quick to get to the stables to speak with Langley.

"City police, you say? Veery interesting, Langley. Veeery interesting."

*****

"Mia," called Stubbs from the front door of the homestead. "We have company." His voice was shaking and was matched by the tremors of his hands. The heat was intense today, but it was the sight of the blacks camped by the river which had unsettled him.

Mia poked her head from the kitchen window. "What do you mean? Can't you see I am baking bread, Stubbs?"

"There's a group of blackfellers Mia, camped by the river. I had to look twice, but Burra is with them. He's changed. No beard and no long hair."

"So long as they don't go robbin' anythin', they'll be fine. If Burra is with them, I think Jacky must know."

But Stubbs was not satisfied with her response. He went to the stables to hitch up his buggy and drive to Wicklow to see Jimmy Boy.

*****

"Mister Jimmy Boy," called Bindi.

"Stubbs is 'ere to see ya."

"That damned menace Stubbs is 'ere to see ya," she muttered, shaking her head.

The last thing Jimmy Boy needed was a conversation with Stubbs. He walked out and greeted the man.

"Mister Stubbs, you are a bit far from home. Any trouble? I am a busy man."

"Maybe yes and maybe no," said Stubbs with a worried look on his face.

"Give me the news Mister Stubbs."

The man was clearly terrified.

"Jimmy Boy, I am surrounded by savages. There is a tribe of blacks camped on the river at Jacky's place. And Jimmy Boy, their leader is Burra. But he has changed. Had a haircut and a shave. But I would recognise those eyes anywhere. I don't think I will sleep at night knowing him and the tribe are so close. Might be murdered in my sleep."

Jimmy Boy wiped his brow with relief.

"If that is all you must tell me, then it's fine Mister Stubbs. Jacky sent them here from up north. They won't trouble you. That is," he added, "unless you bother them."

"I...I... won't bbbother them Jimmy Boy. But is there any chance of me staying in Mister Jennings' hut till they are gone?"

"I have more important things to worry about Mister Stubbs then your fear of the dark. If you are so afraid, then by all means camp in Jennings' hut."

"Thank you, Jimmy Boy. I will go back while it's still daylight and grab some things." The Chinaman gave a wry smile and went back into the house.

✸✸✸✸✸

"Ellie, I think that is them coming over the rise." From their vantage point on the homestead verandah, they watched as six riders came at an easy canter to the gate. Sergeant Connolly was in the lead, but close behind him rode the man

Jimmy Boy assumed to be his uncle. The men dismounted, and Jimmy Boy kept his eye on the imposing figure of the second rider. He was a large man, tall in the saddle, but even taller when he stood on the ground.

*****

Connolly stepped forward. "My uncle, Jimmy Boy. Alistair Fleming."

The man extended his hand and in a gruff voice said, "Heard a lot about you." His grip was firm, and rather than a greeting, it seemed to say, "I know who I am and know what I am capable of." Jimmy Boy felt a mixture of respect and a touch of caution. This was a man who brought confidence and expectations.

"Come on inside, please," said Jimmy Boy to the men.

Fleming turned to the four men with him. "You boys take a rest here in the shade. Connolly and I will handle this."

"I will have cold drinks and cake sent out," said Jimmy Boy to the men, who were content to lie back on the coolness of the grass.

Jimmy Boy led Connolly and Fleming into his study and offered them a chair. Bindi came in with a tray of sliced cake and a jug of orange water, her face filled with curiosity about the strangers in the house.

"May as well get straight down to business, Jimmy. My nephew has told me the story, but I would like to hear more from you. Mind you, it makes for fascinating listening."

Jimmy began his narrative, recounting the tale of the Lambert's murder and the false imprisonment of the Aboriginals. Fleming listened quietly, but Jimmy Boy could see the enormous amount of attention he was paying to his words.

Fleming sipped his drink then asked, "Do you think this Reagan character is responsible for any other murders?"

Jimmy Boy's expression was solemn.

"I cannot say for certain, but the way he operates… well, there could be others. The man craves power and will stop at nothing to get what he wants."

Fleming stroked his chin. "You say you have a witness. What's his name?"

"Kerrigan. Arthur Kerrigan. He worked for Reagan, but with a bit of friendly persuasion on my part, he decided to betray his boss."

"Friendly persuasion? You didn't threaten the man? That would not go down well with a magistrate."

Jimmy Boy smiled and shook his head. "There were no threats, Alistair. I offered him a sum of money to turn on his boss, and he accepted."

Fleming raised his hands in mock surrender. "Whoa, there, Jimmy. Don't tell me any more. A bribe would not sit well with a judge either. I will pretend I did not hear that part of your story."

"My lips are sealed on that part."

"But tell me about the Sergeant. I am led to believe he is on Reagan's payroll."

"I only know what I have been told, but Kerrigan will be able to fill in the details. What I do know is that the Sergeant conducted a very poor investigation into the Lambert murders. And again, it was Reagan who benefited. He may not have the deeds to the Lambert farm, but he has the next best thing: a free run for his livestock."

The three men remained discussing the situation until the shadows lengthened outside.

"I can put you and your men up for the night, Alistair. I have a guest room for you, and I have empty huts at present for your men. You are all welcome to stay and have dinner with us."

Fleming considered the offer and then shook his head. "Thanks, Jimmy, but I think we will head back into Ramsay. Besides, we are not here for a vacation, and we are not paying our accommodation. We will have a few drinks tonight, and I will go over everything you have told me with my men."

Connolly took the lead and stood up. "Be seeing you tomorrow, Jimmy Boy."

*****

Mrs. Wells' keen eyes were centered on the afternoon stage as it rumbled to a halt. She had made it her business to know anyone coming into her town.

"Is that who I think it is, Miss Martie?"

Martha's eyes widened in surprise as she recognised the figures making their way up the street. She had known Will was coming but had not expected him so soon.

"It's Will," Martha murmured, barely loud enough to drown out the squeaking door of the Emporium.

"Well, I'll be. Whatever could bring him here? Seems like he missed you already, Miss Martie. But who is the strange chap with him?"

"Mrs. Wells, do you mind closing? I will go and see Will."

"You can leave everything in the ever-reliable hands of me, Miss Martie," the woman said with a pompous raise of her head. She watched the trim figure of Martha as she walked towards Will. She was still scratching her head with curiosity as she eyed the two figures Miss Martie was headed for.

"Young people," she sighed.

*****

Martha rushed across the street. "Will," she cried, her voice traveling in the afternoon air.

He turned at the sound of her voice and smiled as she approached him. "I have missed you, Martha. I couldn't bear to be away from you any longer."

"Let's go to Jack's Inn. We can talk there," she said.

Remembering her manners, Martha acknowledged Cornelius Deakin's presence. "Welcome to Ramsay, Mister Deakin. I had no idea you were coming."

*****

"Jack!" Martha shouted as she walked into the bar.

Jack looked up from his mopping, a look of surprise on his face. "Martha. Will. What brings you two here?" He looked with interest at the other man.

"Will has come to stay for a few days. I was hoping you would have a room for him. And Jack, this is a friend of Will's: Mister Cornelius Deakin. He will be wanting a room as well."

"Of course. I have rooms." He gestured towards the stairs. "Come on up, Will. Mister Deakin."

At the top of the stairs, Jack opened a door. "You can have this one, Will. Same one as you had last time. It has just been cleaned."

As Will stepped into the room, Martha hovered in the doorway. "Jack, can we have a word?" she whispered.

They were interrupted by Jack's wife, Grace, who was coming from another room. She poked her head into Will's room and watched bemused as he set about unpacking his case.

"The climate here in Ramsay must have some appeal, Will Mckenzie. For you anyway."

Then with an hurrumph of disapproval she wound her way downstairs.

"There you go, Mister Deakin. That is your room. My wife has just finished making it over."

Jack took Martha by the arm and followed his wife, leaving his two guests to unpack and settle in.

"What is happening, Miss Martie?"

She replied, her voice tight with tension. "It's complicated, Jack. All you need to know now is that I need to sort my life out. I cannot talk to my mother or grandmother, because they think I am doing the wrong thing, leading Will on." She paused, searching for understanding. "They don't know what it is like. Being married and… trapped."

Jack squeezed her hand reassuringly. "Whatever is happening, you will figure it out."

She smiled and said, "Tell Will goodbye. I must go home and break the news that Will is here."

*****

"Papa, I have something to tell you. It's about Will."

"Will?" Jimmy Boy maintained his study of the map sprawled out on his desk.

"Yes. He is in Ramsay. With a friend. They are staying at the Inn."

Martha looked at her father, pain etched in her eyes.

"Papa, this is important to me."

Jimmy Boy shook his head. "This news comes at a bad time, Martha. You know what is going on with the affair up north? The Reagan situation? Burra's people? I cannot give any of my time to matters of your own heart, my dear child. I have a special troop of policemen in Ramsay, and we are leaving for Milburra as soon as we can."

"I know, Papa, but Will is only here for a few days. I know he is here to take me back to Sydney with him."

Jimmy Boy was at a loss. Too much of his time had been taken up with the Reagan affair at the expense of spending time with his family. Then suddenly an idea dawned on him. He would take Will McKenzie along with the party of men to Milburra. That would give him time to talk with the man and keep him away from his daughter. For the time being. He knew the risk he was taking. After all, Will would ultimately be in the company of Jacky, the man who was married to the woman he coveted.

"Martha, I will ask Will to accompany our party to Milburra tomorrow. That way I can learn more of his intentions."

Martha felt her stomach twist into a knot. "Papa," she protested. "Jacky is there. I do not think that is a wise move. Besides, Jacky does not know about Will and me."

Jimmy Boy's eyes remained glued to the map. "Then this might be just the solution to the whole problem," he said, his tone unyielding. "Jacky must know of your feelings for Will."

Martha's eyes widened in horror. "No, Papa! Not yet. I want to be the one to tell Jacky. He must hear it from me."

Jimmy Boy's eyes softened. "Martha, I understand your feelings. But Jacky must know the truth before he hears whispers from others."

"I know, Papa. But I am afraid."

"You must realise that this situation cannot continue. We are all going to have to face the truth before long. As soon as we return from our journey, I want this whole business sorted. And I mean all of it!"

*****

Chapter 38

Jimmy Boy guided the light buggy into Ramsay, the newly greased wheels silent on the hard-packed earth. The town was slowly waking up, shop owners opening doors and children playing in the street.

As the buggy rolled by the Inn, Jimmy Boy and Martha caught sight of Will and Cornelius lounging in the sun on the verandah, their hats tipped back and a steaming cup of something in their hands. Will looked up as the buggy passed, but his smile froze as he recognised the father and daughter.

Jimmy Boy halted the buggy and climbed down, and nodded curtly to Cornelius, his eyes never leaving Will's. "Martha, you go on ahead and open the Emporium." Then he added, "You know Mrs. Wells has been asking for a key. Today might be just the day to give her one."

Martha, having noted her father's disposition, picked up the reins and clicked the horse into movement. Her stomach was knotted with nerves as she gave a half-smile to Will. Jimmy Boy watched her go and then approached the two men, with Will's smile fading to be replaced with a look of resignation.

"Good morning, men," said Jimmy Boy, his tone far from jovial. "We need to talk, Will."

Cornelius saw an urgent need to refill his mug and stood and moved away towards the coffee pot on a table by the door.

Jimmy Boy came straight to the point. "What's this I have been hearing, Will, about you wanting to take my daughter back to Sydney with you?" His eyes drilled into Will's, searching for any sign of evasion.

Will swallowed hard, his hand gripped around his mug. "It's true, Jimmy Boy. I care for her deeply, and I know she feels the same. We want to live in Sydney and begin a new life together."

Jimmy Boy continued to search for any sign of insincerity. "Do you intend to take her away from her husband? Then uproot her and take her away from here? And do you truly believe my daughter is suited and ready for city life?"

"I do, Jimmy Boy. And as for city life, I would teach her and show her a world beyond this place. I know this is distressing for you, but I love her and want to give her my life."

Jimmy Boy's face became even more grave. "Love is a powerful word, Will. Can you truly promise her happiness away from here?"

"I believe in Martha, Jimmy Boy, and I believe in us. I know I can make her happy."

"This has all happened at a bad time, Will. There are certain things I must do before I give any consideration to your matter. I have a proposal for you. Come on into the bar. And I will outline the circumstances I am faced with right now."

*****

"Won't I be in the way, Jimmy Boy?" asked Will as he contemplated the story he had just been told.

"No, Will. You won't be in the way. Besides, I would rather have you with me than you staying here at the mercy of Ellie. We will all be risking our lives, Will, and I need to know the kind of man you are." He took a sip of his drink. "I think I know you, Will, but that was when you were younger. You have changed since you left here and went to the city. I want my daughter to be with someone who will protect her."

"I see a major problem, Jimmy Boy."

"That being?"

"Jacky." He had to force himself to say the name.

"There is no problem there unless you create one, Will. You must say nothing to Jacky when we meet. Once we have achieved our goal and are safely back at Wicklow, then everything must come to light. Everything!"

They sat in silence for a while, and Will's thoughts drifted to Martha. He wondered what she would think of him. Joining her father and the policemen on a dangerous quest. Would she see him as a hero, or just another reckless man trying to impress?

"I am in, Jimmy Boy. From all that you have told me, I realise that this whole thing is about freeing the tribe and bringing a man to justice and not about my intentions with your daughter."

"You are right. We have a job to do and must remain focused on it." Jimmy Boy tipped his drink down and pushed back his chair. "I need to go and speak with Connolly and Fleming. There is too much to organise if we are to leave before too long."

*****

The sound of Bindi scratching in the soil was the only sound apart from nature in the otherwise quiet of the morning. Cornelius Deakin watched, fascinated, as the Aboriginal woman pulled juicy yams from the soft earth.

"Look at this one, Mister Cornelius. He be plenty good tucker for us." She dipped the yam in the creek water and wiped the dirt from the skin, revealing the starchy flesh. Cornelius watched in amazement as she peeled the yam and tossed it into the dying coals of the small fire. Suddenly, there came a rustle in the reeds, and Bindi's hand shot out and grasped a black snake just at the back of its head.

"Nice plump one, this one, Mister Cornelius," she said proudly as she held the writhing reptile in front of his nose.

The man took a nervous lean backwards. He had never seen a snake this close before. His hands were shaking as Bindi then turned the snake to face her lips and gave it a mocking kiss.

"Bindi, please. Enough of your showmanship."

She laughed and said, "You tell me that I need to learn to read, so I am tellin' you that you need to learn new things too. No better way to start than by tryin' a feed of this slippery buggar." Then to his amazement, he watched as she carried out a culinary exploit that had been practised for centuries. She put the snake to her mouth and with a quick bite, she ripped off the head and threw the twitching body into the fire.

Cornelius ate sparingly and with a good deal of trepidation. When Bindi had eaten her fill, Cornelius brought up the subject of a move to Sydney.

"Why would I leave this place?" asked Bindi as she waved her arms around. "This is my world, Mister Cornelius. The land of my Dreamtime stories. I can never leave here."

"You disappoint me, Bindi. Here was me thinking we maybe had a future together, but I see that is not the case."

"I like you a lot, Mister Cornelius, but not that much I would leave 'ere and live in the big smoke. Nowwatcha reckon we don't mention that anymore, eh?" She leaned down and plucked a lone greying hair from the inside of his ear.

Cornelius sighed; a deep breath full of resignation.

*****

BOOK 3

He has sent me to bind up the downhearted, to proclaim liberty to the captives, and the opening of the prison to those who are bound.

- Isaiah 61:1

Chapter 39

Jimmy Boy spread the map out on Connolly's desk and traced the route they would take, explaining each leg of the journey with a calm approach that filled the policemen with a quiet confidence. The mission was clear: rescue the imprisoned Aboriginals, take back Jacky's beloved stallion, and bring two men to justice.

"You have a good head, Jimmy Boy," noted Fleming. "But what about this Jacky character? Is he level-headed? We cannot risk him charging in half-cocked."

"I can control him, Alistair. I have learned a lot about him over the years. But I have learned even more from him," he added. "He is a very knowledgeable man."

*****

Jimmy Boy pulled Ellie into his arms, his strong embrace sheltering her from the thoughts of danger that lay before him. "I love you, Jimmy Boy. Please return safely."

"And I love you too, my beautiful princess," he smiled and kissed her again. "It was such a good idea to take Will with you. I do not think I am ready to welcome him here again." He placed a finger on her lips to hush her, his eyes trained on his daughter. "Don't worry, Ellie. All will be sorted out on our return."

Angela stepped forward now and took Jimmy Boy's left hand in her own. "I wish you God speed, my good man. James O'Brien would be so proud of you, and I know he will be watching down from heaven and shielding you from harm."

"Thank you, Angela."

Then it was Martha's turn. She had tears in her eyes as she pushed her body into her father's arms. "Papa, I want to thank you for being the best father in the whole world. Please be cautious and please take care of Will. This is something that is completely out of his world."

"I must go," said Jimmy Boy before he could allow his emotions to take over. "I hope that all goes well, and we will be back within a fortnight."

*****

"Kevin, I am going away again. I don't know for how long, and I need you to do something for me."

The Doctor studied Jimmy Boy's face. He noticed the worry lines that were becoming more prominent. His friend had aged ten years in the space of a few short weeks.

"Jimmy Boy, I am speaking as a friend and not as a Doctor. You need rest. All this business I have been hearing about is taking a toll on your health. Think of your wife and your daughter."

"I will be fine, Kevin. This business will be over soon, and I am going to have one beeeeg long rest." He punched the Doc lightly on the arm.

"I will hold you to that. Now, what is it you want me to do for you?"

"I need you to go to Shanghai and check on the tribe of Aborigines that Jacky sent from up north."

"Aborigines, you say?"

"Yes, Doc. Burra is with them. You need to check and treat any ailments. And do not worry about the cost. I will fix you up when I return."

*****

"Meg, what in heaven's name are you doing in town?" asked Jimmy Boy as he looked at Meg. "And it is not even a Sunday, and you are wearing your finery."

Connolly stepped forward. "I asked her to come, Jimmy Boy. I want my uncle to marry us before we ride out. You could say I am worried I may not come back alive."

Fleming was eager to be on his way. "What's the holdup?"

Connolly pulled his uncle aside and made his request. "I don't know if I can legally marry you, son, but I will say the words. We can carry out the Scottish tradition of jumping the broom handle. Once that's done, you will be married in our eyes, and you can plan a proper wedding on our return."

Connolly's face lit up, and Meg's face flushed with embarrassment at being the centre of attention. The stables transformed into a place of sanctity as Meg and Connolly joined hands.

Fleming hawked his throat. "By whatever powers are invested in me, I declare you husband and wife. You may now jump the broom."

Meg and Connolly stepped forward, and with laughter ringing in their ears, they jumped nimbly over a hay rake, a substitute for a broom which could not be found anywhere. A round of applause greeted the happy couple as they kissed.

Connolly pulled away and said to his bride, "I will come back to you, Meg."

"And I will be waiting."

*****

"You seem to have provided us with some prime horse flesh, Jimmy," said Fleming as he tightened the girth on a sleek chestnut mare.

"Uncle," said Connolly, "hadn't you better do a double check on your provisions?"

Fleming swiveled and drilled his eyes into his nephew's. "Two pointers for you, son. Number one: just because you are a married man, it doesn't give you the right to give me orders. I was about to do exactly that. And number two: don't keep calling me uncle. You are a big boy now and not still shitting in your pants."

The other men laughed, including Jimmy Boy and Will.

"Righto, men, let's do a check."

"Old Bessie has seen better days, Jimmy Boy, but she will be a good pack horse fer ya. I can throw her in fer nuthin'," said Langley.

Fleming cast an eye over the group. Each man had meticulously packed their horses with their weapons and bedding. The packhorse carried their water supply and some basic foodstuffs, plus brandy and bandages as a stopgap medical kit.

Satisfied with what he saw, Fleming gave the order they had waited for. "Lead the way, Jimmy," he boomed.

Georgie Khan was seen quickly scribbling down notes as they headed out of town.

*****

The men camped by a stream that night, after having made sound progress on their first day. The men slept well, lulled by the hooting of owls and the howls of a dingo.

Jimmy Boy and Alistair took the first watch.

"This Reagan," said Fleming as he prodded the coals in the fire, "he's got to be a clever mongrel to have eluded any investigation into his dealings for so long."

"The only thing I know about him is from what I have heard." Jimmy Boy appeared to be thinking something over. "Something has just come to me, Alistair. Kerrigan has mentioned a name quite a bit. It may be a name worth looking into."

"Oh?"

"Mounsie. He is a shady lawyer working out of Milburra."

Fleming screwed his face into a scowl. "That figures. Mostly all crooked men have what they perceive a legal shoulder to fall back on. And crooked lawyers are as plentiful as black flies around this country."

"Reagan is a law unto himself and not a man to take lightly."

"I have good men, Jimmy. They won't let us down. But as a matter of course, how many men are we up against?"

"I cannot answer that. He has lost a lot of men, but just how many he has at his disposal, I have no idea."

"We have the numbers and the firepower, but it's the unknown that worries me. How can Reagan survive?"

"He is a man with nothing to lose, Alistair. Or everything to gain. Either way, we need to be ready for everything."

"What about your man, Jacky? Connolly has a high opinion of him."

"Jacky is as good a man as you could want. He is intelligent and very brave. He has done a lot for my family." Jimmy Boy felt a shudder through his body. He was not looking forward to the moment when the black man found out his wife was leaving him for another man.

"I might turn in, Alistair. We don't need to be so vigilant out here. We are still days away from Richard Andrews' farm."

"Hold on a minute, Jimmy. Before you turn in, tell me a little about Richard Andrews."

"Well," began Jimmy Boy, "Richard Andrews is a decent, hardworking man who just wants to earn an honest living. I admire him and his sister Rachel for their stand against Reagan."

"Then let's hope we can get justice for all, Jimmy."

"I want nothing more, Alistair."

"Night, Jimmy. I will have another cigarette and then sleep myself."

*****

Jimmy Boy and Fleming rode at the head of the men, with the others strewn out in a line and Will bringing up the rear.

"You are traveling all right, Will?" called Jimmy Boy over his shoulder.

Will, facing his fears and inexperience, managed to call back, "Just fine. It's just that it has been a while since I have been on horseback."

"What's the story with that one, Jimmy?"

"Story? A bloody long one, Alistair."

Fleming felt the man's reluctance to talk, so he changed the subject. "How much longer till we get to Milburra, Jimmy?"

"We should arrive at Richard Andrews' farm this time tomorrow, and we will use his barn as our strategic post. It's a safe distance from town, and I will ride in there tomorrow night and stay at the hotel. My presence will not be questioned. The people have accepted me as a businessman, so it's only natural that I come and go."

"Sounds good, Jimmy. Try and track the Sergeant's comings and goings. We need to nab him first before he gets word to Reagan."

*****

Richard Andrews wiped the sweat from his brow and extended his hand. "I am mighty glad to meet you, Alistair. I hope you are the answer to all our problems." He studied the face of the policeman and noted his height and the weathered but determined face.

He studied the face of the policeman and noted his height and the weathered but determined face.Fleming took the outstretched hand and shook it strongly. "I have heard a lot of good things about you, Mister Andrews, and my men and I are keen to get to work." The men around him shifted, and their boots scuffed the dry earth at the front of the barn. Andrews saw they were a rough-looking bunch—just the type needed to bring Reagan down.

"I will ride into Milburra, Richard, and stay the night at the hotel," said Jimmy Boy. "I will leave these men in your capable hands."

"That's fine, Jimmy. Come with me, Alistair. I will show you to the barn. You can wash up and then come to the house. My sister has a meal prepared."

As Jimmy Boy turned to leave, Fleming called after him, "Where is this Kerrigan chap? And your black mate, Jimmy?"

He left Andrews to explain. "Kerrigan is over at my house. As for Jacky, who knows where he is? He comes and goes like a wisp of smoke."

*****

The men slept well that night. There was only the one time that Fleming had to rise from his mattress of hay and silence the noise that was keeping him awake.

"For Jeezus sake man, stop that awful racket."

He slapped Jennings over the head with his pillow, but the only response he got was a loud blast of air from the man's arse.

*****

The hotel loomed ahead as he walked from the stables, and Jimmy Boy felt a strange sense of comfort as he walked up the steps. He pushed the door open, and the soft tinkling of a bell announced his presence. Mrs Peterson looked up from her knitting and smiled, recognising the little Chinaman.

"So glad to have you back Mister Wang," she said as she adjusted her spectacles.

Jimmy Boy returned the smile.

"That's right. It is good to be back."

"I didn't see you get off the coach this afternoon Mister Wang."

"No, you did not. I decided I needed to gain more experience around horses. This time I left the coach at Hardwood and hired a mount."

"I see."

But the woman's curiosity was not yet satisfied.

"How's your business planning going" she asked as she set aside her knitting and reached for the register.

"It's coming along nicely. I have some good leads and a sound plan."

Mrs Peterson nodded.

"I have heard about your expertise Mister Wang. You are just what this town needs to forge ahead."

"My expertise? Who have you been listening to?"

The old woman blushed and tried to cover up her presumption.

"Oh….just people you know. Anyway, let me see."

She squinted at the register.

"Ah yes, your regular room is available."

*****

The bar was quiet, understandable for a weeknight. Jimmy Boy nursed his rum and was about to retire to his room when a figure came through the door. It was none other than

Sergeant Tanner. The man surveyed the room with the practised eye of a policeman, his gaze not settling on anyone.

The barman handed over a large bottle, and Jimmy Boy watched as the Sergeant took a long pull from the neck. He gulped the liquid down, nodded at the barman, and pushed the half-empty bottle back at him. "Save it for tomorrow night," he grumbled, and walked out.

Jimmy Boy felt a peculiar curiosity stir within him and found himself standing and following the man. He trailed him at a safe distance and kept the man's silhouette in sight until he reached the edge of town. In the darkness, Jimmy Boy could make out an old shack, its paint cracked and its roof barely holding the framework together. The Sergeant disappeared inside without as much as a backward glance, but his figure in the doorway was replaced by a middle-aged half-caste woman, who looked around suspiciously and then closed the door behind her.

Jimmy Boy knew what was happening inside. He had heard about it before. The Sergeant had a certain type, and it was not the prim and proper ladies who attended church and town balls. It was one with stories etched into the lines on their faces, the ones who knew the price of survival. He felt a touch of sadness, but he knew the woman was not powerless. She knew how to use her body to keep herself fed.

With a sigh, Jimmy Boy turned and walked back to his hotel room.

"It's time we went into town, Richard. I want to take a look around. Get a feel for the place. And I want to take a close look at Tanner and maybe talk with some locals."

"Is Mister Kerrigan going with you?"

"No. Only my men, Richard. I don't want anybody to see a connection between my party and Kerrigan. Or you and Jimmy, for that matter. We will be just a sorry-looking band of itinerants wandering through. And I will keep this out of sight for the time being." He removed the badge from his shirt and stuffed it into his pocket, and Andrews watched as his men followed suit.

*****

Jacky's grip tightened around Tarni's arm as he pulled her roughly to the ground.

"What do you think you are doing, you black mongrel?" she hissed.

"I hear riders," he answered softly. "Stay low."

Presently, the riders came into view.

"Who is it, Jacky? More men Reagan has hired?"

"No. They are coming from the Andrews' farm. I suspect they are the policemen Jimmy Boy went back to fetch." He rubbed Tarni's head with satisfaction. "It seems that Jimmy Boy has finally put together a plan that may work. Come on. We will follow them for a bit."

The two Aboriginals trailed the riders until they came to the edge of town. It was then Jacky made his decision.

"Tarni, you remain here. It is not safe for you in town. I will go in and keep an eye on what is happening. I want you to go back to our camp and stay there. I may be back this afternoon or the next day or…"

"I understand. You will be working on blackfeller time."

He gave her a mock clip over the ear.

"But Jacky, you can't go into town like that. You don't have the white man's clothes on."

Jacky looked down at the pants he was wearing. He still had on the cut-off trousers he had been wearing for over a week. He gave a low laugh. "And you know what else? I don't have a single penny in my pockets either."

*****

The men were tethering their horses outside the hotel as Jacky passed by a shack on the edge of town. He gave scant attention to the figure standing at the door of the hut until she shouted a greeting.

"Hey, Jacky!"

The mention of his name was enough to attract his interest. The voice came from an Aboriginal woman, but she had fairer skin than any of the other women he had seen around, and he figured she was the daughter of some local white man, her mother one of the many women who gave up their bodies for a cigarette or some cheap drink.

"Hey back," he called. "How do you know my name?"

She ambled across, and Jacky could smell the cheap alcohol on her breath. She had an old clay pipe in her mouth, which had long gone cold for want of tobacco.

"Ever'body in town knows you, Jacky. Big flash blackfeller what was hangin' round Mister Reagan's daughter. Ain't so flash now by the looks of ya," she chuckled.

"You might say I am having a run of bad luck, lady."

"I ain't no lady," she cackled.

"I guess not."

"Got some tobaccy in yer pockets?"

"I have never indulged in that bad habit," he said.

"Wearin' bloody rags and still you talk like an uppity blackfeller. Go on, piss off!"

"Good day to you, ma'am."

"Get the fuck outta 'ere. But you jis better be careful in town, Jacky. Sergeant Tanner don't go much on you, I bin told."

"The feeling is mutual," said Jacky and walked off with the woman calling after him.

"I'll be sure and tell 'im that, Jacky, when I see him."

*****

Jacky

The two men passed each other, close enough for a casual greeting, but Jacky kept his eyes averted from Jimmy Boy's. The Chinaman leaned in slightly, and Jacky could feel his warm breath as he whispered, "The men are here in town."

Jacky's face remained unreadable as he grunted and continued walking. "I know. I followed them here."

Then, satisfied that Jimmy Boy had everything under control, he headed off to find Tarni. As he walked, he heard the same voice again shouting from the edge of town. "Go on, git! A blackfeller with no money ain't welcome in Milburra."

*****

Chapter 40

Fleming's gaze was fixed on a solitary figure leaning across the bar. He whispered across the table to one of his best men, Constable Walsh. "Walsh, see the gentleman drinking on his own over at the bar? It would be a real shame if you somehow managed to upset his beer. Get my meaning?"

"Got you real clear," said Walsh as he stood, his movements exaggeratedly clumsy.

As Walsh staggered towards the bar, the others watched on, curious as to the outcome. Walsh was a favourite among the men, and they encouraged his antics and foolishness to keep their spirits buoyed. His performance of a drunken drifter deserved a standing ovation, and they couldn't hide their delight as he put his acting skills to use.

He wobbled unsteadily towards the bar and grabbed at it for support. His elbow, albeit accidentally to those not in the know, upset the drink of the lone customer, and the precious liquid splashed onto his shirt and down into his crotch. The other men collectively held their breath, not knowing what would ensue. But the man's reaction was not what they had expected.

He simply turned to Walsh and in a calm voice said, "I'd watch my manners if I was you, mister."

Walsh, still playing his part to perfection, raised his arms in mock surrender. His eyes flicked to Fleming for a moment, seeking approval. Fleming gave an almost imperceptible nod.

"Sorry, mister, but you shouldna been puttin' yer drink in me way."

"Listen, mister, I don't know you and do not want any trouble."

"Well, now you know me, mister. And I come with trouble." Walsh threw a punch hard enough to rock the man, but not hard enough to do any harm. He then relaxed and let the retaliatory blow come. Then the fight began, with Walsh mainly covering himself up from the blows being rained on him.

Fleming peeked at his watch. "If our noble Sergeant of Police is any good, he should be here in less than a minute."

But what happened next stunned the men. The obvious winner of the punch-up pinned Walsh's arms behind his back and said, "You are under arrest, mister. I charge you with the assault of an off-duty police officer."

Without further ado, he bustled the bemused Walsh out the door, over the street, and into the Police Station.

*****

"What do we do now, Sub?"

Fleming's men were so close to him he allowed them the liberty of calling him by the nickname of Sub, short for Sub-Inspector. In return, he treated his men like he would his own children, which the man was unfortunate enough never to have. His first wife had died during childbirth, and his second was past the childbearing age.

He scratched his chin and cracked his knuckles, a habit that would stay with him until the day he died.

"Well, this little incident sure puts a different slant on things. But I think for now we will let our thespian spend some time in the cells. He may pick up some information there. In the meantime, we will go and find this man Mounsie and have a little chat with him."

*****

Mounsie's office was not difficult to find. The outside of the wooden building looked as old as the town itself and was badly in need of a coat of paint. A sign with his name on it dangled from a nail driven in above the door. When the men entered, Mounsie was leaning on the window ledge and staring vacantly into the street. He spun around as the men walked into his dimly lit office.

"Can I help you men?" he asked in a business-like tone.

"Are you the only lawyer in town?" asked Fleming. His men stood behind him, their eyes searching the room and taking in the yellowed documents and faded legal tomes on his desk.

Mounsie pushed out his chest and said pompously, "The one and only, mister. And if you want anything done, then you have come to the right place."

"I appreciate your cooperation, Mister Mounsie… that is what the name says on your sign. I am here seeking some information about your dealings with Mister Harry Reagan."

Mounsie's face paled. "I don't have to answer any questions from you," his voice a mixture of concern and caution. "I don't even know you. What authority do you have here?"

Fleming sensed the man's nervousness and decided to push his advantage. He reached into his pocket and pulled out his badge, laying it gently on the man's desk. It was a simple gesture, but it had a profound effect. The implications the badge held turned Mounsie's face into the colour of a thick pea soup.

The badge gleamed under the dull light: it was old and dented, but the emblem was unmistakable.

"Police," murmured Mounsie as his eyes flicked up to meet Fleming's. "What do you think I know about Harry Reagan that our local Sergeant cannot tell you?" The defiance in his voice was clear, but so too was his fear.

"Your Sergeant may know a lot, but in small towns things can become complicated. Sometimes people keep secrets to protect their own."

"I can assure you that I have no secrets."

"Take a seat, Mister Mounsie, and I will see for myself."

Mounsie looked at the doorway. He knew he had to get out and head to the Police Station. His sudden dash to escape the confines of his office was thwarted by the constables standing by the doorway. He was pushed roughly down into his chair.

"You wouldn't mind so much if I looked through your books? Your diary? Any bank books you have?"

"You have no right!" spluttered the desperate man.

Fleming poked at the badge on the desk and said, "I think that gives me every right."

"I have done nothing wrong, mister!"

"Then you have nothing to worry about."

Fleming pulled up a second chair and began scanning through the papers on the desk. His men pulled books and documents from shelves and flipped through them, tossing them aside on the floor. After coming up with nothing on the desk, Fleming pulled the desk drawer open, and and as he did so, Mounsie leaned over and attempted to close it again, but Fleming batted his hand away.

"Must be something important in here, huh?"

"Nothing you would be interested in."

Fleming leafed through the documents and mouthed the titles. "A bill from the bakehouse, a receipt from the Post Office, and some copies of invoices."

Just as Fleming was about to give his search away, he looked at the last paper and his eyes lit up when he saw in large letters at the bottom the word Jacky followed by an X.

He held it up triumphantly. "Lo and behold, Mister Mounsie. The first piece of concrete evidence."

Mounsie was on the defensive. "A Bill of Sale? What sort of evidence is that? It's all legal. A darky sold a horse to Mister Reagan, and I drew that paper up. All legal, mister. All legal!"

"It so happens, Mister Mounsie, although I do not know the man personally…" He paused to add a dramatic flourish to his words, "I do know that this Jacky character is an educated Aboriginal. Why would a man who can read and write sign a legal document with an X?"

Fleming leaned forward and breathed in Mounsie's face. "This is a forgery, Mister Mounsie. A blatant attempt to defraud Jacky of his most prized possession. His stallion. You used your position to cheat a man for your own personal gain, didn't you, Mister Mounsie? Didn't you?" he shouted now.

Fleming cowered. "Sir, this is a genuine document. The man, Jacky, well, he was… he was unusually distraught that day. The X is simply a circumstance of his emotions that day."

Fleming scoffed. "Distraught? A convenient excuse, Mounsie. You are a lawyer, bound to uphold the legal system, and here you are defrauding a man. I can ensure that you never work again."

Mounsie's face dropped. He knew he was a beaten man. "It was all because of Mister Reagan."

"Ah," smiled Fleming. "Now we are getting somewhere."

But then Mounsie had second thoughts. He tried to weigh up whether it was better to tell all he knew and risk the wrath of Reagan, or to button his lip and say nothing and live.

Fleming made the decision for him. "I want to know everything, Mister Mounsie. And if I detect the smallest of lies, I will see you spend the remaining days of your life in a gaol. However, the truth may see you spared from such a fate. The decision is yours."

"But Reagan will kill me, mister," blubbered the pitiful wretch.

"I will ensure your safety. You will be under my protection until we have Reagan in custody. But first, I want to hear about the local Sergeant. I believe he makes for a good story."

*****

Fleming was a very clever man, and that made him a very clever law officer. He had one of his men write down the basics of what Mounsie revealed and enjoyed watching the man's face every time the pen hit paper.

When he had finished all he knew, or all he was willing to reveal, Mounsie gave a sigh of relief. "Thank you, Mister Mounsie. You have been most helpful. Now all you must do is sign the document, and it will be used as evidence in a court of law."

"Are you sure you will protect me from Reagan? And from Tanner?"

"I could not be more sure of anything," said Fleming, handing the man a pen. "And I want a signature, mister. Not a goddamned X."

"Will I go to gaol?" asked Mounsie as he scrawled his signature.

"Your part in all this stems from simple greed, Mister Mounsie. I think I can put in a good word with the judge and tell him how helpful you were. He may then see fit to be lenient and sentence you to a few months for accepting money and shady dealings. But realistically, I can see you remaining a free man. The main rogues we need to witness serve time, and possibly hang, are Sergeant Tanner and Harry Reagan."

*****

"I have come to bail my friend out. I am sorry about the trouble he caused earlier. He cannot handle his drink."

Fleming cast his eyes around the interior of the Police Station. It was clean and orderly, far from what he expected.

The constable who had arrested Walsh was young, but his voice carried a maturity in his tone. "I am afraid that is not possible, mister. It is our policy to keep drunks locked up overnight till they are sober."

"Ah, but I think my friend is indeed sober at this very moment."

The constable gave a laugh, which came out as more of a snort. "Sober? The bastard is as drunk as can be."

"Then maybe I might have a word with your Sergeant."

"Not possible. He isn't in town."

"Is there anyone else above you in rank I can talk to?"

"Mister, this town has two policemen: me and the Sergeant. I am afraid you will have to come back tomorrow morning."

In a slow but firm voice, Fleming said, "I want my friend released. Now."

"I already told you, mist…" His words were cut short as Fleming, with a slow and deliberate movement, for the second time that day, pulled his badge from the confines of his pocket. He placed it gently on the table and kept his eyes on the young constable to gauge his reaction.

"What's your name, son?" Fleming asked in a fatherly voice.

It took a while for him to answer. His eyes were transfixed on the metal on the table. "Alfie, sir. Alfie Sales."

Fleming nodded at his badge. "Do you know what that means, Alfie? It means I am the law around these parts now. Do me the favour of freeing my constable."

Sales hesitated for a second before taking a key from the wall and heading out the back to the cells. Fleming made himself comfortable in the seat at the desk and waited. He heard the creaking of the cell door and then Walsh appeared, a huge grin on his face.

"I wasn't too sure, Sub, just how long you would leave me there."

"I should have left you there for the night, Walsh," joked his boss.

Sales scratched his head. "Never seen a man sober up so fast."

"It doesn't take long when you have had only a small drink, Alfie. It was all a clever ruse by our thespian here."

"Thespian? What is that?"

"Never mind, boy. Just take a seat. I have some matters to discuss with you."

*****

"I have had my suspicions, Mister Fleming." He was in a state of disbelief at what Fleming had told him of his Sergeant's misdemeanours.

"Just call me Sub. I am used to it."

"I have never had proof of anything. Maybe I just didn't want to believe it. But the Sarge has been acting strange lately."

"In what way?"

"Just little things. He used to leave his locker open— that's where we keep the tea rations—and I just used to help myself. But now he keeps it locked, and I must ask him to unlock it. Tea leaves are not that expensive they have to be kept under lock and key."

"All this is a tough pill to swallow, Sales, but I need your help."

"What do you need from me?"

"First, I need to know where you stand. Are you with me or against me? Are you going to be a problem?"

"If you can prove what you are saying, then I am with you. What do I have to do?"

"Absolutely nothing. We are highly trained men and work best on our own. All you need do is go about your daily business as if you know nothing. These two men may see the end coming, and that will make them just that little bit more desperate."

Fleming thought for a moment. "Another thing, Alfie, we have two other men involved with us. No matter what happens, I don't want to see them harmed."

"Tell me the names, Sub."

"Names are not an issue. It is the Chinaman you may have seen getting about and an Aboriginal: Jacky."

"Jacky? The blackfeller? Sergeant Tanner has been sweating on him since he had a fallout with Harry Reagan. He has ordered me to arrest him for any minor breach of the law."

"That sounds like Tanner. He would like nothing better than to have Jacky in a cell where he could suffer some fatal illness or meet with an accident."

"But you don't mean that the Sergeant would stoop to murder?"

"Commit murder? Maybe. Cover up murder? Definitely. Money works in mysterious ways, Alfie. With Jacky out of the way, Reagan is safe from the blacks and has a prize horse given to him on a silver platter thanks to Mounsie."

"Are you saying Mounsie is involved in all this as well?"

"He is, as our thespian would say, only a bit player in the whole affair. He will never take center stage."

"You are confusing me, Sub."

"Never mind. Now, Alfie, there is one important role you need to fulfill."

"Anything."

"Find some excuse to arrest Jacky. But leave it until tomorrow. When you have him in a cell, then find another excuse to go out of town for the day."

"What will I arrest him for?"

"Use your imagination, boy. Anything."

"Drunkenness?"

"No. From what I have learned, he does not drink. Vagrancy is a good nick. Check him for money."

"After I arrest him. Then what?"

"We will be back in town and be watching and waiting. Ready to arrest Tanner for attempted murder."

"Huh?"

Fleming shook his head. The man, although companionable enough, appeared to have no common sense. "Alfie, do you have any idea where Tanner keeps the key to his locker?"

"He keeps it on his person."

"Then you disappear, and we will look in the locker."

"You mean…?"

"Exactly."

*****

Larsson's hands trembled as he fiddled with the lock. It had been years since he had picked one, but the skill was something he would never forget.

"Your past history comes in handy, Larsson," grinned his boss.

Larsson ignored the gibe; he had left that job behind when he first pinned on his badge. He slowly pulled the door open and stood back as Fleming approached.

"You still have it, Larsson," he said as he pulled a bag out and caressed it. "Now, let's see what we have inside here," he said with a degree of harnessed excitement. He reached inside and his hand emerged with a crumpled letter and a dull yellow nugget.

"We have struck paydirt, men. This would be the nugget Jimmy gave Kerrigan. And this…," He unfolded the letter, "This is the bank document which he spoke of. This gives us even more reason to ensure that our Sergeant Tanner faces justice."

"He won't do much time for theft, Sub. Besides, he can lie his way out of this," suggested Walsh.

"You are right, Walsh. But never mind. In a couple of days, he will be under arrest for attempted murder."

*****

Chapter 41

"It's about time we all sat down together," said Fleming, as he looked around the group of men huddled around the makeshift fireplace in the barn. "We need to work as a team."

The barn's wooden beams creaked softly in the cool night air and the flames danced shadows around the huge building.

Fleming reached into his pocket. "What do you have there, Alistair?" asked Jimmy Boy.

He untied the drawstring from the pouch he liked to keep his things in, and the men gave a collective gasp as they saw the nugget. "This came from Tanner's locker. Along with this bank letter."

"The bastard has been in my hut," exclaimed Kerrigan.

It was Jacky who led the discussion now. "So Tanner is double-crossing Reagan now. He is living a very dangerous life. If Reagan were to hear of this, the man would be dead."

"This is all irrelevant, Jacky. Stealing Kerrigan's incentives from Jimmy is a mere pittance. We need to nab the man for something more than petty theft. We want him for something serious."

"Like what?" asked Jacky.

Fleming came straight to the point. "For trying to kill you, Jacky."

"What!"

"Like I said. We will arrest Tanner for trying to murder you."

"And just what is this grand plan, Fleming? Am I to be used as bait?"

"Unfortunately, Jacky, that is exactly the plan. I know it is a risky move. You will return to Milburra tomorrow, and I have instructed the young constable to arrest you for vagrancy. We just do not have enough evidence yet to take the man to trial."

"Does that mean a spell in the gaol again?" Jacky asked wearily. "You may not know it, mister lawman, but us blackfellers have a certain disdain, a terror if you like, of being locked up like an animal. We are free people. The land is ours. We don't need to be behind a white man's bars."

Jimmy Boy could see the logic in Fleming's plan. If Tanner took the bait, then he could be arrested and that would leave only Harry Reagan to deal with.

"Jacky, I know this is hard on you," said Jimmy Boy, "But just think. It is a step closer to freeing Burra's people and getting your horse back."

"And getting justice for the Lamberts," added Richard Andrews.

Jacky went into a kind of trance. The men around him could see he was deep in thought. They sat in silence watching the black man.

"Can I have a word with Jimmy Boy in private?" he finally asked.

"Of course, Jacky. Go outside for a spell."

*****

"Jimmy Boy, you know how I feel about being locked up. My first time was in Hardwood, and I swore it would never happen again. There is just something that terrifies me."

"I understand, Jacky. But it will only be for a short while. And it will help our cause no end."

"Promise me, Jimmy Boy, you won't let anything happen to me," he said with a genuine fear in his voice.

"I swear, Jacky. I swear it."

He pulled the black man into his chest, and they held each other tightly, both fighting their emotions. Jacky pulled away and with a different look shrouding his face asked, "Jimmy Boy, why is Will McKenzie with you? I only had to take one look at him to know he is not suited for this business. He is dressed like a Sydney businessman."

Jimmy Boy had to think quickly and invent a white lie. "He came for a visit, Jacky," he said as he avoided the black man's eyes. "And with his business here, he asked could he come along. He just wants a breath of fresh country air, Jacky."

"Is that so?" asked Jacky sceptically.

"He doesn't strike me as the type to get his hands dirty."

"He doesn't know the full story, Jacky, and we will keep it that way."

"Well, if you say so, but he doesn't want to cause any trouble."

"He won't, Jacky. He will stay here and help on the farm. Richard can do with an extra hand."

Jacky remained silent, thinking things over. He knew Jimmy Boy well enough to know that there was more to Will's visit than the need for fresh air. The two men had a history, and it wasn't one filled with Sunday picnics and fresh air and goodwill.

*****

"Good luck, Jacky."

The two men stopped at the edge of town, and once again Jacky was the target of the woman who dwelt in the shanty. They had both been astride the one horse, and as Jacky leapt down, she began her harangue.

"Hey, Jacky, you black mongrel. Got a bloody Chinaman for a mate now. Waddya 'ave to do fer 'im to 'itch a ride?"

"You know her?" asked Jimmy Boy.

"No. But she sure knows me. I cannot pass by without her abusing me."

"You go on ahead, Jacky, and I will wait for about half an hour and then follow you."

"Be seeing you, Jimmy Boy. And soon, I hope."

The Chinaman watched as Jacky walked off in the direction of the main street.

*****

"Just play along with me, Jacky," the young constable murmured as he grabbed Jacky's elbow. His touch was gentle and surprisingly apologetic.

"You want me to kick up a fuss or what?" hissed Jacky.

"Just imagine that this is a real arrest. Play it by ear."

"It's your call," said Jacky as he let out a scream.

"What the bloody hell am I being arrested for? I ain't done nuthin'."

"Just move your black arse, Jacky. You and me are off to the lockup."

"I tell ya, I ain't done nuthin'."

"I am arresting you on a charge of vagrancy."

He pinned Jacky's arms behind his back and frog-marched him down the street, ensuring the townsfolk had plenty of opportunity to witness the spectacle. Once inside, he let his captive free from his hold and motioned him to the cell at the back.

Jacky hesitated and with pleading eyes he asked, "Can you at least leave the cell unlocked?"

""'fraid not, Jacky. I have my orders. Everything must look real. But never mind, it is only overnight." He slammed the cell door and locked it, pocketing the key with a flourish, and Jacky could not help feeling a twinge of anxiety. The cell was bare and cold, and reeked of the many occupants who had spent time there.

"You are the least troublesome Aboriginal I have ever locked up, Jacky," Sales grinned.

Jacky glared at the young man. "If this was for real, constable, then there would be no way you would have gotten me in here."

And Sales felt a shiver. He knew that Jacky was right.

****

"Mister Mounsie?" said Jimmy Boy as he pushed the door open and walked into the man's office.

"That would be me," he said without looking up.

"Ahem. I need you to do something for me."

Mounsie now looked up to see who had come in. "The Chinaman. What do you want?"

"I have a chore for you."

"I don't do chores, mister. I am a lawyer."

"I think you might like this chore, Mister Mounsie. I want you to ride out to Harry Reagan's farm and tell him that his constable has Jacky locked up."

A change came over the man's face. From being a cock-sure lawyer, he became a frightened man. Jimmy Boy marvelled at how the mere mention of Reagan's name caused panic. His voice croaked as he spoke.

"Why should I do that?"

"I believe you met the policeman from Newcastle yesterday. He told me you were very cooperative."

Mounsie's face turned the colour of a calf's scoured-out backside. He recognised the insinuation. "What is this? Are you all working together?" he stammered.

"The Sub-Inspector also told me that you were quite willing to do anything to save your reputation and maybe stay out of gaol."

The poor man wrung his hands and Jimmy Boy thought he was about to begin sobbing. But he composed himself enough to speak.

"I will go right away. But please, mister, I will go and tell Sergeant Tanner where I am going."

"It is difficult to tell a man something if they can't be found. Tanner is not around. And Mister Mounsie, for your sake, I wouldn't like anyone to know I sent you to carry the news to Reagan. If he asks, tell him you witnessed the arrest."

Mounsie heaved a sigh of relief. He knew where Tanner would be. At the whore's shanty on the edge of town. He had no trust in the man at all, but even one ally was better than none.

*****

Tanner emerged from the shack with a grunt, his suspenders hanging loosely over his shoulders. His face was flushed red, and the stench of whiskey wafting from his breath almost made Mounsie retch.

"You've been at it again, Sergeant," said Mounsie in a disapproving tone.

"Mind yer own fuckin' business Mounsie, else I will clobber you one. What the fuck are you botherin' me so early for?"

The black woman emerged from the hut, and Mounsie noted she looked ten times worse than her benefactor. Her toothless mouth dripped with spittle, and she was wearing nothing but a tattered policeman's issued shirt, missing all the buttons and exposing her sagging breasts.

"What's 'e want? Tell 'im to fuck off."

Mounsie ignored the woman. He had been the brunt of her venom before. "It isn't early, Sergeant, and I am bothering you with something you might find interesting."

"Jis git to the fuckin' point, Mounsie, and stop fuck-arsin' about."

"Your constable locked Jacky up this morning."

Tanner snapped upright. "Jacky? What for?"

"You will have to ask him that. I was on my way to tell Mister Reagan and thought you might like to ride along."

Tanner turned to the woman.

"Git yer arse out back and saddle my 'orse, you useless bitch."

"Do it yer fuckin' self. I aint yer black servant." She pulled her shirt aside and lifted a wrinkled breast and jiggled it in front of Mounsie's nose."'ave a good look Mister Mounsie. I dun seen ya watchin' and starin' at me boobies. Wanna suck on these little beauties?"

She laughed, and the sound reminded Mounsie of a cow calving.

"You disgust me, you horrible excuse for a woman!"

*****

"That's all I know, Mister Reagan," squeaked Mounsie, his voice betraying his nervousness. "I just happened to be at my office this morning, and what do I see? The young constable arresting Jacky. He is in the cells right now."

Reagan cocked his head to one side. "What's the charge?"

"I don't know, Mister Reagan." Mounsie had fulfilled his part of the deal with Jimmy Boy. He just wanted to be away from Reagan and Sergeant Tanner. "Mister Reagan, if that piece of information pleases you, do you think you could spare…?"

"Get the hell off my land, Mounsie!"

"Y-y-yes, Mister Reagan. Right away, Mister Reagan."

Mounsie scurried from the room and was in his buggy and headed back to Milburra in a matter of minutes, leaving Reagan and Tanner ruminating on what action to take.

Reagan leaned across the table, the smoke from his cigar drifting up Tanner's nose. "What do you think, Tanner?" he asked in a flat tone and unblinking eyes.

"About what?"

"Geezus fuckin' Christ! Am I the only one who is capable of thinking 'round here?" He stood up and paced the room before speaking. "This is my chance, Tanner. My chance to be rid of the black man for good. Send your constable on a trip somewhere out of town, and I want you to kill the black bastard!"

Tanner threw his arms in the air. "Whoa back, Mister Reagan! I have done many things for you, but I ain't never killed a man. And I ain't about to start."

Reagan reached into his drawer and pulled out a crumpled wad of cash and tossed it onto the table. He proceeded to tap a pencil against his teeth while staring at the Sergeant. Tanner's hands hovered over the cash, his eyes shifting from Reagan's to the money and back again. He licked his lips nervously then scooped the money up before Reagan could change his mind.

"Right, Mister Reagan, I believe we have a deal. But I am warnin' you. This is the last time I do any business with you."

"You just keep your mouth shut about this, Tanner."

"You think I am a fool? Murderin' a man, even an abo, is still a serious crime. If I swing, then you swing, Mister Reagan."

"Outta my sight, you crooked mongrel!"

Tanner did not need to be told twice. He scurried from the room and slammed the door behind him.

*****

Sergeant Tanner thumped his fist on the door and shouted, his voice cutting through the air, but then mindful of his proximity to town, he lowered his voice.

"Gizelle, you black slut. Open the door."

The red-eyed woman opened the door and said, "What now, Tanner?" her voice a mixture of annoyance and curiosity. He pushed past her and pulled the wad of cash from his top pocket.

"I need you to hide this for a while. Put it with the rest of the money. Pretty soon we are getting' outta this shit town. We'll jis disappear into thin air."

"Yeah, Tanner," she said despondently. "I've 'eard yer shit talk before."

"Jist do it, Gizelle. Don't touch it, don't count it, and don't fuckin' spend a penny of it. Got that?" He drew his fingers across her throat. "Or else you are dead meat."

*****

Chapter 42

Tanner appeared calm on the outside, but inwardly, he was feeling a severe bout of nerves. His guts felt like they were being ripped apart by barbed wire. Although he had carried out many tasks of questionable legality for Reagan over the years, he had never imagined that one day he would be asked to commit murder. He tried to appear casual as he entered the Police Station.

Constable Sales felt about the same as his sergeant. He tried to put on a calm and detached face. He knew he had to play his part.

"Mornin' Sales," grunted Tanner.

"Where have you been, Sergeant? I have good news."

Sales couldn't contain himself and blurted out, "I have the blackfeller locked up, Sergeant."

Tanner feigned surprise at the news.

"Jacky? Good work, Sales. What did you nab him for?"

"Vagrancy Sarge. I searched him and he didn't have a penny on him. In town to do a bit of thieving, I reckon."

"I will see to him later Sales. I need you to ride to Harry

Reagan's place. I saw one of his men just now, and he said Harry is having some sort of trouble."

"Like what?"

"How the bloody 'ell do I know? Just git on yer horse and go."

Constable Sales felt mighty pleased with himself and pleased to be out of Tanner's way. As he headed out back of the Station to fetch his horse, he spied Fleming and his men strolling nonchalantly down the street. He gave Fleming the slightest of nods and walked to the Police stables to saddle his horse. Constable Sales was going to enjoy a relaxing morning by the riverbank fishing for some cod.

*****

Jacky leaned against the cold metal bars of his cell, listening intently to the muffled murmurs. The words weren't clear, but he could tell one of the voices belonged to Tanner. Jacky felt a stab of fear pierce his stomach. He was the bait to bring down the corrupt Sergeant, and he knew it was a risky plan. And now, the moment of reckoning was approaching, and the reality of his situation settled in.

Jacky felt a bead of sweat trickle down his forehead.

The plan hinged on precision. What if Fleming and his team didn't show up in time?

The man had promised him he would be safe, but Jacky could not help the fear he was alone in all this. His breath grew shallower as he heard footsteps, and then he found himself staring into the cold eyes of the policeman. Tanner's grin was a twisted mockery of amusement, and he appeared to be revelling in the fear he inspired.

"Got ya jis where I want you, Jacky," he said, raising his pistol to waist level.

"Now you be a good little black man and turn and face the back wall."

Jacky's heart pounded against his ribs, but he kept his eyes locked on Tanner's. He knew the Sergeant was toying with him, enjoying trying to break his spirit. But Jacky was made of sterner stuff, and he wasn't about to let fear dictate what could possibly be his final moments.

"If you are going to shoot me, Tanner, just like a dog, I will stare you in the face. I am not afraid of death."

But in truth, Jacky was petrified. He did not want to go to the Dreamtime just yet. He thought of his wife Martha and the girl he had grown to love…... Tarni. He wanted to live.

Tanner chuckled.

"Oh, I am not goin' to shoot you, Jacky," he said with a cruel smile on his face.

"A dead aboriginal in my cell would cause me no end of trouble. Besides, the townsfolk would hear my gunshot. Oh no, boy, you are going to 'ang yerself. Then I will go out for the day and let that useless piece of shit, Sales, discover your body. All the town needs know is you committed suicide."

Then, without warning, Tanner swung his pistol and smashed into the left side of Jacky's skull. Tanner stood over the lifeless body, his hands trembling, and watched as blood oozed from the wound. He went to the main office then and returned with a rag and a bucket of water and crouched beside the still figure. His hands felt for a pulse, and he knew Jacky was still alive. The bleeding had stopped by then, and Tanner used rags and water to clean the wound and to remove the traces of blood from the concrete floor. He dabbed at the wound and was satisfied that it was seemingly inconspicuous.

Then, with shaking hands, he untied the rope which had up until now, held Jacky's trousers up. The noose began to take shape in his hands, and he allowed himself a smug smile of satisfaction at what he perceived as his ingenious plan. He knew he had to be careful, mindful that everything looked just right. He struggled with Jacky's body and raised it up so he could loop the rope through the bars.

*****

Outside the Police Station, the men were becoming edgy. Jimmy Boy paced back and forth, his eyes glued on the door of the police building. This was the moment they all feared. Would their plan work? Would their timing be right?

"It's been too long, Alistair. We need to move in now," said Jimmy Boy anxiously.

Fleming remained unflappable.

"Not yet, Jimmy. We need to bide our time and get enough evidence."

Jimmy Boy's agitation grew.

"Evidence won't bring him back if he's dead, Alistair. Tanner is a snake. Who's to say that he hasn't already killed Jacky?"

But Fleming was determined.

"We all knew the risk, Jimmy. Trust the plan. Wait for Jacky's call for help."

"I am telling you, Alistair, how can he call if he has a knife in his belly? He is my friend, and he trusts me!"

Jimmy Boy's fear had reached the breaking point. Without warning, he sprinted across the street and burst through the door of the Police Station. He gasped in shock as he saw Tanner with the rope in his hand and attempting to loop it through the bars.

"Tanner, what in God's name are you doing?" he shouted.

Tanner's startled eyes snapped up.

"It's not what it looks like," he stammered, but Jimmy Boy was beyond reason.

He lunged forward, and his fist smashed into the policeman's jaw.

"You are a murdering bastard!" Jimmy Boy roared as he continued raining punches on the man.

Fleming and his men had sprinted after the Chinaman with pistols cocked.

"Jimmy, stop!" he bellowed.

"I will take it from here. Everything must be done by the book."

Jacky lay slumped on the ground as Walsh grabbed Tanner's arms and pinned them behind his back. Jimmy Boy crouched over his friend.

"Jacky," he whispered and cradled his head.

"Are you with me? Can you hear me?"

The black man's eyes fluttered open, and he managed a smile and said, "Still with you, Jimmy Boy. But how about next time you get here a mite faster. Thought the Dreaming had come."

Fleming poked Tanner in the chest.

"Sergeant Tanner, I am arresting you on the charge of attempted murder and theft of property."

Tanner had all the fight gone out of him now and said nothing.

"Lock him in his own gaol house, Walsh."

*****

"Mighty good of ya, Mister Cornelius, to 'ire a buggy and bring me into town. Been a while since I bin 'ere."

Cornelius Deakin nodded. He enjoyed Bindi's company and wanted to spend as much time with her as possible. He had no idea when Will McKenzie would return and no idea of what would happen when he did. He knew the reason behind his friend's trip to Ramsay, and he also knew of the consequences that could or would ensue.

Cornelius pulled the buggy to a halt outside the Emporium and helped Bindi down. She was reluctant to take the hand he offered.

"Ain't that old I cannot git down off a buggy yet, Mister Cornelius."

"I am only doing what is expected of a gentleman Bindi."

"Well, if you is a gentleman, then ain't no good bein' with me. I ain't no lady to match yer tastes."

Cornelius laughed.

"You are a lady to me, Bindi. Promise me you will never change."

"Not about to change fer anyone. C'mon, let's go in and see Miss Martie."

Bindi was in conversation with Mrs Wells as they entered.

"Bindi!" exclaimed Martha,

"Look what the wind blew in."

Bindi looked around.

"What'd it blow in Miss Martie? Dust? Better git Mrs. Wells some dustin' cloths."

She wiped her fingers along a shelf and gave a snort.

They all laughed at Bindi's simplicity as her eyes took in the array of goods in the Emporium.

Cornelius spied a colourful parasol and picked it up, and opened it over Bindi's head.

"Just the thing for you, Bindi. It will keep the sun off your skin on the hottest of days."

"Sun, don't bother me none. I can't git any blacker than I am."

*****

"You don't need your new parasol in the shade, Bindi."

"I like it, Mister Cornelius. Nobody ever bought me such a nice thing before," she laughed as she twirled her new treasure above her head.

They were sitting by the Bella River, having partaken of cake and bottles of flavoured water which they had purchased in Ramsay. Cornelius was making ready to leave when Bindi raised the subject of Martha and Will.

"Mister Cornelius, what you reckon about Miss Martie and Will McKenzie?"

He stroked his grey wisp of a beard before answering.

"Their affairs do not concern me, Bindi. They are adults and have minds of their own. What I do know is everybody on this earth deserves to be happy."

"In that case, what about Jacky? 'e deserves to be 'appy too. Can't say as he will be pleased if Martie ups and leaves him."

"I will speak no more of this Bindi. It is none of my concern."

"Cranky old buggar, ain't ya?"

Jacky

*****

"Sergeant Tanner, you would be doing yourself a favour by cooperating with me. Charges of attempted murder and actual theft carry a potential death penalty, particularly as I have a certain way of persuading magistrates. Get what I am saying?"

Tanner glared at the man sullenly.

"Nuthin' to say to you, mister."

"Suit yourself."

*****

"Are you sure you will be all right, Jacky?"

Jimmy Boy held concerns for his friend. Although not severely harmed, he had suffered mental torture at the hands of Tanner. And Jimmy Boy, with his innate wisdom, knew how hard it was for his friend to be caged like an animal. He knew how much the Aboriginal people valued their freedom, their independence, and the security of the land around them. A cage was like death to a black man.

"I am all right, Jimmy Boy. But I need time to myself. I need to be in the open spaces around me, breathe the air, and seek the company of the environment. I will return to Richard's farm tomorrow, and you can fill me in on Fleming's plan to take down Harry Reagan."

"Please do not do anything silly, Jacky. I know how headstrong you can be."

"I'll be fine. Till tomorrow," he grinned and loped off into the bush.

*****

Milburra was no different from most country towns, and it was not long before most people learned of Sergeant Tanner's arrest. Gizelle had staggered into town to beg Tanner for some money to feed her craving, but when she heard the news, she went straight back to her hut. The money he had hidden there was a blessing in disguise.

"Jis, a couple of pounds, Tanner," she rattled on to herself.

"This old black gin is gunna git 'erself drunk while you are in yer own gaol."

She took a couple of notes from the stash and went back to town to buy some liquor.

"I got money mister. See if I don't."

Gizelle waved her money at the barman, and his mood changed.

"It'll cost you all that, you black bitch. You most likely pinched it anyway."

By mid-afternoon, Gizelle could barely walk.

Constable Sales rode back into town, a happy man with a bag containing two cod tied to his saddle. He was eager to meet up with Alistair Fleming. Then, suddenly, he winced and rubbed his neck. A sharp stone had come from out of nowhere and struck him, opening a small cut in his neck. He looked in the direction the stone had come from and saw a drunken black woman rolling around and laughing at him. He recognised her as Tanner's woman from the shack on the edge of town. Sales reasoned that she was in town because Tanner had been locked up.

That was one good thing about the Sergeant. He discouraged the woman from entering the town, and although he discouraged talking and being seen in public with her, the whole town knew about his affair with the woman. But at this moment, her presence in town was proof to Constable Sales that Tanner was, indeed, in gaol.

Sales led his horse into Milburra while dragging the drunken woman behind him. He hitched his horse outside the Police Station and then lifted the skinny woman and carried her inside, where he tried to place her delicately on the floor. She rolled on her side, and Sales was rewarded for his kindness with a boot covered in black vomit. He left her there gasping for breath and went out back to the cells. Squatting there on the cold concrete floor was none other than his own Sergeant Tanner.

Sales feigned a look of surprise.

"Sarge, what in hell are you doing there? And where is Jacky? Has he escaped?"

Tanner's eyes pleaded with the constable.

"It's a set-up Sales. Some hot-shot lawman from the city has charged me with tryin' to kill Jacky. I swear on my mother's grave, Sales, I am innocent."

"So where is this law officer now?"

"I have no idea, but now is the perfect opportunity for you to free me, Sales. I have money. I swear, Sales, I will give you all I have if you jis let me outta 'ere."

Sales scratched his chin as if thinking about what he should do. But he had no need to think. He had made his mind up when he agreed to side with Fleming.

"I am afraid I can't let you out, Sergeant Tanner. There is no harm in telling the truth now. I have been working with Sub-Inspector Fleming from Newcastle. They know about your dealings with Harry Reagan."

"This is all Reagan's doing!" Tanner spat out.

"He's the one who fed me cash to keep me trap shut about his shady doin's."

Tanner begged now.

"Please, Constable, let me out. Then I will take you to where I have stashed all my money. If you let me ride outta here fer good, you can have all the money Reagan has given me."

*****

Gizelle pulled herself from the floor. She could hear the faint traces of conversation out the back. On her bony and wobbly legs, she made her way outside, unhitched Sale's horse, and headed for her shack. It was only a mile from town, but each step the horse took hammered a thousand nails into Gizelle's skull.

She dismounted and staggered inside to retrieve more of Tanner's money. The only cure for her, she knew, was another bottle of rum.

The woman felt around in the dark, struggling to find a candle. A screech from beneath her feet caused her to sober up slightly. It was her old tomcat sleeping by the door.

"Git outta the fuckin' way," she shouted as she kicked the cat away and felt in her pocket for a match.

With trembling hands, she struck the match, the sulphur smell masking the stench of decaying food scraps and spilt liquor. She spotted her candle: it had as much life left in it as the empty bottles of rum strewn around the floor. As the wick sputtered to life, it lit up the room, revealing the depravity she was forced to live in. She licked her lips with anticipation as she lifted the lid of the chest containing Tanner's money. Then she grabbed a handful of bills and stuffed them in her pocket. It was more than enough for what she needed.

The candle flickered and almost died as she made her

way back to the door, and the cat, old and frail, was to be her downfall. She tripped and tumbled to the earthen floor, and the candle, with its last attempt at life, fell into a pile of her clothing. For a moment, there was no sound, but then the whole place exploded into a dazzling blaze of colour. Gizelle watched the fingers of flame claw their way up the walls; horror spread across her gaunt features, and unable to comprehend the situation, she gave herself up to the flames, and she died with a smile on her face and the taste of rum in her throat.

*****

It was Fleming who broke the news to Tanner.

"Tanner," he began, his voice low and gruff,

"I have some news for you. Your woman, the black one from the shack just out of town, she's gone."

Tanner screwed his face up.

"What do you mean gone?"

"She is dead Tanner. Burned to a crisp. Her cabin went up in flames a few hours ago."

Tanner's eyes scanned Fleming's, searching for

anything that suggested a twisted joke. But Fleming's face remained stoic.

"But how?"

"It was a fire, Tanner. What do you think happens in a fire? She didn't make it. The rotgut she had inside her wouldn't have helped."

The callousness in his voice was all too obvious.

"One might say she is better off dead, from all accounts I have heard about the woman."

"And the shack?" asked Tanner.

"All gone."

Tanner's face went as white as the ash that remained where Gizelle's hut once stood.

"My money," he moaned.

"All my fuckin' money I 'ad put away. I was gunna piss off from 'ere and start a new life. Was even goin' to take poor Gizelle with me."

"Money wouldn't have been any good to you where you are going, Tanner. And if you were any sort of man, you would be mourning your woman, not your money."

Fleming wheeled about and left the man in solitude.

*****

Chapter 43

The campsite was empty, and there was no fire burning, but Jacky had come to know Tarni and knew she was watching and waiting. He called out her name, his voice disturbing the tranquil clearing.

"Tarni! It's me. Jacky."

A rustle of leaves was the response, and Tarni stepped from the scrub hesitantly until he held out his arms, and she flung herself into his embrace.

"I was worried, Jacky," she said as she stroked his cheeks.

"Not as worried as I was, Tarni."

"Tell me everything, Jacky. Please?" she implored him.

Tarni listened, all the while saying nothing. She was in awe of her man's calmness in the face of possible death.

Jacky continued his narration, and still, the girl maintained her steely silence.

"When Tanner struck me with the butt of his pistol and knocked me cold, I had a vision, Tarni. A powerful one. I was in the Dreamtime, but you weren't with me. It was cold and lonely."

Tarni's eyes grew wide with understanding. She knew the significance of the Dreaming, where the future unfolded and destinies were shaped.

"Go on," she whispered.

"What happened in your dream?"

"I was lost," he continued.

"I was wandering through a wasteland, and I was calling for you, but there was no answer. And then," he paused,

"I saw a rope hanging from a tree. It was calling to me, waiting for me."

She squeezed his hand.

"What does this mean, Jacky?"

"It means that I almost lost everything," he rubbed his hand over hers.

"But I didn't die, Tarni. I was brought back to be with you. Tarni, my life is entangled in the white man's world, but I only want to be with you."

She smiled and moved away further into the shade. Jacky sensed what she wanted, but he wasn't finished just yet.

"Tarni, I need to tell you something. I have been thinking a lot about my life and the choices I have made."

He paused and gulped in fresh air.

"I cannot ignore the connection between us any longer. I know now, without any doubt, I want you for my woman."

Tarni searched his eyes for any insincerity.

"But Jacky, you told me you were married to a white woman. This is not a choice to be made lightly."

"I know," he said rather sadly,

"But my vision…….it showed me what I stand to miss if I do not follow my heart. And my vision told me that I am aboriginal."

*****

"Papa," called Charley as she emerged from the house.

"What's going on?"

Her father and Marty Hope, his new right-hand man, broke from their conversation to acknowledge her.

"It's nothing you need worry about, Charley. I was just going over some things with Hope. You ready to go into town?"

But Charley knew her father was hiding something. She had seen that look before. Hope gave her a nod as he held the reins of the horse hitched to the buggy.

"Yeah, jis business, Miss Charley."

She had a sick feeling in her stomach as she looked at the man, and she saw his eyes wander to the shed in the distance where the aboriginals were being held. Charlene Reagan had a funny feeling that things were just not right.

The trip into Milburra was mostly in silence, and Charley sensed a tension and an urgency in her father. She knew enough about his dealings to know it made him a wary man, but she had never seen him on edge like this before.

As they rolled into the town, Charley noticed the place was eerily quiet, as if it was waiting for something to happen. Reagan pulled the buggy to a stop outside the Police Station, and Charley was quick to question him.

"What business do we have here, Papa?" she asked, and then she saw Constable Sales leaning on the doorpost.

But Reagan was in no mood to answer her. He was too preoccupied with the whereabouts of Tanner. He climbed from the buggy and, in a gruff voice, asked,

"Where's Tanner?"

"And a good morning to you, Mister Reagan."

"I asked you a question, Sales."

Reagan had known from the time he arrived that the young constable would be a thorn in his side. He was too good-looking, too much a by-the-book lawman.

"Sergeant Tanner is asleep out back in the cell, Mister Reagan."

"Well, go and wake him and tell him I need to speak with him."

"I am afraid if you want to speak with him, then you will have to go in to see him. Sergeant Tanner is currently my prisoner, Mister Reagan."

Reagan felt the blood drain from his face.

"What!" he sputtered.

The whole situation seemed to be spiralling out of control.

Feigning ignorance of Reagan's involvement, Sales said,

"An inspector from Newcastle arrested Sergeant Tanner on the charge of attempted murder. He tried to kill an aboriginal by the name of Jacky. You know him of course."

He dropped his voice a notch in volume as if there were unwanted ears.

"This contingent of police is looking for someone. Someone who might be involved with…….. with a certain misunderstanding with the black man."

Reagan's neck muscles tightened, and Charley's face blanched.

"Papa, I need to talk. Now!"

Sales interrupted.

"I can take you in to see Sergeant Tanner if you want."

"Let the bastard rot in there!" came the response, and he walked back to the buggy.

"Papa," she said in a low voice,

"I don't know anything about this murder business with Jacky, but I do know one thing. There is something that needs to be dealt with immediately."

"What are you talking about?"

But then his eyes widened with realisation.

"The blacks," he murmured.

"Yes Papa. We must get home at once and turn them loose. I told you so many times, but you wouldn't listen. Now, see the trouble we are in."

*****

"You ran too much of a risk with Jacky, Alistair. Any longer, and it could have been disastrous."

Fleming gave a smug smile.

"Some people have claimed I live close to the edge, Jimmy. But seriously, I knew what I was doing."

"I just hope you know what you are doing with regards to Reagan. There are more lives at risk than just one. We don't even know how many captives he has."

"It doesn't matter. But the first thing we need to know is how many men he has protecting him."

He looked at Kerrigan.

"He had upward of a dozen or more, but the numbers have dwindled. But I think out of the men still with him. There are only about five or six who would be willing to gamble their lives for him. While I was there, the men began to become restless, and I heard talk that some were leaving. Most didn't like being slave masters."

"So, we will take it as a rough guess that he has ten men. I will take my four men and Sergeant Connolly. You will ride into town and remain at the Police Station with Sales."

Fleming went on to outline his plan. It was simple but risky. He and his men would ride onto Reagan's land under the guise of reports of a tribe of Aboriginals being kept as slaves and forced to work Reagan's land. Then, as Fleming kept Reagan and his men busy, Jacky and Jimmy Boy, along with Kerrigan, would enter the shed where the tribe was being held and release them before Reagan had a chance to send his men to harm them.

"Jimmy Boy, once you have them away from the farm, fire a shot in the air to let us know you are safe. Then, I will arrest Harry Reagan for murder and kidnapping. And throw the charge of corrupting the law and horse theft in as well. With your testimony, Mister Kerrigan," he looked at the attentive face of the man,

"We will have enough evidence to see Mister Harry Reagan dangling from a rope."

The meeting was interrupted by a shout from out beyond the barn.

Jennings and Wells had been quiet, trying to absorb the seriousness of the situation. Both felt an enormous sense of inflated pride being admitted to the inner sanctum of the planning. When one nodded his head in approval, the other, not to be outdone, would nod twice as many times and murmur,

"Good, Good."

But the shout unnerved Wells. He leapt up and, in an alarmed voice, shouted,

"It's Reagan's men. They are a'comin' to git us."

Jennings clipped the man behind the ear.

"Bloody fool, Wells. Can't you tell Jacky's voice by now?"

*****

As Jacky approached the barn, the men ceased their

planning and focussed on the new arrival. Fleming was as pleased to see the black man as Jimmy Boy was.

"Just in time for some tea, Jacky," said Wells as he lifted the billy from the low fire.

Jacky felt the coolness of the barn as he entered, with Tarni shadowing him like a good drover's dog. The first face he saw was the inquisitive face of Will McKenzie. Jacky had known this day would come. He had married Martha for love, he thought, but then he wrestled with the idea that the marriage may have been for some semblance of security, a life beyond the harsh realities of his people. But he had come to know his heart, wild and untamed like the scrub around him, belonged to the young girl behind him.

As he looked at McKenzie, he felt a prickle of unease, a twinge of guilt tight in his belly. He knew Will had feelings for his wife, and the man's eyes held unspoken accusations as he looked beyond Jacky at the figure of Tarni.

The rest of the men had paid no attention to Tarni, but Will Mckenzie saw a chance to drive a barb into his rival.

"I see you have brought company, Jacky. Aren't you going to introduce us to your friend?"

The irony was lost on both men.

Martha had found herself trapped in a loveless marriage and had sought solace in the arms of Will McKenzie, and now Jacky's infidelity mirrored hers, a cruel twist of fate.

"This is Tarni," he said.

"Nullah's granddaughter."

Will's expression remained firm, his eyes betraying nothing but a cold assessment of the situation. He could see the fierce devotion in Tarni's eyes. The unspoken question hung in the air.

How long before this precarious situation was shattered and the truth came out?

McKenzie's silence was more damaging than any outburst. He had no need to voice any disapproval; his eyes said it all. Then the two men nodded to each other; a strange sort of understanding between them, a grim acceptance of the situation. They both knew this was not the ending but a new beginning and one filled with uncertainty. Jacky looked at Tarni, her hand resting on his hip.

"Might have a cup of tea, Tarni. What do you reckon?"

*****

"Jimmy Boy," Will began.

"We need to talk about Jacky. I know I have a vivid imagination, but there is something more than friendship between him and the young girl he brought here today. He is married Jimmy Boy. To your daughter. The girl I love more than life itself. Haven't you got anything to say about his infidelity?"

"Will," said Jimmy Boy in a measured voice,

"I understand your concern. My daughter is a good woman caught in a difficult situation. I know you have strong feelings for her. But what we are doing here is tricky business. And dangerous. The raid on Reagan's place, well, it could go sideways, and someone may be killed. But I don't want to interfere in Jacky's personal life, especially not now. Let's just focus on getting the Aboriginal people to safety. Once that is done, then we can talk things through."

"You are right, Jimmy Boy," he said resignedly.

"But after we have freed those people, we must talk this all out. About Martha. About Jacky. About everything."

Jimmy Boy made a silent vow. He had to address the simmering family trouble once his task was over. The raid on

Reagan's farm loomed, but for now, a sense of purpose gripped him. The immediate future belonged to the fight for justice, but the future beyond that, he hoped, would hold a resolution for his daughter's troubled heart.

*****

Chapter 44

Harry Reagan didn't spare the whip on the pony as he hastened to get back to Dingo's Retreat. Sergeant Tanner's unexpected arrest had alarmed him, and the talk of a police task force in the district was even more frightening.

"Papa, ease up a little on the whip. The poor pony is doing its best."

"Hush Charley. We need to get home as fast as we can. You were right. I must free the blacks and get them off my property. I don't like the sound of unknown police in the district."

"I have been trying to tell you that Papa."

Reagan's mind was in turmoil. For too long, he had held the tribe captive, their lives marked by forced labour, near starvation, and the unspeakable violation of the women. He had convinced himself that it was necessary, that they were no more than animals, useless without a master, and deserved their fate. But the lies he had told himself had slowly faded to be replaced by the truth of an impending doom.

Marty Hope was coming from the stables, where he

had been checking on Jacky's stallion and the mare. He took the lead rein of the pony and rubbed its neck.

"Back so soon, Mister Reagan?"

He looked at the floor of the buggy.

"And no supplies either."

"Charley, you unhitch the pony. I need to talk to Hope," said Reagan as he stepped down.

"Problems?" asked Hope.

"Bloody big ones Hope. Where are the blacks at now?"

"The men have them in the river paddock grubbing out stumps and burnin' off."

"I need you to go across to the shed where the women are and unchain the lot of them. Then, I want you to lead them as far from here as you can. And I mean far, Hope. Don't fucking return till they are out of sight. Tell the men in the paddock to let the other bastards loose as well and force them, at gunpoint, to clear right out of here with the women. I don't want to set my eyes on the heathens ever again."

He thought for a moment. He needed to do this thing properly. There was no room for error.

"And Hope, have the women clean the shed before they go. There must be no evidence of anyone ever being there."

Hope's eyes lit up.

"Any chance me and the men can 'ave some sport with them? Some nice one's goin' to waste."

"I don't give a fuck what you do with them, Hope. Just so long as it is a hundred fuckin' miles from here. Now get started!" roared Reagan as he threw the keys to the chains on the ground.

*****

Hope jingled the set of keys as he walked towards the shed. He had known this day would come. Reagan, the fat-gutted, self-absorbed tyrant, had finally buckled under the threat of discovery. Now, it was up to him to free the women and take them to join their men and get them as many miles away as possible.

Hope and the other men had always known that Reagan visited the black women at night. And now it was their turn. A reward for liberation. He used the biggest key to unlock the door of the shed and stepped inside. No matter how many times he had been in there, he had not become used to the smell of unwashed bodies, rotting food scraps, and the overflowing tin buckets used as latrines. He adjusted his eyesight and took in the miserable wretches cowering on the floor. Their fear was unmistakable. They knew it was not their feeding time. What was the white man doing here at this time of day?

Hope keyed open the lock, holding the length of the chain to a solid post buried deep in the ground, with the rest of the chain running through an iron link around each woman's ankle. He motioned them to stand, using his pistol as an incentive not to cause any trouble.

His voice came as a grunt.

"Waddya black bitches so scared of? Terday is yer lucky day. Yous are free."

The women stood frozen, unable to comprehend what was happening. Those who understood some English had heard whispers of freedom in the past, whispers that had come to nothing. A promise from a black man and his woman that had come to nothing. But there was something in Hope's tone that signified today was different.

Hope made a comical charade of picking up the trash

and scraps from the floor and gestured at the terrified women to do the same. The realisation that their home for the past few seasons was to be cleaned meant one thing. They were being moved. Or better still, freed. It took only a short while to have the shed clean, and the latrines carted outside. When Hope was satisfied, he motioned the group outside with his pistol and pointed in the distance to the paddocks where the men were working.

*****

Hope watched as the women made their way towards the working men. Reagan's farmhands looked at him with puzzled faces. The women had never been made to work in the fields, only in the home paddocks. The aboriginal men were equally puzzled until they saw the smiles on the faces of the women. Then, a wave of emotion spread over them, a mixture of relief and joy. Tools were thrown in the air as the women reunited with their fathers, sons, husbands, and brothers.

"What the fuck is goin' on, Hope?" called one of the men.

"Reagan told me to free the black bastards and get them as far from here as we can. The coppers are on Reagan's arse, and he's runnin' scared. We gotta move."

Hope raised his pistol above his head and fired a shot, then lowered the gun and pointed in the direction of the bushland way off in the distance. The aborigines needed no further encouragement. With some carrying the children and the young men helping the elders, they began their long trek to freedom, the white men following on horseback.

*****

Tarni lay in the gunyah that she had so carefully constructed. She was becoming increasingly restless, hoping that Jacky would return soon. Then she heard it. A faint murmur and the shuffling of feet and the distant sounds of voices, which she knew at once belonged to the Wiradjuri tribe.

But what were they doing way out here?

She made her way cautiously towards the sound, her feet silent over the hot earth. And then she saw them. The tribe of aborigines, moving slowly, their bodies wracked by exhaustion. And behind them on horseback came the white men with Hope in the lead.

Tarni edged her way towards their line of travel, and as

the first of them passed her, she slipped silently into the group and used her spear as a crutch. She saw recognition dawn in the eyes of the women who had seen her with Jacky, and instantly, she raised her fingers to her lips, the universal sign for silence.

Fifteen miles, he had estimated. Far enough away from Reagan's farm. Hope decided that this was far enough. He pulled his horse to a stop and shouted at the blacks.

"Hoy there. Stop!"

Every man, woman, and child knew what the word meant. After all, they had heard it said enough times.

"On the ground," Hope barked.

"Time for some fun, men, before we let the bastards loose."

*****

Rachel Andrews had a big breakfast prepared for the men, and under her direction, they operated as a well-regimented group. They were lined up in a single file with chipped tin platters held in front of them and were served slabs of dried pork and fried eggs. They ate in silence, each man thinking of the role he had to play in the day's mission.

"I don't see why I can't be a part of the team, Mister Fleming," moaned Wells.

"Nor me," echoed Jennings.

"I was in with Jacky from the start. All you fellers are jis blow-ins. Was me and Jacky started the whole thing."

"I admire your qualities, men, but this is a task for the police. I don't want innocent lives lost and be left to bear the guilt."

"Can shoot as well as anyone," mumbled Wells to himself.

Will McKenzie sat silently, watching, his eagerness barely contained. But he was to be let down as well.

"My final orders," announced Fleming, "are as follows. Connolly, you will ride into Milburra and provide support for Constable Sales. We must ensure that Tanner gets no sniff of a way to escape. Will, you will remain here on the farm with Wells and Jennings and see that Richard and Rachel are kept safe. My men and I will ride into Reagan's place, and Jimmy, you, and Jacky trail us by about five or ten minutes.

Then we will listen for your shot and take it from there."

"What about me?" asked Kerrigan.

"I think it is best you are not with us. You ride with Jimmy and Jacky. Your major role begins when I arrest Reagan."

He looked at each man and nodded.

"All clear?"

There were murmurs of assent.

As the men mounted their horses, their movements efficient and unhurried, Will made a split-second decision. He would prove himself to Jimmy Boy and to the black man that he could face danger as well. Will McKenzie decided that he wanted to be in on the adventure.

*****

Will decided that fifteen minutes was enough to start for the last of the riders, Jacky, Jimmy Boy, and Kerrigan. He saddled his horse under the watchful eyes of Wells and Jennings. He had promised himself something he couldn't miss. The freeing of the Aboriginals and the arrest of Reagan.

"Jis, where you headed, Will McKenzie?"

The young man mounted his horse and said,

"I don't think I need to answer that Wells. You know damned well just where I am going."

"Better be careful Will. Jimmy Boy won't take a likin' to this at all."

"I am my own man, Jennings."

As he rode, Will imagined the scene. A dramatic confrontation followed by an even more dramatic arrest. Much better than the story books he was used to reading during his free time in Sydney. But he was to find the reality far different. Will had lived in the city for too long, and soon, the well-trodden tracks he had followed slowly disappeared. He began to feel uneasy, and the realisation struck him. He was lost!

The crack of a gunshot ripped through the incessant buzzing of flies, and Will's heart leapt to his throat. He spurred his horse towards the sound but was almost unsaddled as a bunch of riders, their faces masked by dust, galloped past him. His horse shied, and it took all his skill to stay on its back. The riders were clearly fleeing, but from whom? Or what?

He hesitated for a moment and then pushed his horse forward until he found himself in a clearing. In front of him stood Tarni, a group of aboriginals behind her. Lying lifeless at her feet lay a white man, a spear protruding from his back.

She stood defiant and showed no fear, and he could see the rage and the fire in her eyes.

"Jacky?" asked Will. And she pointed in the direction of Harry Reagan's farm.

He turned his horse and headed in the direction she had pointed, with one thought in his mind. The men who had ridden past him were headed in the opposite direction to Dingo's Retreat.

*****

Chapter 45

"And just who would you be, mister?"

Fleming was taking his first look at the man he had vowed to bring to justice. He saw nothing extraordinary about the man. Just a typical farmer and maybe carrying some excess weight.

"My name is Alistair Fleming, and I am here about a rumour that has spread down south."

Fleming kept his hand near his holster, ready for any unwanted visitors.

"Rumours? What type of rumours?"

Reagan held his shotgun tightly, and Charley stood beside him with a worried look on her face.

"The kind of rumour that says you have a secret, Mister Reagan. A secret that involves keeping people against their will."

He paused, letting the accusation sink in.

"Specifically, a tribe of blacks chained up somewhere in one of your sheds."

Reagan's jaw clenched.

"You have been fed a pack of lies. I don't know what you are talking about. But I do know I don't take kindly to folk who poke their noses in my business. And what gives you the right to make accusations?"

Fleming extracted his badge and turned it up so the man could see.

"The magistrate gives me the right."

Reagan's face took on a pasty shade.

"Now, if you could lead the way, we will take a look."

Reagan glanced at the shed where the blacks had been kept. It had been almost a day. Surely, the blacks were far enough away by now. But Hope and the rest of his men still had not returned. That left only himself and his daughter on the farm. And Bruce. He thought of his son. He loved him, but he was afraid of the hulking giant. And he knew that he was of no use to anyone if there was trouble. His thoughts churned. There had to be a way to stall Fleming and his men.

"What about we have a drink?" Reagan suggested.

"We can talk this over like civilised men."

Fleming warmed to the idea. He had wanted to look in the house, but he couldn't help but feel that Reagan was trying to fob him off. Still, it would give Jacky and Jimmy Boy more time to free the aborigines.

"That sounds a fine idea, Mister Reagan."

*****

Reagan ushered Fleming and his men into his opulent home and set about pouring generous glasses of rum.

"Here's to a speedy resolution, Mister Fleming," he said as he bumped his glass on the lawman's.

Fleming's eyes kept drifting towards the front door, and his ears were tuned, listening for a single gunshot signalling the end of the Aboriginal incarceration.

Then, a loud shout could be heard from across the yard, and Jimmy Boy burst through the door.

"The shed's empty," he gasped.

"There's nobody there."

Reagan's eyes gleamed with satisfaction.

"I told you, Mister Fleming," he drawled with a false innocence.

"There's been a dreadful misunderstanding. I know nothing of any aborigines."

Fleming's calm demeanour dissipated. There had to be a mistake. His evidence had gone, vanished as quickly as the aborigines themselves, and he was left with nothing but suspicion. He consoled himself with the thought that he still had his major trump card to play. The real crime, the one that would finally bring Reagan down, rested on Kerrigan's testimony.

"Where is Mister Kerrigan, Jimmy Boy?"

Reagan began oozing sweat. Hadn't the man left the area? Kerrigan was the last man he wanted to see.

"He will be here shortly. He found a man by the hog pens and is having trouble getting him here."

At the mention of hog pens, Reagan let out a beastly roar.

"Bruce! My son! If you bastards harm one hair on his head, I swear I will not rest until you are all dead! He is but a child!"

Kerrigan and Jacky pushed the giant of a man through

the door. He was snivelling and on the verge of tears.

"Papa, "he blubbered, "these bad men took me away from feedin' my hogs."

Jacky pushed Bruce towards a chair.

"My people were here not so long ago, Mister Fleming. This simpleton was feeding the pigs with human shit. And it was fresh."

"Papa," wailed Bruce, "can I go back to my hogs?"

Reagan showed genuine concern for Bruce.

"Go upstairs with your sister, Bruce. It's time for your hogs to go beddy-byes. And you, Kerrigan, you are not supposed to be here!" he spat.

Charley put her arms out to Bruce, and the big man allowed himself to be led to his room.

*****

The arrest was swift and efficient. Reagan offered no resistance as Fleming said the words he had been dreading to hear.

"Harry Reagan, I am arresting you for the murder of the Lamberts and the solicitation of the attempted murder of

Jacky Wang. There will be further charges laid against you when you are removed from your place of sanctuary here and taken to the lock-up in Milburra. From there, you will be conveyed to Maitland gaol to await trial."

"I have no idea what you are talking about, Fleming. What proof do you have? I want my lawyer."

"You mean Mounsie? I think you are better off without him, Reagan. Your lawyer seems to have less than his fair share of intestinal fortitude. In fact, he has helped us already. And as for proof, Mister Kerrigan can provide all the evidence we need."

Reagan began shaking. From being a tyrant living in luxury, he had become a sad and sorry and beaten man.

But there was still a gaping hole in the investigation. The whereabouts of the aboriginals were of major concern, and that caused a pain in the gut for Fleming and even more so for Jacky. The missing blacks cast a shadow over the case for Fleming and an even darker shadow over Jacky, who was desperately trying to convince himself that Reagan hadn't killed them.

"Mister Reagan, there is no use lying any longer. I

know you had my people in your shed."

Jacky's tone was ominous.

Then, without warning, the black man leapt forward and struck out with his fist, knocking Reagan to the ground.

"What have you done with them, you white mongrel?"

It took all the men to pull Jacky away from Reagan's throat.

"Get him outside, Jimmy," barked Fleming.

"Better still, take him back to Richard's farm. We'll take this gentleman into Milburra and lock him up."

Charlene Reagan returned from upstairs. She was distraught and sobbing with her head on the table, but then, with an effort, she lifted her head and spat her words at Jacky.

"And to think I liked you, Jacky. You are no different to all the blacks 'round here."

*****

"It feels good, Jimmy Boy," said Jacky as they rode back to Richard Andrews' farm.

"What?"

"Being astride my own horse."

He smiled and rubbed Bandit's neck.

"C'mon boy," he yelled and kicked the steed into a gallop, veering off the track, leaving Jimmy Boy wiping dust from his eyes.

"Jimmy Boy, I am going to look for Tarni," he shouted over his shoulder.

*****

Jimmy Boy was in no hurry to get back to the farm. Reagan would soon be behind bars, and Richard and Rachel Andrews could finally breathe easily. But he still held doubts about the aborigines. What had Reagan done with them? Were they alive?

It was one of those perfect days, the kind when a man should have no worries in the world. In the distance, a cloud of dust began to form, swirling like a small willy-willy. He squinted into the sun's glare, and as the dust grew closer, he could make out the shape of a rider-----Will McKenzie. Will was galloping on his horse as if it was a race to the death. Something wasn't right. He eased his own mount under a shady tree and waited for Will.

Will's horse skidded to a stop right in front of Jimmy Boy, who saw the panic-stricken face.

"Jimmy Boy! Thank the Lord Almighty. "

"Will! What are you doing here?"

"I tried to follow you, but I got lost," he panted.

Jimmy Boy leaned across and took the reins of Will's horse.

"Will, you were told to stay at the farm."

"But Jimmy Boy, I am sure glad I didn't. I couldn't pick up your trail, but I stumbled across a tribe of aborigines.

And..." he gasped.

"The aboriginal girl, the one with Jacky, she was with them, Jimmy Boy. And there was a dead man lying there," he began to sob.

"I think the girl speared him."

Jimmy Boy's face beamed with what could only be described as delight.

"Will McKenzie, you bring me good news. It means the tribe is alive, and if Tarni is with them, it means they are safe."

But then his brow furrowed.

"What about the dead man? Was there anybody else?"

"There was a bunch of them who went riding past me, Jimmy Boy. And the speed at which they were travelling, I think they were running scared."

"Which way did they go, Will?"

"As you know, Jimmy Boy, I am not very good with directions, but they went in that direction."

He pointed in the distance to the clouded peaks of a mountain range.

Jimmy Boy heaved a sigh of relief.

"It seems to me that they have cleared out Will. That is nowhere in the direction of Dingo's Retreat. Maybe, just maybe, that is the last we will see of Reagan's men."

*****

Jacky had ridden hard before he saw any trace of a beaten trail. He breasted a rise, and, in the distance, he could see wisps of smoke spiralling into the afternoon air. He craned his eyes, and there, in a sheltered gully, he saw the aboriginal people. His heart yearned for Tarni, and he spurred his horse forward, a triumphant cry echoing through the valley.

As he approached their makeshift camp, a chorus of joyous cries welcomed him, and Tarni, her eyes shining with joy, rushed to meet him.

The men had been busy on the trek, and roasting on the small fires scattered around the gully were plump goannas, juicy witchetty grubs, and sweet native fruits. The air was alive with the rhythm of laughter and the clacking of sticks gathered on their journey.

That night, doing the best he could with the little Wiradjuri he knew, Jacky outlined his plan. He would escort them to his farm where Burra and the other members of the Wiradjuri tribe were camped, and then Burra would lead them back to their tribal lands in the Gulu-Mada, the Blue Mountains.

*****

Under the watchful gaze of the moon, Jacky and Tarni slipped away from the sleeping camp, lured by the sweet scent of eucalyptus and in the darkness, their reunion was complete. After their passion was spent, they lay on their backs, taking in the night sky.

"You are my woman, Tarni. I will leave the white man's ways. I want you forever."

"Are you sure, Jacky?"

"We will leave the camp tomorrow and ride to the Andrews farm. Jimmy Boy needs to know where I am going. Our work is done here now. We just need to return and lead the people away."

*****

Jacky and Tarni found the men resting in the coolest spot on the farm-----Richard Andrew's barn.

Jacky, without any hesitation, blurted out the news.

"We found them, Jimmy Boy. The tribe. They are safe and waiting for my return to take them south and meet up with Burra."

Jimmy Boy smiled, a flicker of weariness crossing his face. He wanted nothing more than to go home to his family.

"I know," he said softly.

"Will told me yesterday."

Will interrupted a trace of smugness in his tone.

"See, Jacky, I am good for something at least."

Jacky ignored him, his look fastened on his friend.

"Tarni and I will take them to my farm tomorrow and meet up with Burra. When they have rested up, he can lead them south back to their tribal lands," he continued, snubbing Will's boastful interjection. But Will was persistent and couldn't help inserting himself into the conversation.

"You seem to be mighty close to the girl, Jacky."

This time, Jacky's patience snapped.

"And what business is that of yours, McKenzie?"

Will, visibly chastened, didn't respond and walked to the back of the barn, and Jacky said nothing more. The unspoken bond between himself and Tarni was on show for all to see.

Jimmy Boy merely nodded at Jacky, a silent acknowledgment of Jacky's anger. He knew he had to find a resolution as soon as possible.

*****

The farewell felt abrupt, rushed even. Jimmy Boy was

anxious to get back to Wicklow. He clapped Richard on the shoulders.

"Farewell, my friend."

Rachel offered a small, hesitant smile as she stood with her hand in Kerrigan's.

"We will pray for your safe journey," she said.

"Thank you for everything, Richard."

"It is us who must thank you, Jimmy. Reagan has finally met his match."

"It is not done with yet. Kerrigan, you become an important player now. Everything rests on your testimony."

Jimmy Boy shook his hand.

"I wish you and Rachel true happiness."

"Goodbye, Richard," said Will.

Jennings and Wells were waiting with the horses saddled. They were tired men and wanted to get home, too. The four men mounted up and set off for home. Jimmy Boy took one last look back, a knot of worry tightening his gut. He knew that even when he reached Wicklow, his worries were not over. But for now, the miles he put behind him were a victory in themselves.

*****

Fleming pushed the bound Reagan through the door of the police station, and in a furious rage, he spat on the floor.

"Put me in a cell with Tanner," he rasped.

"I'll murder the bastard!"

Fleming chuckled.

"Save your breath, Reagan. It's a bit late for settling scores. You both will be swinging before long."

Then he gestured to constable Sales.

"You best get some sleep. Connolly and me and the men, well, we might go to the hotel for a drink and spend the night there."

But Fleming felt a prickle of unease. Years of being a lawman had made him cautious. The arrest of Reagan had been too easy. He had faith in the young policeman, but he issued him a final warning.

"Sleep lightly, Sales. Any trouble, fire a shot out the window."

Sales grinned. He relished the responsibility.

The town was silent, and as Sales looked out the window, he could see that the hotel lanterns were being extinguished. He made himself comfortable on Tanner's chair, placing his revolver on the desk within reach. Then he succumbed to a light sleep, fidgeting with images of the burnt woman he had been made to pull from the ashes of her hut.

He was disturbed by a rhythmic moaning coming from the cells. Tanner, notorious for his cunning, was claiming to be ill, and Sales, on the other hand, known for his compassion, poured the man some water into a tin pannikin. He shoved the water through the bars and helped Tanner drink. This was his mistake. Tanner grabbed him by the neck and pulled him forward with enough force to crack his head on the cold steel. Sales was not unconscious but dizzy enough not to feel Tanner reach for the keys. Having used the key many times as the gaoler, it took mere seconds for the prisoner to free himself and make a grab for Sale's pistol. He used it with enough force to club Sales on the side of the head, and the man slumped to the floor.

Reagan had been asleep, but the commotion woke him, and when he saw Tanner on the outside of the bars, he pleaded with the man.

"Tanner, let me out."

"Fuck you Reagan. You are the reason I was in me own cell in the first place. You can rot there, you mongrel bastard!"

Fleming finished his drink as the last of the lanterns was doused. He had an itchy feeling.

"I think I will check on Sales before bed," he said to his men.

As he walked out the hotel door, he heard the loud scream of Harry Reagan, and the next moment Sergeant Tanner came bolting out of the station.

Alistair Fleming was known for his marksmanship. Rumour had it he had dropped a man at five hundred yards. He didn't panic but unholstered his revolver and fired a single shot at the onrushing Tanner. The bullet sped true and struck the man in the bridge of his nose.

Fleming put his pistol away, and with shouting men bursting from the hotel, he walked over to the dead man.

"Nailed him, Sub," said Walsh in his laconic fashion.

"Saves a trial leastways," remarked Fleming.

*****

"I will be a couple of hours, Tarni. I have some business to take care of. Have the tribe ready to move when I get back."

Jacky decided against telling Tarni the true nature of his errand. He was going to see Charlene Reagan. He felt a pang of sympathy for the girl. After all, he was partly responsible for her father being in police custody. Now with her father gone, she was alone, save for her useless brother Bruce, and she was tasked with the responsibility of running Dingo's Retreat.

Charley met him at the gate, her eyes sparkling with resentment.

"What the hell do you want, Jacky? You have a nerve!"

"I have come to say sorry, Charley."

"It's a bit late for that now."

"And to give you something."

She relaxed her stern face and waved him in the gate.

"Come on in and have some tea."

"I cannot stay long, Charley," he said as he pulled up a

chair on the porch.

"What is it you want to give me, Jacky," she asked in a sultry tone.

"The horse that is tied up at your front gate, Charley."

"You mean…?"

"Yes. I have no need for him anymore. Besides, he may give you some comfort, what with all you have been through."

Charley smiled, a new appreciation of the black man dawning on her.

"Gilmore Cup huh? Two years in a row."

But then she adopted a serious tone.

"Jacky, now, with my father gone, this place is all mine. There are endless possibilities for us, Jacky. You can share all this."

She waved her arms around.

"And we could live here in happiness."

She leaned closer and placed her hand on his crotch.

"Wouldn't you like that, Jacky?"

But the man remained unmoved.

"I have tasted the life you offer Charley and have found it's not the life for me. You may not understand, but my heart belongs to the land."

To his surprise, she didn't press the issue. A strange resignation settled over her face and, with it, an understanding of the black man.

With a wry smile, she said,

"I wish you luck Jacky."

"What will you do?" he asked.

"I have all this. I will rebuild what my father began but Jacky, I will do it in an honest way. And I will see that Bruce is taken away from here. He needs treatment. I will send him to Sydney. This is no life for him."

"I must be going," said Jacky.

"Then take one of the horses from the stable, and when you reach your destination, turn it loose."

Jacky stood and looked at her.

"I enjoyed my time with you," he said sincerely.

She stood and kissed him fervently and pulled him in close to her breasts. He could feel her heat, and her breathing became fast and heavy. He pulled away.

"Be seeing you Charley."

"Fuck you, Jacky," she laughed as he walked to the stables.

"Fuck you!" she said again, still with a grin on her face.

*****

Chapter 46

The letter began with Fleming's meticulous handwriting.

Dear Jimmy Wang,

Reagan's arrest went smoothly with no loss of life, thanks to your and Jacky's tireless work. Your information proved invaluable, and he will hang for the murder of the Lamberts for sure.

No doubt you have heard about Sergeant Tanner's untimely death. He is one less prisoner the government has to feed.

Mister Kerrigan is here with me in Maitland. The man is understandably shaken, but he is ready to testify. He sends you his regards and to Jacky also. He speaks a lot about how his opinion of the Aboriginal race changed after Jacky saved his life.

He is a different man from the one I imagined before meeting him. I think the woman, Rachel Andrews, has had a profound effect on him. She is with him at present. After what she and her brother have been through, I think she deserves a holiday.

The trial is set for one week, and as I do not know how speedy the mail is, it could be over by the time you receive this letter.

No doubt I will be seeing you in a short while at the proper wedding of my nephew and your daughter-in-law Meg.

On a more serious note, I could not help but notice you were carrying grief of your own regarding family matters. I pray to God that all can be resolved. You are a good man, Jimmy Wang.

Regards,

Alistair Fleming.

Jimmy Boy carefully folded the letter and poured himself a small brandy. Resolved. That was the word.

*****

"Papa," whispered Martha as she glanced at her mother and grandmother, who were taking a midday nap.

"When will Jacky be home?"

"Martie," he said,

"It may be two or even three days more. The journey is an arduous one. We were lucky. We had the advantage of horseback, but Jacky is leading the aborigines on foot. He will return though Martie," he said with an emphasis on the word will.

"Papa, I know what you are implying. I am no longer afraid to face the truth. But I need to speak with Will. Can I visit him in town?"

Jimmy Boy screwed up his face, but not with anger. He understood.

"Can't it wait until Monday when you go to work at the Emporium?"

"But Papa, Jacky may be home then."

Jimmy Boy sighed and, in a gentle voice, said,

"You may go Martie. But your mother must not know, and I will go with you. We will make it quick and be back before dinner."

The ensuing silence was comforting. A shared understanding between father and daughter. The weight of her secret eased slightly with her father's blessing. But the shadow of Jacky still hung over her, along with her guilt, which would constantly remind her of the delicate balance between desire and the unrelenting realities of life.

*****

It was mid-afternoon, and Will and Cornelius Deakin were idling their time away on the verandah of Jack's Inn, each man holding a somewhat cold cup of tea. Cornelius took a reluctant sip of the bland concoction and said,

"You seem to be deep in thought, Will. Anything the matter?"

"I was just thinking of Martie, Cornelius. I cannot wait to see her."

Then, as if by sheer chance, they heard the squeaking wheels of a buggy rolling down the street.

"Looks like your prayers have been answered, Will. That's Miss Martha and her father now."

Jimmy Boy halted the buggy and dusted off his hat.

"Afternoon, gents," he said as he helped his daughter from the buggy.

Martha wore a simple cotton dress that fluttered in the

light breeze, revealing the graceful lines of her body. She attempted to avoid Will's eyes, concentrating on the face of his companion Cornelius, but Will stepped off the verandah and embraced her. Jimmy Boy cleared his throat, reminding them of his presence.

"Let's go inside, Will. I think there is much that needs to be discussed."

They entered the Inn and found a secluded spot in the corner.

"You realise that Jacky will be back in a couple of days, Will," said Jimmy Boy to break the silence.

Then Martha surprised all of them with her words.

"Will, I brought Papa with me for moral support. I wanted to tell you in front of him that I am going to leave Jacky and go with you to Sydney."

Will reached across the table and took her hand.

"You are a courageous woman, Martha. But what will Jacky have to say about that?"

"May I add something to this conundrum?" asked Jimmy Boy.

Jacky

Will looked at him, waiting for a disapproval.

"I do not think Jacky will worry about this at all. Because I suspect------no------ I know, Jacky has found someone else. You yourself, Will Mckenzie, have also known this, have you not?"

Will's face reddened.

"I have suspected that, of course."

He gave Martha an almost pitiful look and said,

"Your husband, Jacky, has been spending time with an aboriginal girl from the Kamilaroi tribe up north. Her name is Tarni. I have seen the way he looks at her."

Martha searched his eyes for signs of deception.

"Are you sure about this?"

"I am Martha," he said with a finality.

"All this talking isn't the solution," said Jimmy Boy.

"Martha, you cannot leave Jacky without talking with him first."

Martha's gaze fell to the table.

"But what if he doesn't understand?"

Her eyes searched Will's, seeking reassurance.

"We will work it out together, Martha," he promised.

It was then that Will dropped a huge surprise to them both.

"Martha, we will not be returning to Sydney. We will remain living in Ramsay. I intend to finish the last six months of my training by correspondence. I intend setting up my own legal business right here in Ramsay."

*****

As Jacky led the group towards the light of the fires, his heart filled with elation. He could see the Shanghai homestead in the distance, but his destination was the aboriginal camp by the river. Burra, the aboriginal elder at the centre of everything, emerged from his gunyah and stumbled towards Jacky, and embraced him warmly. While the two tribes became acquainted, Jacky told Burra of the preceding events that led to Reagan's capture and arrest. The relief on the old man's face that it was finally over was all the thanks that Jacky needed.

Later that evening, under the watchful eyes of the stars, Jacky addressed the Kamilaroi people.

Jacky

He announced Reagan's imprisonment, news that sent ripples of joy through the assembled natives. Nullah, the elder who had tried to keep his tribe together against Reagan's oppression and attempts to drive the tribe from their lands, let out a heartfelt groan of relief.

The Kamilaroi tribe, far from idle while resting at Jacky's farm, had spent their time crafting weapons and musical instruments. Jacky eyed a pile of handiwork------- boomerangs shaped to perfection, spears tipped with fire-hardened points and intricately carved didgeridoos. Jacky knew these were not just tools; they were symbols of their culture and unwavering spirit and proof of their ongoing resistance to oppression.

As darkness closed in, the celebration began. The rhythmic drone of the didgeridoos filled the air, and the men, their bodies painted with coloured ochre, danced around the flickering flames. It was a celebration of not just their freedom but a celebration of the bond between man and nature.

*****

Jacky led Tarni away from the rhythmic thud of the didgeridoo towards the homestead on his farm. She was hesitant, but Jacky knew what she was thinking. Here he was, straddling two worlds----- the aboriginal world of his birth and the white man's world because of necessity. Why was he discarding the comforts of the latter and choosing her for his woman?

As they approached the house, Tarni whispered, although there was no one to hear.

"Why would you leave all this for me, Jacky? I am just a poor aboriginal girl. I have nothing fancy to give you."

He turned and pushed his face into hers.

"Tarni, the white man's ways are fleeting. They are shining like precious metal, but they don't fill the emptiness in one's heart. The things that matter are not inside the walls of this house. They are beating in my heart."

He pulled her to the ground, and they made sweet love on the plush, green lawn. When the act was finished, and they lay breathless, Jacky said,

Come on. I will take you inside."

"No! I cannot, Jacky. I belong out here, under the stars. Standing on the earth. I don't belong in there."

He understood and kissed her, and they made their way back to the camp.

*****

Martha was in the garden with her mother, tending to the flowers which were just coming into bloom. She looked up with a mixture of surprise and trepidation as Jacky tethered his horse to the gatepost.

"Jacky," she said, her voice laced with tension.

"You are back."

"Yes, I arrived home yesterday. I hope you don't mind that I didn't come immediately here. I stayed with my people at their camp. Just to reassure them, you know."

Martha sensed his uneasiness.

Eleanor stood, wiped the soil from her hands, and said,

"I think you two have a lot to talk about. I will leave you be."

"Arrived home?" asked Martha.

He ignored the insinuation, opened the gate, and entered the yard.

"I have missed you, Martie," he said, but he felt the weight of his secret resting heavily on his heart.

Images of Tarni flashed through his mind. He heard her laughter and saw her spirit, wild and free. But mixed with the images of the young native girl were images of his wife, Martha. Images of her smiling face splashing in the stream, images of her as she kissed him and brushed the hair from his eyes.

Martha's eyes flickered with something akin to understanding as if she could sense the turmoil raging inside him.

"I have missed you too," she said barely in a whisper.

"But things have changed, Jacky."

"Changed? How?" he asked.

"I have been to Sydney while you were away, Jacky. And I stayed with someone."

He felt a pang of jealousy, but it was quickly overshadowed by his own infidelity.

"Will McKenzie?"

"Yes," she replied with a touch of sorrow.

Jacky

Jacky looked down at his bare feet. They reminded him of who he was and where he had come from.

"What are you trying to tell me, Martie?"

"It is over between us, Jacky. Maybe it has been over for some time now. I never meant to hurt you, Jacky. I have changed. We have changed. And we can never be the same people we were before."

"Maybe we were never meant for each other, Martie."

There was silence. Both had so much to say but so little courage to do so.

"What do we do now, then?" he asked.

Martha sniffled and wiped her eyes.

"We let go Jacky. We go our own way."

Her words struck him like a blow. He knew she was right.

"Jacky---------I know about your new love. Tarni, isn't it?"

"How did you know?"

"I have talked with my father and Will. Jacky, if this

girl makes you happy, then be with her. I want nothing more than your happiness. You know that."

"I am torn Martha. I don't want to lose you."

"You won't lose me, Jacky. But we need to explore who we are. Without each other."

Jacky nodded. He felt a mixture of sadness and anger, but he understood. They had both made choices that had led them to this moment. And now they had to face the reality.

"I hope you have found what you are looking for, Martha."

"I hope for you too, Jacky."

With that, she turned and walked away, hiding her pain and her tears from the man she had once loved. He stood there reflecting on what had just transpired, feeling the weight of their shared past and wondering about their futures. And he knew he had to take that first step into the unknown and find himself again.

*****

Jimmy Boy extracted the folded paper from the envelope and knew immediately what it was. It was an extract from the Newcastle Herald detailing the fate of Harry Reagan. Scrawled on the top was a short note.

Jimmy, thought you might find this of interest. Regards Fleming.

"Ellie. Angela. I'd like you to hear this."

He began to read slowly and deliberately.

Today, at 6 am, Harry Reagan paid the ultimate price for his crimes when he was hanged by the neck at Maitland Gaol. He was tried and convicted for the heinous crime of the murder of Harriet and Bert Lambert, a quiet farming couple whose only offence was to resist his demands to purchase their land. Arthur Kerrigan, a former employee of Reagan, painted a damning testimony of the cold-blooded murders.

A litany of lesser offences compounded the severity of his crime. The bribery of a police sergeant and the lesser crime of imprisoning a tribe of Aboriginals as virtual slaves on his holdings.

"Lesser crimes be damned!" he mouthed to himself before continuing.

The hanging took place out of the public eye, as per the

Government order, which only added speculation and rumours amongst the people.

When asked if he had any last words, Harry Reagan simply said, "May the Good Lord watch over Bruce."

Jimmy Boy screwed the paper up and threw it into the open fire.

Epilogue

"What will you do now, Ma?"

Jacky had never seen his mother cry, and his heart felt as if it was shredded in two as he noticed the first signs of tears rolling down her cheeks. He stretched an arm out and stroked her forehead.

"I guess with Miss Martha moving back here with Mister Will, I might just up and go back to Wicklow and live with Bindi. That old black git needs some takin' care of anyway. Besides, Mister Stubbs is enough to drive anyone away."

Jacky nodded. This was no time for words. He turned to walk away.

"You jis git that black arse back here and give yer mummy a cuddle."

Jacky pulled his mother into a tight embrace and cradled her head.

"It's not like I will never see you again, Mama," he said with a crack in his voice.

Mia untangled herself from his arms and looked at her warrior son.

"That water comin' from yer eyes, boy?"

"Lack of sleep, Mama."

"Tell lies jis like yer daddy Jacky."

"I have to go Mama."

"You be sure to take care of that little girl, Jacky."

Her voice hung in the air as Jacky walked out the door.

"You know I will, Mama," he responded.

*****

As Jacky and Tarni reached the crest of the hill, he turned for what would be his last view of what he had called his own. Then, a sudden cloud of dust caught his eye, and he squinted to see what was causing it. He realised it was the buggy from Wicklow, and he could make out Will at the reins, with Martha beside him.

"Is it….?" asked Tarni.

"Yes. It's them."

From a distance, he heard Martha shout, but it was

barely audible. She waved, and Jacky raised his arm in a final farewell.

"C'mon Tarni. Let's go."

The setting sun cast long shadows behind them as they walked toward the distant smoke from the campfires. Jacky is a man returning not only to his people but to himself.

Terry Pankhurst

The End